IMAGINING WOME

Other Titles in the Series

IMAGINING WOMEN

Fujian Folk Tales

Selected and Translated by
Karen Gernant

INTERLINK BOOKS
NEW YORK

First published in 1995 by

INTERLINK BOOKS
An imprint of Interlink Publishing Group, Inc.
99 Seventh Avenue
Brooklyn, New York 11215

Copyright © Karen Gernant, 1995

Library of Congress Cataloging-in-Publication Data

Imaging women: Fujian folk tales / selected and translated
by Karen Gernant.
p. cm. — (International folk tale series)
Includes bibliographical references.
ISBN 1–56656–173–6—ISBN 1–56656–174–4 (pbk.)
1. Tales—China—Fukien Province. 2. Women—China—
Fukien Province—Folklore. I. Gernant. Karen. II. Series.
GR336.F8I43   1995
398.2'0951'245—dc20   94–38505
                                                              CIP

Printed and bound in the United States of America

10 9 8 7 6 5 4 3 2 1

To my parents
Frances Adams Gernant and Leonard Gernant
with love

And to my good friend Chen Zeping
with thanks

CONTENTS

vii

CONTENTS

ACKNOWLEDGMENTS

I am indebted to numerous persons for their various contributions to this book. Cai Tiemjin and Chen Yulun, editors of *Fujian liushinian miniian gushi xuanping* [Anthology of 60 years of Fujian folk tales], graciously gave their permission for the publication of my English translations of many of those stories. Liu Changhua, who illustrated that volume, has also kindly allowed his drawings to be used in this edition. To Professors Sun Shaozhen and Chen Zeping, I owe thanks for seeking and obtaining those permissions for me. Professor Chen deserves many thanks, too, for generously providing answers to my numerous questions about obscure phrases and literary allusions in the originals. I am also grateful to several administrators at Fujian Normal University—President Chen Yiqin, Dean Zheng Qiao, former President Zhu Hejian, Assistant Dean Zheng Ying, and Foreign Affairs Director Xu Fachang—for their kindness in facilitating my visits to Fuzhou and my work there. At Southern Oregon State College, Provost Stephen J. Reno and Deans Cecile Baril and Claude Curran provided administrative support. I also am indebted to Phyllis Bennis of Interlink for her perceptive and meticulous editing. Finally, I thank my parents, Leonard Gernant and Frances Adams Gernant, for their unwavering confidence and encouragement.

Karen Gernant
Talent, Oregon

INTRODUCTION

I have imposed an outsider's structure on this collection of folk tales. The editors of the original Chinese edition neither structured the anthology nor drew special attention to those stories featuring talented, often independent-minded women in pivotal roles. In afterwords to two of the stories, the editors hint at their views. In partial explanation of "Two Lotus Ponds," they write, "Legends often mixed real life and fantasy, causing the listeners to experience and grasp the essence of reality in a magical, illusory world." About "The Story of Jianlian," the editors comment, "In the world of art, the people have the right to construct a way of life suiting their own ideals and hopes. Hard-working people should achieve happiness. Well-intentioned people should achieve proper recompense." Yet, much more frequently, the editors maintain silence on these issues. I suspect they do not grapple more overtly with the issue of fiction versus reality because the tales in fact reflect a reality taken for granted in China—a reality that the Western outsider finds surprising because it collides with what we think we know about China's past.

Confucian Background

Western study of China typically has been informed by the belief that it was Confucianism nearly alone that shaped the Chinese state and society. By and large, we have accepted the official Chinese historical assertion, amply manifest in both the dynastic and the local histories, that Confucianism was not only widely disseminated in China but that it was also widely accepted and

1

internalized—even by people living in remote and tiny villages. Western scholars have failed, I believe, to be as critical of this interpretation as we might have been. We have failed to ask questions that would challenge this dominant perspective.

Under Confucian precepts, rulers were supposed to foster order and harmony in their world (defined in China as "all-under-Heaven"). They were supposed to be benevolent and kind to their people. Humanity was the central virtue; good men were to study the Confucian texts and commentaries and were to cultivate virtue. Education, therefore, was highly valued. But preparation for the civil service examinations required memorizing thousands of characters and many texts. To acquire an education thus was not a realistic hope for many. The ideal proffered to the people, however, was that it was possible for any male (with the exception of some excluded classes) to study, take and pass the examinations, and become a government official.

Numerous examples of decidedly cruel rulers give the lie to the ethic insisting that emperors and their officials be mindful of the people's welfare. Additional examples make it amply clear that the corrupt were sometimes rewarded with office and wealth, while the upright were executed.

A sinocentric cast of mind meant that China could not acknowledge that it needed anything from the outside world, nor could it acknowledge that any other state might be equal with China. From the Chinese point of view, no other state or people was civilized.

Research in the last few decades on Central Asia and its relationships with China makes it abundantly clear that—if one shifts the angle of vision away from the sinocentric approach—China did indeed need more from the outside world than it liked to acknowledge; and took more, too, than it has cared to emphasize. Thus, a more balanced view than China's own histories give us is that something close to interdependence existed between China and its neighbors.

Confucianism, as it is thought to have most influenced people in general, is characterized by hierarchical relationships always according precedence to the higher generation, to those older than oneself, and to males over females. It is also typified

2

by the marked subordination of the individual to the group, particularly the family. Filial piety was demanded of children: Sons and daughters were expected to submit to their parents' wishes in everything, including arranged marriages. The extended family—five generations living under one roof—was valued as an ideal that should be practiced.

Laws supported the Confucian ethic. For example, punishments for crimes were graded according to the relationship between the perpetrator and the victim. A son could be sentenced to death for striking—or even scolding—his father, whereas a father who struck or even killed his son would be punished only lightly. Mourning was also graded according to the relationship between the deceased and the survivors, so that, for example, a son would mourn the longest for his parents.

Western beliefs forged by ethnocentrism and myopia have fostered the assumption that laws on the books in China must have been followed in practice. Some scholarship has challenged that view, suggesting for instance that when edicts and laws were promulgated—particularly repeatedly—this was probably because they were being routinely violated. We can also challenge the earlier view on the basis of what we know about Chinese law today. For example, the Marriage Law stipulates that the minimum ages for marriage are 20 for women and 22 for men. Yet, in my research, I have encountered countless examples of both women and men marrying below those ages. Such marriages cannot be legally *registered*, but this technicality is an insufficient sanction to delay marriages in the face of human determination. Nor are the fines for early marriages enough to dissuade young people from their decisions.

We know, too, that the ideal of the large extended family could be realized only by a relative few—those wealthy enough to afford such a large household, those privileged enough to enjoy good enough nutrition to make it possible for five generations all to be living simultaneously.

Challenges to Western Views of Chinese Women

In accepting the insistence that Confucianism impressed its stamp on all of China and its culture, Western scholars have accepted—relatively uncritically, it seems to me—the view that, with rare exceptions, women were always subordinate to men, that they were suppressed and oppressed, that they were wholly dependent upon men and upon their families. We have accepted the view that the birth of a son occasioned celebration and joy, whereas the birth of a daughter was at best a "small happiness," certainly not a time to rejoice. We have seen daughters as marginal to their natal families—as property that could be sold into domestic service, prostitution, or concubinage. We have mourned with the daughters whose families considered them financial drains: The families would rear them only to have the daughters marry into other homes. We have agonized with the daughters whose feet were bound to enhance their marriage chances. We have wept with the widows who felt constrained by Confucian morality either to maintain chastity for the rest of their lives or to demonstrate their loyalty to the deceased by committing suicide. We have mined the local histories for examples of these model widows. In short, Western scholars have seen the traditional Chinese woman—an abstraction, at best—as the very epitome of the oppressed woman, imprisoned, constrained, restrained by father, husband, and in-laws.

To do so ignores some other realities. It is acknowledged that little boys were sometimes sold, too: to become eunuchs at court; to become servants; to marry into homes without sons in order to carry another family's name and venerate its ancestors. But the tendency, I think, is to reserve the greater share of our empathy—and our outrage—for the girls and the women.

Western scholars have ignored, too, the fact that in all likelihood the vast majority of Chinese women did not have bound feet. We are told that the tradition began with the upper classes and, over time, spread throughout Chinese society, to include even peasant families. To believe that, one would have to believe that the poor did not need their women's contributions to work.

4

Similarly, to believe that women's lives were confined by the walls of their homes (or, in the case of the wealthy, to the inner chambers), one would have to believe that women somehow did not need to walk to the nearest well or river for water for drinking, cooking, bathing, cleaning, washing clothes. Poor women had to do this; wealthy women, of course, did not. But the female servants attending the wealthy surely did so. When we read that girls and women had no contact with males outside their immediate families, we can accept this perhaps as an accurate description of those in wealthy families. But how could it have been so for those among the poor? In a humble home, where would the women have gone when, for example, male cousins came to visit? How could they always have been hidden from view, even if they wished to be?

Possibility: Rewriting Conventions

In the China field, we are just beginning to lift the corners of the quilt hiding the lives and traditions of the ordinary folk from Western eyes. Not only women's voices, but also those of ordinary men, were muted by the dominant Confucian culture. Nonetheless, they were heard in the past through the voices of anonymous storytellers. The tales they told may have represented escapism and fantasy, or they may have reflected reality. Perhaps it is more likely that the stories combined elements of both. The boundary between imagination and actuality may have been home to *possibility*. Some women indeed succeeded in carving out independent lives for themselves—the historical Qian Siniang stands as an example here—and, in doing so, they may have offered possibility to other women and to their daughters.

We cannot dismiss the fact that many widows maintained chastity or that others committed suicide. What we can do is to question the view that these widows somehow represented the norm. It was in the interests of Confucian scholars to record the instances of loyal widows. What about the many more who did not act out the Confucian ideal? Their lives are lost to us;

5

even their names are lost to us. It may also be argued that the exhortations to chaste widowhood were so frequent for the very reason that certain laws were repeatedly promulgated: It seems likely that women and their families would have preferred not to submit to these admonitions, and thus "needed" frequent reminders of women's "proper role."

When we read of daughters as marginal to their families, we in the West are evidently willing to believe that people in another culture lack the bonds of emotion that are so important to us. Recent research has provided us with evidence, if we needed it, that demonstrates very clearly that mother-daughter bonds, in particular, are very strong in some parts of China. It seems certain that, as more research is carried out in China, evidence of strong mother-daughter bonds will mount. If these ties are quite central in modern times, it is likely that they must have been so in the past as well. My own research on young Buddhist nuns shows, too, that some mothers advise their daughters that they can choose a path that the mothers perceive to be easier: That is, the daughters can choose Buddhist nunhood over marriage. Did mothers begin proffering this sort of advice only in the twentieth century? I doubt it.

It has been assumed that female infanticide is another index of the marginal position of daughters. To argue this we must ignore the fact that male infanticide also occurred. We tend, also, to single out the Chinese in condemning the practice of infanticide. This means ignoring the fact that infanticide by exposure occurred in other countries—in ancient Greece, for example. And to focus on the fact of infanticide of either boys or girls is to obscure its root cause: It was harsh, unrelieved, hopeless poverty that drove parents to such an extreme measure.

It occurs to me that as our research has begun to challenge long-held notions about China and its history, society, and culture, we have moved last of all to a critical examination of the perspectives about women in traditional China. I think that there are reasons for this. One such reason is that outrage has perhaps motivated a great deal of Euro-American feminist research. Perhaps not inappropriately, feminists have been eager to expose example after example of patriarchy overwhelming women, of patriarchy constructing the female gender as it wished it to be—and of enforcing that construction, of patriarchy choking off the voices of women, of women being coopted by patriarchy's values and practices, even of a homogeneity of patriarchy and women's oppression by it across culture, race, and class.

For China, too, white scholars—men and women—have patiently and painstakingly uncovered numerous instances of women shrouded (quite literally) by patriarchy—the widow suicides, the female infanticides, the bound feet, the arranged marriages. Perhaps it was necessary to travel that road. But now more nuanced, and ultimately more persuasive, research is being undertaken by a number of feminists of color. In effect, they argue, "What applies to the white and the privileged doesn't (necessarily) apply to us." They are also saying, "White women have oppressed women of color," and, "Privileged women have oppressed those of different class backgrounds." They assert, too, that the public sphere/private sphere (male/female) dichotomy so often invoked in white feminist scholarship isn't so clear-cut (may not even be applicable) for people of color.

I think back to when I began, quite unconsciously, to question our scholarly, Confucian-tempered view of women in traditional China. I knew strong Chinese women in the U.S., and in Borneo and in Taiwan, and I wondered: Could they be so different from their forebears? Somewhat later, I read the classic *Dream of the Red Chamber*, an eighteenth-century Chinese novel. I considered the strong, domineering role of the matriarch. Could it be that she was only imaginary, or—as seemed more probable—did she reflect reality? Still later, as I read men's poetry and essays revealing their love for their wives and children (including daughters), I puzzled again: Were these men atypical? Or might most men have cherished their loved ones, and respected them too? To cherish does not contradict patriarchy, of course, but it does soften it. When I read Ida Pruitt's *Daughter of Han* and *Old Madam Yin*, I recognized these women as *survivors*, as women whose convictions led them to defy men when necessary. And, finally, on my first journey to China in 1979 and in six subsequent visits, I have been repeatedly struck by the fact that many of my Chinese female acquaintances have

7

indicated that, for them, "women's liberation" would consist in being able to leave their jobs and stay in, and tend to, the home. And when asked about male-female equality, folk living in a poor village assert that equality now exists. They measure equality this way: "Nowadays, boys and girls eat the same food; have the same quality of clothing; have the same chances to play; have the same chances for education." Westerners would not, do not, measure equality in these terms, but—I would suggest—it is not appropriate for us to impose our measurements and our priorities on others. To do so, it seems to me, is to impose a cultural arrogance that is implicitly imperialist.

The Stories: Alternative Values

At last, I came quite by chance to these folk tales. The thirty-seven stories I have selected and translated here represent more than half of the sixty included in an anthology published in 1990 in Fujian. If I had earlier wondered in a rather idle and unsystematic fashion about the position of women in traditional China, these folk tales—originating in and/or set in the Song (960–1279), the Ming (1368–1644), and the Qing (1644–1911) dynasties[1]—forced me to confront my assumptions more critically. The stories challenge Western stereotypes, and they do so largely in a matter-of-fact kind of way. It is clear that those who told the tales did so for a number of reasons: to explain the origin of a certain kind of mushroom or tea, for example; or to explain the reasons behind the construction of certain pagodas; or to depict the accomplishments of important historical personages (Qian Siniang, Li Zhi, Wu Tao). It is just as clear, I think, that the storytellers did not mean to convey a sense that women were taking on, or carving out, roles contradicting conventions. That this un-Confucian behavior is included *naturally*, *matter-of-factly*, without comment, appears to me to be convincing evidence that what outsiders might take to be "unconventional" actions were accepted alternatives among the folk of China's past.

At the most fundamental level, the stories were probably meant

8

simply to entertain, and perhaps also to instill certain values. But if they were intended to inculcate values, the messages were mixed, for the stories not only portray people adhering to traditional Confucian values, but they also portray people resisting those values—and sometimes resisting them successfully. For example, seventeen of the tales deal, at least in part, with persons planning to be married. Of those seventeen, there is clear evidence in twelve stories that both young women and young men either made their own decisions about their marriage partners, or *believed that they should be able to do so*. If these stories reflect reality, as I am increasingly led to believe was the case,[2] this would suggest that although people were doubtless *exposed* to Confucian values, they did not accept them—or, at least, not all of the people accepted them at all times and in all places. It seems likely that it was particularly the inhabitants of villages who rejected or ignored Confucian tenets they viewed as restrictive. If these stories reflect hopes and desires, rather than reality, this would suggest that young people sought to struggle against those Confucian values.

The stories also include four women—three young, one old—who were not married. The storytellers do not call attention to this, thus suggesting that perhaps it was not so unusual to remain unmarried even in a society where—we are told—everyone was expected to marry.

Twenty-one of these folk tales indicate, either explicitly or implicitly, a measure of gender equality. This is frequently demonstrated in the husband consulting his wife about an important undertaking, and sometimes in the wife making a request of her husband—a request which she obviously anticipates will be fulfilled. Some of these stories demonstrate more than gender equality; that is, they depict the women as stronger, more resourceful, brighter, and more capable than the men. The stories also portray the village folk's admiration for, appreciation of, and gratitude to women whose achievements—usually in the face of difficult odds—have saved the villagers from natural catastrophe—flood, drought, or famine.

Numerous women in these stories shaped their own lives, and the lives of those around them. Many of the women do not fit our stereotype of passive, submissive, subordinate, oppressed women. Many, instead, are active, aggressive, engaged—and triumphant. Many of the women depicted here do not occasion our mourning, our sympathy, our pity, or our outrage, as do the stereotypical (and abstract) women. Many of the women in these stories are not subjected to the domination or caprice of men, or to the accident of fate. They are often *acting*, rather than being *acted upon*.

The stories also include examples of nine women who were literate. By the sixteenth century, it was no longer so unusual for privileged women to be literate, but it was not yet common for the less privileged or the poor.

Five of the stories demonstrate the love that fathers had for their daughters. Another shows the love and concern of a father-in-law (Li Zhi), who urged his widowed daughter-in-law to remarry.

Eight of the folk tales deal with female immortals. Nineteen of the stories feature supernatural elements, which are, variously, either benevolent or destructive. Strict adherence to Confucian values would have precluded any suggestion of belief in the supernatural.

Some of the stories blend in one woman qualities reflecting both Confucian and folk values. Most of the women depicted in these stories differ markedly from the stereotype of the traditional Chinese woman. They are strong, fearless, determined, intelligent, sometimes educated, and resourceful. They are talented and skilled. Some lead and organize. Several command the respect, gratitude, and admiration of other ordinary people. Many display an independent turn of mind. Some rely on the threat of suicide to determine the course of their lives. In Confucian society, suicide was a particularly unfilial act—and thus, when the threat of suicide was aimed against parents, women could sometimes forge their own destiny.

Although we cannot be certain whether these folk tales reflect reality or desires or perhaps simply show that there was an audience for escapism and fantasy, I think we can plausibly suggest that traditional China was peopled with many women (and men) whose lives and/or hopes must have been very much like those narrated here. These tales carry authenticity—perhaps particularly because their purpose was *not* to portray women deviating from the Confucian norm. The stories, thus, help us to lift that quilt covering the lives of ordinary folk in China's past. At the very least, it is clear that folk culture not only coexisted with the dominant Confucian culture, but also engaged in passive resistance against that dominating culture. If the carriers of the dominant culture had been more successful in their constant attempts to inculcate that culture's values in the ordinary people, they might well have stilled the voices we hear in these stories and blinded the folk to alternative values. That these alternative values could have found expression in the folk literature suggests that those educated in the Confucian texts were unable to leave a uniform and indelible stamp on all of Chinese society. The folk listened, probably politely, to the Confucian values that were preached to them, and then they simply went their own way, contending with the forces of nature as best they could, and at least seeking—sometimes also finding—whatever happiness they could seize for themselves and their families. Surely, if most Chinese villagers subscribed to Confucian values, they would not have wished women and children to be exposed to the alternative values—particularly the possibility of choice—inhering in these tales.

The Setting

Most of these stories clearly have Fujian province as their setting. For others, the origin is not so clear. It is extremely difficult to comment with any degree of confidence as to whether these particular folk tales were heard only within Fujian province, or whether these tales—and/or similar ones—had more widespread audiences. Were the independent women portrayed here unique to Fujian? I suspect they were not, but we do not yet have enough translations of folk tales from the various regions of China to assert this unequivocally. If further research and translation demonstrate that the alternative values illustrated in these stories were unique to Fujian, we can—with somewhat greater confidence—suggest reasons for this phenomenon.

Several geographical features contribute to Fujian's unique position. Located on the southeast coast, just across from Taiwan, Fujian in the past was difficult to reach: Mountainous terrain separated it from the provinces just to the north and west, while travel by sea was always hazardous. In the early days of the Chinese empire, Fujian was considered remote and inaccessible; its people—known as the Yue—were characterized as "semi-civilized." With the chaotic conditions after the Han dynasty fell in the early third century, however, Chinese began to immigrate to this region, despite the obstacles of the mountains and the dangers of the sea. They tended to settle along the coast, then as now offering more opportunity than the harsh interior region of the province. The population continued to grow until by the end of the Ming dynasty (seventeenth century), Fujian's population was said to be so dense that half its people had no choice but to look for employment outside the province.[3]

With 90–95 percent of the province hilly or mountainous, it was difficult to coax a living from the land. By the middle of the eleventh century, Fujian could not even produce enough rice to feed its inhabitants, necessitating rice imports from more fertile regions of China.[4] Drought, flood, and famine all made dependence on the land unpredictable and precarious, as some of these folk tales illustrate clearly.

The sea promised both opportunity and escape. The people of coastal Fujian struggled with the sea for its food and for the land that could be reclaimed from it. They struggled with the turbulent waters and the typhoons—represented in these stories by a vast array of sea demons. For increasing numbers of people, the sea offered the possibility of flight and hope. Fujianese sailed for Taiwan, and for spots in Southeast Asia. Some of these tales depict persons leaving Fujian, then, in search of better lives. The sea also gave merchants the chance to trade and to smuggle. During the Song dynasty (960–1279), Quanzhou in Fujian province became the greatest port in the world. For about the first century of Song times, trade from Fujian ports was not legal, but in fact it was thriving. Traders from Fujian set sail for spots to the north in China, as well as Korea and Japan, and for ports to the south in Southeast Asia. Late in the eleventh century, the Chinese government took note of this activity by stating that subjects could live overseas. Some years later, the Court also established a trade superintendency for Quanzhou.[5] The first Ming emperor (reigned 1368–98) prohibited overseas trade, yet—undeterred—Fujianese traders carried on a thriving smuggling trade. Finally, in 1567, official sanction was once again given to private trade from Fujian. But in the interim, overseas trade had continued unabated. Geography favored Fujian province, for—located far from the capital in Beijing—central government control was not easily imposed or enforced. Nor, even, was the provincial government in Fuzhou able to impose control over southern Fujian's ports.[6] Of the inhabitants of southern Fujian, one official wrote in exasperation that they "all live alongside the sea and derive their strength from it. They gather in large numbers and rebel. They are vicious and arrogant people. If you are lenient towards them, they will stay at home. If you are harsh, they will take to the sea. We are totally unable to deal with these people." Another official said, "The instructions of the government are not propagated, and the common people can easily resist civilization."[7]

I would suggest that if the people of Fujian could have successfully resisted government orders prohibiting them from engaging in overseas trade, they could have also successfully resisted the Confucian ideals. If the official quoted above was correct, they may not always have even been *exposed* to the ideals. Daniel Overmyer's research on popular religious sects from Ming and Qing times shows that some sects assumed equality between "men and women, rich and poor, noble and humble . . ."[8] Overmyer also argues that Buddhism "provid[ed] the theoretical support for dissent . . . Buddhism at the popular level continued to provide an alternative point of view . . ."[9] I suspect that such an alternative point of view would have been a powerful magnet for those most disadvantaged by Confucian ideals— women, youth, and merchants. I am persuaded that the majority of China's ordinary people were at least as much influenced by Buddhist and other popular sects as by Confucianism; if that is so, then they might have turned to popular religious beliefs for sanction for their choices and their lifestyles—if, indeed, they thought they needed any sanction. This would have been particularly true, I suggest, in places like Fujian—a site far from the center of government and at the same time home to numerous Buddhist temples, as well as temples to local gods and goddesses.

In addition, Fujian was the home of the enormously popular goddess Mazu, protector of sailors and fishermen. Said to have been born near the island of Meizhou in 960 and to have grown up on that island, she is believed to have saved her father and sister from drowning. After her death in 987, the legend runs, a temple was built to her. In subsequent centuries, faith in Mazu spread along the coast and riverways; prayers to her by elite and humble alike were efficacious; emperors honored her with plaques and imperial titles. Whether Mazu existed in fact is probably not very important. More important is that people *believed* in the past, and continue to believe today, that she did. If she did not exist, if—that is—she was created by the people, then there is no need for her to have been created female. She might just as well have been male. Even if she did exist, it is worth asking why she became a goddess. How did it happen that a woman was consciously elevated to a position commanding respect, veneration, entreaties, and sacrifices? This woman would become the most cherished and the best known of women indigenous, either through birth or legend, to China.

For some reason, people wanted this protector of those on the waters to be female. They *chose* to make her female. This is true whether or not she was an historical personage. If she existed, she could have been ignored, or legend could have transformed her into a male entity, or she could have been supplanted by a male. None of this occurred. If she did not exist, the case is even stronger; for in that case, the choice of a female was clearly a conscious one.

We can only speculate about the reasons: 1) Buddhism had drawn believers in part because of the gentle, compassionate

14

image of Guanyin, the goddess of mercy. To her, women went to pray for assistance, primarily for help in conceiving sons. The times in China were not kind to families, particularly the poor. Of the poverty-stricken, perhaps those most subject to the capriciousness of the weather were those whose livelihood took them on the water where danger could strike in an instant and where lives could end minutes later. How, then, could women seek to preserve the lives they had asked to be born to them? Perhaps through prayer to yet another kind, responsive goddess—one whom they would create themselves if need be. And this goddess would be their own, not one imported from a distant land. Perhaps a goddess drawn from their own folk would be even more efficacious than the imported Guanyin. And in influence and power, at least along the ocean and on the rivers, this goddess of the people indeed came to surpass Guanyin. 2) The women might have begun to worship Mazu, and, when their men returned from the sea unharmed, the women might have told their fathers, husbands, and sons that a woman deity was watching over them. 3) The men might have found reassurance in their womenfolk's belief. They might have thought that if prayers offered on land were effective, prayers on the sea would be even more effective and more direct as well. They decided it would be comforting to have an image of the goddess with them on the boat—or ashes from the incense burned to her. Taboos existed, however, against women sailors, for they were thought to bring bad luck. Thus, it is the more extraordinary that a woman became the protector of sailors and fishermen. But perhaps a woman who had become a spirit was considered suitable, for she could represent the men's mothers and wives. Mothers and wives symbolized home, comfort, and safety. They were life-giving, nurturing, sustaining. A goddess would have all of these qualities writ large, and more: She would have power.

Neo-Confucianism, one effect of which—it has been believed—was to further restrict and constrain women's lives, had not yet taken firm hold over scholarship and the state at the time that people began to worship Mazu. Foot-binding was also just beginning. This was conceivably the latest time in Chinese history that a goddess could have been created, that a woman—real

15

or legendary—could have been elevated to a position above men, albeit at the same time a position serving men.

The goddess Mazu was and is virtue and power personified and deified. Come from the folk (and, if indeed she did exist, also unmarried), she may have provided the womenfolk—particularly those of Fujian—with a role model. Her strength and power may very well also have inclined men to believe that mortal women, too, could be much more than subordinate—that mortal women, too, could make contributions to their communities; that they, too, could have independent lives; and that they, too, were worthy of respect and gratitude.

Earlier in this essay, I suggested that the boundary between imagination and reality may have housed *possibility*. I suggest now that, to the ordinary women and men and children of Fujian, Mazu exemplified the *possible*. I suggest, further, that the heroines of these stories inhabited the possible—and that those who fell short of success reflect dreams and aspirations, while those who succeeded reflect reality.

Karen Gernant

HISTORICAL OVERVIEW

FUJIAN: FRONTIER OF OPPORTUNITY

Today, as one travels along the coast of Fujian, it is difficult to imagine that once this land was unopened and forbidding. Now one sees the brilliant red canna defying the winds and the lavender jacaranda and delicate flame trees dancing in the breezes. Narcissus blooms perfume the air. Trees are laden with bananas, oranges and tangerines, lichees and longans, papayas and mangoes. Sugarcane seems to stretch to the skies. Mushrooms dry along the road. Man-made ponds are alive with fish. Salt-flats lend to some of the land an eerie, wasteland appearance, but fields of rice shoots sparkle like clusters of emeralds. At harvest time, the golden-brown plants catch the autumn sun. Vegetable plots are filled with neat rows of cauliflower, beans, cabbage, carrots, onions, tomatoes, and potatoes. Even the mountains in the interior, where poverty does still exist and where life is harsher than along the coast, are painstakingly terraced to yield rice and fruit and tea. Tea from Fujian is highly prized, and connoisseurs are discerning in their choices.

Walking through urban and village markets, one sees a tantalizing array of food: chicken, ducks, geese, pork, beef, clams, crab, shrimp and prawns, fish of all kinds, squid, scallops, eggs, vegetables, and fruit. Gone are the days when meat and fish were only special holiday treats. And gone are the days when fruit was reserved for children and the ill.

Fujian is classified as subtropical, but that designation obscures the fact that the wet winters bring bone-piercing cold.

Without central heating, people encase themselves in six layers of clothing so that—before summer's arrival—the visitor thinks that everyone is fat. Summer is so brutally hot and humid that even the local people complain of it.

Festivals give rhythm to the seasons and to people's lives. During the Lunar New Year holiday, even visitors quickly learn not to try to find people in their offices, which function at that time with reduced staffs. Nor does one try to travel, for at this time—all over China—people are making their way to their homes. There, they celebrate the holiday with their families and enjoy the most lavish feasts of the year. Just before the Lunar New Year, some people still also mark the festival of the kitchen god, whose mass-produced picture hangs in the kitchen. It is believed that the kitchen god keeps an eye on the family the whole year long. At year's end, he goes to heaven where he reports on the family. The family provides him with mouth-watering treats to sweeten his words. Then the family burns his picture, so that the smoke can carry him to heaven

On the fifteenth day of the lunar year—the time of the Lantern Festival—the family gathers for dinner under the first full moon of the year. The full moon—and the spherical dumplings served as part of this meal—symbolize the unity of the family. At this time, too, grandparents typically give children small, colorful paper lanterns—a craft for which the city of Fuzhou has been known since Ming dynasty times (1368–1644).

Early in April, the only traditional holiday linked to the solar calendar is observed. This is *qingming*, "clear and bright." At this time, in honor of their ancestors, families go to the graves, or light incense and candles and leave offerings of fruit and flowers. At the grave sites, they sweep the tombs, weed the surrounding area, and often touch up the red paint on the incised calligraphy.

On the fifth day of the fifth lunar month, wherever there is a body of water, the Dragon Boat Festival is celebrated. Crowds turn out to cheer on the numerous colorfully decorated dragon boats, each rowed by about thirty people, as they race through the waters. This race commemorates the suicide by drowning of the third-century BC poet Qu Yuan, an official whose candor had led to his exile from the court he had served. The dragon boat race symbolizes the attempt to recover his body. Also associated with this holiday is a dumpling made of glutinous rice and steamed in a bamboo-leaf wrapper. Legend relates that in the third century BC such dumplings were tossed into the river to draw the fish away from the poet's body.

It is also just after the Dragon Boat Festival that the weather turns predictably hot. As I wearied of the winter rains that spilled into the solar calendar's springtime, I used to ask my friends in Fuzhou when I could expect hot weather. They replied sagely (and, as I then thought, mysteriously), "After the fifth day of the fifth month." Now I no longer ask, for I have learned that they are right.

There are religious holidays, too, associated with various Buddhist figures and with the indigenous goddess Mazu. But foreigners generally forget to consult the lunar calendar. I recall going one day to my favorite Buddhist temple, where friends greeted me with regret: "Oh, you should have come two days ago for the birthday of the goddess of mercy."

And, of course, since the beginning of Communist rule in 1949, there has also been the October 1st National Day holiday. For this holiday, there is less spontaneity and merry-making. It is observed more formally, with official receptions, dinners, and speeches.

In earlier centuries, hardship would have suggested that Fujian was not necessarily a place where happiness and good fortune could be *found*, but—oddly, perhaps—it was a place where they could be *constructed*. (The provincial name Fujian combines the character meaning "good fortune, blessing, happiness" with the one meaning "establish, build, construct.")

The oldest name for Fujian was Min. In Zhou dynasty times (1122–221 BC), the various Min tribes were part of the southern nationality of the Man (pronounced Mahn) who were considered savage and uncivilized. The area called Seven Min (later Eight Min) included all of present-day Fujian, as well as parts of Guangdong and possibly part of Zhejiang province.[1]

When the Qin state unified China in 221 BC, it created the prefecture of Minzhong, which included present-day Fujian, along with parts of Zhejiang, Jiangxi, and probably part of Guangdong.

19

Although the Qin dynasty claimed this prefecture as part of China, it exerted no effective control over this territory.[2]

In 202 BC, the newly formed Han dynasty appointed a local leader as king for the Min Yue—a territory including most of the Minzhong prefecture of Qin times. The Han took this step because the inhabitants of the area were mostly of the Yue nationality, and, far from the capital, they were difficult to control. The king established Fujian's first capital. In 135 BC, troops dispatched by the Han Emperor Wu achieved victory against the Min Yue. But the victory was short-lived, and in 112 BC the Emperor Wu once again sent forces against the Min Yue. Tired of warfare, this time the Min Yue people did not support their ruler against the Han. Zhu Weigan writes, "As soon as they saw the Han army, it was like boiling water spilling over snow: They immediately melted." For generations, the Min Yue had been influenced by the Han Chinese, even fighting alongside them against the harsh Qin dynasty. Longing for peace, they preferred unification with the Han to death on the battlefield. The Min Yue's surrender to the Han in 110 BC ended the separatist southeastern regime. To eliminate potential rivals to Han control, the Han then moved the Min Yue's aristocrats, bureaucrats, and military to the region north of the Yangzi—effectively separating them from their roots and bringing them closer to the Chinese capital of Chang'an.[3]

Frequent warfare erupted again during the late Eastern Han dynasty (25–220 AD) and the Three Kingdoms period (220–280 AD). The troops of the Wu kingdom in the southeast repeatedly entered Minzhong and finally took control of the region. A civil government replaced the former military rule, and several counties were created.[4]

At last, under the Tang dynasty (618–907 AD), Fujian was integrated into the Chinese state. With the fall of the Tang, Fujian went through a brief period as the separate state of Min (907–945). After coming under the control of other small nearby separatist regimes, it was integrated in 978 into Song dynasty China. Since that time, it has remained an integral part of the Chinese state, although frequently its people have also been difficult to control.

In the fifth century AD, a poet serving as an official in that region wrote: "Leaves fill winter, and flowers color summer: How extraordinary the scenery!" And: "I love the jade-green waters and the immortal mountain [Wuyi Mountain], the rare trees and the miraculous grasses. Submerged my whole life in what I love so much, I don't even feel the hardships of travel."[5]

But that had not always been the outsider's assessment of the region then called Minzhong. In the second century BC, as the Han court deliberated over sending a punitive expedition against the Yue people of Minzhong, forceful arguments were marshaled against taking such action: The forests could serve as havens for the local people familiar with the terrain, but— for the unknowledgeable northerners—the forests housed the hazards of snakes and wild beasts. In the eyes of the northern Chinese, this was a wild frontier—and they feared it. The Yue were skilled at fighting on the water—another advantage over the northerners. Furthermore, it would be costly and difficult to provide clothing, rations, and land and water transport to send armies thousands of miles from the capital. Enemy diseases of the subtropics—"miasmas" and cholera—could also strike. It was predicted that numerous soldiers would be killed and wounded, for the Han dynasty had never fought against such "weapons" as the ones it was now contemplating. Still, after taking all of these risks into consideration, the Han nonetheless sent out its troops and subdued the Min Yue.[6] Somewhat later, Fuzhou was characterized as a "gloomy, marshy swamp."[7] The inhabitants of this region were thought to have had tattoos and to have worn their hair short before they had contact with the Chinese people.[8]

We do not know a great deal about the early people of Fujian, but we know that the Han Chinese thought of them as minority nationalities, as "uncivilized." Like others living outside the Chinese civilization, they were considered by definition "barbarians."[9] These were people who as long ago as about 2000 BC had buried at least some of their dead in "boat coffins," each constructed of a single tree and then suspended in the caves of Wuyi Mountain in the northwest part of the province. Their descendants, it is said, did not understand that it was the suspension that preserved these coffins from rotting: It is thought that they believed that these phenomena represented traces of immortal beings.[10] This practice attests to the ingenuity of even the very early people living in Fujian. It also suggests that they were daring enough to brave risks—a strength also evident in these folk tales.

A legend from antiquity tells of the Lady Taiwu (also Taimu) opening up the land of Min before other people lived there, and of mountains being named to commemorate her. She was believed to be the earliest forebear of the Minzhong people. This legend has been interpreted as evidence of the existence of a pre-Neolithic matriarchal society.[11]

It was probably in the fourth century BC that neighbors of the Min people began moving into the Seven Min from Yue (modern-day Zhejiang province). At that time, after Yue fell to the large and powerful Chu state, some of the Yue royal relatives undoubtedly entered Min territory. They brought with them some of their culture, as well as the culture of the Chinese heartland—the Central Plains region. It seems likely, for example, that they brought along the techniques of spinning and weaving, as well as their renowned military technology. It is also possible that in these times some miners and smelters moved from Yue to Minzhong. Surely the Yue, whose homeland was near the rivers and the sea, took their boat-building and sailing skills with them.[12]

By the third and fourth centuries AD, it is clear that Minzhong had very skilled sailors, as well as able boat-builders. The first recorded instance of people sailing to Taiwan occurred during the third century.[13] Thus, already in place was expertise that would contribute in later centuries to Fujian's leading role in trading.

During this time, too, waves of Chinese immigrants reached Fujian from the Central Plains region. They left their homes and sought refuge elsewhere for many reasons. Warfare drove some to seek stability and peace. Others arrived involuntarily—as soldiers for garrison duty in Fujian, or as exiled criminals or the families of such criminals. Finally, Taoists went to Fujian to collect herbs for pills of immortality. At the end of

the Eastern Han dynasty, one person wrote, "We live in chaotic times. Those who are high officials are in peril. Those with
too much property die." The only escape—the only sure path
to safety—was to study Taoism.[14]

Movement into Fujian continued during the fourth through
the sixth centuries. During this period of disunion, when there
was a succession of dynasties in both North and South China,
significant progress took place in Fujian. More land was opened
up and cultivation expanded. Fields and gardens and villages
appeared. Fields were planted in early-ripening strains of rice,
and tangerines and pomelos were also cultivated. Irrigation works
were also built. Even this early, it is asserted, pagodas 300 feet
high were constructed, as were Buddhist and Taoist temples.
Handicrafts and trade both flourished. Some of the people living in Quanzhou made their homes on boats, thus helping to
foster Fujian's later prominence in sea transport and international trade.[15]

For some centuries, population exploded in Fujian. By the
middle of the eighth century, Fujian registered 100,000 households—almost twenty times the fifth century figure. In the late
tenth century, Fujian had nearly half a million households, while
by the late eleventh century, it had more than a million, and
in the early thirteenth century, it boasted 1.6 million households. Continuing immigration into the province accounted for
much of the population increase; outsiders were attracted by
the growing opportunities in trade.[16] That this was the incen-
tive is worthy of note, for Confucian values dictated that merchants—considered parasites on society, since they were thought
not to produce anything necessary to either state or society—
were disrespected. It seems possible, then, that the people drawn
by the magnet of trade might have already found Confucian
ideals less than persuasive. They might have regarded Confucianism as essentially irrelevant to day-to-day living. This—
along with unremitting poverty—may also have predisposed them
in later generations to emigrate from Fujian to Taiwan and
Southeast Asia.

It was in the Tang dynasty that foreign traders began calling
at the ports of Fujian. Most important in this trade was

Quanzhou—Marco Polo's Zaiton.[17] By the late Song dynasty (960–1279 AD), Quanzhou had overtaken Guangzhou (Canton) as China's busiest port. Marco Polo described it as "splendid" and asserted that "Zaiton" drew a hundred times as many ships as most of the other ports in the world.[18] From the ninth to the thirteenth or fourteenth centuries, Quanzhou was a major port for overseas trade. Accompanying the trade was Islam, and several mosques were constructed in Quanzhou. Of those, one built in 1009 survives today. Arabic influence remains evident, too, in a strict Muslim restaurant in that city.

Overseas trade flourished despite persistent Song dynasty attempts to control or prohibit it in Fujian.[19] The trade was essential to the economy of Fujian, for pressure on the land was heavy and the folk could not expect the land to support them—particularly given the large influx of immigrants. Some peasants began to cultivate cash crops, such as sugarcane, cotton, lichees, oranges, and glutinous rice (for rice wine).[20]

However, the prosperity associated with the trade drew pirates and also led the government to increase the taxes on trade. These twin forces sapped the enthusiasm of the traders, and the registered population of Fujian fell from 1.6 million to 700,000 households in the thirteenth century.[21]

Early in Ming dynasty times (1368–1644), the court eunuch Zheng He, a Muslim, led a series of seven spectacular naval voyages. Begun in 1405 and ending in 1433, the expeditions included more than 60 ships and nearly 30,000 men. The ships called at the port of Fuzhou in Fujian province, and sailed as far as India, Ceylon, Indonesia, Persia, and East Africa. If legend and history are to be believed, Zheng He sought the blessings and assistance of the goddess Mazu for safe journeys.

Official sponsorship of Zheng He's voyages notwithstanding, the Ming dynasty strictly prohibited all *private* overseas trade. Yet Ming times saw a resurgence of overseas trade in Fujian province—a resurgence which violated Ming edicts. Chinese were not allowed to sail overseas, and foreign traders were not allowed to call at Chinese ports.[22] The first Ming emperor stated the policy succinctly: "Let not an inch of wooden board set out to sea."[23] Tribute trade, sponsored by the government, was the only legal avenue for trade between China and foreigners. Late in the fourteenth century, the Ming designated Quanzhou as the official port for tribute missions coming from the Ryukyus. Such prohibitions and regulations should have jeopardized overseas trading in Fujian. But, through smuggling and through the sanctioned tribute trade with the Ryukyus, it persisted.[24] The favored treatment which the Ming extended to the Ryukyus allowed the Fujianese to maintain their skills in navigation and ship construction. China presented ships and expert sailors to the Ryukyus to ensure the continuance of tribute missions.[25] For a fifty-year period, from 1385 to 1435, the ships were constructed in Fujian, and the sailors presented to the Ryukyus were all Fujianese.[26]

By the early sixteenth century, as Ming power waned, smuggling flourished to such an extent that it overtook the tribute trade in importance.[27] Still, by that time, the Fujianese had built their reputations as master shipbuilders and as skilled navigators. The government turned to them to serve in the navy, and the private sector turned to them to build and sail trading ships.[28] Several of the folk tales collected in this book bear witness to these abilities.

In Ming times, peasants began to cultivate cash crops in addition to those noted above for Song times. Grown in the Quanzhou area, both longans and lichees were dried for export overseas. Indigo and safflower, sugarcane and tea were all expanding in cultivation. The thriving industries of this time included textiles, salt, sugar-refining, and the Dehua porcelains. The development of both commercial agriculture and industry led to better transport and more trade; market towns also sprang up.[29] By this time, the silting-up of the harbor had stripped Quanzhou of its prominence as a port, and merchants sought—and located—substitute ports a little farther south. Geography favored these two new ports, for, as Lin Renchuan notes, they were "on the periphery of the Chinese state where central control was lacking and officials were afraid to visit."[30] Inlets and islands made the remote region a labyrinth for clandestine activities. According to a contemporary source, the inhabitants of one of those islands "made their living from piracy."[31] Private trade through these ports flourished, and statistics indicate that, in the last half of the sixteenth century, at least 33,000 people went every year from just one of these ports to the Philippines. Other Fujianese merchants traded with other Southeast Asian countries, and with Korea and Japan. The risks were enormous— sometimes only 20 or 30 percent of the people returned—but so were the profits. Even though farmers were esteemed and merchants were not, people left the mountains and the fields for the opportunities of the sea. Even members of well-to-do families sought to augment their wealth through trade. Some even adopted sons, who—as adults—would represent the family interests at sea. Lin Renchuan quotes from a local gazetteer: "People do not feel ashamed to let [adopted sons] enter their clans."[32] Such action would have been extremely un-Confucian. Confucian practice, it is true, allowed the adoption of sons—particularly when a family had none of its own—but the accepted pattern was to adopt sons from one's own lineage. Ordinarily, a family would not have adopted a son from another clan with a different surname. That families did so during these times suggests again that Confucianism exerted at best a fragile restraint on daily life, especially when overseas trade— and adoption—would help to sustain that life.

During the Ming dynasty, piracy—both domestic and Japanese—frequently bedeviled the court. Defense walls built in those times still stand on the Fujian coast.

As the faltering Ming dynasty ended at last with conquest by Manchu invaders, Fujian figured prominently again in China's history. The Ming loyalist, Cheng Zhenggong (Koxinga), used Fujian as a staging ground for resistance against the alien Qing dynasty from 1646 to 1658. Later, in defeat, he fled to Taiwan, where he forced the Dutch out—thus, ironically, opening the way for the Qing conquest of that island in 1683 and for Taiwan's administrative integration into China as part of Fujian province. The Qing (1644–1911) punished Fujian by moving the coastal population a considerable distance inland. Despite a Qing ban on Chinese emigration to Taiwan, large numbers of poverty-stricken Fujianese made their way to that island—still another indication of the continuing failure of enforcement to reach parts of China remote from the capital.

In the eighteenth and nineteenth centuries, it was also impossible to enforce the laws against opium-smoking. Many of Fujian's poverty-stricken, as well as the wealthy and privileged, became addicted to that drug. It sapped their energy and drained away their incomes. In 1838, the Qing court appointed the Fuzhou native Lin Zexu as imperial commissioner to Guangzhou (Canton). His charge was to end the opium trade. In confiscating and destroying the foreign-owned opium, Lin created the catalyst for the Opium War (1839–1842) with the British. Among other provisions, the treaty settling the conflict stipulated that five ports be opened to foreign trade. Among those ports were Fuzhou and Xiamen (Amoy) in Fujian. Several years later, as part of the self-strengthening movement intended to achieve technological equality with the West, China established a shipyard at Fuzhou—thus building on Fujian's long period of supremacy in this realm.

Over the centuries, then, Fujian has had an uneven relationship with the central government—sometimes accepting it, often resisting it. Turbulence, adventure, economic expansion, and both immigration and emigration have marked Fujian from early times onward. Those entering Fujian during the chaotic times after the fall of the Han dynasty in 220 AD had to battle rugged mountains or the surging waves of the ocean to get there. That fact underscores two points: 1) that the turmoil and instability of the north must have been truly unbearable to push people to leave the familiar behind and set out for unknown territory; and 2) that the immigrants to Fujian must have had a level of determination and daring distinguishing them from those who stayed at home. They were perhaps more open to new experiences and more willing to defy both Confucian tradition and government control. For many of them, Fujian must have seemed beyond the pale—a frontier land. Their willingness to abandon their northern homes may also have made them more receptive later to the opportunity afforded by leaving China entirely. Living near the sea, as many did, would have provided constant reminders that if they wished to seek a better life they need only push away from shore—and set out again for either the unknown or the fabled. The waters, they knew, could be their enemy—but they could also be their salvation. For those with little to lose, as well as for those with much to gain, the sea must have appeared to offer more opportunity than risk. And, after the tenth century, they had their own goddess—Mazu—to protect them from calamity.

Karen Gernant

PART ONE

PASSIVE, SUBMISSIVE, AND LOYAL: IMAGES OF TRADITIONAL WOMEN

DAHONGBAO

In this story, Industrious Old Woman is depicted in a partly stereotypical way: That is, she is willing to share her meager fare with a stranger. The story shows the traditional Confucian value of reciprocity: Because she helps the stranger, he offers his help in return. She helps the other villagers by following the stranger's instructions, rather than through her own ability. She also is seen as working hard at traditional women's work—sewing, mending, and washing clothes. She is atypical, however, in that she is neither married nor living with family members.

"Dahongbao," well-known both at home and abroad, is one of Wuyi's[1] most treasured teas. There are several different folk legends about its origin.

It isn't certain in what dynasty or in what year Wuyi Mountain suffered a severe drought. For 360 consecutive days and nights, not a single drop of rain fell.

The hundred birds of that mountain were so thirsty that they gasped for breath. The village folk were so hungry that they were filled with anxiety. The drought killed the crops. They couldn't harvest rice. How could they eke out subsistence?

They could only cross the mountain ridges and climb the slopes to the mountain and strip the tree bark and pull up grass roots to satisfy their hunger. But before long, the bark and roots had all been eaten. All they could do was dig out some white clay to fill their stomachs. This white clay really did fill the stomach, but it couldn't be digested. So, people's stomachs grew more swollen by the day.

In Huiwan village north of the mountain lived an old woman

30

more than 50 years old. She was a fine person who was well-known for 100 *li*![2] She had no son, no daughter, no husband. She passed her days alone. She also often helped her village neighbors and friends sew and mend, and wash and starch clothes. Because she was so industrious and good-hearted, everyone affectionately called her "Industrious Old Woman."

One day, with great difficulty Industrious Old Woman picked a bundle of green and yellow leaves from trees on a faraway mountain. To satisfy her hunger and thirst, she boiled a bowl of tree-leaf soup. Just as she was about to drink it down, suddenly she heard a moaning sound outside: "Aiya, aiya." Industrious Old Woman immediately set down her bowl of soup, and went out to look. Sitting on the rock outside the door was a white-haired old man leaning on his dragon-head staff. He was out of breath and gasping hoarsely. Dry from thirst, the corner of his mouth and his lips were split open with one cut after another. Industrious Old Woman hurriedly helped him into the stone house, and gave him that bowl of tree-leaf soup. She apologized, "In time of drought, there's nothing good to eat. But eat this bowl of tree-leaf soup while it's hot!"

The old man accepted the bowl of soup gratefully, and slurped it down in several gulps. In a moment his face was glowing with health and he was full of energy. With a laugh, he lifted the dragon-head staff and said, "Good woman, thank you so much for saving me. This old man has nothing to repay you with, so I'll just make you a gift of this dragon-head staff!"

Industrious Old Woman looked at the staff, which was yellow and smooth and gleaming brightly. In the dragon's mouth was a luminous shining pearl. This was an invaluable treasure! Industrious Old Woman was a sincere person. She thought: One bowl of tree-leaf soup—how could she let someone present her with a gift?

Just as Industrious Old Woman was about to return the staff to him, the old man had already read her mind, and he said again, "Good woman! Dig a hole and plant this staff. Then sprinkle some clear water on it. That'll work just fine! It will be useful to you."

The old man pointed. In a moment, Industrious Old Woman

felt a light breeze blowing in. She turned around to look. Ah! The white-haired old man had changed into a Taoist wearing a large, padded red robe and he was riding the light breeze into the distance! Only then did she realize that she had met an immortal!

In accord with the old Taoist's instructions, Industrious Old Woman dug a hole in the middle of the yard, planted the dragon-head staff, and sprinkled a bowl of clear water on it. Early the next morning, she was pleasantly surprised to see a clear spring. That smooth yellow staff had already turned into a glossy green tea bush. The whole bush was bursting with clusters of delicate buds. A light scent fluttered continuously in the morning breeze, attracting the mountain's one hundred birds, colorful butterflies, and bees. It also attracted men and women, old and young, from the village.

Industrious Old Woman warmly called everyone to pick the round clusters of gleaming green tea leaves. It was really wonderful. As people picked the tea leaves, more tea leaves grew. There was no way to pick them all!

Extremely happy, Industrious Old Woman rushed to boil water. She steeped a large pot of strong tea and divided it among the villagers. When they drank it, everyone felt that the light scent was refreshing, that it cleared the air and restored the stomach. Stomachs no longer ached and they no longer bulged. Everyone was laughing happily, and Industrious Old Woman also began dancing around the tea bush with the younger generation.

There is a saying: "The world has no wall that won't let the wind in." Before long, the legend of this miraculous tea bush had flown to the capital city and reached the ears of the emperor. But this emperor was vicious and greedy. In his eyes, any precious grasses or flowers, any marvelous unusual treasures of the people, all belonged only to the emperor. Even more so, this incomparable miraculous tea!

The emperor very quickly dispatched great officials and troops, and they dug up and seized Industrious Old Woman's tea bush and moved it to the imperial palace, where they planted it in the back garden.

When the emperor received this miraculous tea, he couldn't
help but light up with pleasure. He invited the court's civil and
military officials to a grand tea-tasting party. There was instrumental music and singing, and the palace maids danced. In
the midst of the festivities, the emperor went around the tea
bush whose scent was so enticing. He looked at it left and right,
right and left. He laughed until he couldn't hold his lips together. Suddenly, with a great display of music and drumbeats,
and shouts on all sides, it was announced that the emperor
himself would pick the tea! Just as he stretched out his pale
and withered hands with the sharp fingernails, that tea bush—
with a *"wulala"* sound—grew one large section taller.

The emperor stood on tiptoe and raised his arms, but he still
couldn't reach the tea. He told someone to move a stool over
there. The emperor had just climbed onto the stool when the
tea bush made another *"wulala"* sound and grew 10 feet taller.
So angry that he was foaming with rage, the emperor immediately ordered the civil and military officials to bring a long
ladder.

The emperor was shaking as he climbed the bamboo ladder.
The tea bush grew another section taller. The emperor climbed
another rung. And the tea bush grew another section taller.
And so the emperor climbed and climbed, and the tea bush
grew and grew, until it grew to a very high altitude and pen-
etrated the clouds.

The emperor couldn't reach the miraculous tea. In a towering rage, he ordered that the tea bush be chopped down. When
the huge ax fell, a cold light flashed and the gigantic tea bush
fell, crushing the imperial palace and killing the emperor. In
alarm, the civil and military officials covered their heads and
fled in panic.

Just then, a magnificent red cloud drifted down from the
sky. It floated around in a leisurely way and then landed on
the tea bush! In a moment, the tea bush grew a thick trunk
and burst forth with delicate glossy green leaves. The red
cloud floated and floated, and also encircled and drifted around
the tea bush three times. It wrapped up the tea bush—roots,
leaves, and all—and floated out of the capital city, crossed high

mountains, cut across streams and wastelands, and flew toward Wuyi Mountain where Industrious Old Woman lived. Since that day when the emperor's troops had stolen the tea bush, Industrious Old Woman had been distraught. She wept by day, and thought by night. She thought and wept. Every day she was worried. Gradually her thinking turned her hair white and her weeping turned her eyes red and her worrying made her ill. Then one day Industrious Old Woman was lying on the bed when suddenly she heard happy magpies calling "*chacha*" at the window. Leaning on her staff, she got up to look. Ya! Under a red cloud, large numbers of birds and sparrows and bees and butterflies were gathered around a fresh, green tea bush. And they were fluttering in the tile-blue sky, and flying toward her own home.

The tea bush! The tea bush! Wasn't this the miraculous tea bush she had thought of morning and night? Happy again, Industrious Old Woman recovered from her illness and her worries disappeared. Her eyes were clear. Throwing the staff aside, she ran over.

The tea bush circled over Industrious Old Woman's yard, and then, reluctantly, it flew away. It skimmed over Huiwan Cliff, drifted past Liuxiang Ravine, and flew into Nine Dragons' Nest.

When Industrious Old Woman and the villagers chased it to Nine Dragons' Nest and climbed the cliff and drew near to look at the tea bush—Ya! That red cloud was the large padded red robe that the white-haired immortal had worn before! She lifted the padded robe. A puff of clear scent floated in all directions. She saw only that the fresh green tea bush had already turned into a brilliant red one.

So, everyone then called this tea bush "*Dahongbao*."[3] Later this tea bush changed into three bushes. Why did that white-haired immortal want this tea bush to put its roots down at Nine Dragons' Nest, halfway up to the sky? It is said that Halfway-up-to-the-sky is a piece of "precious land." All year long without interruption, a clear spring flows on that cliff. This is the "immortal water" oozing out from the luminous pearl in the mouth of the dragon-head staff! Everyone says that only courageous, industrious people can go up that dangerous cliff that has no path, and pick this miraculous tea, and reap good fortune and happiness!

(Story collected by Liu Xiling)

THE GOD OF MEDICINE

These two stories both depict essentially passive women, who therefore fit the traditional stereotype. Baosheng Dadi's original name was Wu Tao. He was a famous physician in Song dynasty times. A lot of stories about him were passed down in the region of southern Fujian.

Response to the Reward for Curing the Empress

It was in the time of Song Renzong.[4] The country was prosperous and the people were at peace. The weather was good. The common people lived and worked in peace and contentment. It was one vast panorama of peace.

But one day, Song Renzong sat frowning in the palace. His face was heavy with sorrow. All the officials filling the court felt completely bewildered. Song Renzong's wife had come down with a serious disease. All the imperial physicians had tried to cure her. One after another, pots for brewing medicine had been used until they broke. Not only was the empress's illness not cured, but instead it worsened by the day. She was in imminent danger of death.

The empress's illness was in fact very difficult to cure. She was suffering from breast cancer. In the beginning, a small knot—like a yellow bean—was discovered in her breast. It neither itched nor hurt. She wasn't too worried about it. Born into high position, she was embarrassed to ask someone to treat her. Later, the small knot grew bigger and bigger until it was like a small walnut. Only then did she pay attention to it. But when the imperial physicians came, she only told them about her illness; she wouldn't let anyone examine her. So, she drank a lot of soup and medicine, but this did not cure her. Finally it had dragged on to this late stage. It festered, and the pain was hard to bear.

The empress was ill and the imperial physicians could not cure her. Everyone was terribly worried. Song Renzong forgot to eat and sleep. He wasn't comfortable either standing or sitting. Nothing worked. All he could do was order people in the whole country to paste up yellow notices to solicit a fine doctor.[5] Whoever could cure the empress's illness would receive gold and would be made an official. But with this kind of illness—with no evident cause—who would dare respond? The empress's illness became graver by the day. Even the officials filling the court—loyal officials and fine generals—were all at a loss as to what to do. They were at the end of their rope.

One day, the county physician Wu Tao, who had come to the capital Kaifeng from Fujian, saw the yellow notice. He tore it down. This news created a stir all over the capital. Everyone knew that associating with a monarch was like associating with a tiger. If he cured the disease, of course he would reap the promised reward and be made an official. He would receive endless favors. If he didn't cure the disease, though, he would have to watch out for his head.

After Wu Tao tore down the notice, a bodyguard led him quickly to the palace. Song Renzong interviewed him personally. He saw that Wu Tao was wearing a Taoist priest's hat, a long blue gown, cotton socks, and straw sandals. His travel had wearied him. His voice was sonorous. He didn't have court etiquette. Song Renzong thought to himself: This is clearly a very typical country quack. Is it possible that he can cure the empress? But since he had dared to take down the notice, he let him try.

Wu Tao was led into the empress's palace. The empress lay on the bed. The eunuch pulled out a red silk thread, and told him to feel the pulse on top of that. In the past, in ancient times, men and women couldn't be close. The physician could not feel the pulse directly on the empress's wrist. He could only examine the sick person's pulse through the red silk thread.

If the physician was not extremely skilled, this could never be done.

Wu Tao pressed his three fingers lightly on the red silk thread. Inclining his head, he narrowed his eyes. He examined her for a while, and then sighed deeply, "There isn't a cure, there isn't a cure. The empress's pulse has already stopped." He finished speaking and stood up to leave.

Song Renzong and the crowd were startled. The emperor felt the truth of the old saying: "Ocean water can't be measured with a dipper. People can't be judged by their looks." In feeling the pulse, this rustic county physician had shown a few tricks of the trade. In order to test his medical knowledge, they had purposely tied the red silk thread to the bed. In a flash he had determined that there was no pulse movement. This was extraordinary.

Seeing that he was about to leave, the crowd rushed up to stop him. "Doctor, don't go so quickly. Please examine the empress's pulse once more."

Wu Tao had no choice. He sat down heavily, and extended his three fingers again and pressed lightly on the red silk thread. He concentrated all his attention on the pulse, and bent his head in deep thought. Suddenly his eyes brightened, but after a while he said again, "There's no cure, there's no cure. The empress's pulse is jumping as nervously as a cat." He stood up to leave.

This time they had purposely tied the red silk thread to a cat's foot to test him again. He saw through this, too. They quickly asked him to feel the pulse once more.

Wu Tao had absolutely no choice. He sat down again to feel the pulse. He stretched out his three fingers again and pressed on the red silk thread. He lowered his head and inclined his ear. With total absorption, he distinguished in detail the different types of pulse at the three different spots in the wrist. He said, "There's nothing seriously wrong." He asked for writing materials, and wrote out a prescription.

Wu Tao separated the empress with a screen and used moxibustion and acupuncture on her back. He also gave her medicine to be taken orally. After a time of treatment, as the doctor had predicted, that enlarged spot gradually stopped hurting. Song Renzong's joy was boundless. He treated the doctor as a distinguished guest. After more of Wu Tao's treatment, the empress's cancer became smaller by the day. Finally, it disappeared without a trace. The empress recovered her good health and everyone was very happy. The empress and Song Renzong were happy beyond all expectations, and deeply grateful. To express their gratitude, in addition to presenting him with a lot of gold and silver valuables, Song Renzong also appointed him imperial physician.[6] It never occurred to him that Wu Tao would graciously decline. He got up and took his leave. "My aspiration is to cultivate the divinity within and help the common people. Glory and riches are not what I desire."

Song Renzong saw that Wu Tao had already made up his mind to cure diseases among the people. Since there was no way he could keep him at court, he honored him with the title "Taoist saint." Song Renzong commended him for his virtue, and saw him out of the palace personally. So Wu Tao became even more famous.

After Wu Tao left Song Renzong, he led several disciples and carried a box of medicine on his back, and roamed all over.

Everywhere he went, he cured all kinds of unusual diseases for the common folk. He devoted his whole life to helping and saving people. He didn't take money from the sick. He was deeply loved and esteemed by the people. Later, he returned to his home village. In many places in Haicang, he dug wells and located springs, picked medicinal herbs and made pills of immortality in order to provide treatment and medicine for the impoverished sick people. His kindness was known all over.

Before long, the region of southern Fujian had a widespread pestilence. The farmland was laid waste. It was desolate everywhere. The sound of grieving arose on all sides. In order to save the masses of the people, Wu Tao—with his disciples—trekked into the area between the high mountains and the ridges. He didn't expect that when he went up Longchi cliff to pick medicinal herbs to fill prescriptions, he would unfortunately slip and fall from a precipice. He was carried home, but no cure worked, and so he died at home . . .

Breaking the Centipede Case

One day Wu Tao and his disciples arrived at the county seat, and found an inn where they could rest. It was then already time to light the lamp, so teacher and disciples all hurriedly washed up and rinsed their mouths. Unexpectedly, the young shop assistant said, "County Magistrate Liu has come personally to see you."

Wu Tao got dressed and went out. County Magistrate Liu immediately raised his hands high in obeisance and intoned, "I didn't know that you had arrived. Excuse me for not meeting you. Pardon this offense, pardon this offense."

"My comings and goings are unpredictable. You are very busy."

County Magistrate Liu said, "I have something to ask of you. I don't know whether you're willing to help or not?"

Wu Tao laughed and said, "Aside from practicing medicine, I have no other ability."

Magistrate Liu said, "My daughter is 18 *sui*[7] this year. Some days ago, she came down with a strange disease. First her stomach hurt for several days. Later she vomited whatever she ate. If she ate rice, she vomited rice. If she took medicine, she vomited medicine. If she drank water, she vomited water. Now she's already gone three or four days without taking a drop of water. She lies on her bed resting under the covers. I beg you to save my daughter's life."

Wu Tao thought and thought, and then said, "Treating sick people is my responsibility. I am duty-bound to fulfill this responsibility. According to your description, I'm afraid it is a digestive ailment. We'll talk again after I've felt her pulse."

County Magistrate Liu immediately prepared the sedan chair and welcomed Wu Tao and his disciples into the *yamen*.[8] Installed in the *yamen*'s guest house, they were treated as distinguished guests.

The county magistrate's daughter was like flowers and jade. She was young and yet she had contracted this serious disease. She hadn't eaten even a kernel of rice for many days, and she was already so hungry that she looked haggard. This illness was clearly one of the digestive tract. Wu Tao gave her medicine. This time, she didn't vomit it. After one more treatment, she slowly took a turn for the better.

One day, County Magistrate Liu was in court trying a case. Wu Tao had nothing to do, and he went into the court. He saw a young married woman kneeling there in mourning dress. Her tears were like a gushing spring as she shouted loudly of injustice. County Magistrate Liu struck his gavel in a threatening manner, and shouted sternly, "You have a lot of gall, sly girl. It's altogether clear that you killed your husband by poisoning, and you also did not tell the truth and come in right away! You thought you could avoid being sentenced."

That young married woman shouted of injustice and wrong. "You should investigate. We—husband and wife—were loving and affectionate. We respected one another like guests. We never even argued. We never got angry. Isn't it preposterous that I would poison my husband to death?"

"What gall! If you didn't poison him, then how did this person die with no reason? Do you still dare to argue?"

"Official! Every day at noon, I took food out to the field for my husband to eat. It didn't occur to me that that day he would return home and shout that his stomach hurt unbearably. Even before I called the doctor it was too late. I don't know, either, why he died. Truly, I didn't poison him. I implore you to investigate."

"*Po!*" Magistrate Liu slammed the table. "Without torture, you'll never tell the truth. Bring the press quickly, and squeeze her ten fingers."

That young married woman couldn't stand up under the torture. She fainted right away. Magistrate Liu ordered people to splash her with water. After she came around, all she could do was confess under torture to these false charges and admit that she had poisoned her husband to death.

"Let her make her mark. Then take her to the death prison."

Wu Tao felt that a case involving human life should be handled with great care. How could a judgment be reached so carelessly? He sought out Magistrate Liu to ask him about the case.

This young woman's name was Zhu Yufeng. Her husband had been Wu Changrong. They lived in Houxi *xiang*[9] and farmed

41

for a living. They usually had difficulties, yet they lived together in harmony. They farmed two *mou*[10] of poor land. They began work when the sun came out and they stopped when the sun set. They worked hard at plowing and weeding. Generally, Zhu Yufeng cooked the lunch and took it out to the field for Wu Changrong to eat. That day, Zhu Yufeng also especially fried two savory eggs to go with the rice. When she took the food out to him, Wu Changrong was busily cultivating the land. Zhu Yufeng set the food down on the ground and then hurried home to feed the pig. When Wu Changrong took a break from work he must have polished off the food in large gulps and only gradually realized that his stomach hurt. After he got home, he died that very evening.

After Wu Tao heard this, he said, "That young married woman kept on shouting of injustice, and she was also wearing mourning for her husband. The two of them lived together so harmoniously. I dare ask you: Why must she have poisoned her husband?"

"This . . . " All of a sudden, County Magistrate Liu couldn't answer. After a short delay, he finally said, "Wearing mourning is the way of the world! If she poisoned her husband, there must have been adultery involved."

"Is there any evidence of such a villain?" Wu Tao asked.

"In fact, we don't yet know who the villain was."

"So, there must be something odd in this. You've sentenced her to death, but you have no real evidence. Aren't you afraid that this isn't proper?"

"What do you think?" asked Magistrate Liu.

"In my view . . ." Wu Tao spoke into Magistrate Liu's ear. Magistrate Liu nodded his head.

At noon the next day, Wu Tao ordered people to fry two savory eggs as before, and take them to the land plowed by Wu Changrong and then step aside and watch.

Two hours passed, and they only saw a large centipede climb out of a small hole on the embankment. It ate from the savory eggs for a while and also climbed around on the eggs, and then it returned to the hole.

Wu Tao ordered that the plate of eggs be brought back and

fed to a dog. That evening, that dog began to howl. It lay on the ground and rolled around. Before long, its four legs stiffened and it died. Only then did Liu understand.

Wu Tao broke the centipede case and saved that young woman's life.

He also cured the magistrate's daughter.

(Stories collected by Xu Changbo)

MR. SNAKE AND LOTUS-SEED FACE

Virtue triumphs in this story, albeit with a strong boost from the supernatural. Although the lesson is a stereotypical one— reward for the hard-working and virtuous, and punishment for the jealous and wicked, the young woman Lotus-Seed Face is depicted as persistent and intelligent. She was also able to discern the essential worthiness of the man whom she agreed to marry. We also see in this story the love and concern of her father for his pregnant daughter.

In the past, in a small mountain village lived an old grandfather. Early every morning, he went out to pick up pig manure. The people of the village all called him "Pig Manure Grandfather."

One day, Pig Manure Grandfather went to another village to pick up pig manure. The road crossed a small mountain. He discovered that the mountain was covered with all kinds and colors of flowers—chrysanthemums, peonies, orchids, camellias, jade flowers, tree peonies, jasmine, magnolia, plum blossoms— intoxicating people with their fragrant scents. He stood there staring at them and breathing in the fragrance. He was loath to leave.

Just then, a young person carrying a street vendor's load walked across from the clump of flowers, and asked, "Uncle, are you lost?"

"Ah. No." Pig Manure Grandfather waved distractedly, and answered hurriedly, "The flowers here grow so abundantly and so beautifully. If my daughters saw them, they would certainly be very happy."

"Do your daughters like flowers?"

"Yes, yes. I have three daughters, who all love to pick flow-

45

ers. Every time I go out, I always pick some wildflowers for them to wear in their hair."

"Uncle, what are they like?"

"The eldest has a face like a rice sieve; the second has a face like a crab dipper; and the youngest has a face like a lotus seed."

"Uncle, I own this mountain garden, and ordinarily I grow flowers. When I have time, I take up my carrying pole and sell flowers and silk thread. I was born in the year of the snake, so everyone calls me Mr. Snake. I live alone in a remote spot. I wonder if one of your daughters would be willing to marry me?"

"This . . . I see that you are also a farmer. Farm families can't dislike other farmers. I just don't know which one of my daughters would like to marry you."

"Uncle, if you think well of me, please go home and ask them."

Mr. Snake then plucked a large bunch of delicate, fragrant jasmine flowers and gave them to Pig Manure Grandfather. The southern Fujian folk use this flower to request marriage.

Pig Manure Grandfather went home. As soon as his daughters saw the flowers, they all fought over them. Just then, the jasmine made a sound. As though singing, it said:

Fragrant, fragrant, fragrant,
Fragrant, fragrant, fragrant.
Wear this jasmine in your hair,
And give me betel nut!

Dumbstruck, the three daughters crowded around their father and asked why this flower could sing, and what the song meant.

Pig Manure Grandfather smiled and said, "This flower is one given to you by Mr. Snake on the mountain in back. Ordinarily he raises flowers. When he has time, he takes up his carrying pole and peddles flowers and silk thread. He still isn't married. I don't know which one of you would like to marry him?"

"Eeya!" As soon as Rice-Sieve Face heard this, she took off

the jasmine flower and cast it away. "I'm tired of this life of farming. I want to marry a high official or a noble lord!"

"That's right!" Crab-Dipper Face also took off the jasmine flower and pinched it to powder. "I've worn enough of these homespun gowns. I want to marry a rich man in a rich and influential family!"

Only Lotus-Seed Face was still wearing the flower. She said nothing at all.

Pig Manure Grandfather's heart felt cold when he saw this. He was extremely pained that he had reared these children who didn't respect farmers. He went into the bedroom. As soon as he lay down, he had no more thought of getting up.

At noon, the three sisters cooked the rice, and saw that their father hadn't gotten out of bed. They went into his room to check on him.

Rice-Sieve Face said, "Father, why are you so distracted?"

Crab-Dipper Face said, "Father has given up the matter."

Lotus-Seed Face sang:

The fragrant, fragrant good rice,
The salty, salty vegetables and beans and eggs.
Tell your children what is in your heart.
Your children can assume the burden.

When Pig Manure Grandfather heard this, he turned and asked, "You want to?"

"Father can decide."

"You still want to work hard? Still want to suffer? Still want to endure the wind and the rain?"

"I'm not afraid of hard work. I'm not afraid of suffering. I'm not afraid of the wind and the rain."

Pig Manure Grandfather turned over and got out of bed. He happily stroked Lotus-Seed Face's hair and smiled.

So Lotus-Seed Face came to the rear mountain, and married Mr. Snake.

Early each morning, Mr. Snake went out to sell flowers, and Lotus-Seed Face packed a delicious lunch for him. Near evening when Mr. Snake returned home, he saw that the flowers and

47

trees in the garden had all been watered, and that a basin of warm water was ready for his bath. A month passed, two months, three months. Lotus-Seed Face also wove several yarn belts, and embroidered several flowered jackets. Mr. Snake carried these goods in all directions to sell them. Everyone praised Lotus-Seed Face's fine handicrafts.

After a year, the flower garden on the rear mountain was even more extensive. Even more flowers opened. Large numbers of butterflies and bees, birds and sparrows and cicadas all flew in. *Jiji, chacha, enen, wengweng.* It was all exciting. People walked over from the middle of the mountain and often heard Mr. Snake and Lotus-Seed Face singing happily:

Elder brother and little sister are a perfect couple,[11]
They are really like twin lotus flowers on one stalk.
Elder brother's heart is as white as a plum blossom,
Little sister's face is as beautiful as a peach blossom.

Before long, Lotus-Seed Face was pregnant.

One day, Pig Manure Grandfather heard that his daughter was pregnant, and he came to the rear mountain to see his daughter and her husband. Mr. Snake served dainties of all kinds—good wine and fine fruit. Pig Manure Grandfather ate until his stomach stuck out like a mountaintop. When it was almost time to go home, he asked Mr. Snake for a piece of toilet tissue. Mr. Snake gave him a piece of flimsy paper. He saw that it was made from gold. How could it be used as toilet tissue? Loath to use it, he slipped it into his pocket, and picked a section of sugarcane for toilet tissue. Then he left.

Pig Manure Grandfather returned home, and showed the gold foil to his two daughters, and boasted, "Your third sister is really lucky. Husband and wife work hard at farming. They have better lives than do the nobles and great families."

Rice-Sieve Face and Crab-Dipper Face fought over the gold foil. Glaring at each other, they grappled with it until their faces grew even uglier. Incensed at their behavior, Pig Manure Grandfather gave them a tongue-lashing. That evening, Rice-Sieve Face and Crab-Dipper Face were thinking: In the past year, no officials or wealthy people had come to propose marriage. Besides, Third Sister's life was going so well! The two were very jealous, and so they secretly discussed how to steal away Third Sister's money and property.

One day, Pig Manure Grandfather was going to a very distant place to see relatives. Rice-Sieve Face and Crab-Dipper Face took advantage of the opportunity to visit Third Sister. The two reached the flower garden at the rear mountain and saw how wonderful the scenery was. Unconsciously they shouted in unison, "How wonderful it would be if we could live here!" They walked into the cottage, and saw Third Sister weaving cloth—*kala, kala*—at the loom.[12] Pretending to be very happy, the two shouted, "Little sister, we've missed you so much!"

Lotus-Seed Face was overjoyed to see her sisters. She boiled sweet eggs and brewed a tea of dried longans, and said, "Early this morning, Mr. Snake went down the mountain to sell silk thread. If you had sent word a day earlier that you were coming, he wouldn't have gone out."

When Rice-Sieve Face and Crab-Dipper Face heard this, they relaxed and exchanged smiles. They rolled their eyes, and they piled up layers of lies and polite remarks. The eldest sister spoke first:

"Third Sister, you live in such a good place. You become younger and younger, and prettier and prettier."

"*Ai*, you love to joke," Lotus-Seed Face said. "I'm the same as before."

"Yes," Crab-Dipper Face praised Lotus-Seed Face, "you are much prettier than before. If you don't believe it, we'll get a basin of water for you to look at yourself!"

"Why fetch water?" Rice-Sieve Face said. "There's a well in the garden. If you look in it, you'll see!"

Third Sister walked to the edge of the well, and moved her head toward it. Suddenly Rice-Sieve Face shoved Lotus-Seed Face. *Putong*! Third Sister was pushed down into the well. Rice-Sieve Face and Crab-Dipper Face immediately ran to the opening, and covered the well with a rock.

Rice-Sieve Face then said to Crab-Dipper Face, "Second Sister, as I see it, if both of us stay here, and Mr. Snake returns and asks where Lotus-Seed Face has gone, it would be hard to deal with. You go on home first."

"Hunh, *I* go back? Why don't you go back first?"

"I'm the eldest, so I should stay."

"I'm the little sister. As the elder, you should let the younger stay!"

"Your fate is sorrow. What good fortune is there anyway in staying here?"

"Your face is covered with pockmarks. What face do you have to stay here!"

"You have no right!"

"You have no right!"

Talking and yelling, the two of them pushed and pulled and began fighting. They pulled each other's hair out, and their faces were covered with blood. They became uglier and uglier. They held each other and rolled back and forth—rolled straight to the edge of the manure pit outside the gate. The elder had a little more strength. She exerted herself, pushing Crab-Dipper Face into the manure pit. She sank in over her head.

Puffing and panting, Rice-Sieve Face ran and stumbled into the room. She fell down. She didn't have even a little strength left. Just then, Mr. Snake came back. Thinking it was Lotus-Seed Face who had fallen, he rushed to lift her up. He asked, "Little Sister Lotus, what's happened to you?"

"*Aiya!*" Rice-Sieve Face realized that this must be Mr. Snake, and she immediately pressed her face against his chest.

"Little Sister Lotus, what in the world has happened to you? It's a good thing I came back a little earlier today. Otherwise. . . ."

"*Wu!* No sooner had you left than a porcupine scurried up. It was going to bite me. I struggled with him. He lost and fell into the well."

"Ah, into the well?" Mr. Snake was about to walk over to the well when Rice-Sieve Face cried even more pitifully.

"Don't move it, don't move it!" Rice-Sieve Face ran over to the stone slab on the well, and she was weeping and shouting, "In our village we believe that when we kill a porcupine, we can't look at it again. If we look that can cause father to die, mother to die, husband to die, wife to die. You absolutely cannot. . . ."

"*Eee!*" Only now did Mr. Snake notice her face. "How does it happen that your face has so many spots?"

"They're from the porcupine's needles!"

"How does it happen that your face is so large?"

"It's swollen!"

Mr. Snake helped her lie down on the bed. He half-trusted, half-doubted her. But when he saw that her face was covered with bloodstains, his heart softened, and he immediately boiled some snacks for her. While he waited for her to finish eating, he walked to the side of the well. He intended to hoist up some water to wash the dishes, and saw that the stone slab was covering the well. When he moved the stone slab, a black shadow suddenly rushed out. He looked up, and saw a small bird resting on the eaves. It was singing:

Jijiji, gugugu!
Mr. Snake has eyes but no eyeballs.
Sweetness first, bitterness next.
The eldest sister is pretending to be your wife.

Mr. Snake thought this was very odd. He said:

You say something *jigugu*,
Mr. Snake has both eyes and eyeballs.
Little bird, if you're mine,
Fly over and rest on my shoulder.

The bird heard this, and, with a "*puci*" sound, it flew to Mr. Snake's shoulder. Rice-Sieve Face heard this and immediately rushed out from the house. She rushed to Mr. Snake and intended to grab the small bird. She also swore, "Anyone who listens to an unlucky bird won't have good luck!"

The small bird circled over Rice-Sieve Face's head, and sang:

Jiujiujiu, xiuxiuxiu!
Eldest Sister is using my hair cream,

51

And sleeps in my new bed with my new mosquito netting.
Her deception won't fool people very long.

Rice-Sieve Face struck out several times, but never caught
the small bird. She then struck out wildly with a bamboo stick
until the small bird fell to the ground. She caught the small
bird, and cruelly pulled out its feathers, and cursed, "I intend
to boil you until you're very tender. Let's see if you still talk
nonsense!"

The fire was hot, and the small bird was cut into several
pieces and put in the pot to stew. As soon as the water boiled,
the steam from the pot was just like a person talking:

Duoduoduo, duoduoduo!
Eldest Sister occupies my house.
What Mr. Snake eats of me is all flesh.
What Eldest Sister eats of me is all bone.

As predicted, the morsel Rice-Sieve Face was about to eat
turned to bone as soon as she put it in her mouth. She nearly
broke her teeth on it. Furious, she tossed the bone over the
wall.

The next day, a clump of bamboo was growing beside the
wall. The leaves were rustling in the wind—*sese susu*—as if
they were saying:

Sousousou, sousousou!
Mr. Snake should see clearly
That the pock-marked face is really filthy.
Your eldest sister-in-law is pretending to be your you-know-
who.

Mr. Snake was just about to ask about this when Rice-Sieve
Face placed his pole on his shoulders and told him to hurry up
and go out and earn some money. Heavy-hearted, he walked
slowly. Every step he took, he looked back three times. He
didn't stop looking at that clump of bamboo next to the wall.

Near evening, when he returned home, he discovered that

the clump of bamboo had disappeared. Rice-Sieve Face had chopped down the bamboo, and asked people to make two chairs from it. At dinnertime, Rice-Sieve Face brought out the chairs and sat down. Who would have thought that that chair could also sing. It sang without stopping:

Yaoyaoyao, yaoyaoyao!
Mr. Snake is very stable.
The Eldest Sister-in-Law will fall three times.
She will get a large bump on her head.

As predicted, the chair where Mr. Snake was sitting was very steady. But as soon as Rice-Sieve Face sat down, she fell over, and a large bump appeared on her head. Rice-Sieve Face was so angry that she cut the bamboo chair up into little pieces, and stuffed them into the stove for firewood. Burning them, she cursed, "Since you're still making an uproar, I'll force you to turn into ashes!"

Just then, an old woman from below the mountain came to Mr. Snake's home to beg for kindling to cook rice. Rice-Sieve Face told her to take it out herself. The old woman took out a small amount and asked, "*Ao*, where did this red turtle cake come from?"[13] Rice-Sieve Face said, "You're seeing things. Where is there any red turtle cake? If there is, you may have it for a treat."

The old woman took the red turtle cake home with her, and kept it for her grandson to eat when he came home from herding cattle. She kept it warm in a quilt. After her grandson came home and heard that there was a red turtle cake in the quilt, he happily went to look. He was dumbfounded: There was no red turtle cake in the quilt. Instead, a young girl was lying there, sleeping soundly. The grandson quickly drew the old woman over. In surprise, the old woman said, "Isn't this Mr. Snake's bride?"

The old woman was kindhearted. She remembered the woman she had just seen when she went to beg for kindling. She felt that this was all very fishy, so she quietly invited Mr. Snake over.

Mr. Snake came to the old woman's home. He went in and as soon as he saw her, he understood everything. He shouted, "Little Sister Lotus!" Lotus-Seed Face opened her eyes, blinked three times, and sat up immediately and leaned close to Mr. Snake. Weeping, she told of being tricked by her elder sisters.

Rice-Sieve Face was just in the midst of purposely reducing the bamboo strips to ashes. She thought that from now on she would be able to live happily with Mr. Snake. Suddenly she heard a commotion outside. Peering out, she discovered that the villagers were crowding around Lotus-Seed Face and Mr. Snake, and walking up in a great rage. She was so frightened that she jumped out the window and began running away. She ran to the side of the manure pit that Crab-Dipper Face had sunk into. She slipped and fell into the pit. After struggling briefly, she sank in over her head.

From that time on, the good and honest and hard-working Mr. Snake and Lotus-Seed Face began a happy, new life.

(Story collected by Zheng Huicong)

HOW THE "TWO COMMON PEOPLE" ORIGINATED

In the following tales, the female characters are depicted as essentially passive as they acquiesce in the exhortations to marry their brothers and repopulate the earth.

In eastern Fujian and southern Zhejiang, when her husband dies, why does the wife cry over and over again, "Brother—ah—Brother. . . ."? In the past, the She[14] nationality and the Han nationality had the same legend.

This is the She people's legend:

In the past, according to the legend, it was said, "When heavenly oil falls, the race is destroyed." It is said that if heavenly oil fell from heaven, it only needed to strike one spark in the world, and it would immediately ignite a great conflagration which would burn up the grasses and trees, the houses and people and animals, until nothing was left.

One day, suddenly—just like a heavy rainstorm—"heavenly oil" began to fall. Flames rose on all sides. Everywhere, houses collapsed. The land slid and the earth cracked. The people and the mountain beasts and the flying birds all fled in confusion. One brother and sister were unable to run. They hid beside a large rock and wept and shouted loudly. Suddenly a white-haired, white-bearded local god appeared before them. Stroking their heads, he said, "Little brother and sister, don't be afraid. In a moment, this rock will open its mouth. Then the two of you can take refuge there!" Before long, as predicted, the rock opened its mouth, and the brother and sister went in.

The rock then closed its mouth, and rolled and rolled, rolled and rolled. It rolled down from the mountain to the bottom of the sea. It sank and, for seven days and seven nights, it was at the bottom of the sea. Then the rock floated to the coast and opened its mouth into two cracks. Exiting, the brother and sister saw that the world was very quiet. Not one person remained.

"*Du! Du! Du!*" Leaning on his staff, the same white-haired, white-bearded local god walked over. The local god said, "Little brother and sister! The two of you are grown up now, and now the two of you—brother and sister—are the only ones in the world. You must get married! Otherwise, the race will become extinct." The brother and sister said, "We are brother and sister. How can we marry each other?" The local god said, "Just this way! This rock that you took refuge in has now cracked into two halves. Each of you should hold one half and roll it to the beach. If the two rocks join together, then you are married!"

The brother and sister listened to the local god's words, and each of them pushed half of the rock down to the beach. They rolled and rolled—and the two rocks really did join together. The brother and sister then married, and had sons and daughters. Generation followed generation.

This is the Han people's legend:

In the world of a very, very long time ago, there were the "first people of the world." Like people today, they worked industriously and ate sparingly, and passed their days in harmony.

One day, in one household, the little sister took food to the mountain for her elder brother, who was cultivating the land. Her elder brother was just about to rest and eat when suddenly a monkey emerged from the forest, seized the food basket from the little sister's hands, and ran off with it. The elder brother and the little sister chased him over one mountain after another. They chased and chased until the monkey ran into a mountain cave and disappeared. The little sister said, "The monkey has disappeared!" The elder brother said, "In fact, it is in this mountain cave and it can't escape!" The brother and sister then entered the cave to search. This mountain cave was dark, and very large, and very deep. Inside, the brother and sister walked more than one *li* and still didn't find the monkey!

Just then, outside the mountain cave—*huahua*—"heavenly oil" began falling just like rain. It is said, "When heavenly oil falls, humankind is destroyed." As soon as people are drenched by the heavenly oil, they die. Luckily at this time, the brother and sister were penetrating deep into the mountain cave in search of the monkey. They hid there during this calamity.

After the "heavenly oil" had fallen, the brother and sister found the food basket. They left the cave and looked around. The grasses and trees on the mountain had all died and withered. The houses in the village had all collapsed. The people of the world had all died. The brother and sister had no choice but to return to this mountain cave, and live on grasses they pulled up in the cave, and on snakes and rats they caught in the cave.

In this way, year after year passed. The brother and sister emerged from the cave to look around. The world was alive again! Grasses and trees were green again. Mountain flowers had opened again. The elder brother said to his little sister, "The world is alive, but without people that means nothing!" The little sister worriedly asked her elder brother what they could do. Her elder brother said, "If we want people, all we can do is marry!" His little sister said, "That would be shameful!" She dashed into the cave, and covered her face with that broken food basket. Her elder brother chased her into the cave, and married his little sister. They had children, and generation followed generation.

Later, the elder brother died. The She and Han legends both say that the little sister, in weeping for her husband, cried "Elder brother, elder brother." This kind of weeping style has been passed down to the present.

(Stories related by Li Shenghui and Dong Xinyan; collected by Lan Qingen and Dong Enjin)

57

QIU MENGSHE CLEVERLY KILLS
THE COUNTY MAGISTRATE

*Huijie, the woman in this story, is essentially passive, following
the instructions of Qiu Mengshe, but she is also quick-witted
and thus able to take advantage of unexpected occurrences.
She is also depicted as a devoted wife loyal to her husband.*

In the past, on the island of Dongshan, there was a beautiful
and affectionate couple. The man was named Xie Sheng. The
woman was named Huijie. The man farmed, and the woman
wove. They lived very happily together. One day, a shameless,
rude rascal named Cui Hua caught a glimpse of them. Noticing
Huijie's looks, Cui Hua came up with a scheme. If he could
recommend her to the Mao County magistrate, maybe he would
be rewarded with a half-time official position.

The county magistrate was too fond of alcohol and women.
As soon as he heard of this exceedingly beautiful woman, he
was interested. He immediately ordered Cui Hua to take a *yamen*
runner to the Xie home and seize the woman. Xie Sheng had
gone to the fields. The *yamen* runner, who was like a wild
animal, grabbed Huijie and stuffed her into the bridal sedan-
chair. When Xie Sheng returned, she was already gone and the
house was empty. In his anxiety, he took up an ax and was
about to risk his life in pursuit when a kind neighbor firmly
restrained him.

Just then, someone dressed like a warrior made his way through
the crowd and walked over. This was Qiu Mengshe, who enjoyed a great reputation all along the coast. Qiu Mengshe asked
the ins and outs of the situation, thought about it briefly, and
then said something to Xie Sheng and left in a hurry.

Now let's return to the other thread of the story. In the county *yamen*, Huijie couldn't even think of tea and she couldn't eat even a grain of rice. She wept the whole day long. And when she saw the county magistrate, she swore. The county magistrate summoned Cui Hua to admonish her. That Cui Hua had no sense of shame. He went up and chastised her, "Girl, don't you know how to appreciate favors? I, Cui Hua, also admire your incomparable looks. It was because I was afraid your beauty would be wasted that I at last recommended you to the county magistrate. If you—a villager—now become the wife of a county magistrate—isn't this a rare honor?" His words had just fallen when there was the sound of "*po*." Huijie had slapped his face. Before Cui Hua could say anything, suddenly there was a loud commotion outside. The county magistrate immediately told Cui Hua to investigate. He reported that Xie Sheng was demanding to see his wife. The county magistrate was about to refuse, when Huijie said, "If I can see my dear husband one time, I will be ready to die." When the county magistrate heard that she was even willing to die, he thought she should be even more willing to marry him. So the county magistrate agreed to give her two hours with Xie Sheng.

In accord with Qiu Mengshe's idea, Xie Sheng had caused a commotion in coming to the *yamen* to see his wife. As soon as they saw each other, they wept in each other's arms. Only after a good long while did Xie Sheng tell her why he had come. He also warned her repeatedly to laugh only when she should and not to laugh at all when she wasn't supposed to—to avoid making a big mistake. Huijie nodded her head and promised. With tears in his eyes, Xie Sheng left.

After Xie Sheng left, that county magistrate went in, intending to gather Huijie into his arms. Huijie cleverly dodged to one side and said, "If you want my obedience, you must do one thing for me." The county magistrate immediately asked what, and Huijie said, "You have to make me laugh in public before I'll marry you." The county magistrate thought to himself, "What's so hard about this!" So he agreed.

The drums sounded three times.[15] The county magistrate went up to the court and asked someone to invite Huijie to come out. The county magistrate nodded his head, and eight cripples came up to the court and danced the dances of cripples. That was really both ugly and comical, making everyone in the court laugh and laugh. But Huijie's face was as cold as ice. When the county magistrate saw that this hadn't worked, he immediately called out again. Eight people wearing square headscarves walked up. When they reached the court, they danced a nondescript dance, making everyone double over with laughter. You wonder why? These eight people were all bald. Their heads were also all scabby—just like designs. But Huijie still revealed no expression at all.

There's no need to go into great detail. That county magistrate had exhausted all his tricks. From beginning to end he was unable to coax a laugh out of Huijie. After his disappointment, he was so ashamed that he flew into a rage. Huijie saw that her chance had come, and only then did she open her mouth, "Why not put up an announcement asking for a talented person?" This seemed reasonable to the county magistrate, and he immediately ordered an announcement posted outside the city, saying, "If there is someone who can make the county magistrate's wife laugh, the reward will be one hundred ounces of silver. . . ." The notice had just been posted when Qiu Mengshe emerged from the crowd and tore the notice down. He was dressed up as a stone grinder. He was carrying a rack of grindstones on his shoulders. That *yamen* runner saw that the notice had been torn down, and immediately reported to the *yamen*. At this time, the sun had already set. The curtain of night was gently falling. The county magistrate listened to the report, and ordered someone to take a lamp up to the court, and to order the person who had torn down the notice to come to the court. Qiu Mengshe reported immediately. The county magistrate took his measure, and asked, "How are you going to make the county magistrate's wife laugh?" Qiu Mengshe replied, "I'll grind scissors." Half-believing, half-doubting, the county magistrate said, "Go ahead." Qiu Mengshe said, "My grinding stone has a taboo. If too many people are watching, the grinding won't work." When the county magistrate heard this, he immediately told all the *yamen* runners to leave.

Qiu Mengshe didn't say much. He just looked at Huijie, and then concentrated on grinding the scissors. Soon, Huijie began to laugh. When the county magistrate saw this, he was overjoyed, and immediately came down from the court. Following Qiu Mengshe's example, he also began grinding. Huijie stopped laughing. The county magistrate was terrified, and he immediately asked Qiu Mengshe why this was so. Qiu Mengshe said, "If you want to make your wife laugh, you must also change clothes with me." So the county magistrate took off his red robe and removed his black gauze cap, and put on Qiu Mengshe's clothes and head covering, and began grinding again. Then, as expected, Huijie laughed like a hibiscus flower bursting open. This was such a beautiful sight that the county magistrate forgot himself in his happiness and he began grinding even harder.

While the county magistrate was grinding, Qiu Mengshe flew to don the red robe and the black gauze cap. He extinguished the perpetual flame, and turned and sped to the table. He rapped the table: "Come!" The *yamen* runners responded immediately. In the county magistrate's tone, Qiu Mengshe shouted, "This stone grinder—he dared to run into the court and take liberties with my wife. He is guilty of a crime for which he deserves to die ten thousand deaths! Go down and behead him for me!" The *yamen* runners saw that he was wearing the red robe and the black gauze cap. Since the lamplight was dim, they couldn't see clearly. They believed that he was the real county magistrate, so they immediately agreed. Like wild animals, they forcibly brought the real county magistrate to the court. In an instant, that county magistrate became confused and disoriented. He couldn't even shout. Only when the executioner was about to raise the butcher knife did he shout: "Stop! I am still. . . ." They didn't let him finish. The knife had found the spot, and the head had already fallen to the ground.

Qiu Mengshe then ordered that Cui Hua be brought to the court. When Cui Hua got there, he heard Qiu Mengshe shout, "You slave. You're evil. You're a bully. You violate moral principles. It's hard to see to it that justice is served. Look at the knife!" That Cui Hua had no chance to respond. The knife flashed, and his corpse and head were quickly separated.

Off to one side, Huijie saw that this had become terribly serious, and in a moment she was so frightened that her face turned green. She didn't know what to do. Then she heard Qiu Mengshe say, "Don't be afraid. I've already told your husband to come and meet you outside the city. We'll take advantage of darkness and I'll see you out of the city." Huijie asked hesitantly, "Is it possible to escape?" Qiu Mengshe pointed at the red robe he was wearing and laughed, "You forget: I am still the magistrate of Qipin county." Huijie suddenly understood, and immediately followed this "county magistrate." They walked grandly out of the court, and went outside the city.

At this time, outside the city, Xie Sheng had already driven up in a cart and had been waiting for a long time. Just as Xie Sheng was about to say something, Qiu Mengshe said, "We can't talk here. Go home first." Saying this, he jumped onto the cart. Xie Sheng quickly cracked the whip. All that could be seen behind the cart was a puff of yellow earth. When the *yamen* runners realized what had happened, it was already too late to catch up!

(Story collected by Lin Guifu)

JINDING DUCK

In this story, despite maltreatment by her stepmother, the young woman Yalian remains a filial daughter. Consumed by greed, the stepmother creates the conditions leading to her own demise.

Jinding[16] Village on the bank of the Jiulong River abounded with the double-yoked Jinding duck eggs. They were in great demand all over the country. Everyone liked them. But do you know the history of the double-yolked Jinding duck eggs...?

Tradition has it that in this region of rivers and lakes—Jinding Village—the duck-raising expert was Guo Hai. At middle age, he lost his wife and remarried. His first wife left one daughter, named Yalian, and his second wife bore a daughter named Yazhen. The stepmother, the Woman Wang, usually ate well but was lazy. Guo Hai was ill from overwork. It is often said, "The stepmother is cruel to the first wife's children." The Woman Wang maltreated Yalian. She forced the young Yalian to assume the heavy burden of raising the ducks. Every day before it was light, she forced her to go out to care for the ducks. In the summer the scorching sun burned her face and ears red. In the winter she trembled from the cold. Whenever the girl failed to satisfy the stepmother, she hit her and didn't even give her food to eat!

Near evening one day, wind and rain came together. Yalian was hurrying the ducks home. On the way, she discovered that one was missing. What would she do? If she went home and her stepmother found out, she'd be cruelly beaten. Moreover, her father was ill and in bed. She couldn't court his anger! If she didn't go back, where would she go on this windy, rainy night? If the ducks got drenched and then got sick, what would

her family depend on for food? She decided to search throughout the night. So she stealthily drove the ducks into the duck
pen and, taking advantage of her stepmother's absence, slipped
out. It was raining even more heavily now. Yalian was struggling in the wind and rain. She stepped across one shallow
ditch after another. She crossed one footpath after another. She
went through one dense forest after another, calling and searching
without stopping. She didn't know how much time had passed
or how far she had walked. She continued walking straight ahead
and searching.

"*Ya! Ya!*" From ahead came the indistinct sound of a duck
call. When Yalian heard this, she was so happy! She went up
and looked. On the beachhead was a grass hut. A white-bearded,
white-haired old grandfather was sitting there watching the ducks.
Yalian asked him, "White-bearded Grandfather, are you watching
my duck?"

"Maybe your duck slipped in among my ducks!" He led Yalian
to the top of the shallow ditch to look.

"Is this the duck you lost?" The white-bearded grandfather
held up a plump mother duck.

"No. The one I lost isn't that plump."

The white-bearded grandfather then held up a large male
duck. "Is this the duck you lost?"

"No. The one I lost is a small, thin black duck."

Finally, the white-bearded grandfather held up a small, thin
black duck, and asked, "Is this the small duck you lost?"

Yalian looked at it carefully, and said happily, "This is exactly the small duck I lost. Give it back to me, okay?"

The white-bearded old grandfather said, "Honest young girl,
you take it back with you! It can do good things for you."

Yalian carried that small, thin black duck, and ran home
joyfully. When her stepmother saw her, she heaped abuse on
her.

Yalian lowered her head and went in. She ran to her father's
bed. Her father's hands were shaking as he stroked Yalian's
wet hair. "Child—such a heavy wind and rain. Where have
you been?"

"Looking for a duck."

"Did you find it?"

"Yes. Here it is!" Yalian held up the duck that she had carried at her breast.

"Ah!" The father and daughter shouted nearly in unison. They were at a loss for words. What had happened?

The duck that Yalian had carried home wasn't a small, thin black duck. It was instead a plump, large golden duck. It was gleaming gold under the rays of the lamp.

The stepmother and sister Yazhen heard the commotion and rushed in. The whole family was looking at this golden duck. They were so happy they didn't know what to do.

After staring for a while, the stepmother asked Yalian where she had found this golden duck. Yalian had never been able to tell a lie. She told her parents the whole story.

After listening and listening, the stepmother began hurling abuse again. "Hunh. You stupid, unpromising pig. Couldn't you bring back more!"

Near evening the next day, rain was mixed with wind again. The greedy stepmother forced Yalian to lead the way, and she also told Yazhen to help her. She and Yazhen tied cloth bags to their waists, preparing to bring back several golden ducks.

The mother and daughters searched as they walked. Finally they reached the front of the white-bearded grandfather's grass hut. Yalian didn't dare go up to talk.

The stepmother had her mind set on taking several golden ducks back. She ran up and said, "Hey, old man! Our family's flock of golden ducks has run into the midst of your flock of ducks."

"Can golden ducks also run?" The white-bearded grandfather laughingly looked around.

"I don't care whether they can run or whether they can't run. In any case, most of your flock of golden ducks is in fact our family's," the stepmother said forcefully.

"If they're your family's, then just take them home!" the white-bearded grandfather said, still laughing.

The stepmother was only too anxious for the white-bearded grandfather to say this. She and Yazhen hurriedly untied the cloth bags, expertly chose the plumpest, largest mother ducks and packed them into the bags. They held them fast and packed them in. Before long, the two bags were both bulging. The two of them walked like pack animals. They walked to the side of the grass hut, and saw a heap of shining golden ingots, flashing gold. The greedy stepmother opened her mouth and put two golden ingots in her mouth, and then began to hurry homeward.

Along the way, they walked and stopped, stopped and walked. It was nearly dawn by the time they reached Jiulong River. They began wading across. Wading and wading, the stepmother apparently stepped on a round rock. Her foot slipped, her body tilted. The two large heavy bags were lopsided. The stepmother fell into the water. Yalian and Yazhen wanted to pull her out, but they couldn't. The stepmother wanted to shout, but as soon as she opened her mouth, the two golden ingots rolled around and ended up in her stomach.

Yalian and Yazhen were shouting "Ma! Ma!" but they heard no answer. Before long, a large, fat mother duck floated up from the water. But they didn't know where the stepmother's body and the bags had drifted to!

Yalian and Yazhen returned home with this plump mother duck, and related this experience to their father.

It's very strange to say, but from then on, this plump mother duck laid a large egg every day. All her eggs were larger than the other duck eggs. And each one had two yolks!

People said that the stepmother had changed into this mother duck. Because she swallowed two golden ingots, this mother duck's eggs were all double-yolked. Since it was after she swallowed the golden ingots that she turned into a duck, people called this kind of duck "Golden Ingot Duck." This village is also called "Golden Ingot Village."

(Story collected by Ya Ying)

LI ZHI URGES HIS DAUGHTER-IN-LAW TO REMARRY

Li Zhi, a scholar of late Ming dynasty times, is known as an iconoclastic thinker. In this tale, his daughter-in-law exemplifies the Confucian virtues, for, although she would clearly like to remarry, she is prepared to live out her life as a chaste widow serving her father-in-law. Li Zhi is unusual in that he urges her to remarry and takes the tonsure in part to relieve her of responsibility for him.

When Li Zhi[17] was 61 *sui*, his wife was in poor health. He told his daughter and son-in-law to take her home to Quanzhou. He kept only his son, daughter-in-law, and grandson with him. His son was named Li Gui. The son of Li Zhi's younger brother, he had been adopted by Li Zhi. Li Zhi loved him as if he had been his own son. Unfortunately, not long after his wife left, Li Gui died of drowning. Li Zhi was always weeping. He was consumed by sorrow. He took up his brush and wrote three elegies, "Weeping for my son Gui." In the poems, he swore bitterly, "Deep water can kill people," and, "I bitterly hate this pool of water." He saw that his daughter-in-law was still young, and so he wrote in the poem, "Your wife should remarry." So, after his son had been dead for a hundred days, he turned to the matter of his daughter-in-law's remarriage. One day, when his daughter-in-law brought him the steamed rice and vegetables, he asked her to sit down. He said, "My daughter-in-law, you are still young and should find another family. My son Gui is dead, and can't come back to life. You shouldn't waste your youth."

"No!" Holding back her tears, the daughter-in-law answered,

"You treat me even better than you do your own daughter. Now your wife is no longer with you. I want to look after you until you're a hundred years old. I want to keep watch over Siguan[18] until he grows up."

"My daughter-in-law, it's okay for Siguan to stay either with me or with you. Don't worry. I'm old, but I have a lot of friends. They can take care of me. But you. . . ."[19] Pointing at the bamboo outside the window, he said, "Look—there is a green vine climbing the bamboo and growing up and blossoming with white morning glories. Last night's wind and rain blew the bamboo to the ground. The young vine lost its support and now it can only grow up creeping on the ground. How hard this is! We should lift the bamboo up again. Only then will it have renewed support. My daughter-in-law, you are just like that young vine. You need to find support!"

When his daughter-in-law didn't respond, he told her the story of Zhuo Wenjun and Sima Xiangru.[20]

His daughter-in-law listened, and her eyes were brimming with tears. She thought to herself: All the fathers-in-law in the world want their daughters-in-law to remain chaste. It's only my father-in-law who advises me to remarry. The old man is so reasonable!

Li Zhi also said, "Many people come here every day to hear my lectures. Be very discerning. If you respect a young man who is hardworking and honest and who has high aspirations, and if he is unmarried and he also likes you, you just say one word to me and I will help you. Or if you'd like to go home to Quanzhou and then remarry, that's fine too. It's your decision to make. As your father, I certainly won't make things difficult for you."

Later, Li Zhi learned that his daughter-in-law had taken a fancy to a young fisherman who used to come to listen to his lectures. That fisherman was a bachelor. He was kindhearted. He caught lots of fish and always divided them with the villagers. He often came to hear Li Zhi lecture, and he understood a lot of principles. The youth saw that Li Zhi's daughter-in-law was virtuous and sincere, and he liked her very much. Li Zhi was very happy. Just as he was about to arrange things for

68

them, his son-in-law unexpectedly brought bad news: his wife had died. Consumed with grief, Li Zhi fell very ill. While he was ill, he write six poems in memory of his wife, "Weeping for Huang Yiren." At a time like this, how could his daughter-in-law have the heart to leave the wretched, lonely old man? She determined not to remarry. She would devote herself to caring for her aged father-in-law. Li Zhi saw that his daughter was intentionally avoiding that young fisherman, and he was very puzzled. But figuring out the reason quickly, he resolutely shaved his head and said to his daughter-in-law, "I've already shaved my head to become a monk. There is no need for you to worry about me anymore. You have someone you like. I am happy for both of you!" He asked someone to bring the young fisherman over, and said sincerely, "The two of you needn't go on waiting. Get married! I present you with a couplet written in scrolls."

The young fisherman excitedly accepted the couplet, and knelt and kowtowed.

The daughter-in-law said, "Father, I know that you shaved your head for me, as well as to cast off the ordinary world. I know that you want to fight against hypocrisy. We will come to see you often."

Concerning the grandson, Little Siguan: from childhood, it had been his grandfather who had doted on him. He himself wanted to stay with Li Zhi. Later, Li Zhi's son-in-law took him back to the old home in Quanzhou.

Li Zhi's exhorting his daughter-in-law to remarry was a denial of the reactionary Taoist belief that "starvation is a small thing, loss of chastity is a big thing." It was also a display of contempt for feudal moral principles and virtues.

(Story collected by Li Huiliang)

PART TWO

ASSERTIVE, UNFILIAL, RESOURCEFUL: IMAGES OF WOMEN AND MEN IN LOVE

THE STORY OF PHOENIX ROCK

In this story, we meet two strong women: one, a woman in love who intends to marry the man of her choice; the other, her stepmother who intends to thwart the younger woman in her desires. In the end, both die, as do others, but—through supernatural intervention—the young woman, Zhenniang, is able to remain with her betrothed through eternity.

A small mountain with dark green trees stands north of Yongding City—North Gate Mountain. On the mountain peak is an enormous rock that was split open by thunder. It is shaped like a cooper bell that has been split open. Local people call it "Rock Hit by Thunder." Some people call it "Cooper Bell Rock." It is said that when thunder split this rock open, a beautiful phoenix flew out from inside. So there are also people who call it "Phoenix Rock." How could a phoenix fly out from the rock . . . ?

No one knows how many years ago this occurred. At that time, the bustling city of Yongding didn't yet exist. Below North Gate Mountain there was only a very small village. Around this village, aside from several paddy fields, the other places were merely overgrown with weeds. In front of the village was a river—the one we know today as Yongding River. In the village at that time was a young couple, a boy and a girl. The boy was named Wu Bicheng. His parents had died a long time ago; he was a bachelor, and he was extremely talented. He was also very robust. He farmed, fished, hunted, and chopped firewood. He could do everything. The girl was named Lai Zhenniang. Extremely beautiful, she was like a budding mountain camellia. She was also talented. She wove cloth quickly and well. Her embroidered flowers could attract bees. The two of them were innocent playmates. It was puppy love.[1] From childhood, they were together tending the cattle, they were together picking wildflowers, and they were together picking wild fruit. Sometimes they also went to the river together for water fights. The whole day long, they were always together. They were as close as brother and sister. Their feelings became stronger as they grew older. Unconsciously, they fell in love. The boy said to the girl, "I wouldn't marry anyone but you." The girl said, "I would marry someone else only if the river water flowed backwards and the sun rose in the west." The girl gave the boy a small bag that she had embroidered especially for him with a decorative heart pattern. The boy gave the girl a bracelet that his mother had left him. In this way, the two of them were considered to have secretly become engaged. The villagers all said that if they could become husband and wife they would be considered a couple made in heaven.[2] The two of them also contentedly thought that when the time came they would be joined together as a devoted couple. But heaven doesn't obey the wishes of human beings. Difficulty was piled on difficulty in their desire to become husband and wife.

Zhenniang lost her father when she was seven *sui* and her mother when she was ten *sui*. All she could do was live with her uncle. Early on, her uncle lost his wife. Later he took a new wife. That female had bulging eyes and a wide mouth. She was as fat as a ball. Everyone called her Old Woman Frog. Because the uncle was away for long periods, she took care of household affairs. Old Woman Frog had a vicious heart. Her eyes opened when she saw money. She was insatiably greedy. She saw that Zhenniang was like a water lotus. If it was possible to marry her into a wealthy family, she herself would profit from it. So each time she saw Bicheng and Zhenniang together, she was filled with impatience and hatred. She thought, "If Zhenniang marries this impoverished devil, won't I lose out?" So she said to Zhenniang, "You're like a flower. That guy Bicheng is like a pile of cowdung. How can cowdung match a flower?"

Zhenniang said, "If you cultivate flowers with cowdung, the flowers will flourish even more."

Then Old Woman Frog said, "That guy has a pair of shifty

eyes. Just by looking at him, you can tell he is poor now and will always be poor. In the future, if he isn't a thief, he'll be a beggar."

Zhenniang said, "Bicheng is a poor man, but he is not poor in aspirations. He depends completely on his own two hands for food to eat. He has a good moral character. I like him."

Old Woman Frog said spitefully, "If you dare see that son-of-a-bitch again after today, I'll break your legs!"

Zhenniang said decisively, "Even if I had broken legs, I would still get up and go to see him."

Old Woman Frog's face was swollen with anger. She beat her breast and stamped her feet. Crying and sniveling, she gave Zhenniang a tongue-lashing. From then on, no matter what Zhenniang went out to do, she followed along. Even when Zhenniang was weaving cloth at home, she stood guard beside her. Bicheng was unable to be with Zhenniang for warm heart-to-heart talks, so he sang mountain songs, and sang duets with Zhenniang. Bicheng sang:

> If you really want to climb a tree, you must climb to the top; don't stop midway.
> If you really fall in love, you should love to the end; you can't store water in a sieve.

Zhenniang sang:

> On top of the high mountain is a plum. The hands climb the plum tree and wait for the flowers to open.
> Nine out of ten plum blossoms open—saving one for elder brother's arrival.

Bicheng then sang:

> Wearing unlined clothing in the wintry cold twelfth month. You know, too, that I am impoverished now.
> Your family has a great deal of wealth. I don't know what little sister's style is.

Zhenniang immediately sang:

A pot of brown rice gruel. With an unwavering heart I would marry elder brother and not fear poverty.

I hope our love will last forever. If you go out to beg, I will hold the bowl for you.

Old Woman Frog was so angry at hearing this that smoke poured from all the openings in her body. She flew into a rage. Pointing at Bicheng from a distance, she heaped abuse on him. "You're a toad lusting after the flesh of a swan, yet you can't piss and take care of yourself." Bicheng ignored her and continued his rhythmic singing, angering Old Woman Frog so much that her lips turned purple.

How could she make Bicheng drop the idea? Old Woman Frog racked her brains. She thought and thought, and finally came up with a wicked plan.

On a very cold day, she said to Bicheng, "Today, if you can go into the river and catch a live fish weighing twenty *jin*[3] with your own hands, I'll let you marry Zhenniang. If you can't catch it, you give up this idea." Bicheng left without a word.

Looking at the swirling snowstorm, Old Woman Frog thought; "This guy surely doesn't dare go, but if he goes he must freeze to death in the water. And if he doesn't freeze to death, he doesn't have the ability anyhow to catch such a large fish with his bare hands and bring it back." But while she was still feeling smug, Bicheng was carrying back a large, live fish. It weighed exactly twenty *jin*—no more and no less. Bicheng said to her, "You can't take back the water you've poured out, nor can you take back your words. Now you have to let me marry Zhenniang!"

Old Woman Frog was dumbstruck. Her eyeballs rolled, and she had another idea. She said, "I've said it before, and I can say it again. You did something, and you can do some more. Today if you can kill the poisonous snake of West Mountain, I will certainly let Zhenniang marry you. If not, you must still give up this idea."

Bicheng left again without a word.

After Bicheng left, Old Woman Frog thought to herself, "The

poisonous snake of West Mountain can swallow a cow in one gulp. The snake will surely eat that guy." Unexpectedly, in only the time it takes to eat a meal, Bicheng returned, dragging a huge poisonous snake, frightening her so that her whole body trembled and shivered. Bicheng walked over to her and said, "Now there's nothing more for you to say. Now let Zhenniang go with me."

Old Woman Frog tilted her head, thought, and said, "This is my final request. If you can give me a hundred ounces of silver, Zhenniang will be yours. This time I certainly won't break my promise. Whenever you give me the money, I'll give you the person."

Bicheng was a man of iron. Up to now, he hadn't begged at all. He left angrily. From then on, he buried himself in work, going out every day when the stars faded and returning in the moonlight. When the work on the land was finished, he went down to the river to catch fish and up to the mountain to chop firewood and into the forests to hunt. When he thought of Zhenniang, his strength was inexhaustible. Every day until evening, he was like a water cart in a drought, going around without stopping. He tightened his belt, and he didn't spend one copper coin foolishly. After eighty-one days had passed, he had saved ninety-nine ounces of silver. He only needed to earn one more ounce, and he could marry Zhenniang! His joy was boundless.

On that morning when Bicheng weighed the silver, Zhenniang was washing clothes at the river. She washed and washed. When she'd finished washing and was about to stand up, she suddenly heard Old Woman Frog beside her. She was calling out warmly to she-didn't-know-who, "Aiya, Master Wang, what wind blew you in?" Zhenniang looked up. Standing on the bridge was a rich man with an insolent grin. This person was more than thirty. It was as if his pair of triangular eyes were mesmerized as they stared wickedly at Zhenniang. Zhenniang knew that this villain was up to no good. She spat in his direction, and stood up and walked off. Old Woman Frog had observed that rich man Wang, and knew right away exactly what he wanted. She watched Zhenniang walk into the distance. She was afraid there would be complications, and so all she could do was rush to catch up with him. As she approached him, she said, "Master Wang, if you would like to, please come over to my house for a while."

"Fine, fine." With his mouth, Master Wang agreed. With his eyes, he still stared dumbstruck at Zhenniang's retreating figure.

Master Wang was the biggest landlord in 90 *li*. His nickname was Miser Demon. He was also a lusty devil. Although he already had two wives, as soon as he laid eyes on Zhenniang, he was driven to distraction, and determined to take her as his third wife. He went through the village and climbed a small mountain north of the village. This is the North Gate Mountain of today. There was an ancient temple on the mountain peak. In the temple was a mangy monk. You could see him all day long striking the gongs and beating the drum, chanting the sutras, and praying to Buddha. But his intentions were evil. He and Miser Demon often colluded with each other and engaged in immoral acts.

The next day, the mangy monk went down the mountain to look for Old Woman Frog. When he found her, he said, "Congratulations! Congratulations!"

Old Woman Frog cracked open her wide mouth and said, "Ah! Old Buddha is teasing. How could happiness come to my poor family, to my poor path?"

The mangy monk said, "Master Wang wants to marry Zhenniang. Isn't that happiness as big as the sky!"

Old Woman Frog was overjoyed, but she worriedly asked, "Really? Maybe our Zhenniang isn't the lucky one."

"It was Master Wang himself who asked me to talk with you. If you agree, he will give you whatever amount of silver you can carry. He will also add ninety-nine pieces of silk, ninety-nine pieces of satin. . . ." When Old Woman Frog heard this, she was so happy that her wide mouth cracked open larger and larger, and she immediately assented over and over again.

But Old Woman Frog's happiness was premature. Zhenniang adamantly refused to marry Miser Demon.

Old Woman Frog said, "Master Wang has a dignified appearance. He is very good-looking. In what way doesn't he match you?"

77

Zhenniang said, "He has a fat head and big ears. He is pot-bellied. He's a big, fat pig."

Old Woman Frog said, "If you marry him, you'll wear silks and satins; you'll eat delicacies from land and sea. You'll have gold and silver and money and valuables—so much that you won't be able to go through it all in a lifetime."

Zhenniang said, "If I eat his food and wear his clothes, my stomach will rot and sores will cover my body."

Old Woman Frog said, "When the bridal chair comes, even if you don't want to, you'll have to go!"

Zhenniang said, "I would never marry him unless the river water flowed backwards and the sun rose in the west."

Old Woman Frog was furious, "I'll never let you marry Bicheng!"

Zhenniang said firmly, "Alive, I'm part of the Wu family. Dead, I'll be a ghost of the Wu family!"[4]

There was nothing Old Woman Frog could do. She could only go to the temple and find the mangy monk. The two of them exchanged a wink and chattered for a long time. In the end, they hatched a deadly trap.

One day, Wu Bicheng was carrying firewood to sell, and ran into the mangy monk.

"Firewood peddler, my temple wants to buy some wood. Come along with me."

Bicheng accompanied the mangy monk, and carried the firewood to the temple. After he stacked it, he went into the temple to collect his money. When he entered, he saw a landlord sitting there with his whole face shining with oil. This was Miser Demon. Miser Demon rose hypocritically and called to Bicheng, "Ah, Elder Brother, you're tired. Please sit down."

Without responding, Bicheng just turned to the mangy monk and asked for his money.

The mangy monk said, "Not so fast. Master Wang has something to say to you."

"If you have something to say, be quick about it," Bicheng said impatiently.

"Okay. I'll speak frankly." Miser Demon slapped his pocket and said, "I know all about you and Zhenniang. If you'll let her marry me—hey! I'll give you a hundred ounces of silver."

At this, Bicheng's whole body burned with rage.

Miser Demon saw that Bicheng wasn't saying anything at all and that his face had turned an angry color. Unleashing all his fury, he threatened, "How about it? You'd better be sensible. If you don't agree today, you'd better not think you'll leave here!"

Bicheng was angry and confused. He picked up his carrying pole, intending to strike Miser Demon. But the carrying pole just swayed and shook in the air. Caught off-balance, Bicheng fell. The mangy monk had struck him on the back of the head with an iron staff.

The Miser Demon and the mangy monk saw that Bicheng was already dead, and they searched the bag on his person. Then, hurrying frantically, they opened up the copper bell and hid Bicheng's corpse in it. They intended to deal with it later.

Then the mangy monk followed Miser Demon's orders and went rushing out to find Old Woman Frog. As soon as he found her, he immediately gave her the bag, and also bent her ear with a lot of chatter.

Old Woman Frog rubbed her eyes with fresh ginger so that she could squeeze out several teardrops, and then she entered Zhenniang's room. Feigning grief, she said to Zhenniang, "Child—ah—Bicheng—this child—was truly unlucky. This morning he went up the mountain to chop firewood and fell and died at Cut-Off Life Cliff. Here is his bag."

When Zhenniang saw the bag, she knew it was true. She fainted. When she revived, she began weeping loudly and struggled to go to Cut-Off Life Cliff to see Bicheng.

"Even if you go, you can't see him. People have already dragged his corpse to another spot to bury him." Old Woman Frog blocked the door as she said this.

Zhenniang's whole body went weak and limp. Her tears rushed out like spring water.

Old Woman Frog felt she had succeeded. Secretly, she was happy, but hypocritically she advised Zhenniang, "Child—ah—people who have died can't come back to life. You must not grieve too much. Your own health is still important."

Zhenniang merely cried with all her strength.

Old Woman Frog stuck close to Zhenniang and said in a tone of extremely deep concern, "It's good that Master Wang has taken a fancy to you. Marriage to him would be much better than marrying Bicheng!"

When she heard this, a fiery rage rose from the bottom of Zhenniang's heart, and she said, "If Bicheng is dead, I will not marry my whole life long." With those words, she began to weep bitterly again.

"You can't talk this way. When men are adults, they take wives; when women are adults, they take husbands. It's been this way every since Pan Gu[5] created heaven and earth. If you marry Master Wang, you'll have whatever you want. If you want more power and prestige, you'll have more power and prestige. You'll be as powerful as a god." Old Woman Frog watched Zhenniang's face as she talked. She just saw Zhenniang's round and staring apricot eyes. Zhenniang stood up and shouted, "If you mention that fat pig again, I'll die right away, right here!" Zhenniang turned her head, and struck a pose of hitting her head against the wall. She scared Old Woman Frog so much that she went up and hugged her tightly, and said over and over again, "I won't say it. I won't say it."

Old Woman Frog locked Zhenniang's door. So upset that she didn't know what to do, she went again to the ancient temple.

The next day after breakfast, Old Woman Frog picked up incense, paper, vegetables, and fruit, and said she was going to the temple to ask the monks to release Bicheng's soul from purgatory. Pretending to be benevolent and righteous, she also said to Zhenniang, "You are so determined. I approve of this, too. For your sake, I'll ask the monk to chant several sutras for this child. This will also let him be reborn soon." Saying this, she left.

Old Woman Frog had been gone a long time. There was still no sign of her returning. Suddenly someone rushed into Zhenniang's home, and said to Zhenniang, "Something's wrong. All of a sudden, your stepmother had an attack of apoplexy in the temple. She's lost consciousness. You must go immediately." Zhenniang was kindhearted. Although she hated Old Woman

80

Frog, still, when she heard she was sick, she quickly went with that person. When she reached the temple, Zhenniang was led into the side room. There she saw Miser Demon sitting down, laughing heartily, his eyes flashing with lust. Zhenniang realized that she had fallen into a trap. She turned to go, but Old Woman Frog was blocking the door. She pushed Old Woman Frog down and forced her way out. She didn't expect that the outer gate would also be locked. There was no way to leave. Zhenniang saw that there was no way out. She gnashed her teeth and struck her head against the copper bell.

All that could be heard was the sound *"hong."* The bell opened like a door, and admitted Zhenniang, and then closed up again. There was not a crack to be seen. Miser Demon was thinking single-mindedly of Zhenniang. He strained every muscle to open up the copper bell. But the copper bell didn't move at all. The mangy monk and Old Woman Frog rushed up to help, but it was as though the copper bell had taken root. It still didn't move at all. "Smash it with a hammer!" Miser Demon shouted, hoarse and exhausted.

The mangy monk found a large sledgehammer right away. Brandishing the sledgehammer, he pounded at the copper bell with all his might. This pounding wasn't light. They heard the sound of *"honglong"*—the heavens collapsed and the earth shattered. The copper bell spurted out flames dozens of feet high. In a second, the whole ancient temple was enveloped in flames, burning Miser Demon, Mangy Monk, and Old Woman Frog to death.

The fire died out. The ancient temple was reduced to ashes. The copper bell had also disappeared. But on North Gate Mountain towered an enormous rock shaped like the copper bell.

Who knows how many years passed before the small village at the foot of North Gate Mountain developed into a thriving city with a dense population? On a warm and sunny day, a loud sound came from atop North Gate Mountain. A large crack opened in the copper bell rock. Golden light shot in all directions. From inside flew out a pair of multi-colored phoenixes, circling the village, singing happily, and fluttering and dancing like lovers. The elderly people in the village said, "This pair of phoenixes are the reincarnations of Wu Bicheng and Lai Zhenniang in the copper bell."

This is probably why Yongding is also called "Phoenix City."

(Story collected by Li Musen)

KING LICHEE

In this story, the daughter of a wealthy man falls in love with his hired laborer. Despite her father's displeasure, she is determined to marry the young man. The two defy and foil the wicked father, and run away to live together in a distant spot. With the help of two immortals, they prosper.

Nine Treasures Cave in Nine Lakes Village in Longhai is a village with especially beautiful scenery and fragrant fruit trees. In the village is a large lichee tree with thick foliage and a heavy trunk. Local people call it "King Lichee."

In the summer, when the lichees ripen, red fruit hang from all the branches. Eating lichees under the cool shade of the tree, people listen to the old folks tell the story of this "King Lichee."

In the past there was a very rich man, Wang Daba. His family had all kinds of gold, silver, riches, and treasures. He had field after field of orchards and paddy, and garden after garden of peach and pear flowers blossoming. He had a daughter named Qianjin.[6] Truly, she was incomparably beautiful. Her cheeks were as red as peach blossoms, her eyes as light as a clear spring, her hair so black that it shone. Sometimes rotten bamboo bears good shoots: She and Daba weren't at all alike. She was clever and quick and enjoyed work.

The rich man had a long-term hired hand named Lin Datian. He was a brave, diligent, fine person. It was only because both his parents died that he owed the rich man a debt. Unable to repay the debt, he became a long-term hired hand. Qianjin very much sympathized with him, and often, without telling her father, she gave him clothing and food and other things. After a long time, the two had developed very deep feelings and wished to be a couple as devoted as a pair of mandarin ducks. One evening when the lamps had just been lit and the crescent moon was just rising in the east, Qianjin and Datian met in the flower garden. Observing them, Daba was enraged. He pulled them apart. "The toad is lusting after the swan's flesh. If you marry my Qianjin, there will be one disaster after another!" When it was daylight, he drove Datian out the door, and then turned back and pushed Qianjin into the house.

At night, the slivered crescent moon light reflected on the windowsill. Qianjin was locked in for a whole day. She neither ate anything nor drank any tea. She was thinking of Datian. She tossed and turned and couldn't sleep. Suddenly, the main gate opened, and Datian hurried in. For a moment, Qianjin didn't know if this was joy or disaster, if this was dream or reality. Datian helped her jump over the wall from the back flower garden and escape. That night, the two of them left the Wang home.

The next morning, Daba came to see his daughter. The rooms were empty and desolate. Daba was so angry his face turned purple. He searched to the east, and he searched to the west, but he couldn't find her. Still, he didn't dare say anything, nor did he dare shout.

A pair of yellow orioles has flown out of the cage, spreading their wings and flying high toward the blue sky.

Qianjin and Datian are holding hands. How happy they are as they enjoy their freedom!

Qianjin and Datian passed through the lichee village filled with the fragrance of flowers and fruit. They walked through the orchard of tangerines hanging like lanterns. They walked past the spring water whose music was like the *ding-deng* of the *qin*.[7] They walked through the densely forested mountain with its verdant green foliage. They walked past the large clear pool. In one day, they reached the barren mountain slope, and set up a grass hut to settle down. They gazed at the sky—the same as praying to heaven; they looked at the ground—the same as praying to earth. They picked bunches of wildflowers for the wedding ceremony, and a hundred birds of the mountain came to congratulate them.

From then on, every day the two of them rose at four o'clock, and went to bed at midnight. They reclaimed the wasteland. They wanted to transform the barren mountain into fertile land and a flower and fruit garden. One noon, when the two of them were eating lunch on the land, there emerged from the mountain of virgin forest an old couple wearing ragged clothing and leaning on staffs.

The old man said, "Show us your good hearts. The two of us have had nothing to eat for three days!"

His old wife said, "Show us your good hearts. The two of us have neither sons nor daughters."

Qianjin and Datian immediately gave the old man and the old woman the food they'd been about to eat, and they themselves went hungry. The next day, when they were about to eat lunch, the two old people showed up again leaning on their staffs. Again, Qianjin and Datian gave them the food they'd been about to eat. Noon of the third day was just the same.

Picking up the rice bowl, the old man said, "We've tested you for three days. You are a good couple who are kind and hard-working. I tell you truthfully: We are the gods of the south star of the Heavens. We have come to earth to investigate the good and evil in people's hearts. If you have a request, we can help you."

The old people spoke kindly and sincerely. Qianjin looked at Datian, and Datian gazed at Qianjin. For a moment, neither of them could think of any request. At last, Datian looked at the newly reclaimed land and said, "Old Grandfather, Old Grandmother, we've just reclaimed this piece of land, but we still don't know what to plant here. Do you have any rare seeds?"

The old man said, "Yes, yes, this is a rare seed. Here is a rare lichee plucked from Lifang."

When the old man finished speaking, he stuck his staff into the ground, and said:

Precious lichee, quickly put down firm roots.
Precious lichee, sparkle with green buds.
In time, your fruit will flash like rubies.
The sweet flavor will tantalize like perfume.

Suddenly, the two old people disappeared in a puff of thick smoke.

Datian tried to budge the staff, but it wouldn't move. It was as if it had put down roots. The next day, delicate shoots grew from the staff. The third day, green leaves grew. The leaves grew more and more luxuriantly. After three years, this tree was already large, its green leaves creating shade. In the spring-time, small rice-yellow flowers blossomed on the tree and at-tracted countless bees to collect the honey. In the summer, brilliant red fruit formed on the tree, attracting numerous people who wanted to see the wonderful fruit. Datian climbed the tree to pick some for the guests to eat. Everyone praised its sweetness and its fragrance. Datian and Qianjin were busy picking and picking. They picked the fruit for three days before they were finished. They carried it happily to the nearby market town to sell it. Someone asked, "What is this fruit called?" Datian said, "It's called the rare lichee."

The story of the rare lichee spread far and wide. Finally it reached the ears of the rich man Wang Daba. He saw that although he was rich he was also poor, and he said, "If there is this kind of sweet fruit, it must be mine—Wang Daba's!" So Wang Daba asked someone to guide him there. He rode in a sedan chair and, with a show of strength, he arrived at the fruit tree. As soon as Qianjin and Datian saw that Wang Daba had come, they said, "Damn!", and they left by the back door to hide out.

Wang Daba burned the grass hut, and built a large home right next to this fruit tree. Every day, wearing old and tat-tered clothing, he went into the dense forest "to reclaim land." He also wanted to encounter the immortal from heaven, and ask him for some precious seeds.

One day, two white-haired old people emerged from the dense forest. One was carrying a calabash on his back, and the other was holding a rice bowl. They walked over to Wang Daba.

The old man said, "Show us your good heart! For three days, the two of has have had nothing to eat!"

The old woman said, "Show us your good heart! The two of us have neither sons nor daughters."

Daba said, "Come on over. Come and eat." He immediately asked a servant to take out a pot of rice for the old people. With one gulp, the old people ate it all, and then they said they hadn't had enough. Daba ordered that more be cooked. When it was finished, the old people again ate it all and again they said they hadn't had enough. The rich man was very distressed. He said, "You ate half a *jin* of my rice, and you have to give back eight ounces. If you don't have treasures to give me, you must still give me some rare seeds."[8]

The old grandfather said, "We don't have any treasures."

The old grandmother said, "Nor do we have any rare seeds."

Daba noticed the calabash that the old man was carrying on his back, and he asked, "What do you have packed in here?"

The old grandfather said, "I have *babao* . . ."[9] Before he had finished speaking, the rich man reached out and grabbed the calabash and said, "I want all of the eight treasures."

The old grandmother said, "So we'll give you the calabash! But you must open it only when no one else is around."

Suddenly, a puff of thick smoke rose up, and the two old people disappeared.

Daba was very happy. First he looked in all directions. There was no one around. He held the precious calabash to his ear and listened. *Wengwengweng, wengwengweng!* Wonderful! In a flash, Daba took the cover off the calabash. *Weng!* Eight kinds of fierce bees of different colors flew out. Daba threw down the calabash and fled. Chasing him, the fierce bees couldn't be thrown off. He ran to the mountain slope. He climbed a tree. The fierce bees chased him to the tree. He hid in the vegetable garden. The fierce bees chased him the vegetable garden. He jumped into the muddy pool. The fierce bees chased him to the muddy pool. The fierce bees were singing:

"*Wengwengweng, wengwengweng*—we'll sting this big rotten worm to death.

"He takes the people's land and he occupies the orchard. He has plenty to eat, and he is a man of leisure who doesn't have to work.

"*Wengwengweng, wengwengweng*—we'll sting this big rotten worm to death.

"He exploited the long-term hired worker, and he's crazy about money. Today heaven calls your life back to the Western Paradise."[10]

The eight kinds of fierce bees attacked Wang Daba. In the muddy pool, they stung to death this rich man whose evil deeds had known no bounds. Qianjin and Datian heard that Wang Daba had died, and they moved back to the big house. They worked every day, and they opened up a lot of land. They planted a lot of fruit trees. And they lived very happily.

To this day, that large King Lichee is still there. Because the immortals sent the one treasure of the lichee and added the eight kinds of fierce bees as eight treasures, this village is called "Nine Treasures Cave."

(Story collected by Qing Xin and Dan Ju)

NIE BAO

In this tale, it is at last a kindly magistrate who suggests that the two persons might wish to marry, but it is clear that the young woman has loved the man for a long time from afar. In suggesting that they marry, the magistrate is merely facilitating their own wishes. The young woman in this story is also unusual in that she is highly literate.

A leopard carved of stone stands in front of the Li Gong ancestral temple on Renfeng Street outside the east gate of Quanzhou. Besides the usual two ears, there is also an extra one on that carved stone. Think about it: Aren't three ears precisely the "nie" character?[11] This usage then symbolizes a person's name. This is a perfectly wonderful technique. So, who is this Nie Bao?[12] In the reigns of Ming Zhengde and Ming Jiajing,[13] the Fujian provincial governor Nie Bao had a very great reputation. It seems strange: The names of an impressive and important official are entrusted to a stone-carved animal. Originally, this stone carving served to pay a debt of gratitude. The reason for this debt lies in a bizarre story occurring before Nie Bao entered public service.

Nie Bao was from Yongfeng County in Jiangxi. As a youth, he was charming and energetic. His learning was so outstanding that he was called erudite. Before the age of twenty, he was already well-known in Yongfeng County. One of his neighbors, Zhao Yuanwai, had a son and a daughter. The son was named Shitong, and the daughter was named Xiaozhu. Xiaozhu was beautiful and intelligent. Zhao Yuanwai cherished her. When she was a child, he engaged a famous teacher to teach her to read. Before many years had passed, the bright and clever Xiaozhu

89

had become a learned beauty. She first awakened to love when she was still young. She often heard the servant girls praising Nie Bao's talent and appearance. From early on, in her imagination there was already a Nie Bao in her heart. Luckily, Xiaozhu's bedroom faced the street. Sometimes, as she leaned against the window and gazed into the distance, she heard reports from the young servants and she saw Nie Bao's good looks. But Nie Bao was a youth with a pure and honest character. During the time he had sworn to study, he took no interest in women. Xiaozhu was also a solemn and beautiful woman. Although she had long known Nie Bao's reputation, still she didn't let thoughts of sexual desire cross her mind. Her natural disposition inclined her to recite poetry. She knew that Nie Bao was skilled at poetry and essays, and she selfishly hoped that if she were persistent enough there would be a good chance to become friends with him in writing. That would satisfy her desires.

It was her fate that there would be trouble. One day, it happened that she composed a poem, recited it, and wrote it on her handkerchief. Without thinking it through, she added the two characters "Nie Bao" at the top. And at the bottom, she wrote her own name. Then she put it in her pocket. She walked to the window, lifted the curtain, and gazed out. She was spellbound. After a while, a youth approached from a distance. She stared: It was Nie Bao. Xiaozhu playfully threw the handkerchief-poem out toward Nie Bao. Nie Bao noticed a pure white handkerchief suddenly flying through the air. He picked it up and tucked it in his belt. Paying no attention to who had thrown it, he walked on. Before he had walked a few steps, the handkerchief dropped to the ground. It so happened that Zhou Yixing, a notorious blackguard from Yongfeng County, was walking just behind the spot where Xiaozhu had thrown the handkerchief. He noticed that the girl of this mansion was beautiful, and he couldn't help feeling jealous. He saw the handkerchief that Nie Bao had picked up and then lost. How could he not rush to pick it up?

Yixing was a loafer. All day long, if he wasn't cockfighting and horse-racing, then he was drinking and gambling. At that time, although he had also studied several years and knew quite a lot of characters, he was fierce and tough. He didn't have a regular job, so his companions were all hoodlums. Now, unexpectedly, he had picked up this handkerchief. He opened it up and looked at it. There was a poem inscribed there, and a signature. He thought to himself, "The young daughter of the Zhao family is infatuated with someone named Nie. This treasure has fallen into my hands. Isn't this 'a golden opportunity from heaven?'" He thought for a while, and the plan came from his heart, and the tragic case in Yongfeng County began that very night.

After twilight, Yixing donned a slight disguise. Alone, he looked around quietly and furtively in front of the Zhao home. The main entrance was unlocked. After a while, an old woman walked up. She pushed open the door and went in. Yixing took advantage of the murky light to go in, too. He hid in an empty storage room. At about midnight, he stealthily felt his way upstairs and went toward Xiaozhu's room. It was locked tight, and he had no hope of entering. Taking out a sharp knife, he began to prize open the door. How could he have known that Zhao Yuanwai's bedroom was just opposite Xiaozhu's? Although Zhao Yuanwai had extinguished the lamp, he hadn't fallen asleep yet. The night was deep and the people quiet. Suddenly he heard a sound of scraping at his beloved daughter's door. He immediately threw on some clothing and came out to see what had happened. Glimpsing a black shadow, he shouted, "Thief!" Yixing didn't have time to escape. He struck out at Zhao Yuanwai. Zhao Yuanwai couldn't defend himself and, injured by Yixing's sharp knife, he fell in a pool of blood. Yixing thought, "Since I've killed someone now, I'd better carry it through, no matter what the consequences are." So he beheaded him with the sharp knife, and then wrapped the head in a large scarf and carried it away. The handkerchief-poem had dropped in front of Xiaozhu's door. He opened the main door of the Zhao home, made two turns, and arrived in front of a dried-bean shop on a small street. Pretending that he wanted to buy dried beans, he knocked on Lin Jian's door. Now, why do you think Yixing cut off Zhao Yuanwai's head and rushed into Lin Jian's shop? This was not without reason. In the past, if Yixing had no money on him, he

91

would buy dried beans on credit from Lin Jian. When this happened, the matter of old debts would naturally come up, and the two wrangled with each other. Later Lin Jian saw that Yixing repeatedly repudiated his debts, and repeatedly insisted on buying on credit, and he firmly refused to do business with him. So now if Yixing didn't pay cash, he couldn't buy dried beans. So he harbored hatred in his heart. Tonight he intended to shift the blame to Lin Jian. The knocking on the door immediately awakened Lin Jian. He opened the door and offered to sell dried beans. An object was suddenly thrown in from outside. Frightened, he was about to stick his head out and have a look outside, but the person at the door had already taken off without a trace.

Lin Jian thought it was odd. After composing himself, he lit the lamp and opened up the package. A blood-soaked head lay in front of his eyes. He was so dumbstruck that for a long time he couldn't move. Then, trembling, he awakened his partner Cui Xiaonong, and told him of the strange and frightening occurrence.

"God! What can we do about this person's head?" Lin Jian was looking at Xiaonong as he spoke. He seemed to be imploring Xiaonong to think of a workable plan.

"This is enough to scare a person to death! Whose head is this? What . . . What can we do?" Xiaonong was panic-stricken. Finally it was Lin Jian who came up with an idea. He said to Xiaonong, "Bring in the hoe and dustpan from the back. Whatever happens, you have to help me out for a while, and you also have to keep this a secret."

"Don't worry, Boss! But what use are the hoe and dustpan?"

"There's no need to talk anymore. Just get them quickly and come with me. I have a plan." So, with Lin Jian carrying the head and Xiaonong carrying the hoe and dustpan, they walked toward the cemetery mound a little over a *li* away.

It was dark and there was a half-moon. On all sides, it was silent. The two of them rushed to the cemetery mound. Lin Jian told Xiaonong to dig a hole in an empty area and to bury the head along with the scarf. Lin Jian then used the hoe to cover it up with several layers of earth. Seeing that it was all taken care of, Xiaonong wanted to turn and go back. But, behind him, Lin Jian struck him with the hoe. The head of that pitiable, unfortunate Xiaonong was split open—and he died.

Lin Jian had resorted to this murderous treachery to do away with his accomplice. Carelessly, he buried Xiaonong's corpse next to Zhao Yuanwai's head. And he thought that now he'd be able to forget the whole matter.

To return to Zhao Yuanwai's murder and beheading by Yixing. That night, no one in the family knew about it. Only when it became light and the old woman servant Mother Zou got up did she see the handkerchief that had been dropped in front of Xiaozhu's door. She picked it up and put it in her pocket. Then, turning her head, she discovered the headless corpse. She was so shocked that her soul left her body, and she shouted on and on. Her shouting alarmed the whole hosehold—upstairs and downstairs. Everyone recognized that this was the headless corpse of Zhao Yuanwai. Some shouted in shock, some wailed. Xiaozhu fainted several times. When Zhao Yuanwai's son Zhao Shitong got the news at the home of his tutor, he rushed back home, and prostrated himself and wept loudly before his father's corpse. This confused state of affairs lasted for an hour before this strange case was reported to the county magistrate.

Before long, the county magistrate came personally with his runners and coroners to examine the corpse. He ordered that the murderer be arrested, and he summoned the entire Zhao family for questioning. Because it was Mother Zou who first discovered the corpse, her interrogation was particularly detailed. Mother Zou couldn't bear the intimidation of the county magistrate, and turned the handkerchief over to him. She swore that, aside from picking up this handkerchief, she knew nothing. The county magistrate looked at the handkerchief, and saw that not only was there a poem on it but also the names of Nie Bao and Xiaozhu. He thought that Nie Bao and Xiaozhu must have had illicit relations, and that they had plotted together to kill her father. He flew into a rage. On the one hand, he ordered that Xiaozhu be taken back to the *yamen* and locked up in jail to await sentencing; on the other hand, he ordered runners to apprehend Nie Bao to confront her. Nie Bao, who was studying at home, couldn't make head or tail of it as he was arrested and taken to jail. Zhao Shitong knew that his little sister was a girl who observed the proprieties, but still it was also clear that the poem on the handkerchief was his little sister's and that it also bore Nie Bao's name. He was extremely suspicious. He didn't know how to deal with it. After all, the enemy who killed his father couldn't live under the same sky. He made an accusation immediately. He wanted Nie Bao to take responsibility for his father's death. But the county magistrate questioned Nie Bao repeatedly, and Nie Bao wouldn't confess anything. Xiaozhu suffered harsh torture, and admitted that the poem was one she had written and that the handkerchief was the one she had dropped. But she said that she and Nie Bao had never met. She had no idea how her father had died. So the county magistrate had no way to decide the case.[14] For years, he was unable to discover where Zhao Yuanwai's head was hidden. Nie Bao and Xiaozhu were imprisoned for a long time in vain.

Three years passed quickly in the case of the headless Zhao Yuanwai. Finally, since the head couldn't be found, the case was left unsettled. The county magistrate in charge of this case had just finished his term of office. His successor was Guo Nan, from Jinjiang, Fujian. His style name was Shizhong.[15] He was a *jinshi*[16] born in the time of Ming Zhengde. He had already served as county magistrate of Pujiang. He was a famous, honest, incorrupt official. After taking up his appointment, he reviewed the old cases. The most important of these was of course the murder of Zhao Yuanwai. He immediately initiated renewed interrogation of Nie Bao and Xiaozhu. He saw how cultivated Nie Bao was and how bitterly sad Xiaozhu was. And he knew that in this there must be injustice. So he posted a notice, saying that there would be a large reward and making it clear that whoever had knowledge of Zhao Yuanwai's head and reported its whereabouts would receive two hundred ounces of silver. Before three days had passed, someone had torn down the notice and come to the county *yamen* to make an accusation.

This person's name was Zhang Xiaojin. He was from a certain village outside Yongfeng City. He made his living robbing graves. The evening of Zhao Yuanwai's murder, he had been engaged in his "business" at the cemetery. In the dim night light, he had seen two fellows approaching from a distance. So, quick as a flash, he'd gone into a grave and secretly observed the activity. The whole matter of Lin Jian burying the head and killing his partner, he had seen very, very distinctly. Moreover, he also recognized Lin Jian as the proprietor of a dried-bean shop on a certain street. Now he had seen that there was a reward. After Guo Nan received this report, he immediately sent out runners to bring Lin Jian in. Lin Jian was tortured and questioned, and then made a confession that accorded in all respects with the facts of the case—how the head was tossed into the shop, how he and Xiaonong went to bury it, and later how he chopped Xiaonong to death. It only remained impossible to figure out who had murdered Zhao Yuanwai.

Luckily, Guo Nan looked into it with minute attention, and interrogated in detail. Only then did he learn that Lin Jian frequently wrangled with Zhou Yixing because of his indebtedness and he learned that the familiar voice calling at the door that night seemed to be Yixing's. Guo Nan, who was good at solving cases, now had the clues to crack the case. After a few days, as expected, he apprehended Zhou Yixing. After torture and questioning, the whole case was very clear. The results were: The proof of Zhou Yixing's guilt was irrefutable, and the laws and penalties were clear. Because Lin Jian thought only of his own best interests and thus killed Cui Xiaonong, he couldn't be pardoned. But he hadn't started the trouble, so he wasn't responsible for the whole crime. Also it was because he had been so alarmed and his mind had been so muddled that he had rashly committed murder. So his punishment was reduced to exile. Xiaojin's report was meritorious, and he received the reward. Grave-robbing was against the law, however, and he was ordered to reform.

Thus, Guo Nan dealt with each offender and settled it all. On the one hand, he passed the word to Zhao Shitong that he should bury his father's head and body in one place. On the other hand, he proclaimed that Nie Bao and Zhao Xiaozhu were innocent and were free. Because the two of them had been jailed despite their innocence, and had suffered grave injustice, he had a great deal of pity for them in his heart. He thought deeply for a while. Because of the poem written on the handkerchief, he then thought of the two of them marrying. So, in a low, warm voice he asked them, "I would like to bring you together, but I don't know yet if you both wish this?"

Xiaozhu just lowered her head and said nothing. Nie Bao replied, "You are not only redressing a wrong for this student, but you are also offering this lovely idea. In the future, if I advance even an inch, I wish to be your door guard, to repay one-ten-thousandth of this deep debt of gratitude."

Guo Nan gave his attention again to Xiaozhu. He saw that she was still shyly bowing her head and saying nothing, and so without hesitating he chose an auspicious day for their wedding.

Nie Bao and Xiaozhu obeyed Guo Nan's order to be husband and wife forever. From then on, Nie Bao made an even more determined effort to study. Before many years had elapsed, he had passed a succession of exams and had become a *jinshi*.

Ten years later, Guo Nan had already retired and was raising flowers and enjoying his old age at his old residence on East Street in Quanzhou. One day, his gatekeeper suddenly reported, "A great official and his honorable wife have come to see you!" He hadn't finished speaking when the two honored guests, a man and a woman, crept in. They knelt in front of Guo Nan. For a moment, Guo Nan was baffled and didn't know what he should do. "You . . . this . . . this old man is certainly flattered! Please . . . please quickly get up!" Guo Nan said hastily.

"I am Nie Bao, and I've come with my wife especially to thank you."

Guo Nan heard the two words "Nie Bao," and he became even more flustered, because the Nie Bao now before him was not the Nie Bao from the odd case earlier in Yongfeng County, but was the Nie Bao who had just been appointed civil governor of Fujian. He'd already dismissed the earlier incident from his mind. So, on the one hand, he returned the bow. On the other hand, he hurried to help them rise, and invited them to be seated. But Nie Bao and Xiaozhu declined.

"To have the presence of the great governor in my humble home! I failed to greet you, and I apologize. This great honor: How can I accept it at all?"

"Kind master, can it be that you've forgotten that when you were county magistrate in Yongfeng you redressed the wrong for Nie Bao and arranged his marriage? Luckily, Nie Bao has come to Fujian and I can pay my respects to the kind master, and fulfill my hope of being your door guard."

Only when Guo Nan heard Nie Bao say this did he remember that long-ago incident. Nie Bao earnestly expressed his desire to decline his official post and keep his promise to serve as Guo Nan's door guard. Guo Nan repeatedly expressed his thanks and then Nie Bao and Xiaozhu talked with Guo Nan of what had happened since they had all parted. They warmly got to know each other. It was nearly evening before they took their leave.

Several days passed when Guo Nan's gatekeeper came to report again. "Four people have arrived, and have set down a stone-carved leopard with three ears in front of the gate. They said that Nie Bao told them to bring it."

Guo Nan was deeply moved. He knew that this stone-carved leopard held Nie Bao's name. Its placement in front of the gate kept Nie Bao's promise of guarding the gate and symbolized his payment of his debt of gratitude.

(Story collected by Wu Zaoting)

THE *QIN* MASTER OF FUJIAN

In this story, we see several strong women: a widow willing to share her qin-*playing techniques with a* qin *enthusiast; a boat-woman adept at deception lining her own pocket; a madam at a courtesans' establishment, who is able to strike a profitable bargain; and, finally, a professional singer talented also at playing the* qin—*a woman who is determined either to be liberated from the establishment so that she can marry or to commit suicide if thwarted. The marriage she and her husband forge is portrayed as a rather equal, companionate one.*

Zheng You lived in the coastal city of Chongwu in Huian, Fujian. In fact, although we call it a city here, at that time it was just a small village. So Zheng You chose another name for himself, "Bancun."[17] He was not interested in an official career and often traveled all over with his *qin*, visiting masters, making friends, and learning *qin* techniques. Mr. "Bancun's" reputation spread far and wide.

One summer, Bancun went to Yangcheng in Guangdong province. He heard that a military official's widow named Bai Sujuan lived here. Formerly a singing girl in the *yamen*, she was very skilled at playing the *qin*. Bancun was crazy about the *qin*, and wanted very much to study with her. But in feudal times, seeing an official's widow was even more difficult than going to heaven. Luckily, he enlisted the help of a friend in local *qin* circles. He rented a room in a small house in Bai Sujuan's neighborhood. Every day he heard the *qin* next door. Following Bai Sujuan's melody, he fumbled about practicing the *qin*. Although the notes were similar, the style was a lot different. What to do? Bancun was stumped.

He had some good luck. At twilight on the fifteenth day of the sixth month, Bancun saw a small sedan chair leave Bai Sujuan's home. The sedan chair had white gauze curtains. Two servant girls followed it. One was carrying a box of fresh flowers and fruit, the other was carrying a white silk *qin* case. They were heading toward the street. It seemed odd to him, and he made inquiries of the landlord. Only then did he learn that two years earlier on the fifteenth day of the sixth month Bai Sujuan's husband had led troops on a boat patrolling the Pearl River. They'd run into a surprise typhoon attack. The boat had capsized and he had died at the bottom of the river. The only ones left of his family were this widow and the two servant girls. Sujuan was commemorating her deceased husband. On the fifteenth of each month she went to the Pearl River to play her *qin* and sacrifice and mourn, wishing that the deceased would have the same peace and happiness that he had had in life.

When Bancun heard that Bai Sujuan's behavior was indeed reverent, he followed behind the sedan chair and came to the Pearl River. As Bai Sujuan emerged from the sedan chair, he saw that she was wearing snow-white mourning clothes. She was a little over thirty years old. She was sedate and beautiful. Aided by the servant girls, she boarded the boat and it headed toward the middle of the river. Bancun immediately hired a small boat and followed along.

It was early evening. The moonlight was as bright as fine silver. The Pearl River was flowing like a jade ribbon. A lot of pleasure boats were going back and forth on the water. The sound of the bamboo flute and the sound of the *qin* attracted people until they slipped into a trance.

Bai Sujuan's boat stopped on the river at a spot far from the shore. Bancun's boat also moved forward softly. He saw Bai Sujuan stand at the prow of the boat, and only after lighting incense, sacrificing wine, and offering flowers did she sit down, and, facing the river water, begin to play the *qin*.

Under the moonlight, Bancun wanted to watch the plucking and fingering from his boat, but he couldn't see this clearly. He could only hear the *qin* music—the mournful notes bringing tears to one's eyes. Only when the *qin* sound stopped did Bancun finally sigh a long sigh.

At this time, Bai Sujuan's boat turned around and turned toward shore. Bancun's small craft followed behind. After Bai Sujuan had gone ashore and left in her sedan chair, he boarded Bai Sujuan's boat, and made inquiries of the boatwoman. He learned that on the fifteenth of every month, the young woman Bai came to the river and that she always rode in this boat. He asked the boatwoman to let him board her boat, too, the next time, so that he could listen to the *qin*. The boatwoman saw that he was eager to learn the *qin*, and thought she'd take advantage of the opportunity to make a little profit, so she said, "If you board the boat, this old body will have to take the responsibility. The price is ten ounces of silver. No bargaining. After you board the boat, you must hide in the cabin at the rear. You can't show yourself. If by any chance the young woman Bai discovers you, you simply assert that this old body is your dear auntie, and I'll take care of everything. If something goes wrong at the lower reaches—*heng*! Just don't blame this old woman. . . ." Bancun said, "All I want is to learn the *qin*. You have nothing to worry about." The boatwoman then agreed.

In the twinkling of an eye it was the fifteenth day of the seventh month. Bancun couldn't wait for the sun to set behind the mountain. Taking his *qin*, he boarded the boat and hid in the cabin prepared by the boatwoman. When that bright moon had climbed to the top of the willow tree, as expected, Bai Sujuan also arrived. The boat headed toward the middle of the river—just as before. After Bai Sujuan knelt down and burned incense, she sat up straight and played the *qin*. Bancun secretly observed her fingering, and was very much enlightened. But he had bad luck. The *qin* sound had just stopped and the servant girls were just about to put things in order when they discovered Bancun. They reported to their mistress. Trembling, Bai Sujuan interrogated the boatwoman, "Why did you let a man board the boat?"

Quick with her talk and laughing carelessly, the boatwoman said, "This is a nephew on my mother's side of the family. He

100

came a long way to see me. We boatpeople all live on boats, and I am his aunt by blood. I can't tell him to leave just to earn my money. You, lady, understand principles. How can you not understand the ways of the world?" Bancun was also standing to the side. He said respectfully, "I have studied a little *qin* technique. Today I came to find my aunt, and I was lucky enough to see the lady playing the *qin* very expertly. I wanted to learn a little about fingering techniques. Since the lady is not pleased, it's best if I just leave."

Bai Sujuan looked at Bancun. He was close to forty years old. He was like a teacher, gentle and cultivated, and very well-mannered. He didn't seem to be a bad person. She calmed down. But in order to determine whether he'd spoken truth or lies, she said, "Since you are brilliant, I should ask you to play for me." Without hesitating in the least, Bancun took out his own *qin* and played a song. In the *yamen*, Bai Sujuan had seen a lot of the world and she had very good taste. After hearing the song, she said, "Your skill with the *qin* isn't bad. It's a pity you can't use your fingers freely to do what you want." Bancun took advantage of this opportunity to ask a favor. The boatwoman also helped with a few sentences. Bai Sujuan couldn't easily withdraw. She sat down, and taught him various fingering and plucking techniques. Bancun was clever and adroit. He grasped it all very quickly, and wanted to acknowledge Bai Sujuan as his teacher. Bai Sujuan said gently, "It's late. You should also rest." With this, she told the boatwoman to turn the boat back. Once ashore, she left in her sedan chair to avoid suspicion.

Bancun returned alone to his small abode, and day and night he practiced the fingering techniques. He had learned a lot. One day, when he was walking outside the gate, Bai Sujuan's servant girl spotted him, "Sir, why have you come here?" Bancun answered politely, "In order to study with *qin* friends, I'm staying for a while in this small building. I'll trouble you to wish the young woman well for me." The servant girl nodded slightly and walked off.

The sun set and the moon came out. It was almost time for the Mid-Autumn Festival. Bancun had just returned from visiting a *qin* friend when that servant girl called out to him, "It's very hard to find you. The lady has a letter. Please read it."

This is what Bancun read: "The day before yesterday my servant reported that you live in the small building outside the wall. I hear your *qin* through the wall. You are very accomplished. I invite you to board your aunt's boat again on the night of the Mid-Autumn Festival, and play a song for my late husband. The deceased will be comforted; the living will be moved."

This was everything that Bancun wished for. He asked the servant girl to reply for him, "I will certainly be there at the appointed time!"

The evening of the Mid-Autumn Festival, Bancun took his *qin* to the riverside. He immediately boarded the boat, and paid his respects to Bai Sujuan. There was no way not to adopt again the disguise of aunt and nephew, and he and the boatwoman exchanged glances. The boat reached the middle of the river very quickly. Bai Sujuan finished her sacrifice and sat down and played a song. Then Bancun also sacrificed, and respectfully sat down and began to play the *qin*. Bai Sujuan praised him, "Brilliance like yours is rare. On behalf of my late husband, I present this *qin* to you. Please take it home with you. It's probably not very convenient for you to stay in this town for a long time."

Bancun was very clever. He knew that Bai Sujuan was on guard against saying too much. He respectfully accepted the *qin*, expressed his gratitude, and said, "I'll go home tomorrow. Please take good care of yourself!" The boat neared the shore. Bancun saw Bai Sujuan into the sedan chair, and only then did he return alone with the *qin* to the small building. How could he sleep? In the lamplight, he wrote a song. "*Yaoqin*,"[18] and set it to lyrics, and played the *qin* and sang:

The moonlight above the Pearl River is as white as snow.
I met you unexpectedly on this small boat.
You gave me the *yaoqin* decorated with white jade.
Tears at parting: I cannot play it anymore.

This song praised Bai Sujuan's noble and pure sentiments, and it also expressed Bancun's respect for his teacher and his regret at leaving.

The next day, Bancun took his leave of his *qin* friends in Yangcheng, and, carrying the *qin*, he returned to Chongwu. After arriving home, he painted a portrait of Bai Sujuan from memory, and hung it in the small *qin* room to revere her as his teacher. On the evening of the fifteenth of every month, he always burned incense and worshiped, and played that "*Yaoqin* Song." His *qin* friend Su Pingshan was a government clerk in Suzhou. At the end-of-the-year festival, he visited his family in Chongwu. He saw that Bancun had become expert at the *qin* and said, "Suzhou is a bustling world. A lot of *qin* masters are gathered there. If you're interested, come back with me for a while!" Bancun's wife had died long ago. He had neither worries nor cares. So after Spring Festival, along with Su Pingshan, he boarded a cargo boat for Suzhou.

In Suzhou, he heard that the well-known professional singer Ma Xianglan was in the "Song Courtyard." She was like an immortal. She was also expert at the *qin*. People praised her as "incomparably beautiful and skilled." Her rules for receiving guests were very strict. First, they must be distinguished at *qin* songs; next, they must be masters of poetry and painting. Sons of wealthy families went to her door a hundred times, and it was hard to get one chance to meet her. Although Bancun's *qin* technique was very good, the madam wanted him to pay a hundred ounces of silver before he would be allowed to see her. How could he scrape up so much money? The best he could manage was to gaze at the gate and sigh happily!

Two or three months had passed when he heard that the accountant of the "Song Courtyard" had fallen ill and died, and that the madam was looking for a replacement. In order to get the chance to study the *qin* with Ma Xianglan, Bancun implored Su Pingshan to find a reputable local person to make an introduction, and he became the accountant.

Ma Xianglan was just twenty-four *sui*. She was sedate and gentle and refined. She didn't like to talk. Because of his work with the accounts, Bancun met her by chance, but he had no opportunity to express his desire to study the *qin* with her.

Finally he came up with an idea: Often, deep in the quiet of the night, he burned incense and played the *qin* in the back garden. He hoped this would attract Ma Xianglan's attention.[19]

Several nights running, Ma Xianglan heard the beautiful, tranquil sound of the *qin*. She thought to herself, "I've been in Suzhou for three years, and I have not yet heard such sweet *qin* music. This style reminds me of my cousin's!" She told a servant to find out who was playing the *qin*, and ask him with whom he had studied. The servant soon came back, and said, "It's the accountant, Mr. Bancun. To commemorate his teacher Bai Sujuan, he is playing the '*Yaoqin* Song,' which he himself wrote."

When Ma Xianglan heard the words Bai Sujuan, she said, "Ah," and exhorted her servant, "Quickly go and ask that man where Bai Sujuan is now. How does he happen to know my cousin?" This servant was gone for a long time. When she returned, she told Ma Xianglan of Bancun's acquaintance with Bai Sujuan. Ma Xianglan sighed and said, "My cousin is also unlucky!" She thought dully for a long time, and then took a piece of paper, drafted a theme called "Serene Orchid, Delicate and Fragrant," and told her servant to give it to Bancun and ask him to write a song.

In the deep, quiet night the next evening, the bright shining moon in the sky made the buildings and pavilions far and near look as beautiful as the immortal world of Penglai.[20] Ma Xianglan was leaning on the window gazing at the moon when suddenly a gust of *qin* sound floated up from the garden. It seemed as though the evening breezes were blowing the delicate scent of orchids. Captivated, she strolled down the stairs and walked into the garden. The accountant was sitting on a stone stool beside the flowers and grasses. His whole mind was concentrated on playing the *qin*. Ma Xianglan didn't dare startle him. Standing under the *wutong* tree, she listened entranced until the *qin* sound melted away. Then she couldn't help but say, "This is the very essence of the serene orchid, delicate and fragrant!"

Bancun stood up, bowed deeply, and said, "I wrote this 'Serene Orchid, Delicate and Fragrant' for the assignment you gave me, and practiced it once. Please give me more instruction."

Ma Xianglan returned the bow, and sat down on the rock and said, "You not only can play the *qin*, but you can also write songs. If you can write 'Among the Flowers under the Moon' in front of me, this would be even more worthy of this bright moon of the sky and the serene orchids of the garden!"

Bancun realized that Ma Xianglan wanted to test his *qin* skill in her presence. He sat down and thought for a long time. He figured out a draft in his mind, tuned the *qin* strings, and then began plucking lightly. That soft *qin* sound was just like a light breeze blowing through a clump of flowers—precisely echoing the sounds of nature. When the music flowed naturally and rhythmically, the song also soared to the wide horizons—as though Chang-e in the moon were lightly singing and slowly dancing in that cloud-filled heaven.[21] Listening intently to the *qin*, Ma Xianglan began to feel as if she too were floating in the air. Only when the song ended did she seem to be waking from a dream. A hint of a smile brimmed on her face and she walked over to the *qin*-player and said, "Sir, you are really like Sima Xiangru[22] of Han dynasty times!" With this, she sat down and borrowed his *qin* and played Bancun's music again. Bancun admired her good memory and her dexterity, and he took this opportunity to ask her to teach him. Without hesitating at all, Ma Xianglan turned over all the secrets her father had taught her to Bancun.

From then on, Bancun studied diligently and practiced hard. His ten fingers were nimble—by turns strong and soft, quick and slow. He followed his feelings. Ma Xianglan, who was called "the beauty of this generation," often met with this nearly forty-year-old accountant. One would write a song, the other would play and sing, or one would play and the other would sing. All the wealthy young suitors were coldly turned away.

The madam of the Song Courtyard saw that the road to wealth had been blocked[23] and she detested Bancun. She fired him immediately. When Bancun left, he asked to say goodbye to Ma Xianglan. The madam wouldn't allow this. She also summoned several evil rogues, and lashed out cruelly at Bancun, "If you dare take one step in here again, I'll order them to smash your body and break your bones!"

105

Ma Xianglan lived in a high building deep inside the garden. How would she know what was happening outside? For three days, she saw no trace of Bancun, and so she asked her servant to investigate. Only then did she learn that Bancun had already been driven off, and that another accountant had taken his place. She wept for three days straight. How could she be willing to receive guests? Late the fourth night, she felt she wanted to kill herself, when she heard from over the wall the *qin* sound of "Serene Orchid, Delicate and Fragrant." And she knew that Bancun hadn't forgotten his earlier feelings. He was crying out with the *qin*. Relieved, she dashed down the stairs and walked quietly to the back garden, and softly opened the back gate. Searching for the sound, she came to the willow tree at the riverside and saw Bancun; he looked miserable. He was sitting on a green stone playing the *qin*. Ma Xianglan was both sad and happy. She rushed to question Bancun and—*wa!*—she began to weep. Bancun covered her mouth gently and said, "Don't cry. They'll hear, and it'll be hard to deal with." He quietly pulled Ma Xianglan to hide in the thick grasses at the riverside. He vowed that after they parted he would grieve. Ma Xianglan saw Bancun's true heart, and let all the words pressed at the bottom of her heart spill out.

In the past, Ma Xianglan's father was a *xiucai*.[24] He was very talented at the *qin*, chess, calligraphy, and painting. Because of the chaos of war, her father and mother were murdered and their whole house was burned down. With no support, all she could do was sell herself in order to bury her father and mother. It never occurred to her that the buyer would be an evil scoundrel. He resold her to this "Song Courtyard." Afraid of sullying her parents' reputation, she had never before talked of her past. She had thought of leaving the bitter sea, but there was no one she could depend on. For instance, just as she'd been thinking of relying on Bancun for her whole life, the madam had broken them apart forever. She said to Bancun, "Sir, I cannot not speak the truth to you. This life of mine—only you can save it. But this white cloth of mine has been thrown into two dye vats: The first was ash-gray and the second was black. I'm afraid to sully your purity." Bancun felt that Ma Xianglan was both pitiable and respectable. He said, "If I thought this way, why would I have risked coming here? Don't worry. I'll think of something and redeem your freedom."

Ma Xianglan was so moved that pearl-like tears fell. She asked Bancun to wait a moment, and she rushed back to the building, and gave all of the gold, silver, pearls, and treasures that she had collected to Bancun. She said, "Sir, this life of mine— I depend totally on you to save me. If the madam doesn't agree, I have only one death. I give all of these things to you, and ask that you engrave a tombstone for me. Write on it: 'Bancun's wife, the Woman Ma.' After I'm dead, my spirit will still play the *qin* and sing songs for you!" Bancun embraced Ma Xianglan. The two cried so hard that they couldn't breathe.

Early the next morning, Bancun related all of this to his friends. Su Pingshan admonished him, "My younger brother, your talent with the *qin* early on earned you a great reputation. Although you were widowed in middle age, if you want to find a maiden, isn't that still quite easy to do? If you get involved with this prostitute, you'll ruin your reputation!" Bancun just shook his head and said, "She has a good heart. She sold herself in order to bury her parents. She is expert at playing the *qin*. She and I are a very close couple. The world has a lot of court officials and ladies by imperial mandate. In the daylight they talk of protocol and a sense of shame, but at night they behave like thieves and whores. They are known as wealthy aristocrats. In fact they are prostitutes. I cannot be like Sun Fu who let Du Shiniang down![25] If Ma Xianglan dies, I can't live, either. Please, older brother, use this gold and silver, these pearls and other treasures to send our coffins back to Chongwu, and bury us together on Lotus Flower Mountain."

Su Pingshan saw that Bancun's heart was as firm as steel. He helped him borrow some silver and entrusted someone to negotiate with the madam and redeem Ma Xianglan. But how could that madam be willing to let anyone blow down a tree that money grows on? She refused. Seeing that it was hopeless, Ma Xianglan intended to kill herself by jumping from the building. The madam was afraid that she would lose both the person and the money, so finally she could only agree. But she insisted that Bancun pay a thousand ounces of silver to redeem her freedom. Su Pingshan calculated that Ma Xianglan's gold, silver, and pearls—even counting the silver Bancun had borrowed—still would not exceed eight hundred ounces. Just at this critical juncture, he fortunately ran into a Chongwu merchant dealing in pearls and jewels. He had come to Suzhou to engage in trade. When he heard of this matter, he was very moved, and generously opened his purse to help out. He made up the difference in the thousand ounces, thus allowing Ma Xianglan to leap out of prostitution and become Bancun's wife. He also let them return to Chongwu in his own boat.

When Ma Xianglan went into Bancun's home, she saw that the likeness of her cousin Bai Sujuan was still hanging from the small *qin* case, and she was even more convinced that Bancun was a man with a lot of feelings and ties of friendship. She was speechless with happiness. The husband and wife took out the *qin*, and together they played the *"Yaoqin* Song" to express their feelings for Bai Sujuan. From then on, they put their hearts into skillful playing of the *qin*. Bancun's fingering was better than his teacher's. He could also compose songs, and so the people called him the *"qin* master of Fujian." He devoted the last half of his life to collecting all of the southern songs that people loved so much. Ma Xianglan was his capable assistant. She unceasingly gave instrumental performances for him, so that he could revise the songs. Finally, a great many famous ancient songs were passed down!

(Story collected by Wang Qinzhi)

DA WANG AND JADE GIRL

In this story, although the lead female character is an immortal, she has the attributes associated with admirable mortal women: She is intelligent, lovely, and capable. She also knows how to weave and is generous in bestowing her woven cloth on the villagers. When she and Da Wang fall in love and decide to marry, all of the villagers are supportive of them. Finally, her determination is exemplified in her decision to remain on earth as an inanimate object rather than return alive to the heavenly palace.

In ancient times, Wuyishan in Fujian frequently experienced floods, and the ordinary people suffered a great deal. In the mountains there lived a green-faced, long-toothed demon named Tie Bangui. When he dreamed he always wanted to become an immortal, but he was not willing to store up merit and change his ways. He often used crafty tricks to break up loving couples. So as soon as the people heard of a flood or of Tie Bangui, they were filled with hatred.

One spring, black clouds and dark days appeared several days in a row. The wind rolled up flying sand. Thunder roared and lightning flashed. Raindrops as large as copper coins fell without stopping. The whole region of Wuyishan was flooded. Male and female, old and young were crying and shouting, and one by one they were running away. Some climbed big trees. Some climbed up to rooftops. Those who were too late to flee were carried away by the flood. At this time, a handsome young fellow drifted in. His hand grabbed a Shuixian tea bush, and he was struggling in the waves. With great difficulty, he floated near a large tree. Catching him unaware, the crest of a wave tossed him back into the whirlpool. Suddenly, he saw a very long bamboo pole extended from the tree. The young fellow grabbed the bamboo pole and climbed the big tree. Sitting in the tree was a white-bearded old man. Taking the measure of the young fellow, he asked, "What's your name? Where have you come from?"

"My surname is Wang. I'm the oldest in the family, so everyone calls me Da Wang.[26] I've come from a tea village in the foothills of the Seven Immortals. Old man, the flood has covered my home and carried off my relatives. Please save me! I must control the waters, and rebuild my tea village!"

So, after the flood receded, Da Wang settled down in Wuyishan. Day after day and night after night, he and the white-bearded old man led the villagers to blast the cliffs and drill the rocks, to cut the ridges and fill in the gullies. The wind blew in, the rain fell. But Da Wang's eyebrows didn't crease and his hands didn't stop. The thunder crashed in, the lightning flashed. But Da Wang's heart was even more determined, and his gall even stronger. Month after month, year after year: The flowers on the mountain withered and blossomed again. The geese migrating south left and returned. Da Wang's hands were rubbed until they had very thick calluses. He and everyone else exerted a great deal of effort, and finally they detoured around numerous twists and turns, and opened the very long Nine-Bend Stream and controlled the flood waters. Leading numerous assistants, Da Wang heaped up the cut-out rocks to form thirty-six strange ridges and cliffs, and he also planted that Shuixian tea bush beside the Nine-Bend Stream, and every day he watered it with water from the Nine-Bend Stream. Later, if people were sick, they only needed to steep some Shuixian tea and they would quickly recover from the illness. From then on, the people lived contentedly. They happily sang:

> The fragrance of tea skims across the crystal pure water of the Nine Bends.
> The thirty-six ridges are—oh, so lovely!
> Though the flowers and moon of the heavenly palace are beautiful,
> The scenery of Wuyi Mountain rivals their beauty.

In the heavenly palace deep in the sea of clouds, one day the Jade Emperor's daughter Jade Girl was just leaning on her window sighing along with the parrot about the sad and quiet life in the heavenly palace. Suddenly a compelling mountain song floated up from the mortal world. The quick-mouthed parrot mastered it right away:

Though the flowers and moon of the heavenly palace are
    beautiful,
The scenery of Wuyi Mountain rivals their beauty.

When Jade Girl heard this, her frowns smoothed out. Parting the clouds and the fog, she looked down. She saw the beautiful hills and waters of Wuyishan—the songs rising and the hoes at rest. It was a very happy life. She wanted to ride the clouds and go down and become a mortal for a while. The parrot immediately flew to her shoulder and called thrice toward the sky, and also gave her a multi-colored feather. Jade Girl accepted the feather, kissed the parrot, and descended to earth.

When Jade Girl reached the mortal world, she changed into a beautiful village girl. Following Nine-Bend Stream, she toured the thirty-six cliffs and felt absolutely satisfied. Suddenly she saw a handsome and stalwart young fellow with thick eyebrows and large eyes. He was working very hard. Without thinking, she walked up and quietly asked, "Could I beg a bowl of water to drink?" Da Wang saw a young girl like a heavenly immortal looking at him with a smile on her face. Blushing, he lowered his head, picked up the teapot, and poured out a bowl of water. He didn't know if he poured out too much or if his heart was pounding too hard, but he wasn't careful and the tea water spilled out, soaking her gauze skirt. Da Wang hurriedly took off his short white gown and went up and wiped her skirt. Jade Girl saw how straightforward and good-natured and honest Da Wang was, and she secretly liked him. She pushed Da Wang's hand lightly away, and she wiped the spot with her own handkerchief. Da Wang poured out another bowl of tea, and gave it to her carefully.

111

As she sipped, Jade Girl asked, "What kind of tea is this? It's so fragrant."

Da Wang said, "This is Wuyi Shuixian, because it's irrigated by water from the Nine-Bend Stream."

As the two were talking, they heard the laughing sound of *"Hahaha."* This was the white-bearded old man walking up with a large platter of mountain fruit. He said, "Young miss, you've come from some other village? Come, taste the mountain fruit this old guy has grown."

Jade Girl thought to herself, "Wuyi is just great. The mountain is good, the water is good, and the people are good, too. Why don't I . . .?" Thinking and thinking, she said to the white-bearded old man, "Old man, to tell you the truth, I am the Jade Girl of Heaven. I admired Wuyi's scenery and came to the mortal world. It's wonderful here. Keep me in Wuyi!"

So, Jade Girl stayed in the mortal world. She was hard-working and capable, and was on good terms with the local villagers. Everyone liked her. In the spring, she took tea baskets up the mountain, and, with Da Wang, she returned with basket after basket of green tea. On summer evenings, as the moon was rising, she sang mountain songs and struck firewood-cutting knives on bamboo poles. With Da Wang, she danced the Sword and Flowers dance for the villagers. In the autumn, she brought back mountain flowers and copied them in drawings, and then wove piece after piece of tea-flower cloth and gave them to all the villagers. In the winter, facing the white snow filling the sky, she and Da Wang solemnly pledged their love, expressing the hope that their love would be forever pure like the snowflakes. The villagers all said that they were a couple made in Heaven.[27] The white-bearded old man was also happy to be a matchmaker.

On the eve of the wedding, Jade Girl sat in her room thinking, "Tomorrow, what gift should I send to Da Wang? Right, I'll weave a golden gauze hat for him!" So she took out the multi-colored feather and shouted three times for the parrot. The parrot flew to the window. "Bring me some golden thread and a silver needle right away!" Jade Girl had barely spoken these words when the parrot flew off, and, after a while, it returned with the golden thread and the silver needle. In the firelight, Jade Girl quickly began weaving.

Ever since Da Wang had controlled the waters, the people had been peaceful and content. Tie Bangui was not at all happy. One day, he scurried to the side of Nine-Bend Stream, and saw that everyone was jubilant. The women were sewing new clothes. Several carpenters were making a very large make-up mirror. It was very strange. Changing himself into an old person, he made inquiries and learned that Jade Girl had come to earth and was going to marry Da Wang. He thought to himself, "This is my chance to become an immortal." So he immediately went up to Heaven to reveal the secret and to receive rewards.

Tie Bangui reached the heavenly palace. He ran into the Jade Emperor, who had a stomach illness. He had tried a hundred cures, and none had worked. So he hurriedly gave him several portions of Shuixian tea that he had stolen and brought with him. A short time after drinking the Shuixian tea, the Jade Emperor's expression was clear and refreshed. His illness and pain had completely vanished. Tie Bangui then told the Jade Emperor about the Shuixian tea and Jade Girl. The Jade Emperor immediately ordered Tie Bangui to lead the way. He said he only wanted to summon Jade Girl back, and to get some more Shuixian tea, and he would then permit Tie Bangui to enter Heaven as an immortal.

Meanwhile, Jade Girl had finished weaving the golden gauze hat and it was already daylight. Looking into the clear Nine-Bend Stream, she combed her hair and washed and made up — preparing to be a bride. At this time, Da Wang quietly walked up behind her, and placed a multi-colored mountain flower in her hair. With deep emotion, Jade Girl took out the golden gauze hat for Da Wang to wear. The clear blue ripples of the water reflected their images. The two of them felt as satisfied as if they were drinking honey.

Suddenly the wind rolled up black clouds. The mountain howled and the water roared. Next came a crashing sound. Leading the Jade Emperor and the heavenly soldiers and generals, Tie Bangui had reached Nine-Bend Stream. Tie Bangui pointed to the Shuixian tea. The Jade Emperor reached out and took it.

113

Da Wang and Jade Girl tried unsuccessfully to block him. But then something strange happened. Each time the Jade Emperor touched that verdant, luxuriant tea bush, it withered. He issued an order summoning Jade Girl back to Heaven. Jade Girl immediately knelt on the ground and entreated the Emperor to let her stay in the mortal world. At this, the Jade Emperor was enraged. Tie Bangui, with the heavenly soldiers and heavenly generals, surged forward to pull Jade Girl off. Jade Girl embraced Da Wang tightly. Even if she died, she was unwilling to separate from him.

The Jade Emperor shouted, "If you don't return to the heavenly palace, I'll turn you into rocks!"

Jade Girl retorted, "It's better to be a rock and still be in the mortal world!"

Jade Girl had barely finished speaking; you could see only the flash of an arc of light, and the sound of "*honglong.*" The air was full of smoke. As expected, Da Wang and Jade Girl had turned into two rocky cliffs linked together. The Jade Emperor didn't stop there. He also called on Uncle Thunder and Auntie Lightning to split them apart. But Thunder attacked and Lightning struck—and they only broke off some shattered stones, leaving several fissures and several rock caves. The two rocky cliffs were still linked. The Jade Emperor was furious. He took out his double-edged sword and slashed with all his strength. For a short time, the rock cliff was split open. But after a while it slowly drew together again. The Jade Emperor ordered the heavenly soldiers and the heavenly generals to push the Jade Girl cliff to the south side of Nine-Bend Stream. Because he hadn't been able to summon Jade Girl back to Heaven and hadn't been able to get the Shuixian tea, in his great fury, the Jade Emperor also did not permit Tie Bangui to enter Heaven and become an immortal. He changed him into Tieban Cliff, located between Da Wang Cliff and Jade Girl Cliff.

The villagers who were to attend the wedding rushed up from all directions and saw all of this. They all wept. The drops of tears spilled onto the withered tea branches and the tea bushes slowly revived, grew leaves, and blossomed with yellow flowers. Soon, the tea flowers on the whole mountain surrounded all sides of Da Wang Cliff and Jade Girl Cliff. It was extraordinarily beautiful. At this time, the white-bearded old man sadly placed the large make-up mirror in the water. In the twinkling of an eye, a mirror platform gently arose. It reflected the faces of Da Wang and Jade Girl. They could see each other through the mirror. Their eyes could see through to the mutual feelings in their hearts.

To this day, everyone still calls Da Wang Cliff the "gauze hat cliff," because Da Wang is wearing the golden gauze hat that Jade Girl gave him. On the top of Jade Girl Cliff, the fragrance of flowers spills out all over. This is because Jade Girl wears in her hair the multi-colored mountain flower that Da Wang gave her.

(Story collected by Liu Xiling)

THE BEAUTIFUL LASS LAN RUHUA

In this story, the two young people are drawn to one another through the She nationality's singing contests, and they make their own decision to marry. It is noteworthy as well that the young woman refers to her natal home as her mother's home. Lan Ruhua demonstrates strength of character and resourcefulness in taking advantage of the situation confronting her to escape from an unacceptable fate. Although she sacrifices herself, her sacrifice provides her husband with a cause and he fights with determination against the Japanese pirates.

During the time of Emperor Ming Jiajing, outside Ningde's north gate in the She village of Dutou, there lived a girl named Lan Ruhua. She had a melon face and almond eyes; she was very pretty and charming. Just eighteen, she was clever and deft, and brighter than others. She could sing songs that were extremely pleasing to listen to, and she could embroider beautifully. Everyone called her "Beautiful Lass." A lot of people were always coming to the door seeking to marry her, but no one could move her heart.

The first month of the lunar year was the festival of the singing contest for the young She men and women. Led by Beautiful Lass, the singing troupe went to village after village—and won in village after village. They didn't meet anyone able to do better than her. Now Beautiful Lass's singing troupe reached the She village of Yanting, and encountered the young singer Zhong Youwei. The two people were well-matched. They competed for three days and three nights—and you couldn't tell who won or lost. So they continued for another three days and three nights. Beautiful Lass felt that she couldn't hold her own.

116

This Beautiful Lass had never studied. Although she was clever and quick-witted, her intelligence in fact was limited. Besides, Zhong Youwei was cultured. He had great learning. He had a facile imagination. He was able to write. The poems and songs he had inside himself were just like a gushing underground spring—a steady unbroken stream. In contests, he naturally prevailed. This time, Zhong Youwei was also aware of this. He was afraid that if he competed again and Beautiful Lass couldn't respond, she would find it very hard to bear, so he sang:

Banana leaves sway in the blowing wind,
The singing contest and the mountain flowers welcome the
    beginning of spring.
After the blossoming this spring, another spring will come.
Next spring welcomes little sister to come again.

Beautiful Lass realized that the other side was giving her a way out. In her heart she felt very grateful, and she promptly offered a song in response:

People say that Suzhou and Hangzhou are paradise.
How can they compare with the mountains where the She
    live?
Flowers cover the mountains, and songs fill the baskets.
Next year, when the flowers open, I'll come back and com-
    pete again.

The singing contest ended in a tie. At this time, Beautiful Lass had already been completely won over by Zhong Youwei's intelligence, ability, and character, but she didn't realize that she already adored him. Zhong Youwei saw that her ability and her appearance were extraordinary, and he secretly felt this was wonderful. In his heart, he was very happy. The two of them immediately set a date. Their affection was unbroken. They agreed to spend their lives together. Before long, the man's family sent a matchmaker to ask the girl's family for marriage. They settled it immediately.

The time chosen for the wedding was the Mid-Autumn Festival of the fifteenth day of the eighth lunar month. That evening, a bright moon hung in the sky. A beautiful sedan chair was carried into Zhong Youwei's home. With her female companions clustered around, the new bride stepped from the sedan chair and walked into the pavilion and, with her new husband, she worshiped the ancestors and was married. It was a very festive occasion.[28]

Quite unexpectedly, the young chief of the Japanese pirates who were illegally occupying a nearby island led more than a dozen pirates to charge into the gate. They carried off the new bride and bridegroom. They said that their leader wanted the new bride for his pleasure, and the new bridegroom as his servant. Beautiful Lass knew that this was improper, and she thought that she would resist through suicide. But then she thought again. To die in vain didn't have any merit, either. It would be better to think of a way out of this. So she said to the young Japanese pirate chief, "Your leader told you to capture me. Did he want me alive or dead?"

The young chief said, "Of course, he wanted you alive."

Beautiful Lass said, "Since he wanted me alive, you must agree to one condition. Otherwise, I'll kill myself right away, right here."

The young chief thought, "If she kills herself, what will I say to my leader?" So he asked, "What is your request?"

Beautiful Lass said, "We She sons and daughters are most filial to our parents. My mother's home is at Dutou Village, not far from here. You must let us go to see my parents, and say a few words of farewell, so that we can show a little of our filial piety. Only then will I go with you." The young chief had no choice but to agree.

Beautiful Lass led the Japanese pirates to Dutou, and pointed to the opposite shore and said, "My mother's family lives in the village over there by the side of the river. Let us go across." The crafty chief looked at this wide river and at the surging river water. The opposite shore was also very close to the county seat. So he changed his mind, and he didn't let them cross. Beautiful Lass continued to insist, and the young chief allowed Zhong Youwei to go alone and bring Beautiful Lass's parents over to talk. When two Japanese pirates escorted Zhong Youwei onto the boat, Beautiful Lass mumbled a sentence in the She language to the old ferry boatman. Halfway across the river, the boat overturned. The two Japanese pirates were struggling in the water. Zhong Youwei swam toward the opposite shore very quickly. From this side, Beautiful Lass saw that Zhong Youwei had escaped, and she seized the opportunity to dash toward the riverbank. The Japanese pirates quickened their pace in pursuit. When Beautiful Lass realized that the Japanese pirates were about to close in on her, she leaped ahead and jumped into the river. They heard only the one sound of *"putong."* They couldn't see even her shadow.

The next day, Zhong Youwei heard the sad news that Beautiful Lass had jumped into the river and died, and he cried his heart out. He found Beautiful Lass's body. After solemnly burying it, he joined the army and served under General Qi Jiguang.[29] When General Qi led troops to suppress the pirates, Zhong Youwei summoned up all his courage and energy to kill the enemy. He was often decorated for his military achievements. Finally he wiped out the Japanese pirates, and avenged Beautiful Lass.

From then on, the story of Beautiful Lass has been passed down through the generations.

(Story collected by Wang Zhichun)

119

BAMBOO BIRDS

This story deals with a wealthy young woman desiring to marry her father's hired hand. She expresses her absence of filial piety in extremely strong language when she says that—if her father countermands her wish—she will commit suicide and he will have no one to care for him in his old age. Thwarted by her father, she indeed carries out her threat.

In the past, more than a dozen households of the She nationality were living at West Mountain in Liujia Village. There was one She youth named Lei Desheng whose parents had both died when he was a child. He was friendless and helpless. When he was twelve or thirteen *sui*, he began helping a local rich man, Liu Benshan, tend cattle and cut the grass. When he grew up, he became this rich man's long-term hired laborer. He could plow and rake, he could plait square-bottomed bamboo baskets, he could make yokes for the cattle, he could make plows. He was good at everything. He was honest and diligent. He was a good youth, well-known far and near.

Liu Benshan had an only daughter named Fenglian. Her mother had died when she was a child. Liu Benshan absolutely doted on her. He always locked her in the home. He didn't let her go out and play with other children. The young laborer Lei Desheng was two years older than Fenglian. Fenglian saw that he was friendless and wretched, and, since childhood, she'd taken him as her own good friend and called him "elder brother." Every day near evening, the young Fenglian waited at the door for the elder brother to return, and she also helped him feed grass to the cows. The elder brother also never forgot to bring her a bouquet of mountain flowers or a whistle made of bamboo.

When it was rainy, the young elder brother cut less grass for the cows. Liu Benshan wanted to beat and curse him, but young Fenglian always cried and protested. Lei Desheng was extremely grateful to the young Fenglian.

Several years passed. Lei Desheng was now a robust and handsome young fellow. In her heart, Fenglian loved him even more. Time and again her father said to her, "Fenglian, you're grown up now. You're a one-thousand-pieces-of-gold young woman.[30] You can't continue, as you did as a child, to be familiar with that poor fellow." Fenglian shook her head, and at night—as before—she secretly ran out to the cow pen to watch the elder brother feed the cattle. She had heart-to-heart talks with him. She always gave him some good things to eat. Sometimes she also secretly made a small garment for him and one or two pairs of cotton shoes. Lei Desheng felt apologetic and said to her, "Fenglian, you're good to me. I know that. But you are the master. I am the hired laborer. You are the daughter of a rich man. I am a poor person of a She family. What use is it for you to be good to me?" Fenglian said, "These things don't matter to me. I like you. It's just that I like you. I don't care what other people think." Lei Desheng said with a wry smile, "If you want to marry me, I can't marry you. Your father wouldn't be willing, either." Fenglian said, "Don't worry. My father has only I—only one daughter. I want him to ask you to be a married-in son-in-law.[31] If he isn't agreeable, I'll just let him watch me die. Then, when he's dying, who will send him off?" Lei Desheng also thought this was a good idea, and the two of them became even closer.

One day Liu Benshan laughingly said to Fenglian, "Fenglian, you're twenty *sui* old. Your mother died early. I have only you— one daughter. These several years, I've considered one thousand, I've considered ten thousand, and I haven't yet selected a satisfactory married-in son-in-law for you. This rare opportunity has now arrived. Today the rich man of the Zhou family sent a go-between to propose marriage. I have promised you to his young son. You will have rich in-laws and I will also feel at ease."

When Fenglian heard this, it was as though thunder had struck a fine day. She was shocked, and immediately said, "I won't! I

121

won't! Since childhood, all I've wanted is to be with my good elder brother! He is honest and diligent and able. I just want you to ask him to be the married-in son-in-law!"

"What?" Liu Benshan felt this was no trivial matter. Pointing at his daughter, he cursed, "You little witch! I thought you'd grown up, that you could understand. He is a mountain person—a She person, a poor hired laborer. He is absolutely unsuitable. I never thought that you wanted to marry him! I'm telling you—give up this idea! I have already settled this with the Zhou family. The sixteenth day of this month you will become engaged, and the tenth day of the eight month you will be married. If you desire it, you'll go, and if you don't desire it, you'll still go!" Saying this, panting with rage, he walked downstairs. He left his daughter crying and making a fuss upstairs.

The rich man Liu Benshan thought that the hired laborer was the cause of this fiasco. So he called Lei Desheng in and gave him a tongue-lashing, and then fired him.

Lei Desheng was furious. He left the Liu home and returned to West Mountain. When he related the full particulars of this incident to the villagers, they all said, "Since Fenglian sincerely desires this, we cannot disregard her feelings." Uncle Lan said, "Now there's just one way. Before the Zhou and Liu families formally go through the betrothal, Desheng should secretly bring Fenglian out and be the first to marry her. At that time, the wood will already have become a boat, and the rice will already have been cooked. The Zhou and Liu families won't be able to do anything. Liu Benshan will have to acknowledge his married-in son-in-law." Everyone felt that this made sense.

On the night of the fifteenth, Lei Desheng quietly took Fenglian from rich man Liu's home. But before they had walked very far they were discovered by one of Liu's retainers making his nightly rounds. He shouted, "The young miss is running off with Lei Desheng! The young miss is running off with Lei Desheng! The young miss is running off with Lei Desheng!" No sooner had Liu Benshan heard this than he immediately rounded up all his retainers. Taking up lanterns and torches in pursuit, they very quickly caught Fenglian and brought her back. They also beat Lei Desheng until injuries covered his body.

The next day, Lei Desheng died from his serious injuries. The villagers from the She mountain were incensed, but there was nothing they could do. They could only collect money for a coffin and bury Lei Desheng at West Mountain. From then on, every evening, the villagers heard a strange bird cry coming from the bamboo grove on West Mountain: *"Nifuni! Nifuni!"*

The pitiable Fenglian was caught and taken home and locked upstairs. She wept and made a commotion. She neither ate nor drank anything. Three days later, she suddenly heard a strange bird call in front of the house: *"Nifuni! Nifuni!"* It was very much as if Lei Desheng were asking her, "Where are you? Where are you?" She answered the elder brother in the She language, *"Waifuguai! Waifuguai!"* (I am here! I am here!) It was strange. As soon as she responded, the bird cry stopped. It stopped awhile, and then began again. Fenglian responded again. This crying and responding went on for three nights. Later Fenglian learned that Lei Desheng had been beaten to death. She was so angry that she died from hitting her head.

That night after Fenglian died, the She villagers of West Mountain heard two strange bird calls coming from the bamboo grove. First the call, "Where are you? Where are you?" and then the call, "I am here . . . I am here." The call and response lasted until daylight. The villagers felt it was strange, and rushed to the bamboo grove to have a look. Above Lei Desheng's tomb were two birds with heads like thrushes'. The bodies were like small chicks — one male and one female. Back and forth they flew, calling in the bamboo grove. The male called, "Where are you? Where are you?"; the female responded, "I am here . . . I am here." The voices sounded very much like Lei Desheng's and Fenglian's. The villagers all said, "Lei Desheng and Fenglian changed into these two birds. They love each other, and they are both saying what is in their hearts!"

Year after year passed. This pair of birds still flies back and forth in the bamboo grove, and still calls and responds. They also have descendants. The name of West Mountain is now "Bamboo Bird Mountain"!

(Story related by Lan Junde and collected by Lan Tian)

TWO LOTUS PONDS

This story is similar to the previous one, dealing as it does with a young woman determined to marry the man of her choice. And the conclusion is similarly tragic and unfilial in the extreme. It differs somewhat from the previous tale in that the young woman is literate and in that her father holds the highest examination degree.

A very long time ago, there were two neighboring lotus ponds in Xiamen. The one on the south had been dug out by a merchant named Lian. It had red lotuses, and was called Red Lotus Pond. The one on the north had been dug out by Bai, a retired *jinshi* official who had returned home. It had white lotuses, and was called White Lotus Pond. Pavilions, platforms, and other buildings had been constructed on the banks of the two lotus ponds. North and south faced each other, and they were mutual rivals.

Jinshi Bai was already over sixty years old. He had only one daughter. Her name was Bai Yulian. Yulian was beautiful and intelligent. She not only resembled a water lotus, but she was proficient in poetry, calligraphy, the *qin*, and painting. Those in the area who sought to marry her came in an endless stream—so many that their trampling nearly destroyed the Bai family threshold. But Jinshi Bai had resolved to connect his family with one of illustrious status. If it wasn't that he disliked this family's poverty, then he disliked that family's vulgarity. So he hadn't given his daughter permission to marry.

Early one winter morning, Bai Yulian was in her bedroom combing her hair and applying make-up when suddenly she heard the sound of reading aloud. She pushed open the window to look out. In the pavilion of the Lian family's flower garden across the way, she saw a young student absorbed in reading a book. That student was tall. His face was fair and clear. He was very handsome. Bai Yulian was so entranced that she forgot to comb her hair.

"Hey, where did that student come from?" she asked her servant. Her servant replied, "He is a distant nephew of the Lian family. His name is Lian Shicheng. Because both his parents have died, he came to this uncle for help. *Ai*, the Lian family saw that he was poverty-stricken and down and out. They didn't really want to take him in. But they were afraid of hurting their relatives' feelings, and they were afraid people would talk, so they finally let him stay in the study[32] to teach their own child to read. I've heard the Lian family's slave girl say that Lian Shicheng's mind is filled with essays, and that he is also very good at calligraphy!"

From then on, Bai Yulian was at the window every day staring at the Lian family's small garden, and listening to Lian Shicheng read books and recite poetry. Lian Shicheng was truly diligent. It didn't matter if there was wind or rain: Every day he read without interruption. In the pavilion, he read with complete absorption; in her bedroom, Bai Yulian watched with absolute clarity. Bai Yulian watched and watched. She was no longer inclined either to do embroidery or to play the *qin*.

Half a year went by in the twinkling of an eye, and it was once more the season for the lotuses to bloom. One day, as usual, Lian Shicheng was reading in the pavilion and Bai Yulian was leaning, entranced, against the window. In that pond beside the pavilion, crimson lotuses were in full bloom. Bai Yulian lightly plucked the *qin*, and played a song called "Romance of the Phoenixes":

The male phoenix—ah—the male phoenix—ah—returns to the
    home village.
Traveling the four oceans—ah—in search of his female
    phoenix.

125

The sound of the *qin* was long and drawn-out, like a continuous strand of silk thread. Lian Shicheng was moved. What a pleasant *qin* sound! He listened very closely. It was the song "Romance of the Phoenixes." Turning his head toward the sound, he saw that in fact it was the young girl across the way playing the *qin* in her bedroom. When one song ended, that young girl lifted her head, stood up, and faced him. Ah, the hair at her temples was like spreading clouds, her face like the full moon. She was slim and graceful—just like a dew-covered white lotus in full bloom. Lian Shicheng was transfixed.

Seeing Lian Shicheng's stupefied expression, Bai Yulian faced him and nodded her head. With a winsome smile, she fluently recited a poem:

Fragrant, the red lotuses.
Too still, the student on pond's edge.
He should bend to the fragrance of the lotuses.
Why, instead, does he look this way?

Lian Shicheng was clever. He understood her hidden meaning. After a moment's thought, he responded with a poem of his own:

Across the way, a musical rippling lotus pond,
Where reflections send their own silent fragrance.
Why does the jade girl pose these questions?
One song: "Romance of the Phoenixes."

Bai Yulian saw that Lian Shicheng's response was like a stream and that his speech was excellent. In her heart, she was very joyful. The next day she painted a silk painting, and asked her servant to give it secretly to Lian Shicheng. Lian Shicheng looked at it. It was a painting of the emerald-green lotus leaves and the lotus fruit and flowers. Several small characters in the *liti*[33] script were appended: "The moon reflects the mandarin ducks meeting in the lotus pond."[34] Immediately grasping the meaning, he was pleasantly surprised. That evening, when the moon was reflected in the lotus pond, as expected, Lian Shicheng kept the appointment. He and Bai Yulian trysted on the bank of the lotus pond, and the two opened their hearts to one another. Solemnly pledging their love, they promised to spend their lives together.

Before long, Jinshi Bai realized that his daughter was growing older by the year. He appealed to people everywhere for a son-in-law. Bai Yulian was very worried. She urged Lian Shicheng, "Come to my home soon and ask to marry me."

Lian Shicheng sighed, "*Ai*! I have no father, I have no mother. I am alone in my uncle's home. What can I give your father when I ask to marry you?"

Bai Yulian said, "The gift of a poet's family—literary talent. Why is there any need for lavish gifts?"

"*Ai*! Your family doesn't have just average status."

"Okay. But try it first before we discuss it again."

The next day, Lian Shicheng told his uncle of his desire to marry. His uncle didn't say anything, but gave him several ounces of bits and pieces of silver. Lian Shicheng bought a meager gift, changed to neat clean clothing, and went to the Bai home to ask to marry Yulian.

When Jinshi Bai laid eyes on Lian Shicheng, he was impressed by his fine, delicate features. He also realized that he was talented. In his heart at first he was very satisfied. But as soon as he saw the betrothal gift, and then heard that he was the Lian family's poor relative, he said coldly, "Your home is at the red lotus pond. How did you happen to come to the Bai home?"

"Mr. Bai, this. . . ."

Jinshi Bai didn't wait for him to finish, but harrumphed and growled, "Be quiet! You can marry my daughter only if the water of the red lotus pond and the white lotus pond meets!"

Lian Shicheng left the Bai home in low spirits. He was listless. Reaching the embankment separating the two lotus ponds, he gazed up at the sky and sighed, "Ah, God, why didn't you cooperate!"

It was odd. Just then, crow-black clouds suddenly shrouded the sky, and heavy winds and rains came. He heard only the loud reverberation of "*honglong*" before that embankment was split by a large ditch. The two ponds met. The pond water met. In a moment the red lotuses and the white lotuses were united.

Beside himself with surprise, Lian Shicheng ran at once toward the Bai home. As luck would have it, he ran into Jinshi Bai at the entrance. He said loudly, "Mr. Bai, God has fulfilled your wish. Now the two ponds are already joined." Jinshi Bai saw that this was so, and for a moment he was too astonished to say anything. But as soon as he recalled that this meant he must allow his daughter to marry Lian Shicheng, he was very upset. He shot Lian Shicheng a look of disdain, and snorted. Then he ignored Lian Shicheng again, and shouted to his servants, "Fill in that ditch for me!"

The servants immediately began preparations. Just as they were about to begin filling in the ditch, the old lady came out weeping and wailing from the rear quarters. She held Jinshi Bai back with her words, "Quickly! Yulian is about to make trouble by hanging herself!"

Jinshi Bai rushed into the rear quarters. His daughter's hair was disheveled and her clothing a mess. She was crying so much that she was all tears. Jinshi Bai shouted, "This is preposterous! What are you up to?"

Bai Yulian rammed her head against her father's chest. "I can't go on living! You agreed with your own mouth that if the two ponds met you would let me marry into the Lian family. Now, today, the two ponds met. I'm already a member of the Lian family, but you've eaten your words and broken your promise. Tell your daughter how she can have the face to see anyone?!"

Jinshi Bai was perplexed. He thought, "Is it possible that the two of them already had a secret understanding? Can it be that someone has already secretly acted as a go-between for them?" Only when Jinshi Bai questioned Yulian's servant did he learn that his daughter and Lian Shicheng *had* already agreed to spend their lives together, and that it was the servant who had passed the messages encouraging Lian Shicheng to ask for marriage. He lost his temper, and told people to guard his daughter more strictly, and then wheeled around and again ordered his servants, "Quickly! Fill in this ditch today!"

But that ditch of water was like a deep, bottomless pool. There was no way to fill it in. The servants worked on it for three days. Even though they dumped in nine hundred and ninety loads of sand, the two lotus ponds were still joined. Jinshi Bai then ordered the servants to carry up large rocks to fill it in. And they filled it in for three more days. They only saw the water flowing under the rocks with a *"ping"* sound. The only result was some water splashing up.

Jinshi Bai was so angry that he was dizzy and his vision blurred. At night he tossed and turned, unable to sleep. His round sneaky eyes were glaring. He was desperately wishing for an evil idea. After a long time, he suddenly rolled over and got out of bed, slapped his thigh, and said, "Right—this is it!" That very night, he wrote a letter and wrapped up five hundred ounces of silver and told someone to take all of this to the *yamen*. He wanted the government to bring an accusation and arrest Lian Shicheng and put him in prison, so that his daughter would drop this idea forever.

He didn't expect that Bai Yulian would learn of this. It was just like a bolt out of the blue. She didn't know that her father was capable of resorting to such violent treachery! She mulled it over. She was concerned about Lian Shicheng, but the door was strong and she was also being watched very strictly. How could she go out? Finally she wrapped some silver in silk and told her servant to secretly give it to Lian Shicheng so that he could flee from here for the time being.

When Lian Shicheng learned that the government was about to arrest him, he immediately felt dizzy. He pointed at Heaven, and swore, "Jinshi Bai counts on his powerful connections. He bullies people too much! God—You pretend to be deaf and dumb, letting such an inferior person do evil. It truly is wrong of Heaven!" He accepted the silver sent by Bai Yulian and said to the servant, "Please tell Miss Bai that, in life and death, I will never forget her loving kindness. If I don't die in disaster, I will certainly come back to see her!" That very night he boarded a trade ship and set off for Southeast Asia.

From then on, Bai Yulian was guarded in her bedroom. All day she lay in bed and gazed south, waiting for news of Lian

Shicheng. Jinshi Bai proposed many times that she marry. She always refused. Jinshi Bai pressed insistently. She then answered indignantly, "If you badger me like this, your daughter has only death as a way out." Jinshi Bai was too frightened to raise the issue of his daughter's marriage again.

The lotus flowers withered and bloomed again. Bloomed and withered again. In the twinkling of an eye, two years passed—and she hadn't yet seen a message from Lian Shicheng. One day, a stranger suddenly arrived from Southeast Asia. He went to Jinshi Bai's home and said, "Please tell Bai Yulian that Lian Shicheng has died of dysentery." He also took out the painting of the lotus fruit and flowers that Bai Yulian had given to Lian Shicheng, and gave it back to Bai Yulian. When she looked at it, Bai Yulian felt faint.

Suddenly she dashed out the door of her home, and ran directly to the red lotus pond. She ran to the side of the ditch connecting the two lotus ponds. With a "*putong*" sound, she jumped in. Suddenly there was heavy wind and rain, and then a flash of lightning streaked across the sky. Muffled thunder shook the heavens. Jinshi Bai hurried to look for his child. His daughter had disappeared. The bank of the pond was collapsing, and mud and sand and stones filled the ditch. The two ponds were again separated. Jinshi Bai stared woodenly at the two lotus ponds. It was too late for regrets.

Lian Shicheng and Bai Yulian were dead. From then on, the Bai and Lian families declined with each passing day. Before very long, everyone was gone and the buildings were empty, and those two lotus ponds also fell into disuse. But the story of Lian Shicheng and Bai Yulian's love has been passed down through the generations. Today that place is still called "Two Lotus Ponds."

(Story collected by Zhang Yihong)

THE SEVEN IMMORTAL WOMEN

This story is unlike some of the others in that it deals with immortal women. Still, like the mortal women, they wish to marry and they—along with the young men—make their own independent choices.

In the scenic area of the Yuanyang Stream and Shiping are seven steep, tall, and graceful rocks. People call them "The Cliff of the Seven Immortal Women." Below the cliff a pool ripples with jade-green waves. Since the Seven Immortal Women used to bathe here, people call this "The Bathing Pool of the Immortals."

It is said that these seven immortal women of Heaven absolutely loved cleanliness. Every day they had to go into the river water to bathe and play. They delighted in this. Lake Tai, Lake Poyang, Lake Hongze, the Yangzi—all have their traces. But although these places abounded in jade-green water, they always lacked quiet beauty. So they wanted to find a quiet and beautiful place.

These seven immortal women roamed all through the mortal world. They saw men farming and women weaving. They contrasted the life of affectionate married couples with the loneliness of the Heavenly Palace. They longed to live in the mortal world.[35]

In the last days of autumn one year, the seven immortal women traveled to the air above Shiping and Yuanyang Stream. They saw the jade-green waves and the clear pool of Yuanyang Stream, and the green trees and emerald-green vines on both sides of the stream. The scenery was quiet and unusual. In the pool, pairs of mandarin ducks played in the water with incomparable affection. The immortals involuntarily pushed down the auspicious clouds and fell to the sandy beach. Removing their lotus-flower skirts, they skipped into the jade-green water. They swam and played to their hearts' content. They were inexpressibly satisfied. From them on, they often came to this bathing pool.

An old couple lived in the mountain pass of Shiping. They had seven sons, who were called Eldest Son, Second Son, Third Son, Fourth Son, Fifth Son, Sixth Son, and Seventh Son. The seven brothers were handsome, spirited, and stalwart. Seventh Son, especially, was even brighter and more quick-witted. They had all reached marrying age. But the seven brothers were absolutely filial and obedient. It would be improper not to take care of their parents. In the mountain area, they opened up wastelands and farmed and hunted for a living. One day, the seven immortal women came again. After they finished bathing, they watched and admired the mandarin ducks beside the pool. Seventh Son saw them. How had such beautiful girls happened to come to the deep mountains and ancient forests? Seventh Son guessed that they were immortal women. He counted. It was just right. There were seven of them. He realized with a start that there were also seven brothers. Wasn't this the happy fate brought by Heaven? Seventh Son maintained his composure. He waited until after the seven immortal women had departed on the clouds, and then he went home and told his elder brothers of this strange encounter. The brothers immediately thought of a way to marry the seven immortal women.

The next day, the seven immortal women came again to bathe in the pool. They had just removed their lotus-flower skirts and gone into the water when the seven brothers jumped out from the clump of trees beside the pool—and scared the seven immortal women so much that they jumped onto the beach, put on their lotus-flower skirts, and leaped into the air and flew away! At this time, the youngest of the seven girls noticed that Seventh Son, running in the very front, was really handsome and spirited. He was a man of talent. She purposely slowed her steps and Seventh Son took hold of her. Those six elder sisters who had already leaped into the air saw that Seventh

Sister had been caught, and they immediately dropped down again to save her. In a split second, the six elder brothers crowded up. The eldest caught the eldest sister, the second caught the second, the third the third, the fourth the fourth, the fifth the fifth, the sixth the sixth. The seven immortal women saw that the seven brothers each looked impressive, and they longed to have the hearts of mortals. Each one bashfully and blushingly bowed her head and said nothing. The seven brothers saluted in unison and said, "Because we are taking care of our parents who are old and often ill, we haven't married yet. We hope that the immortal elder sisters will help us out. We weren't at all well-mannered just now. Immortal elder sisters, please forgive us!" The seven immortal women saw that the seven brothers' words were sincere. They were hardworking and filially obedient, honest and sincere. They looked strong. In their hearts, they all desired the marriages, but they were also afraid of transgressing the laws of Heaven. They feared they would be punished. None of them dared say anything.

It was Seventh Sister who had the idea. She said, "If we deceive all the immortals in Heaven, we can stay in the mortal world!"

The six elder sisters immediately asked how they could do this.

Seventh Sister said, "We'll change our immortal bodies into seven rocks, and our real bodies will go with these men into the world of mortals, where men farm and women weave. We will live the lives of mortals. Won't this be wonderful?"

The six immortal elder sisters all felt that this was a good idea. They nodded their heads shyly to indicate agreement.

So the seven immortal women used their immortal techniques. They saw the immortal fog rising. The seven rocks were exactly like the seven immortal women—slim and graceful, and yet seven young girls laughingly stood before the seven brothers!

About those seven tall, straight "beautiful immortal women" rocks, people say: The luxuriantly green trees on top of the cliff were originally the beautiful hair of the seven immortal women; the bright and clean stone bodies are the jade-like bodies of the seven immortal women; the several creases and folds are the lotus-flower skirts worn by the seven immortal women! The folk still say: Just as that mischievous Seventh Sister was about to change, she kicked Seventh Son. Pretending to be angry, she said, "It's all your fault!" This kick of hers created a cave in the cliff beside the pool! If you don't believe this, just go and look at the Cliff of the Seven Immortal Women. That Seventh Sister's pretense of anger and the left foot which kicked out are both still indistinctly visible!

(Story related by Zhang Jiaguan and collected by Gan Pengfei)

SNAIL GIRL RIVER

This story, too, deals with an immortal woman who misses the mortal life and comes to be the wife of a man so poor that he believes he has no chance to marry. This tale differs from others about immortals, in that the snail girl has her sights fastened upon this particular young bachelor. Determined to marry him, she succeeds in her goal. She enjoys three years of mortal, married life, including bearing a son.

At the lower reaches of the Min River lies a narrow, long small island called Luozhou. In ancient times, Luozhou didn't even have a name. Only a few peasant families lived there—among them a bachelor named Xie Duan. He was hardworking and honest. Everyone commended him. When old people saw him, they said, "Ah, Xie Duan. It's time for him to be marrying. Why hasn't he found a wife?" He blushed deeply, laughingly went on, and thought to himself, "I'm so poor I can't even support myself. How can I marry?"

At dusk one day, he was driving a flock of ducks to the riverside. Suddenly a ray of sunlight appeared on the river surface—and he saw a beautiful young girl. Collecting his wits, he looked again. He didn't know where the girl had gone. At the roadside, he saw a river snail the size of a twenty-pound rice measure. Multi-colored rays of light shone on its shell. He thought this was very strange—and took it home and nurtured it in a water crock.

After a few days, Xie Duan returned from the fields one day at twilight. As soon as he entered the house, he noticed hot steam rising from the stove. He took the lid off the pot to have a look—and there was a pot full of fragrant white rice. He was

135

dumbstruck: What good-hearted person was helping him? He rushed out and asked a lot of neighbors. They all said that it wasn't they. After eating dinner, he lay on his bed and thought it over—and still couldn't guess who it was. He went to sleep in confusion. In his dream, he saw an old person bent over at the waist and carrying a walking stick. He was coming toward him, laughing and saying, "Xie Duan, congratulations! Congratulations! I'm coming to drink a glass of wedding wine with you!" Xie Duan couldn't make head or tail of this, and said, "Old Grandfather, what wedding wine?" "Haha, you've gotten married—and you're still trying to deceive me! Look—the bridal sedan chair is already being carried in with drums and trumpets." Xie Duan raised his head and saw a bunch of noisy people crowding in with the bridal sedan chair. He saw that he himself was still covered with dirt. He hadn't made any preparations. He awakened in a panic. It was already light. The ducks were already sticking their necks out from the basket. He got up in a hurry and prepared to wash and cook the rice. But when he lifted the lid from the pot, once again he saw a pot full of fragrant white rice. He was completely befuddled.

When he returned home at noon, the rice was again already boiled.

In the evening, he discovered that his tattered clothing had been mended. His shoes had also been brushed. Xie Duan looked and looked again, touched and touched again—and couldn't be sure whether all of this was real or a dream.

He lit the lamp, and, after eating his fill, he lay down on the bed. He wanted to see exactly what was going on. Before long, he heard light footsteps. Then he heard a *tingteng* sound from the water crock. He opened his eyes and saw a beautiful young girl pouring water into the crock. It was that girl he'd seen at the riverside. Xie Duan slid out of bed and went up and said to her, "Thank you so much for helping me. Who *are* you? To take care of me this way!" Blushing and lowering her head, the girl shyly told him that she was formerly a river snail, and had already become an immortal. Because she'd seen that Xie Duan was hardworking and honest, she had come to be his mate. Xie Duan said, "It's hard for me to manage three meals for myself. How can I draw you into this suffering?" The girl answered, "Diligence is capital. Later you'll farm and I'll weave, and we won't worry about bad times!" Xie Duan couldn't answer for a long time.

The next day the news traveled through the village. Male and female, old and young—all came to offer congratulations. From then on, he farmed and she wove cloth, and the days passed in lovely harmony. The next year, she gave birth to a plump, white son.

In the twinkling of an eye, three years passed. One noon, the river-snail girl was washing clothes at the riverside. In a split second, circles of black clouds rushed toward the river. She immediately ran home. Xie Duan saw that she looked flustered. Worry filled her face. Frightened, he asked, "What's happened?" The river-snail girl threw herself at Xie Duan and said through her sobs, "The Jade Emperor knows that I left the Milky Way, that I selfishly rushed to the world of mankind, that I rebelled against the laws of Heaven. He has already sent out the heavenly troops and generals. At 12:45 they will take me into custody and take me to the Heavenly Court. Ah, Xie Duan, I had hoped we could be together happily for a hundred years. I never thought that today would be the day we would part never to meet again! It's already come to this. There is no way to change it. I hope you'll look after our lovely son and take good care of yourself!" When Xie Duan heard this, he held his son in one arm, and his wife in the other, and shouted himself hoarse in calling out for help. But the distant sound of roaring thunder drew closer. In a moment everything was dark. A gale screamed. The river waves howled. You could see that disaster was close. Embracing her husband and son, the river-snail girl said calmly, "Ah, Xie Duan! I've already made my decision. If I am to die, I want to die in the mortal world and not go back to the Heavenly Court." She had barely finished speaking when thunder and lightning suddenly mingled together. The river-snail girl disappeared from Xie Duan's arms. Carrying his child and heedless of everything, he dashed out the gate to search for her. He saw no trace of her. He only saw a large river-snail bobbing up and down with the tempestuous waves and floating toward the middle of the river. Another thunderbolt fell on the river, and the large river-snail disappeared from sight. Alarming waves rose on the river, a white light leaped from the surface. From the crest of the waves came a plaintive lament. It was near evening before the clouds dispersed and the water receded. From then on, Xie Duan took his son to the riverside every day to search and to wait.

To commemorate the river-snail girl, later generations called this river Snail Girl River, and called this bleak and desolate island Snail Island. Even now, a stone plaque—"the historical site of the Snail Immortal"—stands on the riverside.

(Story collected by Ding Tiehong)

PART THREE

EQUALITY AND MORE: IMAGES OF STRONG AND ABLE WOMEN

BRIGHT MOON PAINTING

In this story, the young woman Huang Xian is portrayed as independent and assertive. She goes into the city alone, bargains successfully for a fair price for her father's painting, and later asks her husband for money to redeem the painting. A sense of quiet confidence and more than a suggestion of equality inform this woman's speech and actions.

In the time of Qing Yongzheng,[1] a famous painter named Huang Shen was living in Ninghua County, Fujian. Huang Shen was one of the famous "eight wonders of Yangzhou"[2]—truly wonderful. Although he painted very well, he didn't use this to curry favor with the authorities. So he never became an official. His whole life, he wore cotton clothing. Wealthy people were willing to pay high prices for Huang Shen's paintings. But Huang Shen didn't even look at the gleaming silver coins. Those high officials and noble lords, landlords and big merchants all came in high spirits and left in disappointment. But when ordinary farm laborers and fishermen, woodcutters and old men asked Huang Shen for paintings, he was always happy to set brush to paper, and generously gave the paintings to them. He didn't take a penny. Because of this, although Huang Shen was very well-known, his family was penniless.

Huang Shen had a daughter named Huang Xian. This daughter was innately intelligent. She was also slender and beautiful. Her father loved her dearly. She was absolutely filial and obedient to her father. When she was little, she learned to manage the household, so that her father could concentrate on painting and poetry and didn't need to take responsibility for the firewood and rice and oil and salt every day. Although Huang Shen's family lived in poverty, still they could make do with what they had to eat and wear.

Winters came and summers went; the years passed. In the twinkling of an eye, Huang Shen's daughter was already seventeen or eighteen *sui* old, about to be married.

The night before her wedding, Huang Shen asked his daughter to prepare a pot of sweet wine. *Gudugudu*—he drank it down in one gulp, and then slept soundly. The next day when he awakened, he didn't bother to wash his face or to rinse his mouth, but immediately spread out his paper and ground the ink. Putting brush to paper, he painted pictures. Without a break, he finished eighteen paintings. When his daughter was about to get into the bridal sedan chair, Huang Shen packed these newly executed paintings into the dowry suitcase, and said to his daughter, "Since your father has no money, these paintings are your dowry." At the same time, Huang Shen also took out one painting and particularly admonished his daughter, "This painting is the one I'm proudest of in my whole life. I want you to take it, too. But you must keep it with you. Only when your family is in the direst need can you take it to a pawnshop and pawn it. You must remember this without fail. It must bring a thousand ounces of silver."

Tears in her eyes, Huang Shen nodded her head. She memorized her father's admonition.

Huang Xian arrived at her mother-in-law's home. Her father-in-law and mother-in-law saw that their new daughter-in-law had brought a dowry suitcase. They thought it was all gold, silver, and other valuables. When they opened it to take a look, all that was in the suitcase were ink and wash paintings. Moreover, they weren't even fragments of mountains and bits of rivers, but just withered branches and wilted leaves![3] The father-in-law and mother-in-law's happiness turned to anger. By the time Huang Xian discovered this, the eighteen paintings had all been reduced to ashes. Huang Xian wept for three days and three nights.

Fortunately, Huang Xian's husband was an honest young lad. After their marriage, the two young people were very close and loving and they lived in harmony.

After three years, the father-in-law and mother-in-law died, one after the other. The husband also became very ill. Not well off to begin with, this family now incurred a lot of debt. They were so poor that they didn't even have porridge to eat. Huang Xian had no choice: She remembered her father's admonition. She went into the city to pawn the painting that she had kept with her. In the east part of the city, the accountant in the pawnshop looked at Huang Xian's painting. He saw only that there was nothing on the painting except a full moon. In the lower left corner of the painting were written the three words "Bright Moon Painting." A connoisseur, this man knew at a glance that this painting was rare and valuable. But, still pretending disdain, he asked, "How much money do you want?"

Huang Xian replied, "One thousand ounces of silver."

"Too much. A painting such as this is no more than a scrawled round circle. It is worth no more than five hundred strings of cash.[4] If you wish, you can pawn it for that. If you don't want to, just take it back with you." Despite the way he talked, he still held tightly to the painting for fear it would slip out of his hand.

Huang Xian thought to herself, "My husband is terribly sick. In any case, five hundred strings of cash could help with the emergency"—so she thought she should pawn it. But she thought back and remembered, "When I married, my father repeatedly admonished me: If you don't get one thousand ounces of silver for this painting, you must not pawn it!" So Huang Xian said, "Since you are unwilling to part with a thousand ounces of silver, and that would be barely enough, I'll just have to go to the pawnshop in the west part of the city."

When the accountant heard this, he was stunned. He had to soften. After bargaining and bargaining, he finally could do nothing but hand over a thousand ounces of silver to Huang Shen's daughter. He also signed a receipt—a particularly explicit one: "Pawned the painting 'Bright Moon Painting.' In the painting is a full moon."

This painting—"Bright Moon Painting"—was pawned for a thousand ounces of silver. When the pawnbroker heard this, he flew into a rage. Pointing at the accountant's nose, he heaped abuse on him, "All right! You don't mind attacking other people's children. You want my family to be totally ruined, don't you? Such a trashy painting! If you lost it on the highway, no one would pick it up. In the end, you were audacious enough to let someone pawn this for a thousand ounces of silver. What were you thinking of? Get out of here. I don't want you handling things here."

The accountant had no choice. He rolled up his bedding and left the pawnshop.

Huang Shen's daughter was beside herself with joy at receiving a thousand ounces of silver. She couldn't help but think aloud, "I really wouldn't have believed that my father's words would have this kind of effect!"

After taking several doses of traditional medicine, Huang Xian's husband recovered from his illness. With the money left over from pawning the painting, he went out to engage in trade.

When Huang Xian saw that things at home had taken a turn for the better, she asked her husband for a thousand ounces of silver to redeem the painting. Never imagining that Huang Xian could bring a thousand ounces of silver to redeem the painting, the pawnbroker was wild with joy. He thought to himself that this woman was really stupid. That tattered piece of paper wasn't worth even a penny—and she was still paying a thousand ounces of silver to redeem it! This amounted to refusing to eat tasty meat when given the chance.

The pawnbroker rushed to get that painting out. Huang Xian looked at it, and discovered that the full moon on the painting had changed into a half-moon. Pointing to the receipt, she said, "The painting I pawned was clearly a full moon. How could it become a half-moon?"

When the pawnbroker saw this, he was also stupefied. He had a brainstorm, and told Huang Xian, "The accountant must have done this. Wait until I can ask him about it, and then I'll give you your answer."

That very day, the pawnbroker looked frantically for his former accountant. The accountant laughed and said, "I knew that sooner or later you would come looking for me. That painting, 'Bright Moon Painting,' is a rare treasure. It's a pity you don't recognize treasures. Just do it this way: Wait until the fifteenth, and then ask that woman to come again to redeem the painting. I guarantee you'll be able to give her a bright full moon."

As expected, on the fifteenth—the appointed time for Huang Shen's daughter to come to redeem the painting—the moon in the painting had again changed from a half-moon to a bright full moon. Earlier, the moon in this painting had lacked fullness just as the moon in the sky had at that time.

It is said that after Huang Shen's daughter redeemed this "Bright Moon Painting," she considered it a valuable family heirloom. No matter who offered a high price for it, she never sold it. But when this painting was left to Huang Shen's grandson, the young grandson saw that—because it was already very old—the traces of ink were no longer clear. So he himself cleverly took a brush and retraced the circle. After this, the moon in the painting could never again be less than full.

(Story related by Zhang Maohui and collected by Ji Dongtian)

WALKING TOWARD HUANGNIE

The woman in this story is depicted as able enough to build a Buddhist convent, and intellectual and literate enough to correspond with the learned scholar Li Zhi.

Li Zhi was seventy-four *sui*. Although he was weak and often confined to bed, he still wrote and lectured. He felt that he didn't have many more days left, and that he must treasure this time even more and do a little more for his descendants.

One day, the official Feng Yingjing—with Huang Quwu, a local despotic gentry and a newly appointed *jinshi*, as his guide—led troops to surround Li Zhi's home. They shouted his name, and demanded that Li Zhi come out and answer questions.

An emaciated old man walked out from the courtyard. Calmly and unhurriedly, he asked, "I wasn't aware that I had the honor to receive Your Honor Feng. Is there something you want to see me about?"

Feng Yingjing sneered, "I've come here to preserve morals and decency. I would never have thought that Li Zhuowu[5] would have been a fourth-rank official and then would go so far as to force prostitutes to bathe with you in the daytime. How can this be proper?"

"The one engaging in corrupt morals isn't I, Li Zhuowu, but is the one who has accompanied you here, Huang Quwu!" Li Zhi answered with high-minded principles.

By now, more and more ordinary people were looking on and they were all commenting, "Old Li Zhi is always dignified. How can you charge him with coarse behavior?!" And, "The base guy who behaves coarsely is really Huang Quwu. All the ordinary people of Ma City know that he is a lady killer!" And again, "Huang Quwu blocks the way and takes liberties with women. He is a morally degenerate hypocrite!"

Formerly, Li Zhi had a good friend named Mei Guozhen. He had been Education Commissioner. As an upright official, he was very learned, and Li Zhi very much respected him. Mei Guozhen had a daughter named Mei Danran. She was intelligent and beautiful. She was a well-known talented girl of Ma City. The unfortunate thing was that she was widowed when she was still very young. That year at Qingming Festival,[6] she went up to the new grave to sacrifice to her husband, and was seen by Huang Quwu, the son of Ma City's despotic gentry. He blocked the way and took liberties with her. Mei Danran cursed him roundly, and, after she returned home, she built a Buddhist convent and prayed to Buddha to show that she had cut herself off from the red dust.[7] She had seen her father's friend Li Zhi, and had read Li Zhi's *Fenshu* and other works.[8] She knew that he had researched Buddhism, and she often wrote letters to Li Zhi to ask his help.

Just because Mei Danran had told him off once, Huang Quwu did not break with his evil ways. After he passed the *jinshi* examination and became an official, he was more determined than ever to take Mei Danran as his concubine. When he learned that Mei Danran was studying Buddhism, he told his loving concubine to disguise herself as a disciple and study Chan Buddhism[9] with Mei Danran, and watch for an opportunity to sound her out. Mei Danran saw through this ruse at once: She saw that the woman wasn't a good person, and turned her down flat. After the news got out, everyone treated this incident as a joke. . . .

(Story collected by Li Huiliang)

THE LEGEND OF LUOXING PAGODA

In this story, the woman Qiniang is wise, bright, and clever. She advises her husband not to journey to the capital city. When he ignores her advice, he meets his demise. She cleverly escapes the clutches of the man who plotted the murder by turning to her advantage one of the conditions she has set for marriage. Finally, when her son does not return from taking the examinations, she is so able that she sells the family property and builds a pagoda. At last, near death, she leaves a letter for her son. From this, we learn that she is also literate.

The legend says that Qiniang's husband Liu Huilong was a native of Yongnan township in Min County (now Fuzhou) in Fujian. He was a military *juren*.[10] In Chaozhou in Guangdong province, he served as a sub-district deputy magistrate.

At that time, in Chaozhou a man named Huang Jian owned a silver workshop. It's hard to say how much family property he had. He was connected with influential officials at court. Of all the civil and military officials in the whole city, there wasn't one who wasn't afraid of him. There wasn't one who didn't toady to him.

One day, on the birthday of the Taishan temple goddess, all the young women of the city went to the temple to offer incense and to pray that they would soon bear sons. Huang Jian also mixed among the pilgrims. He commented that the eastern family's daughter-in-law had delicate skin; and that the western family's young married woman had a trim waist. He flirted with the one from the east, and he flirted with the one from the west. When he made his way to Qiniang, he was transfixed. Even if the Taishan goddess herself stepped down from the

shrine, she wouldn't be as enchantingly beautiful as this woman!
He wanted to approach her, but four government soldiers were
with her. He didn't dare act out of line. He could only stare at
Qiniang getting into the sedan chair. As he walked home, he
thought it over. The sub-district deputy magistrate was a low
official. How did he have the good fortune to while away his
time with such a beautiful woman? He was determined that he
would seize Qiniang.

The next day, Huang Jian prepared a generous gift and called
on Liu Huilong at the *yamen*. His pretext for visiting was that
the sub-district deputy magistrate had recently had a law case
which exposed counterfeit silver, that this had been beneficial
to his silver workshop, and so he wanted to express his gratitude. Not only did he have generous gifts of gratitude for Liu
Huilong, but he also presented gifts of silver to everyone working in the *yamen*. Liu Huilong, who had not been in office long
and was inexperienced, actually thought that he was a very
good person who was generous in aiding the needy, and he
talked with him very warmly. They also became sworn brothers. From then on, Huang Jian visited often and they talked of
everything under the sun. Gradually, he came to know Liu
Huilong's state of mind very well.

One evening, bored and depressed, Liu Huilong invited Huang
Jian to drink some wine and admire the moon. They drank to
their hearts' content. In high spirits, Liu Huilong performed a
sword dance under the moon. All you could see was a circle of
cold light spinning on the ground. Huang Jian repeatedly ap-
plauded and praised Liu Huilong's skill in the martial arts.
Liu Huilong lowered his head in silence. There seemed to be
no way for him to dispel his boredom. Huang Jian read Liu
Huilong's mind, and swore loudly at the unfairness of the manners
and morals of that time. Treacherous court officials were in
power and stifled not a little talent. He said to Liu Huilong,
"Younger brother, you are talented in both the arts and the
military. It wouldn't even be too much for you to become a
commissioner in charge of pacification. It's a pity that no one
recommends you." He watched Liu Huilong's expression carefully, and then he continued, "In fact, I have relatives in the

capital city. They can talk with the Grand Tutor.[11] But I don't know whether younger brother wishes to go to the capital and try?" Liu Huilong was overjoyed at hearing this. He repeatedly expressed his thanks. During dinner, Huang Jian wrote a letter, and gave Liu Huilong generous gifts from the silver workshop to present to high officials when he reached the capital.

Liu Huilong, who was eager to woo officials, thought that he had hit the target, and that this was a stroke of very good luck. If he achieved the support of high officials, then in the future he could advance rapidly in his career. He paid no attention to Qiniang's advice not to go. He hurriedly set out alone for the capital. He didn't imagine that before he was far from Chaozhou he would be killed by lackeys sent by Huang Jian to ambush him.

When the bad news reached her, Qiniang cried her heart out. Huang Jian came, and hypocritically comforted her, and took her back to live in his home.

After Qiniang went into his home, Huang Jian used all kinds of threats and lures. He wanted her to remarry and become his wife. From the servants' quarters, Qiniang learned about Huang Jian plotting to murder her husband. She knew that she herself was a fish that had fallen into the net. Only if she was clever enough would she be able to avenge her husband. She brought up three conditions for the marriage. One was to immediately prepare a thousand ounces of fine silver, and send a special deputy to Fuzhou to provide for Liu Huilong's parents in their old age, and also bring back a letter written personally by Liu's father saying that he had received the silver. The second was to arrange a grand and solemn funeral for Liu Huilong, and guarantee that the city officials would all send their condolences. The third was to arrange separately for the wedding. Only after a full hundred days of mourning for Liu Huilong could the wedding occur. Huang Jian agreed to all of these conditions.

On the day when the funeral ceremony for Liu Huilong began, as expected, it was extremely crowded. All the city officials came to pay their condolences. Just at this moment, Qiniang—her hair all disheveled—rushed out of the mourning hall. In everyone's presence, she wept and told them of Huang

Jian's crime of plotting the murder of her husband. Among those present was Lin Yongxiang, pacification commissioner of southern Guangdong. He was also a native of Fuzhou. He sympathized thoroughly with Qiniang's misfortune, but he also had misgivings that Huang Jian's wealth made him very powerful. And he was afraid something unexpected would happen. So he purposely reprimanded Qiniang and slandered her husband and commanded his underlings to throw her out and escort her home immediately. In this way, he was also rescuing Qiniang from the mouth of the tiger.

Qiniang returned to her husband's home village, and gave birth to a posthumous child. She named the child Luoxing. Sixteen years later, he went to the capital to sit for the exams. Qiniang went to the Majiang ferry crossing. Weeping, she said, "Luoxing, the family grievance will wait for you to redress it. Talking now is useless. I'll wait until you have achieved scholarly honor and official rank and then I'll tell you about it!" Who could have known that Luoxing would be away for sixteen years and that there would be no word of him at all. Qiniang was waiting for her son at the entrance to the alley. Her hair gradually turned white. She sold off all the family property, and built a pagoda on the small island in the middle of the river in front of the Majiang ferry crossing where she had seen her son off. Every day she climbed the pagoda to gaze out at the vessels coming into port. From morning to night, she was tearfully calling, "Luoxing, ah, Luoxing! When will you be able to come back?" Several more years passed in this way. Only when she was terminally ill did she write a letter in her own blood telling of her sad memories. After placing it at the top of the pagoda, she died, her husband still unavenged.

Luoxing's official career was rough. He did not pass the *jinshi* exam. He regretted the eager hopes he'd had when he was about to part from his mother, and he felt he had no face to go home, so he just lived in an old temple. During the day, he made his living by writing letters for others. At night, he assiduously studied the classics. When he couldn't pass one exam, he waited for the next. Three years passed, and three years more. It's hard to say how many years went by before he finally passed the *jinshi*. When he returned home to worship the ancestors after he had made good, his mother had already been dead for five years. He climbed up the stone pagoda where his mother had watched for her son, and wept until he grew dizzy. A sudden sea breeze sent waves crashing against the sky, and woke him from his faint. He stared. The top of the pagoda toppled over, and revealed the bloodstained letter. Only then did he learn that his father had been tragically killed by Huang Jian. He immediately vowed to avenge him, to get rid of the bullies, and to bring peace to the good people.

After several years, Luoxing was appointed provincial judge in southern Guangdong. He had no sooner taken up his post than he received a lot of accusations about Huang Jian harming the people. Each of these offenses was enough to sentence him to death. But Huang Jian, relying on his wealth and influence, was infinitely resourceful. No influential official in the court would speak against him. To deal with this through legal channels was impossible. So Luoxing resolutely and quickly killed Huang Jian. Amid the cheers of the satisfied people, Luoxing put the case files in order, hung up his seal of office and abandoned his position. He returned to his faraway home village and never came back.

(Story collected by Wang Tiefan)

AXIU CLEVERLY READS A STRANGE LETTER

This story portrays another kind of very bright young woman. Although she is illiterate, she is able to decipher correctly the drawings on her husband's letter and thus is able to prove that the courier has cheated her. She and her husband also appear to have a warm, companionate marriage.

In the past, a young couple lived at the Fuqing County port. The man, Aming, was honest, sincere, and hardworking. The woman, Axiu, was bright and capable. The couple were very loving, and were always together. Aming took up a plow and rake, and worked the land; Axiu followed behind with an ox. Axiu took up a sickle and cut firewood; Aming took up a carrying pole and walked in front of her. Neighbors always saw them go out and return as a pair, and they all said they were a devoted couple made in Heaven, and like two forks of the same branch. Although their lives were very difficult, they were happy and they lived in harmony.

Once, when Axiu was cutting firewood and grasses on the mountain, a storm suddenly blew up. There wasn't time to take shelter. She was completely soaked. While she waited for Aming to bring a hat and straw rain-cape, Axiu's lips grew purple from the cold. When Aming saw this, his heart ached as though stabbed by needles. When Axiu returned home, she fell ill. In the daytime she was chilly, at night feverish. She couldn't think of tea or rice, and her hands and feet ached. She was in bed for forty-nine days! Aming brought her soup and fed her medicine. Day and night he waited at her bedside.

When Axiu saw that Aming was becoming tired and thin, it

was hard for her to bear. She said, "Aming! You mustn't worry about me. My illness can't be cured in a short time. If I'm cured, there will be a debt. . . ."

"Axiu, you will get better. You'll be well very soon! All that's important is for you to get well. Don't talk of a debt. Even if it's a mountain-sized debt, I—Aming—am willing to assume it!"

Finally Axiu was well again, and Aming really was burdened with a debt. Like mosquitoes in July, the creditors dunned him. Even if he wanted to hide, there was no place to hide! At this time in the village, several poor young men sought out Aming. They discussed going to Southeast Asia to earn a living. Aming was interested, and went home to talk it over with Axiu.

He mentioned it at 8:00, and Axiu didn't say a word.

He mentioned it at 10:00, and Axiu shed tears.

He mentioned it at midnight, and Axiu gritted her teeth and said, "Go ahead. Go to Southeast Asia, but don't ever forget your wife and children at Tangshan!" Then, her head on Aming's chest, she wept silently.

When Aming was ready to go, Axiu saw him off and went along on the road part of the way. On the road, she exhorted him over and over, "When you reach Southeast Asia, don't forget to send us a letter."

"But I. . . ."

"If you can't write a letter, just send a sheet of stationery. When I get it, I'll feel relieved!"

The boat left shore and sped away. Axiu stood at the seaside and watched the boat gradually go farther away and become a small black speck on the horizon. She went home only when she couldn't see it anymore.

Aming went to Singapore and cut bananas and hauled heavy carts. He did coolie labor, working at many odd jobs. Every night, he lay in the shed thinking of his Tangshan relatives. He remembered Axiu's request. But he would wait until he was more settled, and then he would send his family a letter. He bought envelopes and paper, but he gnawed forever at the tip of the brush and didn't write even one character. Finally he drew a wild goose and mailed it back. Before long, Aming received a letter from Axiu. She had drawn one love-sick tree. In this way, the two hearts living far away from each other remained very close.

It would soon be the Spring Festival. Aming was sure that the creditors would approach Axiu again about the debt. He quickly took the small change he had accumulated and exchanged it for a hundred silver dollars, and entrusted a fellow villager, Chen San, to take it back to Tangshan and give it to Axiu. He also asked Chen San to take a letter with him. Chen San took the silver dollars and the letter, and thought to himself, "This Aming is illiterate and he can still write a letter? What a joke!" So, on the sly, he opened the letter. Hunh! What a letter! It just had drawings of some birds, turtles, tortoises, and dogs! He could make a joke of this in conversation.

This Chen San was used to taking money back to the village. There wasn't much profit in doing things for poor people, so he often embezzled from these remittances. This time he thought, "Aming is honest. Aming doesn't even know one character. These birds, turtles, tortoises, and dogs in this letter: Is it possible that they could talk?" So he came up with a wicked plan. When he reached Fuqing, he gave Axiu just fifty silver dollars.

When Axiu received the letter and the silver dollars from Aming, she felt inside just as she did when she was thirsty and ate sweet watermelon—very pleased with herself. "But I must repay the debt sooner, and then Aming will return sooner." As she was quietly praying and hoping, she hurriedly tore open the envelope and looked at the letter. She saw only drawings of four dogs and eight turtles. What did this mean? This letter had been sent back with the money. There must be some reason for it. Axiu was thinking to herself, and guessing. Finally she understood. Laughingly, she asked Chen San, "Elder brother Chen San: Did my Aming really only send this much money?"

"What a joke! Is it possible that I, Chen San, would eat what is yours? If you don't believe this, go and ask the five aunties. When I, Chen San, do things, I have the highest reputation!"

To herself, Axiu whispered, "Who doesn't know that you, Chen San, are wily!" But, aloud, she said calmly and quietly, "Elder Brother Chen San! My Aming ate sparingly and spent

155

very little, and entrusted you to bring one hundred silver dollars. Did you really have the heart to swallow what is mine? I think maybe you're teasing me!"

Chen San was flabbergasted when he heard this: "One hundred silver dollars? Is it possible that she knows? No, it can't be. This woman is just guessing blindly!" So he said again, "Axiu, I—Chen San—can tell other jokes. But I wouldn't dare joke about remittances! Your Aming sent only fifty silver dollars. Just look at other affectionate couples among the villagers. No one has received as large a remittance as yours!"

Axiu thought to herself, "This Chen San is too stubborn." All she could do was lay her cards on the table and say, "My Aming's letter says he sent a hundred silver dollars!"

"Where?"

"Just look!"

"Ha! Ha! Ha! What kind of letter is this, what kind of letter is this? Where does he write that he is sending a hundred silver dollars?"

A lot of people were hovering around. Chen San was so nervous that he broke out in a cold sweat. But no, if he let Axiu give the game away, he—Chen San—would not be able to eat from any more remittances sent home! Anyhow, Chen San was a very experienced bum, and he immediately counterattacked in his own defense, "You, Axiu, have taken my good will for ill intent. You've said I embezzled your money, and you've wrecked my good reputation. All right, all right, all right! We'll ask the village elder to decide!" He took hold of Axiu, parted the crowd, and went to the village elder's home. Axiu had not intended to make a big deal out of this, but when she saw how unreasonable Chen San was, she thought that if he wasn't taught a lesson, he would squeeze dry the money that several other poor brothers in Southeast Asia sent back. So she steeled her heart, and went with Chen San to the village elder's home.

The village elder heard both sides' accusations, and he still wasn't clear about it all. Axiu said, "Old Uncle, look! Didn't Aming write it very clearly in his letter? 'Four dogs' is 'four-nine.' 'Four times nine is 36.' 'Eight turtles' is 'eight-eight.' 'Eight times eight is 64.' '36' and '64': Isn't this exactly 100 silver dollars?"[12] She wheeled around, and said, "Elder brother Chen San, if you haven't embezzled my Aming's money earned from his blood and sweat, then swear that before Heaven and Earth!"

Chen San was stunned. He hadn't thought that the completely illiterate Axiu and Aming could be so smart. Take an oath! He, Chen San, risked his life crossing the ocean all year long. It was not worthwhile to take an oath just to gain fifty silver dollars![13]

The village elder saw that Chen San was speechless, and he was now very certain of what had happened, "Chen San, if you have embezzled people's money and if you give it back within two days, that'll be acceptable. You cannot embezzle people's money!"

Chen San couldn't justify himself. He said, "Little Sister Axiu, tomorrow morning I'll give your money back!"

From that time on, this story of Axiu cleverly reading a strange letter has been passed on among overseas Chinese.

(Collected by Yu Dazhu and Lin Wenfang)

GOLDEN TURTLE CLIMBS THE CLIFF

This story portrays a girl willing to make a pilgrimage alone to a temple. She is also able to entrap the monk, so that, although he passes the test of attraction to her, he remains vulnerable to the lure of valuables. The other female character—the Taimu goddess—embodies traditional Buddhist and Confucian values. She shows a Buddhist compassion for the monk. And she reflects Confucian values in offering reciprocity to the monk: Since he has helped her for so many years, she feels obligated to offer him a way to follow her at some future time.

At Taimu Mountain, a rocky peak towers high into the clouds. People all call it "Golden turtle climbs the cliff!"

Why did this golden turtle want to climb the cliff . . .?

It was the sixth day of the seventh lunar month. It was said that the next day the Taimu goddess would ascend to Heaven and become an immortal. The golden turtle, which ordinarily carried salt and rice on his back for the Taimu goddess, also hoped very much to go with her to Heaven. He revealed his innermost desires to the immortal children who came to meet the Taimu goddess.

This golden turtle had already been transformed into human form for a long time. His name was Monk Muguo.

One night, Monk Muguo was sitting in meditation under the lamp. Eyes closed, he was thinking about ascending to Heaven. Suddenly he heard someone calling at the door. He opened the door and, to his surprise, he saw a beautiful girl, only eighteen years old. She wanted to stay overnight. How could a monks' temple let a girl stay? Monk Muguo tactfully turned her down.

But that girl piteously entreated him, and kept on talking and didn't leave. She said it was the first time she'd made a pilgrimage to a temple and offered incense. It was dark and terribly foggy. She couldn't find the path down the mountain. If he wasn't willing to let her stay, she would have only the path of death. Monk Muguo sighed. Monks and nuns saw compassion and charity as the most essential. How could he see someone dying and not save her? But he was alone in this temple. There were only two rooms. How could a girl stay here? He hesitated, unable to decide. The longer it went on, the more miserable the girl's crying sounded. Monk Muguo was terribly upset by her. Finally he let her stay in the room inside. He kept his eyes shut and continued meditating as he waited for daylight.

In the last half of the night, Monk Muguo heard the girl moaning on and on. She was saying repeatedly, "Master, master, come quickly and save me!" Thinking something had happened, he rushed to the door of the room. The girl said listlessly, "I drank cold water today. Now my stomach hurts so much I will die."

Monk Muguo said, "What medicine do you need?"

The girl replied, "I don't need any medicine. I just need a vigorous massage and I'll be fine!"

Listening to this, the monk groaned inwardly. It was the middle of the night. Men and women are different. . . . He stood outside the door and hesitated for a long time. Should he go in or not? Just then, the girl shouted loudly once, and then there wasn't another sound. If she hadn't died of pain, she had fainted from pain. Monk Muguo was so alarmed that he chanted over and over, "Amituofu,"[14] and then he pushed the door open and went in, and massaged the girl several times. As expected, she revived and expressed her thanks over and over. When Monk Muguo saw that she had recovered from her illness, he felt at ease. As before, he went outside and sat and meditated until daylight.

When it was light, the girl washed and dressed and left. In her hurry, she forgot her gold hairpin. Monk Muguo saw it and at first intended to follow her and call out to her, but then he also thought of the way that gold hairpin sparkled. It must be worth a lot of money. So he stopped his mouth and waited until the girl had disappeared without a trace, and then hastily slipped the gold hairpin into his sleeve.

This was the seventh day of the seventh lunar month. The Taimu goddess was about to move. Monk Muguo came to a spot below the cliff where she would ascend to heaven. He had just climbed up the cliff with the Taimu goddess when he heard someone say from high in the clouds, "Master, you have been transformed for many years. Although you have a certain merit, still your virtue is not deep enough. You passed the test of the beautiful woman, but you still haven't passed the test of wealth." Monk Muguo heard that thoroughly familiar voice, and was greatly alarmed. He felt in his sleeve. The gold hairpin had already turned into a blade of withered grass. Monk Muguo let slip a sound, and appeared in his original shape of a golden turtle. In a moment, he slid down from the cliff. His claws scratched two deep paths on the rocks.

The young girl of the night before had been transformed from an immortal child. At this time, the immortal children told the golden turtle to be patient and cultivate himself for another three hundred years, and then they'd discuss his wish again.

The nine colorful dragons wanted to soar to the clouds immediately and ride the mist, but the Taimu goddess remembered that the golden turtle had carried salt and rice on his back for her every day, and so she removed an embroidered shoe and put it on the top of the peak. Later he could use this shoe as a vehicle for his ascent to heaven. But the golden turtle's legs felt like jelly. There was no way he could climb up. Even now, the golden turtle wants to climb to the top of the peak, and pick up that embroidered shoe.

(Story collected by Xue Zongbi)

MULANBI

The following story is based on fact, and Qian Siniang, who lived during Song dynasty times,[15] is still credited with originating the plan for the dam on the Mulan stream. She was an extraordinary young woman, possessing notable organizational skills. She also had a great deal of determination, persistence, optimism, and patience. It is clear, too, that she was literate. She also evidently was single.

It is said that one time Wang Mu convened a large "peach of immortality" meeting. Gods and immortals from all the different religions were invited up to Heaven. Even local gods and mountain gods went. When the seating was arranged, the mountain god of Putian's Hugong Mountain and the dragon prince of the Eastern Ocean were seated at the same table. They ate until everything was finished, except for the one peach of immortality. This gave rise to an incident: The one was gluttonous, the other was greedy. They struggled with each other until their faces were red and their cheeks puffed up. They nearly came to blows.

The dragon prince was the first to open his mouth and swear, "How can the young mountain god be considered wonderful? He's not fit to polish my shoes!"

The mountain god was not persuaded. "Let's go and settle this in the mortal world. If you win, the peach of immortality will be yours."

Hugong Mountain was in Putian. The Eastern Ocean was also near Putian. The two of them went down to the mortal world and began to struggle in Putian. The mountain god struck out strongly with his fist, and, with a roar, he leveled the top of

161

Hugong Mountain. The dragon prince opened his mouth and vomited water, and the ocean tide rose a hundred feet. So the mountain god acknowledged defeat and gave up that peach of immortality.

The dissolute dragon prince just retreated to the Eastern Ocean to eat the peach of immortality, and gave no attention to the water all over the mountain. Seven days and seven nights passed before the water gradually receded and dried up. It smashed through a large area of farmland, and emerged from the Mulan stream.

The Mulan stream was roaring like a wild unbroken horse, carrying the stream water from the valleys and mountains all around to crash against the plains of Putian. Because of this, year after year Putian was not very peaceful: heavy rain and great disasters, light rain and light disasters. Several thousands of *mou* of farmland were laid waste. Several tens of thousands of households became destitute and homeless. Countless victims fled to the streets of the county capital, and sold their sons and sold their daughters, and endured freezing and starvation.[16]

The county capital had a wine shop. The proprietor's name was Qian Siniang. This woman was loyal and merciful. She saw that the victims did not have enough to eat or wear, and she secretly shed a lot of sympathetic tears. She thought to herself, "When will the people be able to live and work in peace and contentment? If necessary, I'll give up my family fortune."

One day, three guests came to drink wine, and the talk turned to the disaster of Mulan stream. One of them said, "Build a dam to serve to hold the water back, and the peace will be protected for a thousand years and ten thousand generations."

Qian Siniang was listening. She interrupted to ask, "Since this would work, why hasn't such construction begun?"

The other replied, "The water hasn't inundated the *yamen*, so why would officials undertake this project?"[17]

Qian Siniang said, "We can save ourselves by ourselves. Wouldn't it be fine if everyone donated the funds?"

Another guest laughed and said, "Those with money will just move to another district. Wouldn't that be a happy, unfettered existence!"

"If you want to be merciful, then just go bankrupt and build the Mulan dam!" the third guest said sarcastically. Throwing his wine money down on the table, he stalked off.

Qian Siniang stared for a long time without talking. Suddenly she scooped the wine money up from the table and—*dingdingdangdang*—dropped it into the wine jar beneath the table. She took out a piece of red paper, and wrote ten characters on it: "Build the Mulan dam: Saving the people is saving oneself." Pasting this on the wine jar, she began collecting money to build the dam.

A public figure from Changle County, Lin Congshi, was also drinking wine. He had seen everything that had just occurred, and he walked closer and said to Qian Siniang, "One inch of dam will cost one inch of gold. How long do you intend to collect money?"

Qian Siniang replied, "One year, there won't be much, but in two years there will be more. In five or ten years, there will be enough!"

Lin Congshi was dumbstruck. He nodded his head slightly, and left without a sound.

From then on, Qian Siniang saved whatever profit she made from selling wine. When the wine jar was full, she exchanged it for a large vat. When the large vat was full, she exchanged it for another. She exchanged the savings for gold. Altogether, she had a decaliter. It looked as though there was enough money to build a dam, and she hired workers to begin the job.

The first year, they cut into the mountains to quarry until several nearby mountains were bare. On the two sides of Mulan stream, they heaped two very high mountains of rock. The second year, they dammed the water and laid the foundation. At the bottom of the stream, they built a stone wall. The third year, they constructed the high dam. The news spread. Male and female, old and young all came to Mulan stream to offer congratulations. They beat drums and gongs, exploded firecrackers, and offered their thanks to Qian Siniang.

The sounds of the drums and gongs and the sounds of shouting echoed to the Eastern Ocean and were heard by Calm-Wind Ears, the malevolent spirit in charge of the Eastern Ocean. He thought it was very strange: "What can be so exciting?" So he dragged along Thousand-*Li* Eyes to have a look. Thousand-*Li* Eyes took a look, and rushed to report to the dragon prince: "A dam has been built at Mulan stream. Prince, what do you think should be done?"

At hearing this, the dragon prince was alarmed and angry. He roared, "Speed to Mulan stream, and destroy that dam!"

Crossing rivers and crossing the ocean, the two demons followed the bottom of the water and, in the twinkling of an eye, they reached Mulan stream. They quickly destroyed the rock dam. The stream floods rose suddenly and sharply.

Qian Siniang saw that her own effort had all been wasted in the water. She was both grief-stricken and regretful, and so angry that she wanted to jump into the water and commit suicide. Everyone anxiously held her back, and exhorted her, "You would only die, and the flood waters would still ruin people. Why do you so lightly give up your life?" Qian Siniang thought and thought, and swallowed down her tears, and very reluctantly went home with everyone. And she determined to start all over again to save money to build the dam.

As it happened, this very day, Lin Congshi came from Fuqing to Putian. Earlier, when he had heard what Qian Siniang said, he had been very moved. He'd gone home and sold his family property and had also collected some more money—seventy thousand strings of cash altogether—and he wanted to help her build the Mulan dam.

So, work began again on the banks of the Mulan stream. After three years, an even higher, even wider, even longer rock dam was placed across the middle of the stream. On the day the work was completed, the villagers from all around came to offer their congratulations.

As soon as the drums and gongs sounded, Thousand-*Li* Eyes and Calm-Wind Ears came again to do their mischief and the dam was destroyed again.

This time, everyone was enraged. They were of one mind. They cooperated to build the dam. This family contributed gold, that family contributed silver. Women removed their earrings and bracelets. Children saved their cake and candy money. Very quickly, they had accumulated a hundred thousand strings of cash!

But this time wasn't like the last two times. A lot of laborers had gone elsewhere in search of work, and the rocks of the nearby mountains had all been used up. They had money, but they had no way to begin work. Because of this, Qian Siniang had a worried frown.

One day, an unfamiliar old man found Qian Siniang and Lin Congshi and said, "I've come to contract to do the work on the Mulan dam."

Qian Siniang looked at him from head to foot. She saw his silver beard and his white hair. His body was hale and hearty. He was sixty or seventy years old. His left hand held a worn-out gunny sack. He looked very honest. So she asked him happily, "Altogether, how much money will you need?"

The old man waved the worn-out gunnysack and said, "Fill this up. That'll be enough."

The gunnysack didn't seem large. One string of cash after another was packed in. When the entire hundred thousand had been packed into it, it was full.

Two days passed. The old man summoned stone-cutters from a distant place, and turned them over to Qian Siniang. Leaning on a staff, he himself left. The stone-cutters had nothing to do. All day long, they ate their fill and slept. When they woke up, they sat around and shot the breeze. They were all so well nourished that they were full of life. Seven days passed in this way. Then the old man returned. He was driving a herd of mother pigs. Each was fat and large. Some were white, some gray, some black. He was tapping each pig's rear end lightly with his staff, and shouting, "Go to sleep! Go to sleep!" A mother pig then lay on the ground and turned into a large rock. He tapped and tapped, and shouted the two sentences, and another turned into a rock. He saw that this was just about right, and he locked up the remaining pigs.

So, the stone-cutters began their work. They worked on stone-cutting from dawn to dusk. They cut long rocks—square and even—each the same width and the same length.

The mother pigs passed the night and bore piglets. Each one

bore a litter. More and more were born. So the rock materials for building the dam were no longer a worry. It is said that later when the rocks were seen to be sufficient, the one remaining mother pig was set free by the old man at Nang Mountain. Even today, Nang Mountain in Putian still has such a large rock. People call it "Mother Pig Rock."

Year after year passed, and the rock dam was again completed. This time, even more people came to offer congratulations. People beat the gongs and drums again, and exploded firecrackers. Shouting and jumping for joy, they were wreathed in smiles. Suddenly, the stream water rose rapidly again. Turbulent waves arose. The dragon prince had come in person, and had brought Thousand-*Li* Eyes and Calm-Wind Ears to destroy the dam.

The jubilation turned to panic. Some people wept, some fled. There was chaos all over. At this time, you could only see that old man who had contracted for the job. He squeezed out from the crowd, and—*putong*—jumped into the stream. An iron pillar immediately appeared there. It propped up a section of the dam's foundation. But the larger section of the dam was still collapsing. Qian Siniang looked worried, and she also jumped in. And then Lin Congshi jumped in, too.

On the surface of the stream appeared three iron pillars, propping up the rock dam. The flood waters were tamed. But before long, the dragon prince again bored his way out from the bottom of the water, and exerted his strength to churn everything up. He aimed at, and attacked, the sides and the corners of the rock dam. *Hualala*—some of the cliff rocks were smashed. *Hualala*—some more were smashed. Just at this extremely critical point, another person squeezed out from the crowd and shouted, "I'll go!" He leaped into the air, and jumped into the waves. He also changed into an iron pillar. In the chaos, everyone saw only that he was shabbily dressed, but they couldn't see who it was.

The four iron pillars sparkled, and firmly propped up the entire dam. Thousand-*Li* Eyes and Calm-Wind Ears tried futilely to smash them with their heads. They could only make their "*Aioyoyo*" demon sounds and escape. The dragon prince saw that the rock dam couldn't be smashed, and he feared being imprisoned in Mulan stream. So he also slipped back to the Eastern Ocean. The stream water immediately receded.

On the banks of the stream, the drums and gongs were beaten again, and the firecrackers exploded again. Suddenly ten thousand golden rays shot down from the sky. Everyone looked up. They saw four people standing on a rosy cloud: Qian Siniang, Lin Congshi, Lu Banye—the old man who had contracted for the job—and the other, the one who was shabbily dressed. Some said it was the mountain god Tie Guaili. Others said it was an ordinary poor man. People were still talking about it when the rosy cloud had already floated up to Heaven.

From then on, the rock dam blocked the rapid water and allowed the Mulan stream to flow quietly out to the two oceans. And it irrigated several tens of thousands of paddy fields and sugarcane land.

(Story collected by Cai Huaren)

THE STORY OF ZHENG TANG

The woman in this story—Wang Fufu's wife—plays a very minor role. Yet, it is she who is shrewd and insightful. Had her husband listened to her, he would have averted embarrassment, capture, and punishment.

In the time of Emperor Ming Zhengde, a *xiucai*[18] named Zheng Tang lived on Zhuzi Lane in Fuzhou, Fujian. Zheng Tang was straightforward and humorous. His nickname was "Comical Poet." He was well versed in the *qin*, chess, calligraphy, painting, poetry, and songs. He was a well-known student in that city. Zheng Tang's father Zheng Luo had already served as prefect of Ningbo in Zhejiang. He was an honest and upright official. He wasn't good at fawning and toadying. He was disgraced by the eunuchs who flattered officials, and he resigned his post and returned home. From childhood, Zheng Tang was educated and nurtured by his father. His natural disposition was to be upright and outspoken. He liked to speak out from a sense of justice and defend people against injustice. He wasn't afraid of disobeying his parents. At that time, eunuchs held power, and loyal officials were held down. Although Zheng Tang was in his prime, he was not inclined to obtain official rank.

When Zheng Tang was more than twenty *sui*, he was still unemployed and in the home. One day—the first day of the year—Zheng Tang got up early. When he opened the door to greet the new year, people outside were seething with excitement. At last he saw some people arrive with a coffin. Zheng Tang was dumbstruck. He knew that these were his enemies. He didn't show his anger, but he plotted his countermove. He just heard the guy carrying the coffin say sympathetically, *"Xiucai*

Zheng, this year is unlucky for you. To use this inauspicious thing on the first of the year is really bad luck!" Zheng Tang asked who had bought it. The guy carrying the coffin said, "Manager Qian of the porcelain shop on the back street bought it and told us to bring it to your home." Zheng Tang said, "Thank you. You must be exhausted! I'll trouble you to bring it to the main entrance." The coffin was placed at the entrance. Zheng Tang told the guys who had brought the coffin to take an ax and chop it up, and then build a fire. As the wood burned, it sounded just like firecrackers, and attracted not a few people to watch the excitement. Zheng Tang wrote a couplet and pasted it on the door.

The first line said, "Our neighborhood happily explodes firecrackers to expel evil."

The second line said, "New Year's Day good luck wishes for promotion and property."

Those guys looked at the couplet and couldn't hold back their guffaws. They all said simultaneously with admiration, "*Xiucai* has said this well!" An old man stepped forward from the crowd: "I'll recite some doggerel, okay?" The guys said, "Sure!" The old man recited, "In the new spring, spirits are high. Becoming an official is linked to becoming rich. The Zheng family burned firecrackers, and got rid of death, and there was no big disaster!" The guys all exploded again with guffaws, and they all praised this as a "good poem!"

Half a month passed. On the day of the Lantern Festival, Zheng Tang got up very early again. Carrying a vegetable basket and a rice bag, he went out to purchase some things for the festival. He purposely went to the porcelain shop on the back street to look for Manager Qian, who sold all kinds of large and small water vessels. While bargaining, Zheng Tang suggested selling them by the *jin*. Manager Qian was only too anxious to make more money, and he readily agreed. Both sides agreed that the coarse large water vessels should sell for two cash per *jin*, and the large glazed ones should sell for four cash per *jin*. Zheng Tang selected one of each kind, and asked the manager to deliver them to his house.

Since marrying, Manager Qian had dismissed his partner. So

all he could do was carry the vessels himself. Along the way, Zheng Tang bought pork, chicken, duck, fresh vegetables, and rice, oil, salt, soy sauce, vinegar, and wine—and put it all in the water vessels that Manager Qian was carrying for him. Manager Qian was gasping for breath. He was sweating a lot, and only with great difficulty did he make it to Zheng Tang's home. He put down the load and breathed deeply. After Zheng Tang took the holiday foods into the kitchen, he picked up a scale with one hand and held a firewood knife in the other, and went over to Manager Qian. He broke a coarse large water vessel with the knife, and, lifting the scales, he said, "I'll buy one *jin* of this water vessel. Please weigh that amount." Manager Qian was dumbfounded by Zheng Tang's action. He stood there transfixed, and for a long time he couldn't say anything. Zheng Tang turned around, planning to break a glazed water vessel. Manager Qian stopped him: "*Xiucai* Zheng, you can't break another. I won't sell by the *jin*! I won't sell!" "We had this all settled. Why won't you sell?" "Excuse me. I'd rather accept my loss and give up one vessel and sweat in vain. I'm going back." Manager Qian picked up the shards and left dejectedly.

The next day, Zheng Tang went to Manager Qian's shop again. He wanted to buy a set of quite beautiful tea utensils. The fixed price was only fifty cash. Zheng Tang purposely paid him an extra fifty cash. Manager Qian had taken to heart the lesson of the previous day, and didn't dare ask more, but Zheng Tang urged him strongly to take it. Manager Qian thought to himself, "This person Zheng Tang is not one to trifle with." If he accepted more money from him, he would just be asking for trouble. Zheng Tang asked him repeatedly to take it, and Manager Qian declined repeatedly. Zheng Tang said, "Manager Qian, this additional amount is what I myself wish to give you. I wish to buy and you wish to sell. Just take it." With a slight smile, Zheng Tang added, "The proverb says it well: Just don't do anything that gives you a guilty conscience, and you needn't fear a knock at the door at midnight." Then he firmly pressed the extra fifty cash on Manager Qian. When Manager Qian heard these last two sentences, he knew that Zheng Tang was up to

170

something, and he was even less willing to take the money. Zheng Tang put the money on the table and left. Manager Qian rushed to catch up with him, and pleaded pitifully, "*Xiucai* Zheng, enemies should separate; they shouldn't come together. You take the money back. On the first day of the year, I did something to you that has left me with a guilty conscience. Let me tell you all the facts of that case." Zheng Tang purposely acted astonished, and said, "On the first of the year, you did something that gave you a guilty conscience—what was that?" Manager Qian was like olives spilling out of a jar. In great detail, he told the story of Landlord Wang of Wang Village giving him money and ordering him to buy a coffin and send it to Zheng Tang's home on the first of the year. After Zheng Tang listened to all of this, he comforted him, "Manager Qian, you needn't explain. You're not my enemy. I believe that you wouldn't make fun of me without reason. It is simply that you are anxious to gain advantage and you fell into Landlord Wang's trap. I came here today just because I wanted you to tell me this. Enemies have heads. Debts have creditors. I won't bother you again." Zheng Tang finished speaking, and stalked off with his fifty cash and his tea set.

Zheng Tang left Manager Qian's place. As he walked, he remembered something that had happened the year before—also on the first day of the year. Landlord Wang of Wang Village had sent someone with an invitation. He was inviting the village gentry and distinguished personages to a Spring Festival banquet. Zheng Tang couldn't easily decline, so he went. Lots of different kinds of meat and three rounds of wine were served. Landlord Wang toasted Zheng Tang, "*Xiucai* Zheng, please drink one cup." Zheng Tang could only say, "Fine, we'll drink together." Then Landlord Wang told a servant to place writing brush, ink stick, ink slab, and paper in front of Zheng Tang, and—his faced wreathed in smiles—said, "I especially invited the *xiucai* to come today for no other reason than to ask you to execute an ornamental tablet to make my newly built mansion look even grander!" Everyone added flattering words, "Right, right. Landlord Wang sees that Younger Brother is very good at calligraphy. You certainly must not betray his great kindness!" "Landlord Wang has built up a family fortune and is very wealthy. He has brought honor to his ancestors. It is worth writing about." The words "Landlord Wang has built up a family fortune and is very wealthy" especially grated on Zheng Tang's ears. He blinked his eyes, and he took up the brush and waved it on the Xuan paper,[19] and wrote two large characters: "*Danbai.*" Landlord Wang was stupid and didn't know what "*danbai*" meant. In order to curry favor, a government clerk rushed to explain to Landlord Wang: "This is a good phrase, a good phrase. 'In the early dawn, it is clear and bright.' It praises and honors Landlord Wang's family financial situation as pure and stainless." Landlord Wang was extremely happy, and immediately told someone to make it into a large tablet with gold characters and hang it in the hall as a means of showing off. This large tablet hadn't been hanging many days when several people went to the landlord and secretly told him that the "*danbai*" that Zheng Tang had written referred to the "*Danjiao zibai*" in plays[20] when they said "My family." The character was the same as the pronoun used by women. This satirized the rich man's family as a family of lackeys. Landlord Wang was infuriated. He took down the tablet, and watched for his chance for revenge.

Landlord Wang's original name was Wang Fufu. He had formerly been a gatekeeper for court eunuch Wang in Fuzhou. Eunuchs had power in the Ming dynasty. Evil eunuchs filled the court. From the local level to the central level, if they wanted to be promoted, important and minor officials all had to go through the back door of the eunuchs. So the thresholds of the eunuchs were all trampled by high and low local officials. Before many years had passed, the gatekeeper Wang Fufu was using his job as a means of exacting bribes, and he quickly became the biggest rich man of all of Wang Village. He bought land and built a house. He was very illustrious. Now Zheng Tang had exposed his past. He was so ashamed that he flew into a rage, and hatred congealed in his heart. Day and night he thought of revenge. But he couldn't find the way to do it. He thought and thought. Finally he came up with the coffin plot related above as a way to vent his hatred.

Recalling all of this, Zheng Tang couldn't help but laugh. He swaggered home.

In the twinkling of an eye, it was *qingming* festival. Zheng Tang went to the suburbs outside East Gate to sweep the tombs and go for a walk in the country. On his way back, he passed the gate of rich man Wang's home, and saw a banyan tree in front. The branches and leaves were full and luxuriant—lush and green. He made a point of circling around the banyan tree. He looked up with appreciation, and he repeatedly said admiringly, "A good tree! A good tree!" After a while, someone told Wang Fufu of Zheng Tang's odd behavior. Because of the "*danbai*" incident, rich man Wang had long been at odds with Zheng Tang. So all he could do was hide behind the gate and surreptitiously watch what Zheng Tang was doing. Zheng Tang was still talking to himself, "A good tree. A good tree." Continuing to circle around the banyan tree, he praised it profusely. Wang Fufu was completely baffled by this. With a coughing sound, he walked out with a measured tread. Pretending not to recognize Zheng Tang, he called out, "Who is taking liberties at my gate!"

Without budging an inch, Zheng Tang answered, "It's old Zheng here admiring your precious tree!"

When Wang Fufu heard the words "precious tree," he knew there was a trick in this. He didn't dare be rash. It would be best to adopt a smiling expression. In a currying-favor tone, he said, "Ah. It's *Xiucai* Zheng who's come. Please come in!"

Zheng Tang said, "I'm doing my own thing. This has nothing to do with you being a rich man. A *xiucai* doesn't enter a slave's home. Each does what is appropriate for him!"

Wang Fufu had been snubbed. It was very hard to take. He was just about to flare up when—to one side—Zheng Tang shouted again, "A good tree—ah—a good tree!"

Wang Fufu shouted at Zheng Tang, "A good tree has nothing to do with you. You're resting at my gate and being a nuisance."

Zheng Tang purposely struck a conciliatory pose and said, "If a good tree elicits people's praise for a short time, what's wrong with that?"

"The tree is my family's property. I have the power to refuse your looking at it!"

"True, true. This tree is yours. Don't let me look at it. That's okay. Are you bargaining to sell me the tree!"

"Sell it?"

"Yes. Good jewelry is the gift for beauty, and a sword is the gift for a hero.[21] You should help someone fulfill his wish!"

Wang Fufu thought to himself, "What's wrong with Zheng Tang? Is he drunk?" He scanned Zheng Tang's face. It wasn't red, it wasn't white; it was just very ordinary. He also inspected Zheng Tang's eyes. They looked normal, too. He didn't seem to be bewitched, nor did he seem demented. Wang Fufu calculated to himself, "Is it possible that he came to embarrass me again, to make fun of me? Okay, if you dare to visit me and contradict me, I won't let you take advantage of me!" Wang Fufu figured this out, and then began bargaining: three hundred ounces of silver.

Zheng Tang heard this price, and replied with satisfaction, "That's not expensive, not expensive. It's worth three hundred ounces! Rich man Wang, let me trouble you to bring out the writing implements."

"What do you want them for?"

"To write a receipt for you so that I can go home and get the silver right away."

"You don't need to write a receipt. Just go home and bring back the silver."

"No, that's not acceptable, not acceptable at all. An oral agreement isn't reliable. If, when I return with the silver, you have changed your mind again—your rich family only sees money and it is always fickle with people!"

"You really want to buy it?"

"Who would lie to you?"

"Three hundred ounces?"

"I wouldn't think of giving you half an ounce less!"

"So, please come in!"

"I won't go in. I already just explained. A *xiucai* doesn't go in . . ."

"Okay, okay, okay. Don't say any more. I'll go and get the

brush!" Wang Fufu was afraid Zheng Tang would leave. He went into the house, but he emerged right away empty-handed.

Zheng Tang said, "What? Rich man, the writing implements?"

Smiling radiantly, Wang Fufu said, "I just discussed it with my wife. She said that this banyan tree is the legacy from our ancestors. If we want to have descendants, it's not smart to sell it."

"Oh? I said a long time ago that people like you are like this—fickle. One minute you say one thing, the next minute it doesn't count." Zheng Tang angrily washed his hands of this and was about to go. He said, "This tree is yours. If you don't want to sell it, I won't press you to buy it. Casting pearls before swine—alas! Alas!" He sighed as he left.

Wang Fufu saw Zheng Tang walk the distance that two arrows can reach, and then he ran over and stopped the *xiucai*, and dragged him back, and shouted into the gate, "Bring us some chairs!" The servant moved out two recliners for the guest and host.

"You don't sell the tree, and still you drag me back here. Why is this?" Zheng Tang purposely assumed an angry air as he asked this.

"*Xiucai* Zheng, don't be angry. When guests are detained, there's always an urgent matter to be discussed."

"Are you thinking again of selling the tree?"

"No."

"Is it that you suspect the price is a little too low? No problem. I'll increase it another hundred ounces!"

"No, no, no. It isn't that I suspect the price is low. The tree—I'm not selling it."

"If you're not selling the tree, there's no need to detain me. Who has the time to shoot the breeze with you?" Zheng Tang got up to go.

Rich man Wang held him back, and said anxiously, "I want to ask. Where is the value of this tree?"

Zheng Tang began to laugh with a loud "haha": "So this is what the rich man wanted to ask."

"Yes! Yes! Please tell me!"

Zheng Tang shouted loudly, "This is great. If I am able to

tell you clearly this tree's value, why would I offer a high price to buy it?"

"Blame me for being a fool. If you're willing to explain it to me, I won't begrudge you a lot of gold!"

"How much?"

"A hundred ounces!"

Zheng Tang shook his head, indicating that this didn't satisfy him.

"A hundred and fifty?"

Zheng Tang suddenly stood up: "I'll take my leave. I have no time to keep you company."

Wang Fufu moved forward again and detained him: "Okay, okay—two hundred ounces—a total of two hundred ounces!" Only then did Zheng Tang grudgingly sit down. Rich man Wang hastily shouted, "Servant, find my wife and bring out two hundred ounces of fine silver!" Soon, the servant brought out the two hundred ounces of fine silver and handed it over to the rich man. The rich man then passed it over to Zheng Tang.

Zheng Tang said to Wang Fufu, "This is a very significant matter. Please ask your servant to withdraw." Zheng Tang made a great show of being in earnest and went up to Wang Fufu. Close to his ear, he said, "On top of this precious tree is a valuable leaf. It is called a hide-body leaf. If there's something you want, you can get it without extra trouble!"

"Which branch is the leaf on?"

"Ah, this—there's no way to tell you. It just requires that you be earnest and sincere. Abstain from meat and wine, and purify yourself. Light incense, and climb the tree. If you don't pick it in one day, then you must continue picking leaves the next day. You can stop only after you've picked the hide-body leaf. When you're holding this precious leaf, then you can conceal it on your body and hide your whereabouts. No one would be able to see you. This way, if you go out to steal, nobody would be able to apprehend you."

Hearing this made Wang Fufu extremely happy. Slapping Zheng Tang on the shoulder, he said, "You've seen a lot and you have vast knowledge. You've made me suddenly see the light."

As Zheng Tang was leaving, he exhorted him, "It is only the

rich man climbing the tree himself who can pick the leaf. Ask your honorable wife to help you under the tree. Whatever you do, don't tell any outsiders!"

"I understand! I understand!" Rich man Wang very happily saw Zheng Tang off.

Wang Fufu went into the inner apartments and immediately related this important matter to his wife, the Woman Ma. The Woman Ma half-believed and half-doubted, but for the time being she left everything to her husband. Wang Fufu acted according to Zheng Tang's instructions. He didn't dare ignore even half a point. The next morning, Wang Fufu ordered his servants to close the road off, and ordered travelers to make a detour. Wang Fufu was already over sixty years old. In order to become rich and still richer, he would risk his old life and climb the tree and pick the leaf. The Woman Ma was below the tree serving as his assistant. He picked a leaf and asked the Woman Ma, "Wife, can you see me?"

The Woman Ma looked up carefully and answered, "Yes!"

Rich man Wang dropped that leaf and picked another. He asked again, "Can you see me?"

"I can still see you."

The first day, Wang Fufu picked leaves the whole day without the slightest result. The second day, he was busy again the whole day, and still couldn't locate the hide-body leaf. Wang Fufu had never done manual labor before. After two days of repetitious work, he was so tired his waist was sore and his legs were weak. His vision was blurred. He drank a lot of ginseng soup. The third day, Wang Fufu climbed the tree again and picked leaves. He picked leaves from early morning to near evening, and he still hadn't picked the hide-body leaf. Altogether, he had picked for three days. Wang Fufu had picked 33,333 leaves, and the Woman Ma always answered, "I can see you." Wang Fufu was exhausted from picking.

The Woman Ma answered that she was also tired of this. The Woman Ma thought to herself, "My husband has certainly been deceived." She herself shouldn't also be deceived. To pick all of the leaves from this large banyan tree would take she didn't-know-how-many-more days. Rather than suffering and sharing the fatigue with her husband for much longer, it would be better to say "I can't see you" and let her husband leave the tree a little sooner. And then she would admonish him not to fall into Zheng Tang's trap again. So, when Wang Fufu weakly asked again "Can you see me?" she replied loudly, "Old man, I can't see you!"

"What? Say that again!"

"I can't see you!"

Wang Fufu happily half-climbed, half-slid down the tree. He was earnestly holding the "hide-body leaf" in both hands. On tiptoe, he half-ran into the inner apartments and hid the leaf in a closet, and added three locks to the door.

While they were eating, the Woman Ma admonished her husband not to fall into Zheng Tang's trap again. Where is there a hide-body leaf?! When rich man Wang heard his wife talk this way, he became suspicious. He had eaten only half his meal when he put it down and ran into his room and opened the closet and took out the "hide-body leaf." He was afraid his wife would swindle him and walk off with this treasure. From that night on, he slept alone in the study.

That night, rich man Wang slept especially soundly. The treasure had reached his hands. The lovely thing of having riches enough to topple a country could be realized in just a few days' time! He slept straight until between eight and nine the next morning. After eating breakfast, he donned the "hide-body leaf." He was going to the market to test this treasure. That day, from the spice store, he deftly stole a large plate of smoked *doufu*.[22] The next day, from a butcher shop, he picked up a pork liver without the slightest effort, and took it home. Rich man Wang's happiness was sweeter than honey and sugar. His courage was even greater. The third day, carrying this treasure, he went to the *yamen* of Houguan county. He thought he would play a joke on County Magistrate Jiang, and repay the disrespectful hatred he had experienced in the past. He was holding the "hide-body leaf" very properly as he swaggered into the county *yamen*. The gatekeeper Uncle Wang recognized rich man Wang. Noticing the way Wang Fufu looked today, he thought he must have some urgent reason for seeing the county official, so—without asking him anything—he just let him in. Wang Fufu was secretly happy. He thought that the "hide-body leaf" was working as expected. Even the county *yamen* was allowing him in without any hindrance. He walked straight to the great hall of the county government, and took the great seal of office, and swaggered out of the *yamen*. As it happened, when he reached the main entrance, County Magistrate Jiang was just returning from a party. He ran into Wang Fufu and saw that he was holding his own great seal of office. He was bewildered. The county government's great seal was the life of the country official. How could he just let someone take it away? From his sedan chair, County Magistrate Jiang shouted, "Catch that old man who stole the great seal!" Several people caught him right away and wrested the great seal from Wang Fufu's hand and then tied him up.

County Magistrate Jiang heard the case. It had never been possible to forgive anyone who stole a seal—much less Wang Fufu! When County Magistrate Jiang had first gone to the eunuch's door, he had put up with Wang Fufu's obstruction and extortion many times. He had never guessed that Wang Fufu would someday fall into his own hands. Wang Fufu suffered fifty floggings with the bamboo rod, was fined three hundred ounces of silver, and was displayed for three days in a cage for the crowds to see.

The theft of the seal caused a sensation in Fuzhou. The managers of the spice shop and the butcher shop both rushed up to watch the excitement. When they saw rich man Wang in the cage, the two of them began laughing loudly. The shouted simultaneously, "Rich man Wang, the smoked *doufu* and the pork liver that you walked off with—we've already put it on your account. At the end of the month, we'll go to your honorable home to demand payment!" Wang Fufu raised his head, opened his weary eyes, and stared blankly at these two managers.

For three days, he stood in the cage and then his sentence was finished. Rich man Wang was released and returned home. Before he even got close to his bed, his eyes were black and he became weak and limp. He vomited white spittle and he lost consciousness.

(*Story collected by Zhang Zhuanxing*)

TIGER BOY AND DRAGON GIRL

Dragon Girl and Tiger Boy are equally determined to save their home area from the Serpent King. They display equal courage and ability. When the Serpent King kills Tiger Boy, Dragon Girl embarks alone on a long and perilous voyage to seek help from the Buddhist goddess of mercy. Upon her return, she forces the Serpent King and his demons to flee. Fearing that they will return, she maintains vigilance on the hillside for years. The source of the potential devastation in this tale is supernatural, as is the source of the aid Dragon Girl receives, but she is depicted as a real person—one of perseverance, determination, and ability. She is also portrayed as a self-sacrificing woman saving the people of her district. This story could also have been placed in Part Two, for Dragon Girl and Tiger Boy make their own decision to marry—a decision commanding the whole-hearted approval of the other villagers.

A very long time ago, Xiamen and Gulangyu were joined together. At that time, it was a very fertile place. The land was rich. Each stalk of rice had lots of tassels. Each grain of rice grew round and smooth, like strings of pearls. The blue waves of the sea rippled. The fish and the shrimp were abundant. When a net was cast, it often returned full. The ordinary people of the island farmed the land and fished the sea, and lived and worked in peace and contentment.

On the mountainside of this small island lived a young fellow named Tiger Boy. He was bright and robust. He was not only an expert farmer, but he was also an expert hunter whose arrow never missed its target. During the slack agricultural season, he always took his bow and arrows, and climbed the mountain and crossed the ridges to go hunting. With just one arrow, he could penetrate the chest of even a ferocious wild animal.

On the seashore of the small island lived Dragon Girl, whose family were fishermen. Dragon Girl was extraordinarily beautiful. She was also quick-witted and talented. Applying her make-up, she often attracted the songs of a hundred birds. When she embroidered, this beckoned crowds of butterflies fluttering around. If she went into the ocean, she caught all kinds of rare sea delicacies and brought them back.

Even though Tiger Boy and Dragon Girl lived in different places, they had a lot of opportunities to see each other. Dragon Girl frequently saw Tiger Boy chase and kill the wild animals as far as the seashore. Tiger Boy also often saw Dragon Girl embroidering and weaving nets on the seaside. Dragon Girl admired Tiger Boy's industriousness and courage; Tiger Boy liked Dragon Girl's beauty, intelligence, and talent. Over time, the two came to love each other. There was no one on the island who didn't say approvingly that they were a couple made in Heaven.

Finally, the sweethearts were married on the evening of the fifteenth day of the eighth month. The villagers of the whole island—some bringing rice and wine and glutinous rice cakes, others bringing crab and sea cucumbers—came to congratulate Tiger Boy and Dragon Girl. Everyone talked and laughed and celebrated joyously until midnight. It was nearly dawn before they gradually dispersed.

After the guests left, Tiger Boy and Dragon Girl were just about to enter the bridal chamber when suddenly layer after layer of crow-black clouds shrouded the moon and huge waves rolling up on the sea rushed straight toward the island.

The Serpent King who lived deep in the bottom of the Eastern Ocean had coveted the fertile land of Xiamen Island for a long time. This particular day, taking advantage of the rising tide of the fifteenth day of the eighth month, he led a large group of serpent demons to stir up the wind and waves and raid Xiamen.

As soon as these serpent demons raided Xiamen, they began shoving and bumping. Everywhere, they unleashed violence. When they saw fishing boats, they bumped into them. When they saw fishing nets, they ripped them apart. When they saw cattle and sheep, they swallowed them whole. When they saw people, they bit them. In a split second, the island's fishing villages and farm homes were ravaged and scattered.

Tiger Boy and Dragon Girl couldn't bear seeing any more of the ruthlessness of the serpent demons. From the wall, Tiger Boy took up his bow and arrows, and from behind the door, Dragon Girl picked up a fish spear—and they attacked the Serpent King.

The ferocious Serpent King was just opening his large bloody-basin mouth to swallow down a water buffalo. When he saw Tiger Boy and Dragon Girl, he gulped it down in a hurry. His serpent's head held high like a mountain, he opened his large mouth and shook his long tongue and glared at Tiger Boy and Dragon Girl with his brass-gong eyes. And the serpent demons next to him also all held up their heads and arched their backs, opened their mouths and spit out their tongues, and made a very strange "*si-si*" sound.

Dragon Girl was not the least bit afraid. Taking a step forward, she fiercely stabbed at the opening to the Serpent King's chest with her fish spear. The Serpent King hadn't guessed that Dragon Girl would be able to show off her skill so quickly, and he didn't have time to dodge out of the way. In a moment, that sharp spear cut his tongue into two pieces. The Serpent King was in so much pain that he rolled around on the mountain slope. His tail flailed around in all directions like a whip. In a short time, the mountain had become an expanse of large and small crushed stones, and had turned into a cliff of ten thousand rocks of strange and grotesque shapes.

But the wounded Serpent King was still struggling and creating havoc. Straightening up, he spurted black water mixed with blood at Dragon Girl.

When he saw the Serpent King spurting out poison, Tiger Boy quickly stepped in front of Dragon Girl. Protecting Dragon Girl with his body, he took out his bow and arrows, and, with a whizzing sound, he shot an arrow at the serpent's head. This arrow didn't waver at all, but hit the Serpent King's right eye.

The Serpent King was in so much pain that he let out a loud howl. He immediately leaped halfway up to the sky, and then fell heavily to the ground. People heard only the loud sound of *"honglong."* One corner of Xiamen had been cut off. This small corner became a separate small island, which people later called Gulangyu. The area between the two islands became a small strait. The wounded Serpent King was terrified. Again, he quickly spurted out poisonous fog at Tiger Boy, and then, following this small strait, he escaped back to the Eastern Sea.

At this time, when Dragon Girl turned around to look for Tiger Boy, she discovered that Tiger Boy had already been harmed by the poisonous fog. He had fallen to the ground, and his head was like a small mountain. Dragon Girl bent over Tiger Boy's body. She was so brokenhearted that she didn't want to live. She wept until dark. No matter how the other villagers urged her to, she never wanted to leave.

Suddenly, in a trance, Dragon Girl saw a kindly, beautiful girl in front of her. The girl said to her, "Dragon Girl, you mustn't cry. That Serpent King was wounded. He hasn't abandoned his plans. After he has recovered, he'll return to the island to cruelly kill the people. Hurry to Putuo Mountain in the Southern Ocean and ask the Guanyin Bodhisattva[23] to lend you a double-edged sword to subdue the demons!" In a flash, she disappeared.

This seemed strange to Dragon Girl. She wiped away her tears and went down the mountain and told the villagers of the girl's instructions. The villagers said, "That was certainly an incarnation of Mazu![24] Hurry up and go!"

The next day, Dragon Girl set out in a small boat and rowed toward the Southern Ocean.

She rowed and rowed. She went through seven stormy days on the ocean, fourteen days of high winds, twenty-eight days of hunger, and only after a full forty-nine days did she finally reach Putuo Mountain.

Dragon Girl knelt before the Guanyin Bodhisattva, and burned incense and recounted in detail the serpent demons' violence and the villagers' misfortune. She implored Guanyin to lend her a sword to subdue the demons.

183

After hearing this, the Guanyin Bodhisattva opened her wise eyes and said, "This beast is simply too wanton!" She chanted silently for a while, and then said, "That serpent demon has honed his skills for a thousand years. He has already achieved future bliss. I have no way to deal with him. But you have suffered, and, in all sincerity, I cannot let you go back empty-handed."

Saying this, the Guanyin Bodhisattva walked down to the Lotus Pedestal, and led Dragon Girl to the Lotus Pool. She picked a sparkling, translucent pure white lotus flower and gave it to Dragon Girl: "As long as you have this flower, that beast won't dare come and do evil things! Take the boat. I'll see you off."

Dragon Girl accepted the white lotus flower with both hands, thanked the Guanyin Bodhisattva, and went down the mountain and got into the boat. The goddess of mercy stood on the mountain and lightly waved a willow branch. It was as though the small boat was speeding across the sky as it skimmed the surface of the sea. In the twinkling of an eye, it had returned to Xiamen Island.

The villagers had been waiting anxiously for forty-nine days. When they saw Dragon Girl returning with a white lotus flower, they all happily thronged around her and asked detailed questions. Dragon Girl told of her experiences, and then discussed with everyone the plan for resisting the Serpent King.

Several days later, the Serpent King—now recovered—opened his big eyes, assembled a squad of serpent demons, and rode the spring tide to attack Xiamen Island. Who would have guessed that as soon as they entered Xiamen Bay, they would only hear drums and horns all over. An army of strong hunters was defending the beach with sharp arrows.

When the Serpent King saw that column of strength, he was already rather afraid, so he summoned his serpent demons and turned around to attack Gulangyu.

Unexpectedly, when the Serpent King had just reached the shore, Dragon Girl, who was standing on the hillside, immediately fluttered a white lotus flower lightly in the Serpent King's direction. In a moment, the white lotus flower emitted a glorious radiance. The Serpent King and the crowd of serpent demons were all greatly alarmed. The brilliant shining rays of light pierced their eyes until they couldn't open them. The whole crowd of serpent demons pushed and shoved one another in their confusion. In a panic, one by one, they plunged deep to the bottom of the sea and fled back to the Eastern Ocean. The Serpent King, too, could only flee in anger.

The villagers of Xiamen Island had finally defeated and repulsed the Serpent King's invasion, and saved the peaceful lives of the people.

But the Serpent King hadn't yet been eliminated. No one could say for sure when he would come and attack again. In order to guard against future disaster, Dragon Girl held the white lotus flower all day long and remained on the hillside of Gulangyu. She didn't eat, she didn't drink, she didn't sleep. Day after day, month after month, year after year. In the course of time, she changed into a mountain. In the middle of the mountain was a pool of water, with a brilliant white lotus flower growing there.

Later, to commemorate Tiger Boy and Dragon Girl, people called the mountain that Tiger Boy had turned into, "Tiger Head Mountain," and the one that Dragon Girl had turned into, "Dragon Head Mountain." In order to control the Serpent King, people also built the White Lotus Nunnery on the middle of the mountain where the lotus flowers grew. Today, Tiger Head Mountain and Dragon Head Mountain still face each other, north and south, defending the port of Xiamen and protecting the peace of the Xiamen people.

(Story collected by Zhang Yihong)

THE IMMORTAL LINGZHI

Lingzhi convinces her superior to allow her to go to earth. Once there, she cures people's illnesses. Because she wipes out diseases and does not accept payment, the people are endlessly grateful. It is noteworthy that the common folk place their faith in the efficacy of an immortal female. Lingzhi is portrayed here as fearless, strong-willed, and benevolent.

In her jade palace one day, the Goddess Xiwangmu[25] was concentrating on eating the elixir of immortality that Lao Tzu had respectfully presented to her. It was too hard, and it made her gums and cheeks tingle and ache. Xiwangmu angrily dug the pill of immortality out of her mouth. With a fling of her hand, she threw it toward Immortal Mountain. This pill of immortality went through trees, branches, and leaves, and then fell onto a straw mushroom.

Before very long, this straw mushroom changed. It became even brighter than a mirror. The mushroom stalk was like red coral. Through and through, it was purple-red, glittering and translucent, sparkling and flashing. The mushroom also had a brilliant red heart that allowed it to become an "immortal." This female immortal on Immortal Mountain often looked down on the mortal world. The days were long. She saw that the poor people on earth suffered too much, and she wanted to help them. But to go down secretly to earth was to transgress the laws of Heaven! Did she want to go to earth? She thought about this every day. She thought for a long time. She saw the poor people endure suffering and hardship, while she herself was on this Immortal Mountain—staring and doing what? The more she thought, the sadder she became. Finally, she decided to go down surreptitiously to the mortal world.

That day, she whirled around and bright colors flashed: She changed into a beautiful young fairy maiden. But, as it happened, Xiwangmu emerged just then from her palace to take a stroll—and she saw her.

Watching this incomparably beautiful young girl, Xiwangmu was extremely happy. She drew the girl over to her side, and said with pleasure, "You must thank me. It was I who changed you into a heavenly immortal! From now on, it's best if you remain beside me. Oh, you still have no name. I see that you're so clever that you should be called 'Lingzhi Immortal.'" Then she told Lingzhi Immortal to go back with her.

Head lowered, Lingzhi Immortal neither spoke nor moved. She was still thinking of going to the mortal world. Reading her mind, Xiwangmu was angry. She said, "You have to appreciate favors. I changed you into an immortal. You must be my attendant. Otherwise, I'll send you into the cold palace of the heavenly prison."

Xiwangmu wasn't one to be provoked. Lingzhi Immortal could only go with her. Xiwangmu's anger hadn't yet dissipated. She didn't want Lingzhi Immortal to sit around with idle hands, so she entrusted her with the golden needle and silver dipper that she herself often used. She insisted that Lingzhi Immortal stay beside her and wait on her whenever she was needed. It was not at all easy to wait on Xiwangmu, whose moods were so changeable! If she put the golden needle too close to her, she was treated with disdain. If she was too slow in giving her the silver dipper, she was cursed. So, Lingzhi Immortal was always being criticized by Xiwangmu.

One day, Lingzhi Immortal surreptitiously took a look at the mortal world. She was spellbound. Xiwangmu called to her several times in a row, but she heard nothing. This wouldn't do. After Xiwangmu took her to task, she added, "If you give up the life of an immortal, it won't be easy for you, but all day long you're just thinking of the mortal world. Okay, now I will permit you to go to that remote area of mountains and old forests—that area where you can't see anyone for a hundred *li* all around. I order you to go and taste several days of hardships and then come back here." After saying this, she waved her long sleeve, and Lingzhi Immortal grew cold all over and went to earth in a daze. Only after her feet had touched the ground and she had composed herself did she realize that she had fallen into the gloomy old forest. But she wasn't sad. This was just fine. She could do whatever she wanted to. But how to do it? What should she do to help those suffering people? She opened her hands. The golden needle and silver dipper were still with her. She smiled. Xiwangmu really was so angry that she was mixed up. She even forgot to ask her to return the golden needle and silver dipper. But these precious things from Heaven—what could they do for poor people? Lingzhi Immortal then went to ask instructions from the old mountain god. Old Mountain God said, "This precious thing can conquer demons and get rid of monsters, but if you want to use it to make the weather favorable for agriculture, this just isn't possible. As I see it, poor people fear getting sick more than anything else. If you go to the Immortal of a Hundred Medicines and ask him for some immortal medicine and immortal herbs and then give them to the poor people who are sick, this will help them. But you must be careful. Don't let Xiwangmu know."

Lingzhi Immortal felt that this was reasonable. That very night, she flew to the good Immortal of a Hundred Medicines, and asked for a basket of immortal medicine and immortal herbs. The next day, she changed herself into an itinerant herbal medicine doctor, and—carrying the medicine basket—left the remote mountain area. Along the road, she went through village after village and cured the poor people of their illnesses. Because the medicine wiped out diseases and she didn't accept even a penny, the crowds of people all burned incense and lit candles to express their gratitude to this living immortal.

This news quickly reached the ears of Xiwangmu. She quietly opened the clouds to look. As expected, what she had heard was so. She immediately issued a decree, telling the Gold-Armored God to go down to earth and order Lingzhi Immortal back to the heavenly court.

The Gold-Armored God left the southern heaven's gate and found Lingzhi Immortal practicing medicine in a small village. He shouted in a high voice, "Lingzhi Immortal, the

Goddess Xiwangmu orders you to speed back to the heavenly court!"

Lingzhi Immortal saw that the god had recognized her, and she knew that it would be useless to hide. She could only change herself back into a girl. She begrudged leaving the mortal world, but the god's stern voice compelled her. She could only hold back her tears and leave the earth, and, inch by inch, slowly ascend to Heaven. The village people knelt down to implore her to remain in the mortal world.

Lingzhi Immortal was incomparably sad. But she was afraid if she contravened Xiwangmu's decree she would be severely punished. She couldn't help sighing as she continued to ascend. And the villagers couldn't help weeping loudly.

Lingzhi Immortal couldn't bear it any longer. Facing the Gold-Armored God, she said, "Please go back and report to Xiwangmu: Lingzhi will become a human being and won't return to the heavenly court!" Then she descended again to the mortal world.

After Xiwangmu heard the Gold-Armored God's report, she was beside herself with rage. She immediately ordered the Rock God beside the Milky Way to go and strike Lingzhi Immortal to death, and smash her medicine basket, too. From the village, Lingzhi Immortal suddenly heard a roar in the sky: it was a large boulder heading straight toward her. In this emergency, she fiercely raised the golden needle in the direction of the enormous boulder. She heard a loud noise and the boulder was smashed into a thousand pieces which fell to the wasteland of the remote mountain and forest. Xiwangmu was so frightened that she was filled with anxiety. She looked down, and only then did she remember that the two precious things were still in Lingzhi Immortal's hands. Angry and vexed, she issued a decree to the Milky Way God: Drown the mortal world.

In a second, heavy rains rushed down from Heaven, and in a short time, great floods flowed over the land. They rose higher by the day.

Lingzhi Immortal saw that the people were struggling and shouting for help. It was as if her heart had been cut by a knife. She took out the silver dipper to try to scoop up the water. It was strange. As soon as this precious thing ladled out one dipper of water, the water receded a foot! Lingzhi Immortal was delighted. She ladled dipper after dipper without stopping. The heavenly water kept coming straight down, and yet the water on the ground never rose above the ankle.

As soon as the Milky Way God saw that this wasn't working, he was afraid he would use up all the water of the Milky Way, so he quickly stopped the rain, and asked Xiwangmu to come up with another idea.

Xiwangmu was foaming with rage. She immediately made the sky murky. And Lingzhi Immortal knew that there was about to be a major catastrophe. But she reached a decision: Even if her body was smashed to pieces, she still wanted her heart, her blood, her bones and flesh to remain in the mortal world. So she stuck the golden needle into the ground, and let it put down roots and blossom in the earth to serve as medicine and vegetables for the people. She also poked the silver dipper onto a tree trunk so that the people could use it forever. Later the golden needle blossomed with magnificent golden yellow flowers. People called this the "golden needle flower" and also called it the "golden needle vegetable." Others called it "forget-your-worries-grass," because if you ate it you could banish illness and be free of anxieties and forget your worries. On the tree, the silver dipper blossomed with gleaming silver white flowers that could cure disease and nourish the body. They could also be used as a drink to moderate heat or cold.

Lingzhi Immortal had just put the two precious things in place when black clouds rolled up in the sky and thunder roared. In the clouds, several dozen bright blue, eye-stabbing rays shot out. They were accompanied by an alarmingly sharp noise. The gale swept Lingzhi Immortal halfway up to the sky. In a moment she was changed into ten million multi-colored shooting stars which fell to the ground and changed into five types of beautiful brilliant-colored wild mushrooms. Because these mushrooms were what Lingzhi Immortal's heart, blood, bones and flesh had become, and because they also fell in different places and grew in different ways, people classified them and called them rock *zhi*, wood *zhi*, grass *zhi*, flesh *zhi*, and mushroom

191

zhi. Together, they were called the "Lingzhi grasses." There were red ones, black ones, blue, white, yellow, and purple ones — six colors in all. These mushrooms could cure a lot of illnesses, and they could also bring longevity.

(Story collected by Gao Zhongliang)

GOLDEN CUP AND HUNDRED LEAVES

The young woman Hundred Leaves has a great deal of strength, determination, courage, ability, and confidence. She is able to complete the mission her brother began, thus saving the lives of her home villagers. Like her brother, she sacrifices her own life. Earlier in the story, she is seen as submissive to, and supportive of, her brother, as she prepares necessities for his journey. As she waits for her brother's return, we also see her anxiety and her loyalty. At the beginning of the story, the sister and brother are portrayed as quite equal. By the end of the story, Hundred Leaves' ability is seen as superior to her brother's.

In Zhangzhou's South Village is an immortal lake. Beside this lake lived a brother and a sister. The brother was called Golden Cup; his younger sister, Hundred Leaves. Their parents died long before, leaving several *mou* of land on the lakeside. The brother and sister diligently and conscientiously farmed this land. Also on the lakeside, they cultivated oranges and tangerines, pomelos, red lichees, longans, loquats, and other fruit trees. In the four seasons, the flowers were fragrant and the fruit sweet, and there was a bumper crop of grain. Relying on this immortal lake, they feared neither drought nor flood. The families in the villages of this region also depended on the water from this immortal lake for irrigation. The thousands of *mou* of good farmland near South Village became the flower-and-fruit village and the rich rice-producing area of Zhang prefecture. The people lived and worked in peace and happiness. Their lives were contented.

One day a strong typhoon suddenly blew in. Crow-black clouds

193

gathered, blotting out the sky and covering the earth, weighing everything down. In an instant, it was dark all over. There was no light from sun or moon! The hurricane destroyed homes and uprooted trees. The torrential rains and thunder and lightning displayed their power. The people of South Village had suddenly met with this enormous disaster. Convulsed with fear, they sank into wailing despair. Golden Cup and Hundred Leaves held each other closer. They were afraid they would be separated by the storm and the flood. Just then came a sound so deafening it seemed that the sky had collapsed and the earth had split. A large black object fell heavily from the sky, scaring Golden Cup and Hundred Leaves so much that they fainted. When they regained consciousness, the wind had stopped and so had the rain. The sun was shining again. But a large round mountain had come flying in from somewhere—they didn't know where—and was pressed tightly on top of Immortal Lake! After surviving this disaster, the people of South Village were absolutely destitute. Houses that had been destroyed could be rebuilt; crops that had been washed away could be replanted. But there was no way to save that immortal lake that had been destroyed by the round mountain pressing down on it. So, the source for water was cut off. Each year they suffered from drought. The land was full of cracks. The fruit trees withered and died. The crops and grain weren't harvested. To stay alive, the people had to eat grass roots and tree bark. Golden Cup and Hundred Leaves arranged for the young people of the village to dig wells. They dug and dug. Day and night, they dug without stopping. They dug a hundred feet deep and still they didn't see a drop of water. The elderly wept and sighed. Children wept and wailed that they were starving. Young women cried until their innards snapped. Day and night, everyone recalled Immortal Lake, and longed for that jade-green lake water to irrigate good farmland, and restore the contentment of their earlier lives.

One evening, Golden Cup and Hundred Leaves dreamed at the same time that they saw an old man with a silver-white beard and a large, wide yellow robe. Standing under the light of the moon, he said to them amiably, "Where can you find the immortal lake? Go west to Eighty-One Peaks. Chop open White Crane Ridge. This will lead the water out from Dragon's Pool." After saying this, he changed into a red-crested white crane. With a long cry he flew toward Heaven.

After the two woke up, they spoke of the revelation of the old man of the dream. Golden Cup said, "I think this was an immortal who came to give us instructions. I want to go and cut open White Crane Ridge, and attract the water from Dragon's Pool." Hundred Leaves said, "Older brother, I'll go, too! We'll go together and lead Dragon's Pool water back here, and let the villagers all enjoy good days." Only after Golden Cup argued with her for a long time did Hundred Leaves agree at last to stay home and look after the house.

Hundred Leaves couldn't bear to see her elder brother go alone. Holding back tears, all through the night, she prepared good dry rations for Golden Cup, and clothing and straw sandals. She neatly packed a cloth bag for him. Golden Cup prepared an iron hammer, a chisel, and other tools for opening up the mountain. At daylight, Hundred Leaves saw Golden Cup to the door. She looked up and saw a flash of light streak across the edge of the sky—and a red-crested white crane flew up and dropped to the roof of the house. Golden Cup said to the white crane, "White crane, oh, white crane. Is it possible that you came especially to be my guide?" The white crane fanned his two wings, and made a high long cry. Golden Cup then held his little sister's hand and exhorted her, "Little sister, remember. If by this time next year, I haven't brought the water back, you must then follow my footprints and go to White Crane Ridge and take my place in chopping open the mountain and attracting the water." Golden Cup saw that Hundred Leaves was restraining tears and nodding her head slightly. Then he set out. The white crane flew slowly in front. Golden Cup kept up closely in the rear, and walked directly to White Crane Ridge.

After Golden Cup left, Hundred Leaves walked to the top of the round mountain every day to look out into the distance. Every day, she hoped. Every night, she hoped. She didn't know how many days she hoped. But she never saw a trace of running water, nor did she see a shadow of a cloud or a rainbow.

The pitiable Hundred Leaves. From spring to summer, she was expecting him, and she saw only the fire-hot sun roast the land until it died and cracked. And no news had come of Elder Brother Golden Cup.

The pitiable Hundred Leaves. From autumn to winter, she was expecting him. A lot of villagers had been forced to lead the elderly and the young to flee from this famine to other places. And still there was not even a shred of news of Elder Brother Golden Cup.

The pitiable Hundred Leaves. From winter to spring, she was expecting him. The appointed day would soon be here. And she still hadn't seen her brother bring back the water.

Hundred Leaves grew more and more worried. The more she thought about it, the more uneasy she became. On the appointed day, she wiped her tears, bade farewell to the villagers, and determined to find Golden Cup. At this time, the white crane came flying back. He let out a long cry, and dropped down before her. Stroking the white crane, Hundred Leaves said, "White Crane, lead me there! I must go and take my elder brother Golden Cup's place. Without fail I must bring back Dragon's Pool water."

So, White Crane flew slowly in front, and Hundred Leaves kept up closely behind. She walked directly toward White Crane Ridge. She walked and walked. She walked without stopping, crossing one mountain and then another, climbing one ridge and then another.

On a steep precipice, she discovered traces of blood left by her elder brother Golden Cup.

On brambles and vines, she found strips of cloth ripped from elder brother Golden Cup's clothing.

In the mud of the deep mountain gullies, she saw elder brother Golden Cup's footprints.

Hundred Leaves became more determined. And she became more confident. Following the small path taken by Golden Cup, and stepping in his footprints and traces of his blood, she closely followed White Crane. Without stopping even to rest, she walked ahead. When she had walked forty-nine days and nights, she finally reached the foot of a high mountain. That was White Crane Ridge.

White Crane Ridge was so high it went through the Gate of Heaven. White clouds encircled the middle of the mountain. Even apes and monkeys couldn't climb to the top. The cliffs and precipices seemed a hundred thousand feet high. To get to the top, you had to use the climbing vines; there was no other path. Hundred Leaves thought to herself, "Elder Brother Golden Cup climbed up. I must, too. For the sake of the villagers, even if my body and bones are smashed and splintered, I am willing to climb up." At this time, the white crane let out a long cry. He floated in the air, and soared to the top of the clouds. He stopped and rested at the entrance to a cave barely visible on the cliff—and clapped his wings in her direction, as if encouraging Hundred Leaves to climb up bravely. So Hundred Leaves took hold of the hanging vine and, keeping close to the cliff, heedless of her safety, she dashed up. In the end, she climbed up to the cave entrance where White Crane was perching. Hundred Leaves ran excitedly into the tunnel. In the dimness, she saw Elder Brother Golden Cup's tall, large body, standing straight in front of the rocky cliff—one hand swinging a hammer, the other holding a chisel, as if he was just chiseling the stone cliff! Only when she threw herself in front of him did Hundred Leaves discover that Elder Brother Golden Cup's body had long since become stiff and ice-cold. Bending over in front of his body, she wept bitterly, "Elder Brother, I came too late! I should have come earlier and helped you!" Grief-stricken, Hundred Leaves wept for a long time. She thought of South Village's drought. She thought of the villagers' pain as, day and night, they hoped for water. She thought of her elder brother's exhortations as he was about to leave. She bore her sorrow stoically and dried her tears. Then she took the hammer and chisel from her elder brother's hands, and began to chop open the mountain.

Risking her life, Hundred Leaves chiseled and chiseled. Both her hands were rubbed raw until blood blisters appeared, and still she didn't stop. She kept on chiseling and chiseling. The blood blisters broke. Blood and flesh mingled. Enduring pain penetrating her heart, she still didn't stop chiseling. Later, calluses thickened on both hands. She summoned even more strength

197

for chiseling. In the black tunnel, she couldn't tell if it was daytime or night. With all of her energy she chiseled inward. She must chisel through the rock cliff, and lead out the spring water. When she was thirsty, she licked the drops of water seeping out from the cliff. When she was hungry, White Crane brought tender grasses and mountain fruit. But her strength was being exhausted by the day. Her body was becoming thinner and weaker by the day, and it was difficult to hold up. But—not discouraged—she still chiseled and chiseled. Finally, one day, she used up the very last bit of her strength and fainted onto the ground. She didn't know how much time passed before she slowly came to. From the side of the cliff, she suddenly heard the gurgling sound of running water. In excitement, she struggled to stand up. She pressed her ear close to the cliff to listen: "Ah, water!" She shouted in astonishment, "Dragon's Pool water is right next door!" She exerted all of her strength. Outside, people threw themselves violently against the rock cliff. They heard only the enormous sound of *"honglonglong"* shaking Heaven and earth. The spring water rushed out of the rock cliff and—with a *huala* sound—surged into the tunnel. Along with this sound came the reverberation of the heavens collapsing and the earth splitting. The violent torrent had dashed White Crane Ridge into two halves. The flooding stream of the rushing current picked up the bodies of Golden Cup and Hundred Leaves. Following the waterfalls, they were dashed down the hundred thousand-foot cliff. They flowed at great speed toward the foot of the mountain.

The surging spring water flowed through ninety-nine channels to the foot of the round mountain of South Village. It allowed the dried, cracked earth to grow lush green crops once again. The withered yellow fruit trees once again bore sweet, fragrant fruit. The villagers who had fled disaster were wild with joy as they returned to their homes. But they were worried at not seeing Golden Cup and Hundred Leaves.

At the foot of the round mountain, a fragrant flower suddenly opened in full bloom. It was beautiful and miraculous— a kind of single-petaled flower, like a hexagonal white jade platter holding a wine cup of golden yellow. Wasn't this Golden Cup? Another flower was double-petaled like that girl's dyed, woven skirt—light yellow and pale white. Wasn't this Hundred Leaves? This brother and sister had given their lives in order to bring Dragon's Pool water to benefit the villagers. After their deaths, they had become fresh flowers beautifying their home place. The South Village people called this flower the "narcissus flower."

(Story collected by Xie Hua)

A LEGEND OF JIULONG RIVER

The young woman in this story uses her supernatural powers to vanquish the dragon which has been terrorizing the people. It is also noteworthy that the young man's mother tells the young woman that her son will treat her well. This suggests then that there was some attention given to the proper treatment of wives.

Tradition has it that a very, very long time ago, a husband and wife were living on the bank of North River. They were already more than fifty years old before they had a son. When that son came crying into the world, it was just as the drum tower was sounding the midnight drum, so the old couple named their son "Drum." The two of them were overjoyed, and so they also planted a clump of red-stone bamboo.[26] Before long, the father died from overwork, and the mother reluctantly endured her pain and sorrow and passed the days. Every day, she cut firewood to earn money to bring up Little Drum. And every day she watered that clump of red-stone bamboo. The rays of the sun were like arrows. Twenty years passed in a flash. Now Drum had bushy eyebrows and big eyes. His waist was round and fat and wide. He went up the mountain to cut firewood and down the river to go rafting. He came in in the wind and went out in the rain. He struggled on the wild mountain and in the waters. He was a person of few words, honest and tolerant and unbending. In the evening, Drum took up the bamboo flute and played mountain songs to dispel his mother's depression. The realization that Drum was already grown up made his mother happy, but then she thought of their poverty that would prevent him from marrying. When she was alone, she often sighed deeply.

Spring came. The withered trees revealed new buds. Bamboo shoots broke through the earth. The mountains and the wilds all around were covered with red, yellow, and white mountain blossoms. One night, under the dim moonlight, Drum was playing a moving love song on the bamboo flute. He noticed that behind the house his mother's red-stone bamboo was fluttering in the spring wind—and he heard the *"xi-su"* sound of the bamboo shoots breaking through the earth. In a trance, Drum saw a slim, graceful young girl exuding tenderness and love. Standing in the clump of bamboo, she was smiling slightly at him. He looked again. Under the moonlight, that clump of bamboo was as it was before—waving in the breeze. Drum thought his vision had been clouded, and he sighed softly and went back into the house. Early the next morning, Drum had to go to the riverside to make wooden rafts. When he got there, he saw that the wooden rafts had already been lashed together. A pole was also propped up on the sandy bank. Who had helped with this? Drum was puzzled. When he went home, he told his mother of this. She couldn't figure it out, either. Three days in succession, the wood that Drum hauled down from the mountain to the river was all already made into rafts, and the neighbors and villagers all said that they hadn't helped. The mother and son wanted to get to the bottom of this matter.

The fourth day, just as dawn was breaking and thick fog was winding around the mountain peaks, Drum and his mother hid in the clump of trees in front of their house to observe the activity at the riverside. After a while, a *"sha-sha"* sound came from the clump of stone bamboo behind the house. A young girl walked out from behind the house. This young girl was gentle and graceful. She was wearing a yellow dress. Her face was like the peach blossoms of spring. Her eyes were like a pool of autumn water. The young girl flicked the dewdrops off her body, and, gracefully following the path in front of the house, she walked to the riverside. With unusual skill, she made the wood into rafts. The more Drum watched, the stranger it seemed to him: This young girl was the same girl he had seen in the clump of bamboo several days before when he was playing the flute! Drum hurriedly dragged his mother below the clump of red-stone bamboo behind the house. They discovered that a bamboo shoot that had just broken through the earth had disappeared. All around was layer after layer of peeled bamboo shoot husks. Drum guessed that this young girl had perhaps been transformed from bamboo shoots.

He hastily gathered up the bamboo shoot husks, and rushed to the riverside. The young girl—deep in concentration as she made the rafts—suddenly raised her head. When she saw that it was Drum standing in front of her, she became flustered. She lowered her head. At a loss as to what to do, she fiddled with her clothing. Drum was facing this girl who was like flowers and jade. His heart was pitter—pattering like a fawn's. He was so excited he couldn't say a word. The young girl suddenly remembered her own position and hurriedly took a shortcut and ran back to the clump of stone bamboo. But the bamboo shoot husks in the bamboo clump had disappeared. The young girl was so upset that she ran around in circles. The mother drew close and said to the young girl, "Kindhearted young girl, come and pass the days with us! Although our family is poor, we're good people, able to get along with others. Drum is honest and sincere. He wouldn't treat you unfairly." The young girl looked at this old mother. She looked at Drum who was walking toward her. Blushing deeply and smiling shyly, she lowered her head slightly. In this way, Heaven brought a happy destiny. Drum and the stone bamboo shoot girl were married. The next spring, they had a boy and a girl. The whole family was overjoyed. Drum cut firewood and made rafts. Stone Bamboo Shoot spun and wove cloth. The mother took care of the children, and raised pigs and ducks. In every possible way, the husband and wife were a loving couple. In every possible way, the son and daughter-in-law were filial to, and respectful of, their mother. The days passed in absolute bliss and good fortune.

But the mountain valleys had a lot of evil winds. The rivers and seas had a lot of evil dragons. One year at the height of summer, not a drop of rain fell for forty-nine days. The sun was like fire. The river water completely dried up. The trees and cereal-crop seedlings withered. Worried, the villagers knelt under the scorching sun and offered prayers to Heaven for rain. But day after day passed, and not even a thread of a cloud appeared in the sky, nor even a thread of wind on the earth. The sun's rays were still burning the ten thousand things. Drum had no way to make rafts. There was only a little bit of sweet potato left in the home—and that would soon be gone. The whole family had plunged into catastrophe.

One noon, a fierce wind suddenly blew up. From the western horizon drifted innumerable crow-black clouds. In a second, they spread over the whole sky. The sound of rumbling thunder was deafening. People cheered and shouted for joy, "The rain will soon be here!" Mother's hot tears tumbled down. Stone Bamboo Shoot's worried expression smoothed out. Drum was so happy that he ran crazily all over the mountain. A flash of lightning suddenly streaked across. The huge sound of thunder exploded in half the sky. A ball of fire broke up in the sky. In the flashes of fire appeared several large red, orange, yellow, green light blue, blue, purple, black, and white dragons. Baring their fangs and brandishing their claws, they were flying and dancing up and down. Slowly the large dragons of nine colors flew toward the south and fled. In a moment, the crow-black clouds covering the sky all vanished. A bolt of yellow silk drifted down from the sky in leisurely fashion. Everyone rushed to surround it. Written on the yellow silk were the words: "Every day, offer one pair—a young boy and a young girl—to the Nine Dragon Pool for the nine dragons to enjoy. Otherwise, rain will never fall." It was as though a sound of enormous thunder had suddenly exploded. The villagers were dumbstruck. What could they do in the face of these nine fierce and malicious dragons? In order to save everyone else's lives, the mothers reluctantly gave up the flesh and bones they'd given birth to. Each household of each village took turns every day in sending a pair—a young boy and a young girl—to Nine Dragon Pool as sacrifices to the nine dragons. But ten days passed and the weather was just as fiery hot. Not even one drop of rain had fallen. The villagers felt sorrowful and hopeless.

One night, Drum's family was lighting an oil lamp. Stone Bamboo Shoot embraced her two children tightly. Drum let out a long sigh, and said to Stone Bamboo Shoot, "Mother of these children, if these nine dragons aren't done away with, the people won't have peace. I want to sacrifice my life and kill the dragons and save the villagers, but I don't have a good way to do this!"

Stone Bamboo Shoot said, "There are ways to get rid of the nine dragons, but the nine dragons are venomous. This bodes ill rather than good."

Drum said, "If the nine dragons aren't wiped out, disaster will befall us, too. It's best to let me go and die—and protect the villagers!"

Holding back her grief, Stone Bamboo Shoot agreed and took a gold hairpin from her make-up box. She also cut a length of bamboo in the red bamboo grove and heated it until it turned to ashes. She then gave these two things to Drum and carefully told him how to use them. That night, the two of them sat facing each other until the morning light.

The next day, Drum brushed away his tears and said farewell to his mother and wife. He carried the offering—one young boy, one young girl—in a square-bottomed bamboo basket. Accompanied by the villagers, he took them down into Nine Dragon Pool. As usual, the villagers lighted incense and burned paper, and prayed to the nine dragons for rain. At midnight, cold winds gusted in and suddenly they saw the pool water ripple lightly and then rise like a seething cauldron. The water rumbled loudly. The two children in the square-bottomed bamboo basket were crying in fear. The villagers were so frightened that they all took cover under the large rocky cliff. Drum looked undaunted. He was standing firm and tall. Suddenly, a pillar of water several hundred feet high gushed out. The nine huge dragons surged up and—opening their mouths which were like large basins of blood—they rushed at the square-bottomed bamboo basket. It takes a while to tell of it, but it happened quickly then. Drum pulled out the stone bamboo ashes, and threw a handful at the nine dragons, and turned around and picked up the square-bottomed bamboo basket and ran home.

In a second, everything was hazy with smoke. The smoke stabbed people's noses. In the midst of it, eight of the huge dragons were blinded by the stone bamboo smoke. They were confused and disoriented. They fled in distress, and died when they ran into the large mountain. The light blue dragon had dodged quickly, and hadn't been struck by the ashes. He looked around and discovered that Drum was carrying the children and running home. He immediately spat out the crow-black smoke and went in pursuit. Drum saw that he was about to catch up, and he quickly hid the children under the rocky cliff, and turned around and ran toward the beach. With a shout, the light blue dragon dived down from the sky. He stretched out his huge claws to grab Drum. Drum had trouble seeing but was deft of hand. Pulling out the golden hairpin, he hurled it savagely at the light blue dragon. He saw only a gleam flash by. The golden hairpin pierced the light blue dragon's back. The light blue dragon let out a huge yelp, and again spat out a puff of smoke and fire at Drum, and only then did he escape in a rush with his injuries. The smoke and fire enveloped Drum. And before long, the burning fire had transformed Drum into a large black rock. When they heard the news, Stone Bamboo Shoot and his mother hurried up. Hugging the two children and the rock, they wept loudly. Their tears soaked the beach. His mother cried until her tears dried up and she died beside the water.

Just then, crow-black clouds suddenly appeared, flying in from a distance. After the light blue dragon was injured, his barbarity became very clear. He turned around and again rushed toward Stone Bamboo Shoot and the children. Fury was burning in Stone Bamboo Shoot's breast. She made up her mind to take revenge by killing the light blue dragon. Stone Bamboo Shoot turned the children over to the villagers, and then ran up the hill, raised her hand, and waved to the green hill. The mountain wind immediately roared fiercely. On the mountain, innumerable bamboo trees turned into an untold number of bamboo slips and shot toward the light blue dragon. Sweeping his tail, the dragon spouted out raging fire at Stone Bamboo Shoot. Stone Bamboo Shoot waved a green handkerchief—and the flames were extinguished. Stone Bamboo Shoot then turned into a large bamboo shoot and was swallowed in one gulp by the light blue dragon. Before long, the light blue dragon had a very bad stomach ache. Stone Bamboo Shoot had already stabbed him from inside. Just then, there was a heavy downpour—the tears shed by the light blue dragon as he was dying. The storm was flowing into Nine Dragon Pool where Drum and his mother had died. From then on, the sweet rain moistened the ten thousand things, and the earth's lease on life was restored, and everyone could again live peacefully.

Tradition has it that this light blue dragon turned into Qinglong Mountain Range.[27] The dragon's head became "Dragon's Head Mountain." The place where Stone Bamboo Shoot bored out of the dragon's body became "Stone Bamboo Shoot Peak." It was tall and straight, delicate and beautiful. People call the rock that Drum became "Drum Rock"; the place where his mother died, they call "Crying for the Children Ravine." The place where Drum threw the stone bamboo ash to exterminate the dragons, people call "Clearness of All Ages," because the pool of river water is clear year around.[28] The large river where the nine large, colored dragons lived is called "Nine Dragon River."

(Story collected by Ye Tengfeng)

THE STORY OF JIANLIAN

In this story, Lotus Girl is able to vanquish the thugs who are bent on destroying her. She is then able to live happily with the young man of her choice.

Many years ago, a diligent, honest youth named Li Zhi lived outside the west gate of Jianning. His father and mother had died long before, leaving him alone, orphaned, and helpless. But since childhood his diligence and honesty had earned him the love of his uncles and aunts. They all regarded him as their own child.

One day, Li Zhi went to Raoshan, Jianning's highest mountain, to chop firewood. He climbed the mountain and crossed the peaks. Without being aware of it, he walked into the dense forest deep in the mountain. Hungry and thirsty, he walked on into the remote mountain area to look for water. He found a clear spring, where he drank his fill. Just as he was about to leave, suddenly—at the side of the spring—he saw a wonderful pink flower swaying in the wind. People would love it, he thought. He carefully dug up the flower—roots, earth and all—and took it home, where he planted it in the pool beside the house. Every day after work, Li Zhi gazed at this wonderful precious flower. Under his painstaking nurturing, this flower turned from one into ten, from ten into a hundred, from a hundred into a thousand. It grew into a vast expanse, which soon filled the entire pool. In the summer, a pool of beautiful flowers were in full bloom. Jade-green cones also clustered like a bee's nest. If you pulled off the outer shell, the inside of the cone was white and delicate like pearls. Its faintly scented taste was good to eat. Li Zhi happily divided this unusual fruit among the poor villagers, so that everyone could taste the delicacy.

At that time, outside the west gate of Jianning lived a rich man named Li Waizui—Crooked-Mouth Li. Very ugly and vicious, he loved riches as if they were life. When he heard that the poor fellow Li Zhi had this wonderful flower and unusual fruit, he flew into a rage. He thought that he—Crooked-Mouth Li— should be the only person in the whole world fortunate enough to have this flower and fruit. So, the next day, he took a group of wicked lackeys and hired thugs and—panting with rage— rushed to the side of Li Zhi's pool and cursed loudly, "Who is so audacious as to plant these things in my pool, and yet not pull them all up for me!"

Li Zhi swallowed the insult and said, "Master, I dug this flower up from the mountain and planted it in the pool that my grandfather built. How can you say it is yours?"

When Crooked-Mouth Li heard this, he was even angrier: "Everything here must be mine." He ordered the hired thugs and slaves to scatter and pulverize that expanse of lovely flowers, along with the stalks and the leaves.

Li Zhi was so angry that he sat beside the pool and stared blankly—straight until midnight. Only then did he shed tears. He picked up petal after petal of the wonderful ruined flowers, and bundled up all the broken roots and stalks. Then—*po*— came a sound from the pool. And a new flower bud bubbled up. A beautiful young girl stood in the slowly unfolding, glossy white, lightly scented stamen. Blown lightly by the evening breeze, she dropped down beside the bewildered Li Zhi. She said, "Elder Brother Li, I am called Lotus Girl. Don't grieve. I'll give you even better lotuses." Then she flicked her sleeves lightly, and, in a moment, many lotus leaves and lotus flowers were growing again in the pool.

The next day, as the poor villagers exulted over the rebirth of the lotus flowers, this news also reached Crooked-Mouth Li. Leading a group of hired thugs, he rushed over. Ah! These lotus flowers were even better than yesterday's! Angry and agitated, Crooked-Mouth Li thundered, "Wreck these for me— and be quick about it!" The hired thugs clubbed and beat and raked them back—and again ruined the pool of lotus flowers.

Li Zhi detested Crooked-Mouth Li and wept sorrowfully until midnight. At this time, the Lotus Girl again blew lightly from the stamen, and said affectionately, "Elder Brother Li, don't grieve. I am determined to stay here. Don't be afraid that evil people will break things. Like the fibers of the lotus root, I can't be snapped away from good people." She flicked her sleeves again. And in a second, the pool filled again with an expanse of beautiful lotus flowers.

The next day, Crooked-Mouth Li heard that the pool was full of lotus flowers again. He shook his head like a peddler's drum and said, "I don't believe it. I don't believe it." He sent a lackey to investigate whether this was true or false. He learned that it was true. Panting with rage, he hurried with his lackeys to the side of the pool again. Without a word, he got to work pulling up and wrecking the pool's lotus flowers along with the roots and the leaves. It looked as though the lotus flowers had all been thoroughly destroyed. Now just one lotus flower floated on the water—now in the east, now in the west. No matter what they did, the hired thugs couldn't catch it. Crooked-Mouth Li was so angry that he roundly cursed the lackeys as useless. He himself went into the pool to seize it. It's strange to say, but that lotus flower moved from the shallow water to the deep— now submerged, now visible—leading Crooked-Mouth Li and his wicked lackeys toward the deep part of the pool. One by one, they were all trapped. They were all drowned in the pool.

When Li Zhi saw that the rich man and the wicked lackeys had all drowned, he was delirious with joy, but he was grieved not to see the lotus flower girl he loved. He sat beside the pool until midnight. Suddenly Lotus Girl came again. With deep emotion, she said, "Elder Brother Li, don't grieve. The bad people who cheated us are all dead. We can live happily." The lotus leaves in the pond were green. The lotus flowers blossomed even more beautifully, and they also formed a lot of lotus seeds.

From then on, lotus flowers took root outside the west gate of Jianning. Outside the west gate, Li Zhi and the villagers also opened ninety-nine more lotus pools and painstakingly nurtured the lotus flowers. The lotus seeds here are better than those anywhere else. So the "Jianlian" is renowned at home and abroad.

(Story collected by Zhang Bingxun)

211

LIAN LI GIVES BIRTH TO HAN QI

This story depicts two very strong women: The older woman is cruel, jealous, and possessive, while the younger woman is independent and able. She leaves a note, thus indicating that—despite her slave status—she is literate, and then lives out her life in a Buddhist nunnery.

In the past, in Quanzhou was a lane called Lian Li. "Lian Li" was a slave girl's name. That a lane would be named for a slave girl and be preserved and passed down through the ages is very unusual. Although Lian Li was a slave girl, in the Northern Song dynasty she was also known as the natural mother of Han Qi. A play called *The Story of the Climbing Flowers Twig* tells the story of Lian Li giving birth to Han Qi.

It is said that in the time of Zhenzong[29] in the Northern Song, Han Guohua was the hardworking prefect of Quanzhou. He set up an equable granary for selling grain to help those in distress and poverty. In the eyes and the hearts of ordinary people, he was a good official, but he was fifty years old and still had no offspring. He was often melancholy.

Asleep in the dim moonlight one night, Han Guohua suddenly saw the city god leading a child forward. He said, "Today I'm giving you the god of Qingyuan Mountain to be your son." Looking carefully, he saw an absolutely beautiful youth. His eyes were crystal like the spring water of Qingyuan Mountain. His black hair was thick like the forests of Qingyuan Mountain. Han Guohua was happy beyond all expectations. He was about to thank the god when the morning songs of birds awakened him from his dream.

Still lost in thought, Han Guohua suddenly looked up to see

213

the slave girl Lian Li holding a twig of climbing flowers. She pushed the door open and walked in. All smiles, she said, "Sir! Just look, this twig of climbing flowers has opened to a brilliant red!"

"A twig of climbing flowers?"

"Sure! The banyan bore the climbing twig! Your wife sent me especially to give you this twig for your enjoyment."

This twig of climbing flowers used to be simply a parasite of the local banyan trees. This was extraordinary. Today this flower had opened to be a brilliant red. After the people in the prefecture heard about this, everyone came forward to enjoy the sight. Everyone said that it was unusual, and that it was an omen that Prefect Han would have good fortune and great riches. Han Guohua's wife, the Woman Zhu, had seen that this twig of climbing flowers was an unusual brilliant red, and so she had ordered the slave girl Lian Li to take it to her husband. When Han Guohua heard that this was a climbing twig yielded by the banyan tree, he felt his happiness had dropped down from Heaven, and he speculated, "'That the banyan tree gave birth to a climbing twig,' isn't this simply 'to show that I will have descendants?'[30] In my dream last night I saw the god of Qingyuan Mountain. Isn't it likely then that I will have descendants with this Lian Li?" Although Lian Li was a slave girl, she was also very pretty and sedate and charming. All along, Han Guohua had regarded her warmly and had treated her well. Today he saw her carrying that twig of brilliant crimson climbing flowers. As she stood under the red light, the flowers and her appearance set each other off nicely—making her all the more tender and beautiful and charming. Unconsciously, he was aroused. So, while accepting the twig of climbing flowers, he also said excitedly, "The banyan (I) has borne a climbing twig (descendant). How wonderful!" Then he smoothly drew her to him, "Come, Lian Li! How long have you lived here?"

Lian Li's heart leaped. Uneasily, she responded softly, "Ten years."

"How have you been treated?"

"Better than my own relatives treat me." Lian Li went on to say that when she was a child she lost her parents and had no

214

one to depend on. Destitute, she had wandered the streets. If it hadn't been for Master Han taking her in, she didn't know where she would be now! She was infinitely grateful, but she hadn't repaid him.

Han Guohua saw that she was reasonable, and he loved her even more. He sighed deeply. "I'm sighing because I still have neither a son nor half a daughter. You have ties of friendship like this—but. . . ." Han Guohua stopped short of saying what he wished to say.

Lian Li said, "If Master agrees, I wish. . . ."

"Wish what?"

"I wish to be your adopted daughter."

Han Guohua had thought at first that Lian Li had immediately understood what he wanted, and he'd been overjoyed. Who'd have guessed that what Lian Li thought was completely the opposite. The thought chilled him.

But Han Guohua longed desperately for sons. How could he willingly let go? So he said, "An adopted daughter is still the weaker sex. How can this give me posterity?"

Lian Li lowered her head.

Han Guohua said, "Didn't the banyan tree give birth to a climbing twig? This climbing twig represents descendants! Think about it. Our relationship can be considered predestined by Heaven!"

Lian Li's heart jumped and her ears flamed. Her cheeks reddened. "Ah! Master, Lian Li doesn't dare accept this kind of good fortune!"

"Heaven brought us together!"

"Ah! Master! No! No!. . . ."

But then, in spite of herself, Lian Li submitted.

Before long, Lian Li was pregnant.

The Woman Zhu, Han Guohua's primary wife, was cunning, disagreeable, and jealous. She had not yet had a child. Han Guohua suffered because he had no posterity. Each time he considered taking a concubine, she blocked him. Now she saw that Han Guohua had illicitly married Lian Li, and saw, too, that Lian Li was already pregnant. Her jealousy made her doubly angry, and she often picked quarrels, made trouble, and beat

Lian Li. Lian Li was subjected to all kinds of humiliation. Although Han Guohua had taken her into his heart, he was no match for this cunning woman. There was nothing he could do. One day, when Han Guohua had gone out, the Woman Zhu sent for Lian Li. She insulted and cursed her in a hundred ways, and also demanded that Lian Li obey her in three things: 1) she wasn't permitted to take even half a step outside; 2) she must entertain the master wholeheartedly; and 3) she would have the name "small wife" but not the authority. Lian Li was naturally stubborn. From start to finish she refused to surrender, and she sneered, "Who would value the status of being the small wife in the Han household! I'd rather be a village woman in the mountain wilds."

"Hunh? You cheap slave girl. You wreck the reputation of the Han household, and you still dare talk back!" The Woman Zhu saw how stubborn Lian Li was, and she flew into an angry rage, and raised her own hand to strike Lian Li. Luckily just at this time Han Guohua returned and only then did the Woman Zhu desist.

Later, the Woman Zhu fastened on a deadly scheme. After the slave girls heard it, they urged Lian Li to escape from the Han household soon.

One evening, the moon was cold and the stars few. Cold wind stabbed the bones. Lian Li had a premonition that her child would be born. She hesitated briefly, and then picked up a little clothing and left silently by the back door. She walked with great effort to the alley entrance—and then she couldn't walk any farther. She looked up and saw that the small town god temple was nearby. She hurriedly reached the entrance and went in. There, she lay down on a rock plank in front of the altar. Before long, the child came into the world with a cry.

She'd given birth to a son and she was very happy. But she realized that this place was very close to the government offices. When someone from the Han household arrived, she was sure to lose her life. Her tears gushed like a spring. She thought that it would be better to commit suicide than be killed by the Woman Zhu. But her son had just been born: How could she bear to part with him? Just then, the sound of her pursuers came from the alley. She ripped a piece of her silk gauze skirt and dipped her hand in the blood and scrawled several words: "This is Guohua's son. Lian Li has drowned herself." She wrapped up her child and embraced him, and offered prayers to the town god. She asked the town god to protect and bless her son so that he could grow to adulthood. She kissed her son and murmured to him, "Your mother's life is one of hardship—so much so that as soon as my son is born he has no mother. Oh, my son! You must not blame me!" Reluctantly, she put her son down and ran out the door.

Lian Li staggered along, groping her way through the blackness, and ran out of the city. When she reached the edge of a stream, the birds were already singing. She was about to cast herself into the water when a passing nun pulled her back. So Lian Li went with the nun, shaved her head, and became a nun herself.

That evening, after Han Guohua learned that Lian Li had left, he immediately dispatched Han Fu to lead people to look for her everywhere. Near that small local god's temple, Han Fu heard a baby crying. He went in and discovered the baby and the blood note. He guessed that Lian Li had already escaped. But he didn't know if she had really thrown herself into the water. He didn't want to go and search, so he carried the baby back to the household and made his report.

Han Guohua saw that the baby had already been brought home. He didn't know which direction Lian Li had taken. He himself wanted to send people out again to look for her, but he had no choice but to submit to the Woman Zhu. He could only grieve in silence. But he had a descendant. The two people devoted themselves to rearing the child, whom they named Han Qi.

Time slipped by, and in the twinkling of an eye, eighteen years passed. At first, Lian Li had been a nun in the Deji nunnery and the Qili nunnery. Later she had entered a nunnery on the large and remote Luoji Mountain.

This nuns' temple was at the side of the highway leading to the capital. The rear of the mountain was near water. The ancient pines were hardy. The clear stream gurgled. Birds sang and flowers were fragrant. There was the sound of the morning bell and the evening drum. The incense smoke curled upwards. It was a place of absolute peace. After Lian Li arrived here, all day long the wooden-fish drum and the clear bell made her heart as cold as water. She frequently thought of the past. In her dreams, she went back. She never forgot the son whom she had so painfully left behind. The red fish drum and the clear bell were the companions of dawn and dusk, eighteen springs and autumns of a lonely heart, the Pure Land was a thousand *li* from home. Lonely, she was facing a lonely lamp and deeply missing her son. Eighteen years passed. Her son surely must be grown up, but she didn't know what he was like today. One day, as she burned incense and prayed and methodically struck the wooden fish, she suddenly saw the sky turn to dusk and the ground become dark. A violent rain fell as though the heavens were being turned upside down. She was astounded. This rain was astonishing. In a second, a group of men and horses entered the temple to take refuge from the rain. Among them was Han Qi, who had gone to the capital to sit for the examination. His name was inscribed on the golden list of those passing the exam. He had been named the Number One scholar, and was return-ing home. He had come in for a while to get out of the rain. The old nuns knew that he had come here before. They promptly led him in, gave him tea, and said, "To come here twice to avoid the rain. This is destiny! Destiny!"

Lian Li looked up, and saw that his banner bore the charac-ters of the Han household of Quanzhou. This youth who had just scored first place in the exams was brilliant. He looked like Han Guohua, and suddenly she wondered if he was her own son. She looked then at the steward. Plainly, it was Han Fu. She felt both sorrow and joy. Drops of tears filled her eyes. Han Fu had already recognized her. "Ah! Lian Li! Lady Lian, so this is where you've been!" Han Fu then introduced Han Qi and Lian Li. "This is your natural mother. Come quickly and meet her." To Lian Li he said, "The young master is the Number One scholar and is returning home. This is worthy of congratulations!"

When Han Qi heard that the nun before him was his natural mother, he flew into a rage. "Nonsense! Isn't my mother at home right now? You are really dense!"

Han Fu then told Han Qi of Lian Li giving birth to him.

Han Qi asked, "What evidence is there?"

Han Fu said, "There's a blood note written on a silk gauze skirt. Wait and I'll get it."

After obtaining the child, Han Guohua had forgotten Lian Li. Han Fu had been very uneasy about this. He guessed that Lian Li hadn't really drowned herself, but he didn't know which direction she'd taken. So he secretly kept and hid the blood note that Lian Li had left behind, hoping that a day would come when he could help Lian Li and her son meet. Today, finally, it had become true that Heaven doesn't ever disappoint those with hope.

Han Qi looked at the blood note written on the silk gauze skirt, and he was very moved. Tears in his voice, he knelt before his mother and shouted, "Mother! Forgive your child's unfilial crime in not coming much earlier to ask you to come home!"

Lian Li bowed and embraced her son and began to weep. In several dreams, she had thought of her son but it was difficult to *see* him in dreams. Now today her son who was the Number One scholar was kneeling before her. How could she not be moved! She shouted, "Son! Can you understand how filled with grief your mother's whole life has been? In twenty years I've had only dreams." She had already cried so much she was all tears.

Han Qi said, "Mother! Today your son has placed first on the list and is going home in robes of silk. Mother can live in comfort! I invite you to go home with me."

Lian Li was grateful that she and her son had been able to meet, but she was mortified at the thought of going home. She remembered when the three feet of silk gauze skirt were filled with blood and tears. It seemed to be before her eyes. So many tears, so much hatred. It was rare for a son to be filial and sincere. It was also hard to give up her disillusionment with the mortal world. She sobbed, "Son! You and your mother have met. My hopes have been fulfilled! I absolutely cannot go home!"

Han Qi said, "Mother! That year, my father's wife was jealous and ungenerous. She was too harsh, when in fact she shouldn't have been. For my sake, I hope you will go home with me."

Lian Li said, "Son! Long ago, your mother's heart was already as cold as ice. My life today is only that of a Buddhist follower. And that will be so for my remaining years."

Although Han Qi was absolutely sincere and respectful in asking his mother to go home with him, Lian Li refused. He could only leave.

The next day, accompanied by joyous music and drumbeats loud enough to overturn the heavens, Han Guohua, his son, the Woman Zhu, and Han Fu, as well as the maid Xian took clothing and went to the nunnery to see Lian Li and invite her home. When Lian Li heard this, she cried of the suffering in her heart, "Son! Your mother has suffered from longing for twenty years, and endured loneliness day and night. How can you only now welcome me home? That day of the concubine . . .!" And she immediately escaped inside.

Han Guohua couldn't see Lian Li. All he could do was to leave some silver for temple repairs.

Later, just before her death, Lian Li was taken to the Han home. When the funeral procession was held, Lian Li's coffin was carried out from the main entrance. There, the Woman Zhu blocked its movement. Han Qi was furious. "If it were I who had died, would I be carried out from the main entrance?"

The Woman Zhu said, "Since you are the Han family's posterity, of course you would." When Han Qi heard this, he lay on top of his mother's coffin, and ordered people to carry them out from the main entrance.

Han Qi later became prime minister. He held every important position. His service was meritorious and his achievements were great.[31]

So, the lane where Lian Li gave birth to Han Qi is called Lian Li Lane. The small local god temple was also changed to the palace of his birth. The stone plank in the temple bears traces of blood from the time Lian Li gave birth. It is said that when water is spilled there, the color of the blood is even more discernible.

(Story collected by Zhang Xidong)

LIN AIZHI BRINGS AN ACCUSATION BEFORE THE EMPEROR

In some respects, Lin Aizhi is a stereotypical traditional Chinese woman—particularly in her final decision. But, in many respects, she is not. She is portrayed as extremely intelligent and quick-witted. She follows through on her decision to accuse her brother for the murder of her husband, and—with the aid of a benefactor—brings this accusation to a successful conclusion. Doing so involves not only travel to the capital, but also travel with a man. This suggests then that, in pursuit of justice, she is willing to risk her own reputation.

Lin Aizhi's mother's home is in Huqiu Chiling Village in Anxi County in the Quanzhou region. Her parents died one after the other when she was a child. She had only one brother whose name was Jiamu and who was seven or eight years older than her. Jiamu was savage and cruel, greedy and vulgar. He usually had no regular work. He loved associating with young hooligans. It was when Aizhi was about eighteen *sui* that he went with the local hooligans across the mountain to Weizhanshe. Someone named Zhan Dian heard that Aizhi was beautiful and graceful and that she had the feminine virtues of kindness and worthiness. He asked a go-between to see Jiamu and make the match. When he learned that Zhan Dian's family was well-off, Jiamu agreed. Before long, Aizhi was married to Zhan Dian.

After Zhan Dian married Aizhi, the married couple was very much in love—like a pair of birds sleeping together. They lived a happy life. That could truly be called a time of perfect married bliss. The local Anxi tea specialty brought in a lot of money. Zhan Dian usually engaged in the tea trade. He sold tea three or four times a year in other locales. He took the tea out and he brought the capital back. He went back and forth a lot. After Aizhi had been married three or four months, it was time for Zhan Dian to go out and sell tea again. She hadn't been married long and couldn't help but have a woman's dragging skirt and a tear-damp shirt. She couldn't bear to part with him.

Aizhi thought that it would be at least several months before her husband could return. She prepared wine for a farewell dinner for Zhan Dian and also invited her elder brother Jiamu to join the feast. In this lurked Zhan Dian's misfortune.

They drank until they were warm with the wine. Zhan Dian saw that Aizhi looked unbearably hurt, and so he said to Jiamu, "When I first asked your little sister to come to my home, she wasn't yet very familiar with everything. I know that I must be away several months. Of course, she will feel very lonely, but I already have a plan. This time at most I'll be gone no more than. . . ."

"At most it won't be more than how long before you return?" Jiamu asked attentively.

"I've already figured it out. I'll return in three months."

"So, three months from today you'll return?"

"Yes. Of course I'll pass through Chiling on the way back, so at that time you'll know in advance."

Aizhi interrupted, "Although you can say this, you can't guarantee it. The proverb says 'When out of the home, you live by the road and you can't decide things on your own.' So how can you decide on your own?"

"Really. I can guarantee the time of my return," Zhan Dian said solemnly.

No one knew then that the speaker's words were tossed out carelessly, but that the listener was attentive. Zhan Dian stated his return date in order to console his loving wife, but he didn't guess that Jiamu was fixing every sentence firmly in his memory. There was no more talk that night. The next day at daybreak, Zhan Dian took his leave of Aizhi and began his sojourn.

Jiamu was a rogue with no regular work. He had been in cahoots for a long time with the local white-haired thief. Ever since his sister's dinner, he'd had evil ideas. He schemed to collaborate with the white-haired thief and rob Zhan Dian of his money when he returned.

Zhan Dian had been away selling tea for nearly three months. He counted on his fingers. The date he'd set with Aizhi would soon arrive. It goes without saying that a traveler, not married for long and far away, is impatient to return. He began his trip home, traveling by day and sleeping by night to keep his promise. There was bound to be an exchange of conventional greetings. Sure enough, as soon as he entered the Lin home, Jiamu treated him solicitously. Jiamu insisted that he stay. He said he had already prepared a little wine and that he wanted to give him a dinner of welcome. No matter what, he had to agree to stay a night. At root, Zhan Dian was a sincere and honest person. It was only grudgingly that he stayed at Jiamu's home.

That evening, needless to say, Jiamu's invitation to Zhan Dian was a plot. Among the guests was also the white-haired thief. He was Jiamu's collaborator. So, using the pretext of the great happiness of guest and host, they toasted Zhan Dian with cup after cup of wine. Although Zhan Dian couldn't handle this much alcohol, still he couldn't ward off the double-pronged attack. Before long, he was so drunk that he fell into a heavy faint. When the night was deep and all was quiet, Jiamu and the white-haired thief put their scheme into action.

Only when Zhan Dian felt the first cut of Jiamu's knife did he let out a loud shout in his drunken stupor. Then when the white-haired thief added a cut, Zhan Dian rolled down from the bed. When they started all this, Jiamu's six-*sui*-old son was asleep in another bed. Zhan Dian's tragic cry woke him. He saw Zhan Dian rolling around on the floor. He was too frightened to make a sound. After the two villains had killed Zhan Dian, they packed the corpse into a gunnysack and buried it at Tiantai Mountain in the vicinity of Zhenyiling.

When they came back, they opened up Zhan Dian's small suitcase. It held a thousand ounces of silver. After dividing it in half, the two separated.

Lin Aizhi realized that this was the date Zhan Dian had set. She gazed anxiously until her eyes were strained, and she waited. Day after day passed, but her husband didn't return. At first

223

she sighed resentfully, then she felt puzzled, and finally she was worried. She was so fatigued that she turned wan and sallow and very thin. Women are superstitious. They can never give up imploring the gods and divining, and asking whether the time set for the husband's return has not yet arrived. After about one springtime had passed, Aizhi's hope snapped. It was the end of the world. She could think of no plan. She just determined to return home, and ask Jiamu's help to get news of her husband.

She had no sooner reached her mother's home and had not yet opened her mouth when Jiamu consoled her. He also treated her much more warmly than usual. He told his wife to kill a chicken as a special treat. Jiamu's wife also expressed her great respect. It was unusual solicitude. No sooner had her husband told her to kill a chicken than she went to do that. That innocent nephew—Jiamu's son—shouted very warmly, "Auntie! Auntie!" and dogged her every step. Before very long, Jiamu's wife was killing a rooster.

"*Yi! Yi!*" The rooster rolled around on the floor and made struggling sounds. Its two feet were still moving.

Just then, Jiamu's son suddenly shouted, "Look, all of you. That rooster is still rolling around, not yet dead. It's just like— just like Auntie's husband that night that. . . ."

Jiamu heard this, and stopped him in a hurry. He cursed him in a loud voice, "Damn! Get out of here!" He then turned and said to Aizhi, "Little sister, this child is only seven *sui* this year. He's naughty and useless. When he talks, he just rambles. Really . . . *Ai!*"

Just then Aizhi's spirit seemed to leave her body. When she heard what her nephew said, she was greatly shocked and suddenly she realized what had happened. She thought to herself, "The fact that there's been no word of my husband since he left is connected with this greedy, cruel elder brother of mine." When she didn't see her husband return, she was also suspicious of her elder brother. Before, she had always blamed herself and thought that her longing was too unrealistic, and that she indulged in fantasy. No matter what, she and her elder brother were siblings born of the same womb. He couldn't have this great an absence of conscience! But now she knew that her elder brother had killed her husband.

Aizhi was extremely bright. When she heard Jiamu's son tell the circumstances surrounding her husband's death, although her heart was as pained as if cut by a knife, she pretended she hadn't heard. When Jiamu went out, she took advantage of the opportunity to lead Jiamu's son to a secluded spot. She used a lot of ingenious methods to ask questions about her husband's death. The next day, she returned to her husband's home.

Aizhi hadn't been home more than a few days when the news of the charge against Jiamu spread. That was at dusk one day. A clerk in the county was Jiamu's blood brother. In the Anxi county government office, he saw "the case of Lin Aizhi accusing Lin Jiamu of murder for profit." He went into action at once and rushed immediately to Jiamu's home and told him what was in the document. Jiamu was panic-stricken. That night, he detained the clerk in his home to talk over ways to respond. The clerk agreed to handle things for him in the county office. The most important thing was to get a hundred ounces of silver ready to present to the county magistrate, for the Anxi county magistrate was well-known for his venality. Sure enough, Lin Aizhi's accusation was rejected for "lack of evidence."

When cases were handled during the imperial period, the first trial at the county magistrate's level was the most critical. Since the case had been settled in Anxi County, after that—at whatever level Aizhi brought her accusation—in the end they only replied that the county should investigate accordingly. As before, the county magistrate said there was "no evidence." Because of this, the tragic case of Zhan Dian sank unjustly to the bottom of the sea.

When Aizhi had exhausted her resources and her strength, in the end, she accidentally ran into a liberator. Who was this liberator? His name was Lu Qiujin. Originally Lu Qiujin was a very skillful and crafty person full of strategies for getting along in the world. He was a fortune-teller in Fuzhou. One day, Aizhi was walking around the streets. As soon as Qiujin saw her, he asked her a lot of detailed questions. Aizhi of course told him everything, and asked his help. To her surprise, Qiujin readily promised to help. But what he planned couldn't be done at the side of the road, so Aizhi went home with Qiujin. Although Aizhi went home with Qiujin, Qiujin hadn't yet stated clearly what he had in mind. He had only said a few comforting words to Aizhi. He said that if she wanted to avenge her husband she must first stay in his home, and that she must also wait patiently for the right day. At the end of her tether, Aizhi agreed.

In Qiujin's home, she did the laundry and cooking for him. As before, Qiujin engaged in fortune-telling. Aizhi had already lived there several months and Qiujin still hadn't revealed his plan. Aizhi waited impatiently, and incessantly implored him. Qiujin replied, "This case of yours. You must bring it before the emperor. But to bring it before the emperor, we need money for travel. Since you've come to my home, I've gone out every day to tell people's fortunes. That was just to help raise money for the journey. Don't worry. The time isn't ripe yet. As soon as it is, of course I'll tell you." There was nothing Aizhi could say to this; she could only be patient.

One day, Lu Qiujin smiled and said to Aizhi, "Sister-in-law Dian! Your chance for revenge has come. We will set out tomorrow. We must go to Hangzhou in Zhejiang."

"Hangzhou? What will we do in Hangzhou?" Aizhi asked nervously.

"You are after all the weaker sex, and you don't know about court business, such as the fact that now Emperor Qianlong[32] has said he will travel to the lower Yangzi region. West Lake in Hangzhou is the main attraction there. No matter what, Qianlong will certainly go there during his southern travels."

"But what does the emperor's travel to the lower Yangzi region have to do with my husband being wronged?"

"You can make the accusation to the emperor!"

Only then did Aizhi fully understand.

Here we need to add a section. After Aizhi ran into Qiujin in the provincial capital, the two lived together. Some people said: Aizhi might do something desperate, but she would not be tricked into losing her dignity. Other people said: Qiujin wanted to take revenge on her behalf, and Aizhi was determined to have revenge, so 1) she temporarily gave her body to him; and 2) it was hard to control her emotions, so they became emotionally attached to one another.

When the two of them reached Hangzhou, sure enough, Qianlong had already been at West Lake for several days. Immediately after Qiujin arranged for a hotel, he composed the written complaint for Aizhi, and gave it to her so that she could wait for the imperial carriage in the vicinity of West Lake and block the way and cry out about the injustice. She herself would present the accusation. At this time Lu Qiujin simply hid in the inn. He didn't even venture one step out the door.

Lu Qiujin didn't want to reveal himself because he and Aizhi were already living together. He was afraid the trouble he had taken would come to nothing. In fact he secretly directed Aizhi's every movement.

Aizhi took the accusation and waited several consecutive days on the West Lake road. Nowhere did she see even a shadow of the Qianlong emperor. She was disheartened. Each evening she returned to the inn and told Qiujin everything. They made plans every night. There was never any way to see the imperial carriage. This they greatly regretted. Qiujin decided to masquerade as a beggar. He would follow Aizhi on the road to see whether the emperor had really traveled to West Lake.

One early winter morning, the two of them were no more than a hundred steps away from each other when they saw a crowd of people and horses in the distance, crowding around a sedan chair carried by four persons, with an honor guard and retainers. It seemed to be an important official. It seemed to be a high official. In the previous several days, in fact, Aizhi had noticed this high official two or three times. Each time, there were shouts in front and crowding behind. This time Qiujin noticed that on all sides it was particularly solemn and quiet and serious. There was only the "*de-de*" clatter of horses' hoofs; almost no crow or sparrow could be heard. So, Qiujin signaled Aizhi to make her accusation.

Aizhi saw his secret signal. When this crowd of people and horses drew near, she knelt prostrate. Wailing and shouting of injustice, she blocked the road. The group of retainers walking in front were angry and worried. The person in the sedan chair thought all this was quite strange, and he ordered the group in front to ascertain what was happening. Thus he learned that it was an ordinary woman blocking the way and making an accusation. Hearing the sound of wailing, the official felt pity and he ordered that the accusation be received. Eight characters were appended to the accusation: "Fujian has no officials; injustice extends 10,000 *li*." He guessed that there must be a real sense of injustice in this accusation, and he immediately ordered the footman to tell the woman, "Our grand secretary has received your accusation. After he returns to Beijing, he will present your accusation to the emperor. He instructs you to also go to Beijing and wait for the emperor's imperial edict. When you reach Beijing, you must be sure to report personally to the Ministry of Punishments. Go now!"

Aizhi told Qiujin what the footman had said. Half-believing, half-doubting, the two decided to go to Beijing.

In fact Qiujin's eyesight wasn't bad. That person to whom the words were entrusted on the West Lake road seemed to be a grand secretary; but in fact this was Emperor Qianlong. He was disguised as an important official—needless to say, because he was afraid if he went out he'd meet with something unexpected. So, Lin Aizhi's accusation had been accepted.

After Qianlong accepted this appeal, he headed north to Beijing. Aizhi and Qiujin crossed the difficult and dangerous roads, reached the capital city, and hurried straight to the Ministry of Punishments. The Ministry had already received Qianlong's edict, and they were waiting for her.

After several days, Qianlong issued an edict proclaiming that Aizhi should go to the court. After receiving the imperial edict, Aizhi immediately followed the imperial envoy there. On the way, what terrified her most was that she was wearing white flowers in her hair and wearing plain clothing. But the skirt she was wearing, was red. She and Qiujin had lived and traveled together for a long time. She wasn't wearing mourning clothes. How could she have known that the imperial envoy would have come suddenly like this and want her to go with him immediately? There was no time for her to change her clothing and make-up. Finally, it was the red skirt that helped bring success.

It is said that after Qianlong returned from his southern travels, the empress had given birth to a prince. He was overjoyed. At that time, each time an emperor married or had a son, there was a general amnesty in China—or a reversal of unjust verdicts. Since receiving Aizhi's accusation in Hangzhou, the emperor had had the joy of having a son. In his jubilation, he had summoned Aizhi to come to the court.

Aizhi went into the court. Qianlong saw that she was wearing a red skirt, and, sure enough, he was shocked. His first sentence was, "Your husband was killed. How can you still be wearing a red skirt?"

When Qianlong asked this question, Aizhi was frightened indeed. Luckily, on the way to the court, she had already thought this through. She had recalled that it was widely known in the capital city that "today the emperor had a prince." So now she answered with deep feeling, "When this ordinary woman first reached the capital, people were congratulating the emperor on having a prince. In order to show that the whole world joins in the jubilation, I especially changed into a red skirt."

"But you're wearing white flowers in your hair, and a plain shirt. Why did you change only your skirt to red?" Qianlong asked.

"This ordinary woman's husband was killed. I'm wearing white on my upper body to show that my grievance hasn't yet been avenged. About wearing a red skirt: Because a skirt is below, that expresses congratulations for the emperor's having a prince— meaning that the people below all congratulate the emperor on this happy occasion."

When Qianlong heard this, he was quite happy. He privately gasped in admiration that here was a woman who knew ritual. So before asking about the case, he had already made up his mind to approve her request. After a while, he also asked, "This Lin Jiamu, whom you accused of killing your husband Zhan Dian, is your own elder brother; if according to your accusation, we punish him, then you will be killing your own elder brother!"

Aizhi replied, "The conjugal love of husband and wife is in the bedroom. The friendly affection of siblings is in the living room."

"No, husband and wife, and sibling and sibling are all part of the five relationships. If you get justice for your husband, you probably cannot have justice for your elder brother," said Qianlong.

"It is the husband and wife who remove their clothes and look at each other. It is siblings who wear their clothes and look at each other. The relationship between husband and wife is more intimate than that between siblings. This ordinary woman's elder brother first was not righteous toward this ordinary woman. It's clearly not that this ordinary woman is unrighteous." Aizhi responded like a stream. Her speech delighted Qianlong. He took up his vermilion brush and immediately approved her accusation. He also bestowed upon her the title "Chaste Lady." He also read the words appended to her accusation: "Fujian has no officials; injustice extends 10,000 *li*," and he issued an edict dispatching a special deputy to accompany her home to deal with this case.

Before long, Aizhi, along with the special deputy dispatched by the emperor, reached Fujian. Needless to say, at that time the officials connected with this case were all removed from office and prosecuted. When they returned to her home of Anxi, her elder brother Lin Jiamu had already gotten wind of this and fled. Perhaps it was that justice had a long arm. Jiamu fled to the border to Tongan, and in the end someone secretly reported this to the Tongan county magistrate. Jiamu was nabbed and sent to Anxi and turned over to the special deputy for prosecution. That special deputy ascertained the true state of affairs and immediately ordered the criminals Jiamu and the white-haired thief to be executed.

After Aizhi had avenged her husband, she recalled that she had lost her virginity to Lu Qiujin and thought of her status as "Chaste Lady" and felt ashamed. So she committed suicide by hanging.

(Story collected by Wu Zaoting)

230

SISTERS-IN-LAW PAGODA

This story depicts women who are patient and loyal. In that they build a pagoda of stone, they are also seen as capable and strong. They must also be literate, for they send a letter to Haisheng. The younger sister apparently has remained unmarried; the writer does not draw attention to this, suggesting that remaining single was probably not as unusual as is usually thought.

A very, very long time ago, below Baogai Mountain at Jinjiang in Qiao township of Minnan, there lived a family—an elder brother, his wife, and his little sister. They rented several tenths of *mou* of poor land from a landlord, and they also had one broken-down boat. All year they cultivated the land and fished in the ocean and depended on each other to get through the difficult days.

Haisheng, the elder brother, was very tough and determined. Strong and stubborn, he was like the pine tree that the Baogai Mountain wind couldn't snap. Both in and out of the village, people all said that he could row a boat faster than arrows left a bow, that he could cast a net rounder than the full moon, that the land he plowed was as clear as lake water, and that the grain he grew was like pearls.

The two sisters-in-law looked like the moon. And their handicrafts were famous far and near. Everyone praised them. The birds they embroidered could fly, the flowers they drew could flutter, the fish nets they wove intoxicated the fish and the shrimp, the clothing they made was better than that of tailors.

Although they had difficult lives, they all got along well together.

They stuck together. Often they sang fishing songs. In the midst of suffering there was still happiness.

One year Minnan had a great drought. The large rivers had no water. The small rivers dried up. The rice paddy was roasted until it was like charred grass. Farmers were gazing at heaven from the depths of disaster. Out of ten families, nine went hungry. People begging for fish came in the wind and left in the waves. One net of fish couldn't be exchanged for one liter of rice. But the ruthless landlord ate and drink his fill. The grain filling his storehouse mildewed and rotted. And he still dispatched his servants and lackeys to all corners to press for the rent—pressing so hard that not a few people jumped into the water or hanged themselves.

One morning, the landlord's lackeys truculently showed up at Haisheng's home. Scowling, they said, "You must pay the rent, understand?"

"This year what family has grain to pay?"

"If you can't," the lackey said, "that's okay—we'll just take your wife and little sister as rent!"

"Horseshit!" Haisheng was furious. "You'll have my wife and sister only when the Eastern Ocean is dry!"

The two sisters-in-law were also pointing at the lackeys, and cursing them as dirty swine.

"Okay. You swear at us. Even if you are stones, you must press out some oil for us!" The lackeys fiendishly began shouting fiercely, "Give us your boat. Give us your land! Hunh, it's not over yet!"

The lackeys stalked off.

With no boat and no land either, how could they go on living?

As long as the mountains were green, one need not worry about firewood. After Haisheng and his wife and little sister talked it over, they made up their minds to make a wooden raft so that Haisheng could brave the wind and risk going to Southeast Asia to earn a living.

At twilight on the day of his departure, the sisters-in-law held back their tears and bid farewell to Haisheng. The vast ocean and sky reverberated with the sorrowful song of the sisters-in-law:

The clouds of the sky flutter toward a distant place.
The water rolls in the sea, flowing toward the east.
Clouds of the sky, when will you flutter back here?
Water in the sea, when will you return?
Darling—ah—darling!
Brother—ah—brother!
Leaving home, going to the end of the world—when will we
  meet again?

Haisheng gazed at the sisters-in-law at the ferry. Drop by drop, their tears fell like broken strings of pearls into the sea.

Year after year passed. The flowers wilted and then blossomed again. The moon contracted and then became full again. Every day, the sisters-in-law watched the returning boats. Every year they gazed at the returning geese, but they didn't see Haisheng coming home!

Day and night, the sisters-in-law watched. They watched until their eyes were hollow. They watched until color and scent drained from them. They watched until their hair turned white. But they didn't see Haisheng return!

Day and night, the sisters-in-law moved rocks to the top of the mountain. From dawn to evening, from spring to autumn, each day they moved several dozen rocks. In a year they moved several thousand. They built a platform for gazing out for their husband and elder brother. They stood on the platform to watch. They watched—ah, they watched. If they couldn't bring Haisheng home by watching, they would watch until the sea ran dry and the rocks crumbled.

The sisters-in-law were exhausted from watching, and still they didn't see Haisheng returning. Haisheng, is it possible that you fell ill in a foreign country? Is it possible that you met with danger on the ocean? Is it possible that, separated from mountains and water, you forgot your hatred and the injustice? The sisters-in-law watched until they were burning with impatience. They had no alternative. They tore a strip from a skirt, bit their fingers and wrote a letter in blood, and attached it to a kite and let it follow the south wind and drift to the place where Haisheng was staying.

On an island an indeterminable number of thousand *li* from Baogai Mountain, Haisheng—together with the local people—was plowing and weeding and sowing on a piece of land with weeds growing up to one's neck and old trees reaching to the sky. He was remembering his home village, remembering his wife and his little sister. Every day at dusk, he stood at the seaside and gazed hopefully at the sea. One day, a kite with a broken string floated down before his eyes. He picked it up and looked at it. It was the blood letter written by the sisters-in-law. His tears gushed out like a spring. His heart had already flown home! The islanders tried to detain him, but they couldn't. They tried to advise him not to go back, and then day and night they helped him cut down trees and make a boat, and prepared provisions and water. And on a fine morning, they saw him off, following the wind home.

Sailing a small boat, Haisheng went through dozens of days and nights and went through a lot of hardships and dangers. Finally, in the mist and haze, he saw the Baogai Mountain that he had thought of by day and dreamed of by night. As his boat drew near, his heart thumped in alarm. He saw a stone pagoda on the mountain. He was stupefied; when he left for Southeast Asia to seek a living, he had left from this ferry point. There was certainly no stone pagoda here then! Had he made a mistake?

At this time, the sisters-in-law, who came to Baogai Mountain each day to await Haisheng, were standing on the high rock platform gazing out. Suddenly they saw a small boat surging up on the sea. On the boat was one person. They looked carefully. It was Haisheng! It was the husband they'd watched for day and night! It was the elder brother they'd watched for day and night! The sisters-in-law waved and shouted in excitement. They shouted loudly. Unexpectedly, just at this time, an enormous breaker struck from mid-air. In an instant, Haisheng's boat was swallowed up. It vanished from sight. The sisters-in-law called out in alarm. They jumped into the large sea from the high Baogai Mountain. In a moment, everything darkened. The wailing wind and the weeping rain wept in grief in the ink-black sky and earth! Before very long, the rain passed and the clouds were gathered in, the winds stilled and the waves calmed. On that towering stone pagoda on Baogai Mountain stood two beautiful young maidens. They stared intently at the tempestuous ocean. They seemed to be watching their relative who had been separated from his native home. They seemed to be glaring at the unjust world!

From then on, the people of Qiao township in Minnan called this stone pagoda "Sisters-in-Law Pagoda."

(Story collected by Li Canhuang)

WIDOWS' PAGODA

In this tale, the women decide to build a pagoda to serve as a lighthouse for boats returning to port. One of the women organizes the others to save and collect money for this project. They hire stone-cutters to undertake the construction. When the pagoda is completed, they take turns each evening lighting the lamp at the top. The women of this story are portrayed as extremely capable and determined.

The port of Shangjing lies at the northern part of Xinghua Bay in Fujian. Southeast of Shangjing a small rocky mountain extends into the sea. This small mountain is like the huge legendary turtle squatting on the beach. It seems that it need only stretch out its neck to create waves. It is called Turtle Peak. On the back of Turtle Peak towers a seven-story pagoda of granite. On the lintel are engraved the four characters: "Turtle River's Precious Pagoda." People also call it "Widows' Pagoda."

Three hundred years ago, the Shangjing wharf bustled with activity. An endless stream of vessels called here. To the south lay Southeast Asia, while to the north was the Tianjin garrison. In fact, this was an important port in Fuqing County. Eighteen families named Lin cooperated to construct a large, three-masted sailboat. Every spring, the men of these eighteen families loaded it with silks from Hangzhou and Suzhou, medicines and red tangerines from the Min River area, and longans from Xinghua, and crossed the ocean to engage in trade in Southeast Asia. Then they loaded up the local Southeast Asian products and returned in the twelfth lunar month to celebrate the New Year. They left in the spring and returned in the winter. The women of the eighteen families passed year after year worrying and

236

waiting to be happily reunited with them.

One year, just a month before Spring Festival, it was the time when the men should be returning. The sisters-in-law and aunties were really happy. They spent all the money they had saved by cultivating vegetables, catching fish, and weaving cloth. They wanted to give their menfolk more clothing, and they wanted to buy food especially for them.

It was the time when they should be returning. How could it be that their loved ones hadn't yet come home? Among the women was a young daughter-in-law who was virtuous, kind, and beautiful. Her family name was Ou. People called her Elder Sister Ou. Elder Sister Ou's husband Achun was the boat captain. The two had been married for a long time, but they were still as affectionate as newlyweds. These days, Elder Sister Ou often counted on her fingers to figure out what day Achun would return. She often ran to the top of Turtle Peak to gaze out, lost in thought, at the boundless ocean. Gradually, the other seventeen elder sisters-in-law and younger daughters-in-law also climbed Turtle Peak and looked out in search of their loved ones.

One day near evening, a very strong wind blew in from the southeast, and the ocean was shrouded in fog. Someone said that this mid-winter southeast wind was because of the year of Kongming. After fire burned the Red Cliff, they'd totally forgotten to give the southeast wind back to the god.[33] Looking at the thick fog above the ocean and facing the wind shouting in their faces, Elder Sister Ou felt tired beyond endurance! This strong a wind, this thick a fog: Could Achun hold the boat steady? Could he recognize the village he set out from? The next day as it became dark, several fishing boats arrived from Wheat Island and Cucumber Island. The fishermen said that last night when the sky was black with fog a large three-masted sailboat sailed to just outside Shangjing port. It couldn't distinguish directions, and had turned out again. As a result, it had struck a reef near Cucumber Island, and the boat had been smashed to bits. The people died, the goods disappeared: That was tragedy enough! Elder Sister Ou and the other women listened. Their hearts numbed. It couldn't be. They hoped it wasn't the boat of Achun and the others! Without a thorough investigation, Elder Sister Ou and the others always felt their hearts were dangling! So they went to the fishing boats to ask questions, but the fishermen couldn't say, either, where this boat was from.

That night, the lamps of these eighteen families remained lighted until dawn. No one could sleep. Just as the sky grew light, Elder Sister Ou and the other women climbed to the top of Turtle Peak. They stared at the place in the southeast where the boundless ocean and the sky met. They needed only a black dot to appear at the edge of the sky—and that would be enough to make everyone happy for a long time. When this black dot gradually enlarged, they saw that it was a fishing boat from another place and they were numb again. Just in this way, in worry and waiting, they passed day after day.

The third day was the one of the full moon and the high tide. The tidewater rolled and rumbled, slapping the reefs and setting off *huala-huala* answer. Elder Sister Ou and the others all gazed out, but they still didn't see the shadows of their loved ones. The tidewater swept in several pieces of broken wooden boards. Everyone went to look. They were the flooring from the boat. The tidewater also swept in a part of the hull. Someone said it looked as though it was from their own boat. When they looked more closely, they saw that the red lacquer was still on it! Elder Sister Ou didn't want to believe this evidence. She said, "Where is there any boat without flooring? What side of a boat *isn't* lacquered red?" The ocean tide also brought in a wooden box. Elder Sister Ou looked and looked and became numb. Ah, wasn't that Achun's wooden box? She herself had painted that red peony on the lid.

Elder Sister Ou wept. The seventeen others also began shedding tears in unison. Elder Sister Ou wept until she fainted. The other seventeen women were also paralyzed from weeping. They didn't know how much time passed, nor did they know how many tears they shed before some of the older aunties finally recovered their senses. They had been weeping big tears and crying in desperation, but they had made a mighty effort to bear the grief. They consoled Elder Sister Ou, Little Sister Chen, and Auntie Wang, and several other young daughters-in-

law. Everyone supported each other, and they staggered home
by turns. That night, the birds of the village didn't sing and
the dogs didn't bark. They only listened to the sound of the
women weeping.

After several days, a commercial boat from the next village
returned. They said that Achun's boat had started back earlier.
So everyone was sure something had happened to it. They all
blamed the fog. But Elder Sister Ou didn't believe this. She
said that Achun's eyes were so clear: How could he be afraid
of the fog! Everyone damned the storm, but Elder Sister Ou
didn't believe this. She said, "Achun's arms were so strong:
How would he be unable to control the storm!" As before, every
day, she stood on the top of Turtle Peak and gazed out, staring
until her pupils were ash-gray and her eyes red, but still she
didn't see Achun's shadow. People said that Elder Sister Ou
was crazy, that her soul was following Achun.

Staring and staring—one day, two days, three days. Staring
and staring—one month, two months, three months. In the end,
Elder Sister Ou woke up: Achun couldn't come back again!
Elder Sister Ou still went up Turtle Peak every day and sat on
the top of Turtle Peak. Staring blankly out at the spray, she
felt that innumerable boats were arriving on the ocean, and
that Achun was standing on each one of them. It was as if she
saw Achun thrusting out his shoulders and shouting, "My home
village—where are you?"

Elder Sister Ou understood: She must erect a sign here to let
loved ones sailing back in the fog and blackness from distant
places distinguish the village they'd set out from. At night, Elder
Sister Ou dumped out the ounces of silver from the pottery jar,
and counted it and recounted it. In the daytime, she donned
mourning clothes and hurried from home to home. She led the
eighteen suffering sisters to Turtle Peak, where she said, "That
day, Achun and the others' boat had reached the gateway to
their home. It was just because of the fog and the blackness
that they couldn't distinguish the village they set out from, and
only then did something go wrong. Although *they* can't return,
people here can't stop going to Southeast Asia. We mustn't let
these later ones meet that kind of misfortune!"

239

"Elder Sister Ou, tell us, what can we do?"

"We'll build a pagoda here and light a lamp at night. Then boats returning from afar can always see their home village!"

"Constructing a pagoda costs a lot of money!"

"I saved ten ounces of silver to buy clothes for Achun. Now I'll donate it! If we sisters all donate money, and also collect from our village and the neighboring villages, all we need is good faith. How can we think we can't construct a pagoda!"

So, the eighteen widows donated their own savings, and also solicited contributions from the neighboring villages. Before long, they had collected enough money to construct the pagoda. Elder Sister Ou and the others engaged stone-cutters from Huian, and the young men and women from all the neighboring villages brought along dry rations and hurried to do the work. In less than a year, they had constructed a seven-story pagoda eight or nine hundred feet high. From then on, even in wind and rain, the eighteen widows went up to the pagoda every night to light the lamp.

One night, there was a violent storm. It was Elder Sister Ou's turn to go and light the lamp. The others all said, "In such a strong wind and rain, will any boat come to port?"

Elder Sister Ou said, "No. The stronger the wind, the fiercer the rain, the blacker the night, the more boats will come into port to get away from the wind, and the easier it is for something to go wrong." Taking up the lamp and risking wind and rain, she went up Turtle Peak. The others all went along. Elder Sister Ou carried the lamp up one flight after another of the stone steps, and exerted a lot of energy before finally reaching the bottle-gourd point at the top of the pagoda. Placing the lamp on the shelf in the bottle-gourd point, she lashed it securely with silk twine. The gale was rolling up huge waves, and slapping the huge reefs below Turtle Peak—echoing in a frightening way. Standing at the top of the pagoda, Elder Sister Ou gazed out at the ocean. Far away on the ocean, a little light pulsated on the tips of the waves. She knew that it was a boat coming into the port, and she turned up the wick of the lamp, and then began her step-by-step descent. At this time, a strong wind blew in, blowing Elder Sister Ou around like a flying bird. She drifted lightly down into the ocean.

Little Sister Chen and Auntie Wang saw this, and shouted miserably, "Elder Sister Ou, Elder Sister Ou!"

The Old God of the Heaven saw this, and shouted angrily, "*Honglonglong.*" The Wind God was frightened and quietly slipped away. The Rain Uncle grew nervous, and slowly and calmly retreated. In the boundless ocean, two white seagulls were moving toward the wind and waves—and leading that boat safely into port. From then on, this pair of white gulls flew around, over and below the precious pagoda, doing a fluttering dance. Someone said that these were the reincarnations of Elder Sister Ou and Achun. The fluttering of the white gulls drew the boats home. The sound of the tide called to the loved ones. From then on, when travelers neared Shangjing port, they saw this precious Turtle River pagoda towering high—and, in their hearts, they felt a special closeness, as if the loved ones of their home villages were beckoning them. As soon as a boat entered the port, a pair of white gulls—dipping and soaring—circled the boat. They felt that Elder Sister Ou and Achun were solicitously guiding them.

(Story collected by Ming Qi and Meng Yu)

THE GOOD FORTUNE OF THREE FAMILIES

In this story, the relationships between women and men are depicted as relatively equal. Moreover, it is generally the women who proffer advice to the men—and the men follow the advice.

Formerly, a peasant named Shi Pan lived in Kuzhu Village on the bank of Qingshui River in Minnan. Because he was unable to repay his rent debt to the landlord, he was forced to sell the land and go to Southeast Asia to look for work. He had only an old father and a young wife. These several years, Shi Pan hadn't sent any money home, and no news had come from him all this time. The family still had to borrow in order to live.

One winter, Shi Pan sent word that he would return home at the end of the year. But, day after day, no one saw Shi Pan come home. On New Year's Eve, the creditor came to the door, and Shi Pan's father told his daughter-in-law to go out and ask for news of his son. On the road, Shi Pan's wife heard people say that a foreign boat had hit a reef outside the harbor and sunk. Shi Pan had been lost. After hearing this, her heart hurt as if cut by a knife. Thinking of her husband dying tragically, of her old and ill father-in-law, and of the debt that couldn't be paid, she didn't have the courage to go on living. She walked unsteadily through Kuzhu forest, and came to Qingshui River, and was about to jump in and commit suicide.

But, as luck would have it, just then a teacher walked up on the bridgehead. He was named Su Yi. He taught in another village, and was just on his way home for the New Year. Suddenly he saw that his neighbor Shi Pan's wife was about to jump into the river and commit suicide. He immediately ran across and pulled her back. He asked her why she wanted to die. Shi Pan's wife wept as she told him the situation. Su Yi was so sad at hearing this that he shed tears, and immediately came up with a way to save them. He said, "Shi Pan certainly didn't die. The day before yesterday, he entrusted someone to bring you a letter. The person couldn't find your home, so he brought it to my home. I was just on my way to inform you. It's lucky I ran into you." After hearing this, Shi Pan's wife calmed down, and hastily said, "If there's a letter, then that's fine. But the end of this year is certainly a difficult one to get through! Did he send money?" Su Yi thought to himself, "If you're going to help people, then don't stop halfway." So he said, "Yes, yes. But you'll have to go to the city to get it. I'm afraid there won't be time to do it by New Year's. But I have some money with me. You—you take this first and use it. After you get your money, you can repay me!" Shi Pan's wife accepted the money, and left after thanking him repeatedly.

Su Yi had done a good deed. With a joyful heart, he walked on a little way. Only then did it occur to him that he had given Shi Pan's wife all the tuition money that he had just received. His wife was waiting at home for this money for the New Year. How could he go home with empty hands? After thinking a while, he consoled himself: "A gentleman can be generous in aiding needy people. Sacrificing one's own interests for the sake of others is really important." Relieved, he took long strides home. Because he'd walked so far, he was unbearably hungry. When he went in the door, he couldn't say anything. His wife asked him what the trouble was. Pointing to his stomach, he said, "Hungry!" She asked him for money to buy rice. He rested a long time before he spoke of what had happened on the road. His wife grumbled, "This is a fine thing! For the New Year, our family will have to drink the northwest wind!" Earlier, the Su family had had no rice to put into the pot, and had been waiting for Su Yi to collect the tuition. Who would have guessed that this would come to nothing?

Su Yi admonished his wife, "We did a good deed, and saved the family of Shi Pan's wife. If we go hungry a few days, it doesn't matter. On the fifth day of the first month, I'll go to the school and figure something out." His wife asked him, "How will we manage at New Year's?"

"We'll think of something! If we think of nothing, we'll just eat a little less. If there still isn't anything, plain water can also satisfy hunger!" Su Yi said firmly.

Su Yi and his wife at first thought they would borrow a little money for the New Year, but whom could they ask on New Year's Eve? They considered pawning some things, but they couldn't find anything of value in their home. His wife thought a while and then said to him, "Go to the Shi home, and get a little money from Shi Pan's wife and bring it back." But Su Yi dismissed this idea: "Getting money from them could mean death for Shi Pan's wife and father." Later, his wife thought of another not very satisfactory alternative, and told Su Yi to go to a garden and dig up some yams to satisfy their hunger. Su Yi felt this would be very embarrassing. He said angrily, "If I am worthy of the name teacher, how can I be a thief?" His wife said, "There's nothing else to do. If you won't go and dig up yams, then we must go hungry at New Year's." These words stabbed Su Yi's ears, and he thought to himself, "Because of saving others' lives, I have no alternative but to steal yams to fill the stomach. Although I'll lose face, still it is reasonable." But then he thought again: he would never have face if he stole. He turned it over and over, but he couldn't come up with an alternative. Finally, as his wife continued nagging him, all he could do was steel himself, pick up the bamboo basket, and go out.

In one farm household lived Lin Jie and his widowed mother, the Woman Liu. Mother and son were hard-working. They grew a lot of yams in their garden. It was the end of the year—New Year's Eve—and they were afraid people would steal their yams. Every night, Lin Jie guarded the garden with a bamboo pole. After eating the New Year's meal that day, Lin Jie said to his mother, "I'm going to the garden to look around and I'll be right back." As he was about to go, his mother exhorted him, "If people are stealing, just forget it. Those who come out and steal on New Year's Eve are all poor suffering people!"

Su Yi—with racing heart and trembling feet—groped his way

along the road. He walked to Lin Jie's yam garden, and felt conscience-stricken. He wavered a long time and still he didn't want to steal. Turning around, he saw a local god temple. It was as if he saw the saying, "If you have a request, it must be answered." He walked into the local god temple and prayed: "I, Su Yi, am far from being greedy. It's just because Shi Pan's family is poor and his wife wanted to jump into the water and die. In order to save his family's lives, I gave her all the year's tuition I had struggled so hard for. Now my own family has no rice tonight for the New Year, so I had to come and beg a few yams to satisfy our hunger. If you agree, bless and protect me so that I won't be seen. Just give me one 'sacred sign.'" After saying this, he felt on the floor for a pair of wooden divination blocks.

As it happened, Lin Jie heard these words from his hiding place in the corner. He very much respected Su Yi, and stretched out his hand to quietly help him form a sun and moon pattern from the wooden blocks. This was "the sacred sign." After Su Yi saw this, he went to dig up yams. Lin Jie followed him out, and in the dark he secretly helped him fill the basket. So, very quickly, Su Yi had dug up a basket full of yams. He picked it up and hurried home with it.

Lin Jie went home and told his mother of Su Yi stealing the yams. His mother said in amazement, "You're talking nonsense. How could a teacher do this sort of thing?" Lin Jie said, "You don't believe it? I also helped him fill up the basket!" The Widow Liu said, "Perhaps his wife is sick and wanted to eat yam soup!" Lin Jie said, "No!" Then he told the story in great detail. The Widow Liu listened, and praised her son for doing the right thing. She also told him not to speak of Su Yi stealing the yams. At the same time, she prepared some things to give to Su Yi for the New Year.

When Shi Pan's wife received the good news and money from Su Yi, she and her father-in-law had a happy New Year. On New Year's morning, her father-in-law told her to go and wish Su Yi a Happy New Year, and to pick up Shi Pan's letter at the same time.

Shi Pan's wife hadn't been gone long when Shi Pan arrived.

He had been in Southeast Asia several years. Illness had prevented him from sending money home. Only because of a friend's help was he able to come home to visit, but he'd missed the boat and hadn't been able to get back for the New Year. His father said, "Su Yi has already given us the money you sent." Bewildered, Shi Pan took his father with him to see Su.

On New Year's morning, Su Yi and his wife were eating yams when they heard Lin Jie's shout at the door. Frightened, they quickly gathered up the not-yet-eaten yams. When they opened the door, they saw that it was the mother and son wishing them a happy New Year and giving them many gifts. Su Yi and his wife politely refused them. They said they had plenty to eat. Lin Jie said candidly, "Teacher Su, I heard everything you said in the local god temple!" Su Yi and his wife were very embarrassed. The Widow Liu said, "We know you are good people! So we have brought these things especially for you."

Just then, Shi Pan's wife also arrived and wished Su Yi and his wife a happy New Year. She said, "Teacher Su! It is especially to wish you a happy New Year and to thank you that I came. And by the way, to pick up the letter Shi Pan sent."

Su Yi stammered, "Ah! You want the letter . . . letter?"

"What happened to it?" Shi Pan's wife asked worriedly.

Su Yi thought he'd write a fake letter. He said, "I have it. I have it. Sit down for a while. I'll go and get it!"

Su Yi had just gone out the door when he saw Shi Pan and his father walking up in the distance. Overjoyed, Su Yi ran back into the house and said: "He's come, he's come. Look! Isn't that Shi Pan coming?"

Shi Pan went in and wished everyone a happy New Year. Su Yi said happily, "I knew long ago that Shi Pan would come back."

After everyone had talked for a while Shi Pan's father asked Su Yi, "Teacher Su, that twelve ounces of silver you gave our family the other day: Who in fact entrusted you with this silver?"

Shi Pan said, "Maybe Teacher Su made a mistake?"

Lin Jie spoke first, "I know about this." And then he told

the story from beginning to end. When the Shi family heard this, they were even more grateful for Su Yi's compassion and virtue. Su Yi said, "I should thank Lin Jie and his mother!" The three families thanked each other, and wished each other a happy New Year and good fortune. They were jubilant. When the villagers heard of this, they all said that they were "three families of good fortune."

(Story collected by Xie Jiaqun)

THE SEVEN-*JIN* BRICK

*In this tale, we observe three women. The daughter-in-law is
unfilial and cruel to her mother-in-law. The young woman about
to marry the young man in the story learns of this cruelty and
devises a plot to convince the vicious daughter-in-law to change
her ways. Elements of the traditional inhere in this story, but
the young woman is also clearly intelligent and capable.*

Formerly there was a family of three—the grandmother, the
daughter-in-law, and the grandson.

This daughter-in-law was very sly. When her husband died
prematurely, she resentfully blamed her mother-in-law, and
heaped abuse on her: "Old evil mother-in-law, you heart is
poisonous. You gave birth to a son who would die young and
make me endure the suffering of widowhood." The old woman
was suffering but she didn't dare voice it. She just shed her
tears in secret. She used all her energy to rear her grandson—
striving for the hope of the future. Who would have guessed
that the sly daughter-in-law had still another complaint? "The
old one doesn't die. She has an evil, poisonous heart. She wants
to incite the grandson to sow discord between mother and son."

The grandmother suffered and served her daughter-in-law,
but she could never turn her sly daughter-in-law's expression
to smiles. The grandmother boiled rice—and boiled it thick.
The other one cursed: "Old evil mother-in-law, do you want
me to choke to death?" If she boiled a thin gruel, the other
one also swore: "Old evil mother-in-law, do you want me to
starve to death?" If it was undercooked, she cursed: "Old dog
of a mother, do you want to stab my intestines and stomach?"
If it was overcooked, she also cursed: "Old dog of a mother, do

you want to paste together my intestines and stomach?" The whole day, not only did she curse her whenever she felt like it, but she also readied a two-foot-long wooden club. When she got angry, she beat the old woman with abandon. Beating her wasn't enough. She also took her bowl and chopsticks away and forced her to cope with hunger. This sort of sly, savage, vicious woman: You could look all over the world, and there was only one of them. There weren't two.

The old woman's tears mingled with her food. One day of suffering followed another. With difficulty, she endured it until the grandson grew up. Finally, it was the day of her grandson's marriage. The suffering would soon be over. It never occurred to her that this would not be a happy event. The sly daughter-in-law told her mother-in-law to boil green beans and prepare to make red rice dumplings.[34] The weather that day was very cold, and the old woman hadn't eaten enough at breakfast. Cold and hungry, she fainted at the stove. And so the green beans boiled until they were scorched.

The sly daughter-in-law smelled the scorched food, and shouted curses from the other room: "Old dog of a mother, you should die! Old evil mother-in-law, you have no life. . . ."

At this time, the mother-in-law regained consciousness. The green beans had already burned to black ashes. Trembling with fear, she immediately ran out the door. The sly daughter-in-law cursed her way into the kitchen, but no one was there. She was extremely angry. She pulled a five-*jin* brick down from the stove, and went in pursuit.

One was crying and running ahead; the other was cursing and pursuing in the rear.

The chase reached the side of the stream outside the village. The old grandmother saw that the road had ended. Thinking of her daughter-in-law's cruelty, she jumped into the water— *putong*—and committed suicide. When the sly daughter-in-law got there, she only saw spray rising in the stream. Throwing the five-*jin* brick across, she cursed all the way home.

But the grandmother hadn't drowned. After swallowing some water, she floated up again and was dragged out and saved by a woman washing vegetables. As luck would have it, this woman was her grandson's mother-in-law.

The grandson's bride-to-be was named Xiuying. She was beautiful, intelligent, and good-hearted. When the old grandmother finished telling of her experience, the girl immediately removed her pearl head ornaments and her red dress, and said, "An unfilial daughter-in-law becomes even more poisonous— even more evil—as a mother-in-law. Who wants to marry into such a family, and give up life and endure suffering!"

This worried her mother greatly. The sedan chair was about to come and pick her up. How, at this time, could the wedding be canceled and the relationship ended! She coaxed and pleaded with her daughter. "Looking at my pitiful daughter, it's hard for me to be an upright person. This affects the whole family's reputation. Today is the wedding day. You can't not marry!" The old grandmother also spoke up for her grandson. Finally Xiuying turned tender-hearted. But she set three conditions: 1) the old grandmother would remain in her home, and no word of this would leak out; 2) she wouldn't take along her trousseau; and 3) she would take a three-foot-long club and a seven-*jin* brick with her. These three conditions weren't hard to arrange. Her mother thought and thought, and then agreed completely.

After the wedding, Xiuying thought of a plan. She talked it over with her husband until midnight. The next morning, the young husband and wife purposely slept until after 8:00.

The sly daughter-in-law ran over and knocked on the door. "You still haven't gotten up to boil the rice?"

From the bed, Xiuying asked, "Who boiled the rice before?"

"The old evil mother-in-law."

"Who is the mother-in-law now?"

"I. . . ." The sly daughter-in-law had nothing to say. She just boiled the rice. When she guessed the rice was almost ready, Xiuying got up, lifted the lid of the pot, filled a large bowl, and ate. Then she set her bowl down and asked, "Who washed the dishes before?"

"The old evil mother-in-law."

"Who is the mother-in-law now?"

"I. . . ." The sly daughter-in-law again had nothing to say.

251

She just washed the dishes. After a while, Xiuying took out the carrying pole and water buckets, and asked, "Who fetched the water before?"

"The old evil mother-in-law."

"Who is the mother-in-law now?"

"I. . . ." The sly daughter-in-law was panic-stricken. Laying aside the wooden club, she covered her face and cried, "The daughter-in-law is disobedient and unfilial. Heaven's thunder will come roaring, and heaven's fire will burn!" She wanted her son to come to her support. Instead, her son said, "If the upper beam isn't straight, the lower ones won't be straight, either. You set the example for her. She learned from you. What's wrong with that?"

The sly daughter-in-law was so ashamed she was angry. She shouted, "'One does evil, one does right.' You want to force me to jump into the well!" Her mouth was yelling that she would die, but her rear end was planted firmly on the stool. She wanted to summon the neighbors to come and support her. How would she know that the neighbors all detested her? They just watched the excitement; they didn't intervene. Xiuying took out that seven-*jin* brick, and said, "Whatever is done comes around. If you jump into the water, I'll throw the brick!"

So, at last, the sly daughter-in-law was stung into awareness. Now she finally understood. When she had mistreated her mother, she had lost her conscience and hurt the old woman. She suddenly burst out crying, "A bitter vine forms bitter fruit. A slanted tree forms crooked forks. Blame me, not God. Don't blame my daughter-in-law for any of this."

Xiuying immediately said, "*Aiya*! One person's wrong doesn't mean that there should be two people's wrongs. One generation of crookedness doesn't mean that every generation will be crooked." She apologized. She changed out of her wedding dress, and fetched water, swept the floors, did the laundry, and ladled out the rice and respectfully gave it to her mother-in-law to eat.

So, the sly daughter-in-law was stung to even more awareness. She understood. If she had treated her mother-in-law this way, the whole family would have been really happy, and her mother-in-law would not have committed suicide. The more she thought about this, the sadder she was. She began to cry again, "My suffering mother-in-law, ah, my suffering mother-in-law. If you were still alive, you could curse me and beat me today. I'd be in pain, but I wouldn't dare moan!"

Xiuying saw that she was truly repentant. She happily returned to her mother's home to meet the old grandmother. And she also told people to carry her trousseau across the threshold. Then she clearly related everything from beginning to end to the sly daughter-in-law, and also said, "My mother said to give you this three-foot club and seven-*jin* brick. If in the future I dare to be unfilial and disrespectful, tell me to kneel on the brick and you can beat me with the club."

The sly daughter-in-law accepted the three-foot club and the seven-*jin* brick, and then gave them to the old grandmother and said, "If in the future your daughter-in-law dares to treat you badly, tell me to kneel on this brick and then beat me with this club."

The old grandmother accepted the two things. She looked and looked at her daughter-in-law, and then she looked and looked at her grandson's wife. She began to laugh. She snapped the three-foot club into two pieces and burned them in the stove, and slammed the seven-*jin* brick down until it splintered into pieces and threw them out the door. She didn't need them. She said happily, "None of us has any use for them!"

From then on, the family was united and at peace. There were no arguments, no fights. Love came from above. Respect for the aged came from below. They passed happy days.

(Story collected by Cai Huaren)

THE SILVER-NEEDLE LASS

Accomplishing a mission that her brothers are unable to complete, the young woman in this story saves her fellow villagers from drought and earns their gratitude. Granted, she receives supernatural aid, but so do her brothers—and she succeeds where they do not.

Among China's famous export teas, one kind is internationally known for being especially enjoyable: the white-haired silver-needle tea. This tea—pure white like silver—is shaped like fine embroidery needles. When you bring it to your lips to drink a little, your whole mouth is filled with fragrance gladdening the heart and refreshing the mind. It leaves a lingering, pleasant taste. This tea not only replaces the body fluid and quenches thirst, but it also cures the "great fire disease." So the local people always have some on hand to use as a home remedy.

This silver-needle tea grows in Zhenghe County in the mountainous district on the borders of Fujian and Zhejiang, and this legend comes from there.

It can't be said exactly when it was, but long ago in this bleak and desolate and remote area were scattered some farm families. As the saying went, the mountains were high and the emperor far away. With favorable weather, the mountain people could farm and weave. The tea was crude and the food plain, but the days were also without restraints.

But one year, the old god in Heaven suddenly became hostile. He didn't send down the spring rains, and he didn't drive away the summer winds. In the autumn, he also blew a hot dry wind into the area. This drought lasted for 360 days. The land dried out. The river dried up. Don't even speak of the harvest:

Even drinking water was hard to find. When you add in the illnesses on all sides, countless people died at this time. It was a real tragedy! Observing this situation, the older generation all said sadly, "The old god of Heaven wants to harvest the people of this mountainous region. Quickly! Run for your lives!" Some fled and some died. Most of those who stayed suffered from lingering diseases. In this mountainous area, you couldn't even hear a cock crowing.

It was hard to endure the days and months of suffering. Everyone hoped that a "lucky star" would descend and save the suffering people from disaster and resolve their troubles.

Just at this time, people began to say that, to the east, at cloud-covered, fog-shrouded Donggong Mountain, there was a dragon well. Beside the dragon well, several magic grasses grew. You only needed to gather the magic grasses, press out the grass juice, and, not only could you cure a hundred diseases, but also if you sprinkled the grass juice on the land, the land would be filled with water. And if you sprinkled it in the river, the river would flow with water. If you wanted to save the people of this mountainous region, you must go and gather these magic grasses!

So, some courageous young fellows filled their backpacks with dry provisions, and, facing in the direction of the sunrise, they set off in search of those magic grasses.

But the mountain people only saw people set out. They never saw anyone come back. It must be hard to find these magic grasses! The mountain people's hearts sank.

At that time, a certain family lived in Tieshankun. The parents had long been dead. There were only the three siblings who lived by farming and hunting. The elder brother was Zhigang. He was a spitfire of a guy: With one blow of an ax, he could chop down a hazelnut tree. The younger brother Zhicheng— although very gentle and quiet—was an excellent archer. The third one, the sister Zhiyu, had learned swordsmanship from her elder brother and archery from her second brother. She was an extraordinary lass.

One day, Zhigang took out his double-edged mandarin duck sword passed down through the generations, and said to his younger brother and sister, "To save the suffering villagers, I will overcome all obstacles to find those magic grasses at Donggong. You two stay at home and look after this double-edged sword. Take it out of its scabbard twice a day. If it becomes rusty, that means that I am no longer alive. At that time, you two must take my place in searching for the magic grasses." Then he took up his ax and hurried directly toward Donggong Mountain.

Zhigang walked and walked. He walked for thirty-six days, at last reaching the foot of Donggong Mountain. He tightened the laces of his straw sandals. Just as he was about to climb the mountain, he suddenly saw a white-haired, silver-bearded old grandfather who shouted and stopped him, "Brave young fellow, do you mean to go up the mountain and gather the magic grasses?"

"That's right, Old Grandfather. If I can't gather the magic grasses, the villagers can't go on living," Zhigang replied.

Pointing to the mountaintop enveloped in clouds and fog, the old grandfather said, "Young fellow, just look. The magic grasses grow up above. If you climb up, you must remember: You can only go ahead. You cannot look back. The moment you look back, you'll have no more chance to gather the magic grasses."

Zhigang nodded his head. He was about to thank the old grandfather, but when he looked around, the old man had disappeared.

With just one breath, Zhigang climbed to the halfway point of the mountain. All that met his eyes were jumbled rocks, each taller than a person. The gloom was terrifying. Every time he took a step, strange sounds came from behind him. At first, he bore in mind the old grandfather's words: Just go ahead. But when he was almost out of the area of jumbled rocks, he suddenly heard from behind him an explosive, thunderous shout: "Gutsy Zhigang, you still dare to rush ahead!"

Zhigang felt numb. He thought someone was blocking him. For a moment, he forgot the old grandfather's words—and turned to look back. If he saw nothing he would just forget it. But as soon as he looked around, he was immediately changed into a large new rock.

That day, Zhicheng and his little sister suddenly noticed that the double-edged mandarin duck sword had lost its gleam and had become rusty. They turned pale in alarm. They knew that their elder brother was no longer alive, and they then decided that they would take their brother's place in searching for the magic grasses.

The next day, Zhicheng gave some iron arrows to his little sister Zhiyu. He said, "I'm going to Donggong Mountain in search of the magic grasses. If these arrows turn rusty, then the task of finding the magic grasses has passed to you." Then Zhicheng slung his bow and arrows over his shoulder and left.

Zhicheng walked and walked. He walked for forty-nine days, at last reaching the foot of Donggong Mountain. He was gasping for breath. Without even pausing to tighten the laces of his straw sandals, he immediately set out to climb the mountain. Just then, a white-haired, silver-bearded old grandfather stopped him.

"Brave young fellow, do you really want to climb the mountain to gather the magic grasses?" the old man asked.

"That's right. My elder brother went up the mountain to gather the magic grasses to save the villagers. But he hasn't yet returned. This time—no matter what—I must bring the magic grasses back," Zhicheng replied respectfully.

Pointing again at the mountain peak enveloped in clouds and fog, the old grandfather said, "Young fellow, look: The magic grasses grow up there. You must remember: You can only go forward. You simply must not look back. If you do, there'll be no way you can gather the magic grasses." When he had said this, the old grandfather disappeared.

Zhicheng climbed and climbed. He climbed to the halfway point on the mountain, but he saw that the mountain was covered with a jumble of rocks. Cold air assaulted him. The farther up he walked, the more he felt that the gloom was terrifying. But he summoned his courage and continued up. Just then, all kinds of furious cursing sounds came from all directions behind him, but he remembered the exhortations of the old white-haired grandfather. He didn't look back. He saw that he needed only to climb over the mound of jumbled rocks. Suddenly, he

257

heard his elder brother Zhigang's voice booming out, "Younger brother Zhicheng, younger brother Zhicheng, come quickly and save me!"

Zhicheng couldn't bear it any longer. He turned his head to take a quick look. And because of this, he was also immediately turned into a large rock, and was firmly implanted on that mound of jumbled rocks.

Hoping that her second brother would soon come home, his little sister Zhiyu suddenly noticed that her brother's arrows were full of traces of rust stains—and she knew that her second brother had also met with calamity. She couldn't help but shed tears of sorrow. But she was a strong-willed, firmly determined lass. When she recalled the exhortations of her two elder brothers, she knew that now the important responsibility of gathering the magic grasses and saving the villagers had fallen to her shoulders. Even if there were a thousand difficulties and ten thousand dangers, she must bring back the magic grasses!

The next day, Zhiyu took up a sword and shouldered a bow, took her leave of the crowd of villagers, and rushed directly toward Donggong Mountain.

Zhiyu walked and walked. Because she was after all a girl, altogether she walked eighty-one days before reaching the foot of Donggong Mountain. In her heart, she was determined to gather some magic grasses rather quickly and then go back and save the villagers. So she didn't even stop to take a breath, and was about to start climbing the mountain. Just then, she suddenly saw an old white-haired, silver-bearded grandfather sitting at the roadside, tending a fire and roasting rice cakes. So she went over and respectfully asked him, "Old Grandfather, could you please tell me whether this path goes to the mountaintop?"

It was as though the old man hadn't heard—as though he hadn't even seen her. He just concentrated on roasting his rice cakes.

Zhiyu saw that the old man was ignoring her, but she didn't think this was at all strange. She just sat down and, while helping the old man light the fire, she asked respectfully, "Old

Grandfather, could you please tell me: Is there a dragon well on top of this mountain?"

Only then did the old man lift his head and stare at her.

"Young lass, do you mean to go up the mountain to gather the magic grasses?"

"That's right. I'm risking my life to save the villagers of our mountainous area. I must take the magic grasses back!" the girl answered.

"What a fine lass!" The old man was very happy when he heard this. Pointing to the mountaintop, he said to Zhiyu, "Look. That place covered with clouds and fog: That is Dragon Well. Three stalks of magic grass grow next to Dragon Well. But you must remember: No matter what you hear on the mountain, you absolutely must not turn around."

"Thank you, Old Grandfather. I'll remember."

"Also"—the old man restrained the lass and exhorted her again—"next to that Dragon Well, a small black dragon guards the magic grasses day and night. After you reach the mountaintop, first you must blind the black dragon's eyes with your arrows, and then go and gather the leaves and shoots of the magic grasses. After that, sprinkle Dragon Well water on the magic grasses. The magic grasses will then immediately blossom and form seeds. When you take the seeds back home, scatter them on the mountain slopes and they will grow. Boil soup from the prickly shoots. Drinking that soup can cure a hundred illnesses. Sprinkle the grass juice on the fields, and the fields will fill with water. Sprinkle it in the river, and the river water will flow. And then don't be afraid anymore that Old Heaven will not send the rains down."

The lass thanked the old man and was about to climb the mountain when the old man exhorted her again, "Remember: When you come down the mountain, be sure to sprinkle one drop of magic grass juice on each large rock in the mound of jumbled rocks." As he was speaking, he casually picked up a rice cake and pressed it on the lass: "Take this with you. It will be useful to you."

Accepting the rice cake, she made a deep bow to the old man. When she straightened up, he had disappeared.

The lass climbed up the mound of jumbled rocks. From behind her she heard an endless stream of all kinds of furious, cursing voices, but she didn't pay any attention to them. She continued climbing. Then, from behind her, she heard a lot of desolate weeping. She was terrified, but she still didn't look back. As before, she summoned her courage and climbed up. When she had almost finished crossing the mound of jumbled rocks, she suddenly heard from behind her the sound of her elder brother Zhigang calling to her to save his life. Her heart was moved; her footsteps slowed. But she composed herself and continued climbing. Just then, the lass also heard behind her the voice of her second brother shouting to her. This time, she was even more confused, and her footsteps stopped. But she steadfastly remembered the white-haired grandfather's exhortations. And she thought of the suffering villagers who were hoping that she would bring back the magic grasses. So, in the end, she didn't look back. The lass put her hand to her fluttering heart. And her hand made contact with a soft ball at her breast.

"Rice cake!" The lass suddenly had an idea. She quickly pinched off a small piece from that rice cake that the white-haired grandfather had given her. She rubbed it into two balls, and pressed them into her ears. This was really effective: Now she couldn't hear any sound at all. Bracing herself, she climbed over the mound of jumbled rocks and walked directly toward that place at the mountaintop enveloped in clouds and fog.

As expected, when she reached the mountaintop, she saw a small black dragon rushing at her with bared fangs and brandished claws. She hurriedly drew her bow and arrows. Shooting two arrows in succession, she blinded the black dragon in both eyes. In a moment, he had been transformed into a wisp of black air and had drifted off toward the Western Paradise.

The lass took up the sword and hurried directly to the edge of Dragon Well. In accord with the white-haired grandfather's exhortations, she quickly gathered the leaves and shoots of the magic grasses, and then scooped up some Dragon Well water and sprinkled it on the magic grasses. As expected, in just a second, those magic grasses blossomed and formed seeds. The lass packed up the seeds she gathered, gathered some more leaves and shoots, and began the descent. On the mound of jumbled rocks, again following the white-haired grandfather's instructions, she squeezed out the juice from a blade of magic grass, and sprinkled one drop on each large rock. It was really strange: As soon as the grass juice was sprinkled on a rock, that rock immediately turned into a person. Among them were her own two elder brothers! Those people were all young fellows who had gone up the mountain to gather magic grasses and had met with disaster.

Zhiyu and her elder brothers and their companions returned to their village. Even though it was night, they scattered the seeds from the magic grasses on the mountain slopes. At dawn the next morning, magic grasses half as tall as a person were growing all over the mountain wilds. Everyone immediately picked grass shoots still heavy with dew. Some boiled soup for the sick. As expected, as soon as they drank it, the illness was cured. Some pressed out the juice and poured it on the land. As expected, as soon as it was sprinkled on the land, the land filled with water. In this way, the people of the mountainous area were saved—and the farmland could also grow crops. Year after year, those magic grasses became more and more abundant.

Public spirit on the mountain was good. People thought: Poor suffering people in other areas also had trouble averting numerous adversities and calamities. So, every year, they gathered those magic grass shoots and dried them in the air and distributed them to the poor, suffering brothers of nearby villages. In this way, the reputation of the magic grasses spread everywhere. Also, since these grass shoots had been dried out in the air, they were covered with soft white hair. Each one was just like a silver needle. People called these shoots "silver needles." It is said that this is the origin of the famous present-day white-haired silver-needle tea.

Everyone remembers with gratitude that the lass Zhiyu went through all kinds of hardship to gather the silver-needle magic grasses for the people, and that she saved the impoverished villagers of the mountainous area, so they all affectionately call her "the silver-needle lass." They also say, "Our 'silver-needle lass' is the 'lucky star' who—on behalf of everyone—reversed our fortune and resolved our difficulties."

(Story collected by Xiong Yuanquan)

THE GODDESS OF THE SOUTHERN OCEAN

These stories tell of the extraordinary efficacy of the Goddess Mazu. Believed to have lived from 960 to 987, the young woman— known in her lifetime as Lin Moniang—was endowed with supernatural talents. She used these powers especially to protect those who went out to sea. Over the ensuing centuries, the common folk and high officials alike have entreated her to lend her protection to them. Upon their safe return from voyages, some officials petitioned the throne to give her titles and bestow plaques on her as expressions of their gratitude. Over the centuries, too, countless temples have been built to her, not only in China but also in Hong Kong, Macao, Taiwan, and various other parts of Asia. Her image is a familiar one to most Chinese who live near the ocean or near rivers. And, even today, many people trust in her and seek her assistance.

– 1 –

Legend has it that long ago, in the southeast coastal region, sea demons stirred up the winds and the waves. A lot of unfortunate people died in calamities at sea, and their complaints of suffering reached the heavens. The Woman Wang, wife of the official Lin Weiyi, accompanied the ordinary people every day to light incense and pray to the Buddha. At last, she touched a responsive chord in the compassionate Guanyin Bodhisattva, the goddess of mercy.

One night, when the Woman Wang was lighting incense, she suddenly began to yawn and fell sound asleep in her chair. In her dreams, rosy clouds seemed to fill the heavens. Walking on a lotus flower, Guanyin was slowly approaching. She said compassionately, "Your family has done good works and accumulated virtue. Today I am giving you a special pill so that you can conceive." After saying this, she quickly floated away. When the Woman Wang awakened, her belly hurt. Two or three months later, when she felt nauseated, she knew she was pregnant.

On the twenty-third day of the third month of the first year of Song Taizu's reign [960], the Woman Wang's belly shook. The pain was unbearable. She thought to herself, "I've already had one son and five daughters. Never have I experienced this kind of difficulty. This baby must indeed be extraordinary." So she grit her teeth to keep from moaning and just let the baby stir restlessly. Suddenly, a ray of red shone into the room. Rays of light shot in all directions inside the house. A fragrance filled the air. All around came rumbling sounds, like the rolling of spring thunder. Just at this moment, the Woman Wang gave birth to a daughter.

This infant neither cried nor wailed. For a full month, she was absolutely silent. So the Woman Wang named her Moniang— Silent Girl.

– 2 –

Even as a child, Moniang was clever and bright. The Woman Wang doted on her. The Woman Wang taught her reading and etiquette. She taught her to chant the Buddhist sutras. She frequently also took her to the Guanyin pavilion to gaze out at the sea, and to view and admire the heavenly bodies. By the time she was six or seven, Moniang could distinguish the constellations. She could also tell countless strange stories. Her whole family—especially her father, who was an official—thought this was very odd. By the time she was fifteen or sixteen, Moniang had already become a perfectly beautiful young woman.

That year, in the southeast coastal region, drought and flood followed in succession. The dangers at sea were incessant. Moniang often reflected that if she could only resolve the hardships for the people, she wouldn't hesitate even if it meant facing a mountain of swords and a sea of flames.

One day, Moniang went alone to the garden, where she walked to the edge of the well. Looking into it, she saw the well water reflecting her own beautiful face. Suddenly from the well came the music of immortals, followed by a group of immortal officials slowly emerging from the well. In the leader's hand was a small brocaded box, which he placed in front of Moniang. Then he floated off into the air. Moniang thought it was strange. Summoning her courage, she opened the box. Inside was a pair of copper charms sparkling brightly. On them were engraved numerous closely-written characters. Guanyin was bestowing these magic weapons on her to quell the demons and resolve the people's difficulties. Moniang was truly delighted. Following the techniques indicated by the characters for "auspicious," "ominous," "calamitous," and "fortunate," she experimented several times. As expected, they worked.

At that time, the places along the sea were suffering from pestilence. For several months there had been no rain. The drought was extremely serious. Day and night, Moniang diligently studied the copper charms. At last, she had mastered the technique of using this magic weapon. That very night, she wrote an incantation on a paper charm and posted it, summoning all the folk to come to the marsh and pick sweet flowers. She also shredded a paper incantation and, after simmering it with some water, she used it as medicine to drive off disease. Although the people were dubious, they nonetheless followed Moniang's instructions. As predicted, those who were ill all recovered. Before long, the pestilence had been totally wiped out. She also told the people to go to Zhou Mountain to excavate the spring, and combat the drought with its water. When the people did this, the clear gurgling spring became a brook—and the damage wrought by the drought ended. The crops were such that the people joyfully reaped a bumper harvest—and they all called Moniang "goddess."

– 3 –

When Moniang was sixteen, her father Lin Weiyi responded to an imperial edict to cross the sea with his son and go north to take up a position. Moniang saw them off. She took out the copper charms and spread them on the incense altar. As she was reading them intently, she suddenly became so alarmed that she went white. The sea demon was leading Thousand-*Li* Eyes and Smooth-Wind Ears to come in secret to stir up trouble on the sea at Meizhou Bay. They meant to capsize boats and carry the people off to eat them. Moniang had only two copper charms: She couldn't deal with three sea demons. What could she do? She immediately burned three tall sticks of incense and prayed three times before the image of Guanyin. Mumbling incantations, she entreated Guanyin to come and help in the battle. Then, along with the family servant, she sailed out in a small boat. She took along the copper charms and set off at top speed along the route her father had taken.

Braving the wind and the waves, Moniang stood at the prow of the boat and sailed straight for the sea. Suddenly, there was an enormous noise. Black clouds split open a path and created an opening, revealing the ferocious features of Thousand-*Li* Eyes and Smooth-Wind Ears. Oblivious of even her own safety, Moniang cast out the two copper charms. All that was heard were two shouts from the demons. Two streams of blood cascaded from the skies. Immediately, the wind calmed and the waves quieted. The day turned bright and sunny. Just as Moniang was feeling very happy, the sea demons once again came from behind and raised huge waves dashing against the heavens and relentlessly striking the small boat. An enormous wave hit the small boat and carried it more than a hundred feet away. The sea demons stood on the sea and swaggered around showing off their strength. Just as they were about to make more trouble, suddenly they saw colored ribbons fluttering in the sky and shouting, "That's wrong!" Frantically, they tried to escape, but they were captured by Golden Boy and Jade Girl. Earlier, when Guanyin received the incense burned by Moniang, she had known that Moniang was in trouble, so she sent Golden Boy and Jade Girl to help in the battle to defeat the sea demons.

Standing at the prow of the boat, Moniang clapped her hands and prayed reverently. She thanked Guanyin for her kindness

in coming to the rescue. Then she ordered the family servant
to turn the boat around and head for home.

– 4 –

After Moniang vanquished the sea demons, her reputation shook
the earth. In the southeast coastal region, because Moniang
protected them, the fishermen hoisted their sails and went out
to sea. They returned loaded to capacity. People lived and worked
in peace and contentment. The port was thriving and prosperous. One after another, merchant ships arrived safely to engage
in trade.

One year, at the beginning of spring, a merchant ship arrived from eastern Zhejiang on its way to southern Fujian. As
luck would have it, the south winds were very strong just then,
and a heavy fog hung in the air. You couldn't see ten feet
ahead. When the merchant ship went through the straits, the
current was rushing. It took great care to avoid the reefs. The
people on the boat wailed and shouted for help. Their voices
reached the heavens. When Moniang heard the uproar on the
sea, she knew that a merchant ship had run into trouble, so
she told her family servant to organize the villagers to go to
the rescue. But the crowd saw that the waves were dashing to
the skies, that the tide was as high as a mountain, and that the
dense fog shrouded the ship and its people from view. They
didn't dare proceed. Moniang arranged the altar and chanted
incantations. She took a bundle of chopsticks and walked rapidly to the edge of the sea. Standing on a large towering rock
on the seashore, she hurled the chopsticks in the direction of
the shouting. On the sea, there immediately appeared innumerable large China firs to shield the leaking boat and press down
the enormous waves. The wind gradually quieted, and the fog
dispersed. Because the leaky ship was surrounded by the large
China firs, it stabilized again. The people on the boat speedily
plugged up the leaks and sailed toward the shore.

Just as the sailors were rejoicing that they had avoided calamity at sea, suddenly the China firs were nowhere to be seen.
They were all dumbfounded. Only when they made inquiries

on shore did they learn that it was the goddess's powerful magic that had saved them.

– 5 –

On the eighth day of the ninth month of 987, Moniang said to her mother and her older sisters, "Tomorrow is the Double Ninth Festival. I want to climb alone to watch from a high spot. Please forgive me for not inviting you, my sisters, to go with me." Laughing, they all said, "Little Sister will meet with fresh and unusual experiences. When you come back, you can regale us with these stories." Moniang gazed at them and only smiled.

The next day, on the Double Ninth Festival, Moniang arose very early. She rowed a small boat toward Meizhou Island. Once there, Moniang slowly ascended the peak. She stood on a large rock on a high spot, and lifted her eyes to look at the clouds. The sun was just rising in the east. The sky was blue, and the water jade-green. Like a golden highway to paradise, the rays of the sun reflected on the water's surface. Moniang sat in repose with her eyes closed. Suddenly an unusual fragrance wafted her way. Opening her eyes, she saw a rosy cloud drift from the top of her head to her feet. She stood on the rosy cloud, and her body ascended. Moniang made a circuit of the sky over Meizhou Bay and then—riding the rosy cloud—she slowly departed.

– 6 –

After Moniang ascended to Heaven and became an immortal, she still frequently appeared in dreams and made her presence felt, bringing good fortune to the people. At the spot where Moniang ascended to Heaven, the people of her home village built a temple and a statue to commemorate her.

A merchant named Sanbao had a ship loaded with valuable goods. As he was about to set out, the anchor seemed to be attracted by something. There was no way to pull it up. Alarmed, Sanbao went ashore on Meizhou Island. He went to the temple to burn incense. When he returned to the ship, it was easy to weigh anchor. From then on, his whole voyage to Southeast Asia was smooth. For about three years, he engaged in trade in the Philippines and Malaysia. He made a large profit. After returning safely, he went to Meizhou Island and donated a great amount of money for the construction of a temple. It was called Mazu temple.

During the reign of Ming Hongwu [1368–1398], the Quanzhou garrison commander Zhou Zuo led a maritime expedition of several battleships. All of a sudden, the battleships ran aground on the reefs. Everyone prayed for Mazu's blessings and protection. Suddenly there was a rustling sound on all sides. As if it were high tide, the ships began to float. Not far away there was a ball of fire—now hidden from view, now appearing. Zhou Zuo said to the others, "This must be Mazu's efficacy—a miraculous fire to lead the way." The battleships followed the magic fire, and made their way through the openings in the reefs. Not until daylight did they approach shore. Fortunately, they had averted disaster at sea.

Mazu's miraculous power was vast. Frequently her effective protection accompanied the boats, and saved them from calamities. In the last thousand years, all coastal places in China, as well as foreign ports where overseas Chinese people live, have erected temples to sacrifice to Mazu. In the minds of coastal people and overseas Chinese, Mazu has become a protector goddess.

(Stories collected by Lin Xianjiu)

NOTES

Introduction

1. Many of the stories have no discernible date, but rather begin with such phrases as "A very long time ago..." or "We don't know just when this occurred, but it was very long ago."
2. See Chapter IV, "Grandma's Story," in Trinh T. Minh-ha, *Woman, Native, Other: Writing Postcoloniality and Feminism* (Bloomington: Indiana University Press, 1989). She writes, "If we rely on history to tell us what happened at a specific time and place, we can rely on the story to tell us not only what might have happened, but also what is happening at an unspecified time and place" (p. 120).
3. Eduard B. Vermeer, "The Decline of Hsing-hua [Xinghua] Prefecture in the Early Ch'ing [Qing]," in E. B. Vermeer (ed.), *Development and Decline of Fukien [Fujian] Province in the 17th and 18th Centuries* (Leiden: E. J. Brill, 1990), p. 132.
4. Hugh R. Clark, "Settlement, Trade and Economy in Fukien [Fujian] to the Thirteenth Century," in Vermeer, pp. 52–53.
5. Clark, pp. 46–49.
6. Lin Renchuan, "Fukien's Private Sea Trade in the 16th and 17th Centuries," in Vermeer, p. 171.
7. Both are quoted in Lin Renchuan, p. 172.
8. Daniel L. Overmyer, "Values in Chinese Sectarian Literature: Ming and Ch'ing [Qing] *Pao-chüan* [Baojuan]," in David Johnson, Andrew J. Nathan, and Evelyn S. Rawski (eds.), *Popular Culture in Late Imperial China* (Berkeley: University of California Press, 1985), p. 221.
9. Overmyer, p. 253.

Historical Overview

1. Zhu Weigan, *Fujian shigao* [Draft history of Fujian] (Fuzhou: Fujian renmin chubanshe, 1984), Vol. I, pp. 15–16.
2. Zhu, pp. 23–24.
3. Zhu, p. 23, pp. 28–30, pp. 36–38, pp. 40–44.
4. Zhu, pp. 47–51.

5. Quoted in Zhu, p. 59.
6. Zhu, p. 35.
7. Zhu, p. 42.
8. Zhu, p. 58.
9. The Chinese characters for minority nationalities typically include an element meaning "insect," "worm," or "dog." This in itself suggests the low esteem in which the Han Chinese held those on their borders.
10. Zhu, p. 9.
11. Zhu, p. 7.
12. Zhu, pp. 19–20.
13. Zhu, p. 54.
14. Zhu, pp. 60–62.
15. Zhu, p. 57, pp. 75–76.
16. Hugh R. Clark, "Settlement, Trade and Economy in Fukien [Fujian] to the Thirteenth Century," in E. B. Vermeer (ed.), *Development and Decline of Fukien Province in the 17th and 18th Centuries* (Leiden: E. J. Brill, 1990), pp. 39, 56.
17. The origin of the appellation "Zaiton" is uncertain. Some writers suggest that Muslim traders called Quanzhou Zaiton and that the term is Arabic for "peace and tranquillity." Others suggest that "Zaiton" may derive from the Chinese pronunciation (*citong*) for thorn trees, planted in abundance in Quanzhou in the tenth century.
18. Ronald Latham (trans.), *The Travels of Marco Polo* (New York: Penguin Books, 1958), p. 237.
19. See Clark, pp. 46–47.
20. Clark, pp. 51–56.
21. Clark, p. 57.
22. Chang Pin-tsun, "Maritime Trade and Local Economy in Late Ming Fukien," in Vermeer pp. 65–66.
23. Cheng K'o-ch'eng, "Cheng Ch'eng-kung's Maritime Expansion and Early Ch'ing Coastal Prohibition," in Vermeer, p. 218.
24. Chang Pin-tsun, p. 66.
25. Chang Pin-tsun, p. 66.
26. Chang Pin-tsun, pp. 66–67.
27. Chang Pin-tsun, p. 67.
28. Chang Pin-tsun, p. 68.
29. Lin Renchuan, "Fukien's Private Sea Trade in the 16th and 17th Centuries," in Vermeer, pp. 165–168.
30. Lin Renchuan, p. 171.
31. Quoted in Lin Renchuan, p. 172.
32. Lin Renchuan, p. 175; see also pp. 179–187.

Part One: Images of Traditional Women

1. Wuyi Mountain is a scenic spot in the northwestern corner of Fujian province.
2. A *li* is one-third of a mile.
3. Large red robe.
4. Ruled 1023–1064.
5. That the notices were yellow denoted the fact that they were issued by order of the emperor.
6. This carried the same salary and rank as those of other high-ranking officials.
7. In China, ages are reckoned in *sui*. A person is one *sui* at birth, and becomes one *sui* older on each New Year. Thus, by western reckoning, a person 18 *sui* would be 16 or 17 years old.
8. In traditional China, the *yamen* comprised the offices and residence of the county magistrate.
9. A *xiang* is a township.
10. A *mou* is one-sixth of an acre.
11. Wife and husband often referred to each other as "elder brother" and "little sister," and others also used these terms for them.
12. In traditional China, women engaged in weaving, while men engaged in farming.
13. Red turtle cake is a typical kind of southern Fujian food. Made of sweet rice flour, it is a cake shaped like a turtle.
14. The She are one of the 55 minority nationalities in China. They live in Fujian.
15. This occurred each time a magistrate went to the court.
16. *Jinding* means golden ingot.
17. Li Zhi (1527–1602) was an iconoclastic thinker who combined elements of Confucianism, Taoism, and Buddhism.
18. Her son.
19. Li Zhi was unusual in his willingness to let his grandson grow up with his widowed daughter-in-law. Both widowed daughters-in-law and grandchildren typically continued to reside with the widow's in-laws.
20. The woman Zhuo and Sima Xiangru were celebrated lovers from Han dynasty times. Zhuo ran away from home to marry Sima. Treating each other as guests, the two were mutually respectful of one another. (Sima was Zhuo's second husband.)

Part Two: Images of Women and Men in Love

1. The concept of puppy love is derived from the expression "green plums and toy bamboo horses," used in a poem by Tang dynasty poet Bai Juyi to refer to a little boy going to a girl's home on a

bamboo horse and waving a green plum branch.

2. Contrary to what we believe of marriages in traditional China, then—that they were virtually all arranged—in this story the villagers clearly support the young couple's wishes.

3. A *jin* is equal to 1.1 pounds—half a kilogram.

4. This is meant to suggest her attachment to Bicheng. With these words, Zhenniang makes it clear that she considers herself committed to Bicheng and that she intends to marry him and no other.

5. According to legend, it was Pan Gu who created heaven and earth.

6. This means "a thousand pieces of gold"—sometimes used as a way of referring to a daughter, for a daughter might bring this price in marriage.

7. The *qin* is a traditional stringed instrument.

8. Half a *jin* and eight ounces, of course, are the same amount. Wang Daba is essentially saying that the old couple must repay him exactly what they "owe."

9. *"Babao"* means eight treasures.

10. In Buddhism, the soul is thought to go to the Western Paradise after death.

11. The traditional form of the character "nie" is made up of three of the pictographs meaning "ear."

12. "Bao" in this instance means "leopard."

13. Ming Zhengde ruled from 1506 to 1522, Ming Jiajing from 1522 to 1567.

14. Under traditional Chinese law, a confession was essential for conviction. If necessary, torture was used to extract these confessions. Obviously in this instance, even torture did not lead to confession.

15. A style name, or *zi*, was the personal name taken at the age of twenty.

16. In traditional China, a *jinshi* was a man who had passed the highest level of the imperial civil service examinations. It was through passing examinations that men received appointments to offices.

17. "Bancun" means "half-village."

18. A kind of *qin*.

19. This is a reversal of the usual situation, in which a young woman uses music to attract a man's attention.

20. Penglai: the Chinese Methuselah.

21. Chang-e is the goddess of the moon.

22. Sima Xiangru had used *qin* music to make his intentions known to Zhuo Wenjun. For more on Sima Xiangru, see note 20, p. 264.

23. That is to say, since Bancun was monopolizing Ma Xianglan, Ma Xianglan was not interested in any of the young men who would have paid a great deal to be with her. So the madam's profit was vanishing.

24. That is, he had passed the first level of the examinations.
25. This is a reference to characters in the traditional folk tale, "Du Shiniang angrily sinks a suitcase filled with a hundred treasures." The writer, above, states that Sun Fu let Du Shiniang down. This is an error; the one who betrayed her was Li Jia, a merchant, who went to Yangzhou where he met the prostitute Du Shiniang. He fell in love with her and spent all his money, intended for business transactions, on this prostitute. Finally, he purchased her. On the boat *en route* home, he met Sun Fu, another merchant, who persuaded Li Jia to sell Du to him. Li Jia was afraid his father would punish him because of the money he had frittered away, and he was also afraid of taking a prostitute home as his wife. So he secretly sold her to get his money back. During her time as a prostitute, Du had received and saved a great many jewels. She had planned to surprise Li with this fortune worth millions. She had not told him that he had not only a beautiful wife, but a fortune as well. After she learned that he had betrayed her, she threw her suitcase filled with jewels into the river, and then committed suicide by drowning.
26. "Da" means large, and is sometimes used in the sense of "elder," as in "elder brother" or "elder sister."
27. As in "The Story of Phoenix Rock" above, we see the villagers here, too, supporting young people making their own choice of marriage partner.
28. In traditional China, it was customary to worship the ancestors as part of the wedding ceremony. It was also customary for the bride to ride in a sedan chair to her husband's home.
29. Qi Jiguang was a famous general of this period.
30. See note 6, p. 265.
31. Families without sons typically tried to arrange a marriage in which the husband would move to the woman's home and take her surname. In this way, the family line would be continued.
32. This is essentially a private school in the home.
33. This is an ancient style of writing characters. The fact that Bai Yulian could write in this style shows her talent.
34. The term "mandarin ducks" (*yuanyang*) is also used to refer to lovers.
35. That is to say, they wanted to marry and have children. Gods and goddesses were not permitted to do so.

Part Three: Images of Strong and Able Women

1. Ruled 1723–1736.
2. This refers to eight great poets who lived around the Yangzhou region early in the Qing dynasty and remained loyal to the Ming

dynasty. They were eccentric, and were not only good poets but good painters. Huang Shen was one of them.

3. That is to say, Huang Shen hadn't chosen great scenery for his paintings, but only odd bits of scenery.

4. A string of cash was made up of a thousand copper coins. One such string was equal to a tael, or 1.1 ounces, of silver.

5. This is another of Li Zhi's names.

6. The festival in early April (solar calendar) for paying homage to the ancestors.

7. Red dust—the mortal world.

8. *Fenshu* can be translated "Burn the Books." Li Zhi had criticized much of the classical writing as nonsense. During the Cultural Revolution (1966–76), the Gang of Four praised him as a Legalist.

9. Chan Buddhism is the same as Zen Buddhism—focusing on meditation and sudden intuitive enlightenment.

10. That is, he had passed the provincial level examinations for the military—examinations parallel to the civil service examinations.

11. *Taishi*, or Grand Tutor, was the emperor's tutor, and, as such, one of the highest officials at court with power similar to that of the prime minister.

12. All of this takes advantage of plays on words. The word for dog is *gou*, which is rather close to the word for nine, *jiu*. The word for turtle, *bie*, is rather close to the word for eight, *ba*.

13. The point here is that, in the dangerous ocean crossings, he needed Heaven's protection, and that it would be foolhardy to risk losing the gods' blessings for just fifty dollars.

14. This is calling on the name of the Amida Buddha. In Pure Land Buddhism, this is thought to be enough to achieve salvation.

15. Qian Siniang is believed to have moved to Putian in 1064 and to have begun organizing the work of dam construction at that time.

16. It is striking that the story refers to selling both sons and daughters—and mentions the sons first.

17. In other words, since the *yamen* (the complex of offices and residences for the county officials) hadn't suffered, the officials had not taken the initiative to deal with the problem.

18. See note 24, p. 266.

19. A kind of paper which is especially good for calligraphy.

20. This phrase means "female impersonators vindicating themselves."

21. That is, good things are made to be bestowed on just the right people.

22. Beancurd.

23. Guanyin is the Buddhist Goddess of Mercy.

24. Mazu is the folk goddess who protects sailors and fishermen; see Introduction, pp. 14–16. See also "The Goddess of the Southern Ocean," pp. 255–261.

25. Xiwangmu traditionally is the powerful fairy princess of the Kunlun Mountains. In this tale, she becomes a ruler of the Heavens.
26. This is simply a variety of bamboo.
27. "Light blue dragon mountain range."
28. Because of the sediment from the ash.
29. Reigned 998–1023.
30. This is a play on words—"*rongsheng panzhi*" and "*rongsheng pianzhi.*"
31. Han Qi (1008–1075) served as prime minister to three Song dynasty emperors.
32. Qing Qianlong reigned from 1736 to 1796.
33. This is a reference to the third century military figure Zhuge Liang, also called Kongming, who is said to have borrowed the southeast wind in the wintertime (a time when the wind should have been from the northwest). In order to attack Cao Cao's fleet with fire arrows, he needed the southeast wind. He is said to have reassured his men by saying, "Don't worry. I can borrow the southeast wind from Heaven." Since he knew something about geography, he was able to predict that there would be a southeast wind just when he needed it.
34. For good luck.